M(

E. H. YOUNG

WITH
INTRODUCTORY POEMS

By

EDWIN WAUGH

and

EMILY BRONTË

First published in 1916

Read & Co.

Copyright © 2020 Read & Co. Books

This edition is published by Read & Co. Books, an imprint of Read & Co.

This book is copyright and may not be reproduced or copied in any way without the express permission of the publisher in writing.

British Library Cataloguing-in-Publication Data
A catalogue record for this book is available from the British Library.

Read & Co. is part of Read Books Ltd.
For more information visit
www.readandcobooks.co.uk

CONTENTS

E. H. Young..5

OH THE WILD, WILD MOORS
By Edwin Waugh...7

LOUD WITHOUT THE WIND WAS ROARING
By Emily Brontë..9

CHAPTER I...13

CHAPTER II..19

CHAPTER III...26

CHAPTER IV..33

CHAPTER V...41

CHAPTER VI..48

CHAPTER VII...55

CHAPTER VIII..62

CHAPTER IX..70

CHAPTER X...77

CHAPTER XI..87

CHAPTER XII...94

CHAPTER XIII...103

CHAPTER XIV..111

CHAPTER XV...123

CHAPTER XVI..133

CHAPTER XVII...141

CHAPTER XVIII	148
CHAPTER XIX	157
CHAPTER XX	168
CHAPTER XXI	177
CHAPTER XXII	185
CHAPTER XXIII	193
CHAPTER XXIV	204
CHAPTER XXV	212
CHAPTER XXVI	220
CHAPTER XXVII	228
CHAPTER XXVIII	236
CHAPTER XXIX	246
CHAPTER XXX	255
CHAPTER XXXI	266
CHAPTER XXXII	272
CHAPTER XXXIII	282
CHAPTER XXXIV	289
CHAPTER XXXV	298
CHAPTER XXXVI	309
CHAPTER XXXVII	317
CHAPTER XXXVIII	324
CHAPTER XXXIX	329

E. H. Young

Emily Hilda Young was born in born in Whitley (now known as Whitley Bay), Northumberland, England, on 21st March, 1880. She attended Gateshead Secondary School and Penrhos College, in Colwyn Bay, Wales. As a young woman, Young developed a keen interest in classical and modern philosophy. She became a supporter of the suffragette movement, and started publishing novels. Her first two works were *A Corn of Wheat* (1910) and *Yonder* (1912). When World War I broke out in 1914, Young worked first as a stables groom and then in a munitions factory. Her husband was sadly killed at the Third Battle of Ypres in 1917. The following year she moved to Sydenham Hill, London to join her lover, now the headmaster of the public school Alleyn's, and his wife in a ménage à trois. Young occupied a separate flat in their house and was addressed as 'Mrs Daniell'; this concealed the unconventional arrangement. This drastic change in circumstances seems to have been a creative catalyst. Through the twenties and thirties, Young published seven novels: *A Bridge Dividing* (1922), *William* (1925), *The Vicar's Daughter* (1927), *Miss Mole* (1930), *Jenny Wren* (1932), *Celia* (1937) and *The Curate's Wife* (1934).

In the mid-thirties, Young and her lover (Mr Henderson) moved to Bradford-on-Avon in Wiltshire. During the Second World War, Young worked actively in air raid precautions. She lived in Wiltshire with Henderson until her death on 8th August, 1949, aged 69. Although popular in her time, Young's work has nearly vanished today. In 1980 however, a four-part series based on her novels was shown on BBC television as *Hannah*. Around this time, the feminist publishing house Virago also reprinted several of her books.

OH THE WILD, WILD MOORS

By Edwin Waugh

I

My heart's away in the lonely hills,
    Where I would gladly be—
On the rolling ridge of Blackstone Edge,
    Where the wild wind whistles free!
There oft in careless youth I roved,
    When summer days were fine;
And the meanest flower of the heathery waste
    Delights this heart of mine!
    Oh, the lonely moors, the breezy moors,
        And the stormy hills so free;
    Oh, the wild, wild moors; the wild, wild moors,
        The sweet wild moors for me.

II

I fain would stroll on lofty Knowl,
    And Rooley Moor again;
Or wildly stray one long bright day
    In Turvin's bonny glen!
The thought of Wardle's breezy height
    Fills all my heart with glee,

And the distant view of the hills so blue
   Bring tears into my e'e!
Oh, the lonely moors, the breezy moors,
   And the stormy hills so free;
Oh, the wild, wild moors; the wild, wild moors,
   The sweet wild moors for me.

III

Oh, blessed sleep, that brings in dreams
   My native hills to me;
The heathery wilds, the rushing streams,
   Where once I wandered free!
'Tis a glimpse of life's sweet morning light,
   A bright angelic ray,
That steals into the dusky night,
   And fades with waking day!
Oh, the lonely moors, the breezy moors,
   And the stormy hills so free;
Oh, the wild, wild moors; the wild, wild moors,
   The sweet wild moors for me.

LOUD WITHOUT THE WIND WAS ROARING

By Emily Brontë

Loud without the wind was roaring
   Through th'autumnal sky;
Drenching wet, the cold rain pouring,
   Spoke of winter nigh.
      All too like that dreary eve,
      Did my exiled spirit grieve.

Grieved at first, but grieved not long,
   Sweet—how softly sweet!—it came;
Wild words of an ancient song,
   Undefined, without a name.

"It was spring, and the skylark was singing:"
   Those words they awakened a spell;
They unlocked a deep fountain, whose springing,
   Nor absence, nor distance can quell.

In the gloom of a cloudy November
   They uttered the music of May ;
They kindled the perishing ember
   Into fervour that could not decay.

Awaken, o'er all my dear moorland,
   West-wind, in thy glory and pride!
Oh! call me from valley and lowland,
   To walk by the hill-torrent's side!

It is swelled with the first snowy weather;
   The rocks they are icy and hoar,
And sullenly waves the long heather,
   And the fern leaves are sunny no more.

There are no yellow stars on the mountain
   The bluebells have long died away
From the brink of the moss-bedded fountain—
   From the side of the wintry brae.

But lovelier than corn-fields all waving
   In emerald, and vermeil, and gold,
Are the heights where the north-wind is raving,
   And the crags where I wandered of old.

It was morning: the bright sun was beaming;
   How sweetly it brought back to me
The time when nor labour nor dreaming
   Broke the sleep of the happy and free!

But blithely we rose as the dawn-heaven
   Was melting to amber and blue,
And swift were the wings to our feet given,
   As we traversed the meadows of dew.

For the moors! For the moors, where the short grass
   Like velvet beneath us should lie!
For the moors! For the moors, where each high pass
   Rose sunny against the clear sky!

For the moors, where the linnet was trilling
　　Its song on the old granite stone;
Where the lark, the wild sky-lark, was filling
　　Every breast with delight like its own!

What language can utter the feeling
　　Which rose, when in exile afar,
On the brow of a lonely hill kneeling,
　　I saw the brown heath growing there?

It was scattered and stunted, and told me
　　That soon even that would be gone:
It whispered, "The grim walls enfold me,
　　I have bloomed in my last summer's sun."

But not the loved music, whose waking
　　Makes the soul of the Swiss die away,
Has a spell more adored and heartbreaking
　　Than, for me, in that blighted heath lay.

The spirit which bent 'neath its power,
　　How it longed—how it burned to be free!
If I could have wept in that hour,
　　Those tears had been heaven to me.

Well—well; the sad minutes are moving,
　　Though loaded with trouble and pain;
And some time the loved and the loving
　　Shall meet on the mountains again!

MOOR FIRES

CHAPTER I

In the dusk of a spring evening, Helen Caniper walked on the long road from the town. Making nothing of the laden basket she carried, she went quickly until she drew level with the high fir-wood which stood like a barrier against any encroachment on the moor, then she looked back and saw lights darting out to mark the streets she had left behind, as though a fairy hand illuminated a giant Christmas-tree.

Among the other trees, black and mysterious on the hill, a cold wind was moaning. "It's the night wind," Helen murmured. The moor was inhabited by many winds, and she knew them all, and it was only the night wind that cried among the trees, for, fearless though it seemed, it had a dread of the hours that made it. The fir-trees, their bare trunks like a palisade, swayed gently, and Helen's skirts flapped about her ankles. More lights glimmered in the town, and she turned towards home.

The moor stretched now on either hand until it touched a sky from which all the colour had not departed, and the road shone whitely, pale but courageous as it kept its lonely path. Helen's feet tapped clearly as she hurried on, and when she approached the road to Halkett's Farm, the sound of her going was mingled with that of hoofs, and an old horse, drawing a dog-cart, laboured round the corner. It was the horse Dr. Mackenzie had always driven up the long road; it was now driven by his son, and when he saw that some one motioned him to stop, the young doctor drew up. He bent forward to see her.

"It's Helen," he said. "Oh, Helen, how are you?"

She stood by the step and looked up at him. "I'm very well. I'm glad you knew me. It's three years."

"And your hair is up."

"Miriam and I are twenty," she said gravely, and he laughed.

The horse shook himself and set the dog-cart swaying; the jingle of his bit went adventurously across the moor; heather-stalks scratched each other in the wind.

"You haven't lighted your lamps," Helen said. "Somebody might run into you."

"They might." He jumped down and fumbled for his matches. "The comfort is that we're not likely to do it to any one, at our pace. When I've made my fortune I shall buy a horse from George Halkett, one that will go fast and far."

"But I like this one," said Helen. "We used to watch for him when we had measles. He's mixed up with everything. Don't have another one."

"The fortune's still to make," he said. He had lighted the nearer lamp and Helen's slim figure had become a thing of shadows. He took the basket from her and put it under the seat. She was staring over the horse's back.

"There was a thing we used to do. We had bets about Dr. Mackenzie's ties, what colour they were; but we never won or lost, because we never saw them. His beard was so big. And once Miriam pretended there was a huge spider on the ceiling, but he wouldn't look up, though she screamed. He told her not to be a silly little girl. So we never saw them."

"I'm not surprised," the young doctor said. "He didn't wear them. What was the use? He was a practical man."

"Oh," Helen cried, "isn't that just like life! You bother and bother about something that doesn't exist and make yourself miserable for nothing. No, I won't do it."

"Do you?"

"It's a great fault of mine," she said.

He went round the back of the cart and lighted the other lamp. "Now I'm going to drive you home. That basket's heavy."

"I have been shopping," she explained. "Tomorrow a visitor is coming."

"Your father?" he asked quickly.

"No; he hasn't been again. He's ill, Notya says, and it's too cold for him here. Dr. Zebedee, aren't you glad to be back on the moor?"

"Well, I don't see much of it, you know. My work is chiefly in the streets—but, yes, I think I'm glad."

"We've been watching for you, Miriam and I. She'll be angry that I've seen you first. No; she's thinking too much about tomorrow. It's an uncle who's coming, a kind of uncle—Notya's brother. We haven't seen him before and Miriam's excited."

"And you're not."

"I don't like new things. They feel dangerous. You don't know what they'll bring."

"I thought you weren't going to make yourself miserable," he said. "Jump up, and we'll take home the fatted calf."

She hesitated. "I'm not going straight home."

"Let me deliver the calf, then."

"No, please; it isn't heavy." She went to the horse's head and stroked his nose. "I've never known his name. What is it?"

"Upon my word, I don't believe he has one. He's just the horse. That's what we always called him."

"'The horse'! How dreary! It makes him not a person."

"But the one and only horse!"

"I don't suppose he minds very much," she murmured. "Good-night, horse. Good-night, Zebedee. My basket, please. I'm very late."

"I wish you'd let me take you home. You oughtn't to go wandering over the moor by night."

She laughed. "I've done it all my life. Do you remember," she went on slowly, "what I once told you about the fires? Oh, years ago, when I first saw you."

"The fires?" he said.

"Never mind if you've forgotten."

"I don't forget things," he said; "I'm remembering." His mind was urged by his sense of her disappointment and by the sight of her face, which the shadows saddened. The basket hung on her arm and her hands were clasped together: she looked like a child and he could not believe in her twenty years.

"It doesn't matter," she said softly.

"But I do remember. It's the spring fires."

"The Easter fires."

"Of course, of course, you told me—"

"I think they must be burning now. That's where I'm going—to look for them."

"I wish I could come too."

"Do you? Do you? Oh!" She made a step towards him. "The others never come. They laugh but I still go on. It's safer, isn't it? It can't do any harm to pray. And now that Uncle Alfred's coming—"

"Is he a desperate character?"

She made a gesture with her clasped hands. "It's like opening a door."

"You mustn't be afraid of open doors," he said—"you, who live on the moor." He grasped her shoulder in a friendly fashion. "You mustn't be afraid of anything. Go and find your fires, and don't forget to pray for me."

"Of course not. Good-night. Will you be coming again soon?"

"Old Halkett's pretty ill," was his reply and, climbing to his seat, he waved his hat and bade the old horse move on.

The moor lay dark as a lake at Helen's feet and the rustling of the heather might have been the sound of water fretted by the wind—deep, black water whose depths no wind could stir. At Helen's right hand a different darkness was made by the larch-trees clothing Halkett's hollow, and on her left a yellow gleam, like the light at the masthead of a ship at sea, betrayed her home.

Behind her, and on the other side of the road, the Brent Farm dogs began to bark, and in the next instant they were answered from many points of the moor, so that houses and farmsteads became materialized in the night which had hidden them and Helen stood in a circle of echoing sound. Often, as a child, she had waked at such a clamour, and pictured homeless people walking on the road, and now, though she heard no footsteps, she seemed to feel the approach of noiseless feet, bringing the unknown. For her, youth's delights of strength and fleetness were paid for by the thought of the many years in which her happiness could be assailed. Age might be feeble, but it had, she considered, the consolation of knowing something of the limitations of its pain. She wished she could put an unscalable wall about the moor, so that the soundless feet should stay outside, for she did not know that already she had heard the footsteps of those whose actions were weaving her destiny. Helen Caniper might safely throw open all her doors.

The barking of the dogs lessened and then ceased; once more only the whistling of the wind broke the silence, until Helen's skirts rubbed the heather as she ran and something jingled in her basket. She went fast to find her fires and, while her mind was fixed on them, she was still aware of the vast moor she loved, its darkness, its silence, the smells it gave out, the promise of warmth and fertility in its bosom. She could not clearly see the ground, but her feet knew it: heather, grass, stones, and young bracken were to be overcome; here and there a rock or thornbush loomed out blacker than the rest in warning; sometimes a dip in the earth must be avoided; once or twice dim grey objects rose up and became sheep that bleated out of her way, and always, as she ran, she mounted. For a time she was level with the walled garden of her home, but, passing its limit, she topped a sudden steepness, descended it with a rush, and lost all glimmerings from road or dwelling-place.

A greenish sky, threatening to turn black, delicately roofed the world; no stars had yet come through, and, far away, as though in search of them, the moor rose to a line of hills. Their rounded tops had no defiance, their curve was that of a wave without the desire to break, held in its perfect contour by its own content. The moor itself had the patience of the wisdom which is faith, and Helen might have heard it laughing tenderly if she had been less concerned with the discovery of her fires. She stood still, and her eyes found only the moor, the rocks and hills.

"I must go on," she said in a whisper. And now, for pleasure in her strength, she went in running bounds over a stretch of close-cropped turf, and space became so changed for her that she hardly knew whether she leapt a league or foot; and it was all one, for she had a feeling of great power and happiness in a world which was empty without loneliness. And then a creeping line of fire arrested her. Not far off, it went snake-like over the ground, disappeared, and again burned out more brightly: it edged the pale smoke like embroidery on a veil, and behind that veil there lived and moved the smoke-god she had created for herself when she was ten years old. She could not hear the crackling of the twigs nor smell their burning, and she had no wish to draw nearer. She stretched out her arms and dropped to her knees and prayed.

"Oh, Thou, behind the smoke," she said aloud, "guard the moor and us. We will not harm your moor. Amen."

This was the eleventh time she had prayed to the God behind the smoke, and he had guarded both the Canipers and the moor, but now she felt the need to add more words to the childish ones she had never changed.

"And let me be afraid of nothing," she said firmly, and hesitated for a second. "For beauty's sake. Amen."

CHAPTER II

After her return over the moor, through the silent garden and the dim house, Helen was dazzled by the schoolroom lights and she stood blinking in the doorway.

"We're all here and all hungry," Rupert said. "You're late."

"I know." She shut the door and took off her hat. "Miriam, I met Zebedee."

"Oh," Miriam said on a disapproving note. She lay on the sofa as though a wind had flung her there, and her eyes were closed. In her composure she looked tired, older than Helen and more experienced, but her next words came youthfully enough. "Just like you. You get everything."

"I couldn't help it," Helen said mildly. "He came round the corner from Halkett's Farm. Ought I to have run away?"

Miriam sat up and laughed, showing dark eyes and shining little teeth which transformed her face into a childish one.

"Is he different?"

"I couldn't see very well."

"He is different," Rupert said; and John, on the window-seat, put down his book to listen.

"Tell us," Miriam said.

"Nothing much, but he is older."

"So are we."

"Not in his way."

"We haven't had the chance," Miriam complained. "I suppose you mean he has been doing things he ought not to do in London."

"Not necessarily," Rupert answered lightly and John picked up his book again. He generally found that his excursions into the affairs of men and women were dull and fruitless, while his book, on the subject of manures, satisfied his intellect and was useful in its results.

There was a silence in which both girls, though differently, were conscious of a dislike for Zebedee's unknown adventures.

Miriam laid her head on the red cushion. "I wish tomorrow would come."

"I bought turbot," Helen said. "I should think he's the kind of man who likes it."

"I suggest delicate sauces," Rupert said.

"You needn't be at all anxious about his food," Miriam assured them. "I'm going to be the attraction of this visit."

"How d'you know?"

Her teeth caught her under-lip. "Because I mean to be."

"Well, don't make a fool of yourself, my dear."

"She will," John growled.

Helen spoke quickly. "Oh, Miriam, I told Zebedee about Dr. Mackenzie's ties, and, do you know, he never wore any at all!"

"Old pig! He wouldn't. Mean. Scotch. We might have thought of that. If Daniel had a beard he would be just the same."

"It may surprise you to learn," Rupert remarked, "that Daniel takes a great interest in his appearance lately."

"That's me again," Miriam said complacently.

"Ugly people are rather like that," Helen said. "But he wears terrible boots."

"He's still at the collar-and-tie stage," Rupert said. "We'll get to boots later. He needs encouragement—and control. A great deal of control. He had a bright blue tie on yesterday."

"Ha!" Miriam shouted in a strangled laugh, and thrust her face into the cushion. "That's me, too!" she cried. "I told him blue would suit him."

Rupert wagged his head. "I can't see the fun in that kind of thing, making a fool of the poor beggar."

"Well," she flashed, "he shouldn't ask me to marry him!"

"You'd complain if he didn't."

"Of course I should—of course! I'm so dull that I'm really

grateful to him, but I'm so dull that I have to tease him, too. It's only clutching at straws, and Daniel likes it."

"He's wasted half a crown on his tie, though. I'm going to tell him that you're not to be trusted."

"Then I shall devote myself to Zebedee."

"You won't influence Zebedee's ties," Helen said, "or his collars—the shiniest ones I have ever seen."

"She won't influence him at all, my good Helen. What's she got to do it with?"

"This!" Miriam said, rising superbly and displaying herself.

"Shut her up, somebody!" John begged. "This is beastly. Has she nothing better to do with herself than attracting men? If you met a woman who made that her profession instead of her play, you'd pass by on the other side."

Miriam flushed, frowned, and recovered herself. "I might. I don't think so. I can't see any harm in pleasing people. If I were clever and frightened them, or witty and made them laugh, it would be just the same. I happen to be beautiful." She spread her hands and waved them. "Tell birds not to fly, tell lambs not to skip, tell me to sit and darn the socks!" She stood on the fender and looked at herself in the glass. "Besides," she said, "I don't care. I'm not responsible. If Notya hadn't buried us all here, I might have been living a useful life!" She cast a sly glance at John. "I might be making butter like Lily Brent."

"Not half so good!"

She ignored that, and went on with her thoughts. "I shall ask Uncle Alfred what made Notya bring us here."

She turned and stood, very slim in her dark dress, her eyelids lowered, her lips parted, expectant of reproof and ready with defiance, but no one spoke. She constantly forgot that her family knew her, but, remembering that fact, her tilted eyebrows twitched a little. Her face broke into mischievous curves and dimples.

"What d'you bet?"

"No," Helen said, thinking of her stepmother. "Notya

wouldn't like it."

"Bah! Pish! Faugh! Pshaw—and ugh! What do I care? I shall!"

"Oh, a rotten thing to do," said John.

"And, anyhow, it doesn't matter," Helen said. "We're here."

"Rupert?" Miriam begged.

"Better not," he answered kindly. "Not worth while." He lay back in a big chair and watched the world through his tobacco smoke. He had all Miriam's darkness and much of her beauty, but he had already acquired a tolerant view of things which made him the best of companions, the least ambitious of young men. "Live and let live, my dear."

"I shan't promise. I suppose I'm not up to your standards of honour, but if a person makes a mystery, why shouldn't the others try to find it out? That's what it's for! And there's nothing else to do."

"You're inventing the mystery," Rupert said. "If Notya and our absent parent didn't get on together—and who could get on with a man who's always ill?—they were wise in parting, weren't they?"

"But why the moor?"

"Ah, I think that was a sudden impulse, and she has always been too proud to own that it was a mistake."

"That's the first sensible thing any one has said yet," John remarked. "I quite agree with you. It's my own idea."

"I'm a young man of penetration, as I've told you all before."

"And shoved into a bank!" John grumbled.

"I like the bank. It's a cheerful place. There's lots of gold about, and people come and talk to me through the bars."

"But," Helen began, on the deep notes of her voice, "what should we have done if she had repented and taken us away? What should we have done?"

"We might have been happy," Miriam said.

"John, what would you have done?" Helen persisted.

"Said nothing, grown up as fast as I could, and come back."

"So should I."

Rupert chuckled. "You wouldn't, Helen. You'd have stayed with Notya and Miriam and me and looked after us all, and longed for this place and denied yourself."

"And made us all uncomfortable." Miriam pointed at Helen's grey dress. "What have you been doing?"

Helen looked down at the dark marks where her knees had pressed the ground.

"It will dry," she said, and went nearer the fire. "Zebedee says old Halkett's ill."

"Drink and the devil," Rupert hummed. "He'll die soon."

"Hope so," John said fervently. "I don't like to think of the bloated old beast alive."

"He'll be horrider dead, I think," said Helen. "Dead things should be beautiful."

"Well, he won't be. Moreover, nothing is, for long. You've seen sheep's carcasses after the snows. Don't be romantic."

"I said they should be."

"It's a good thing they're not. They wouldn't fertilize the ground. Can't we have supper?"

"Here's Notya!" Miriam uttered the warning, and began to poke the fire.

The room was entered by a small lady who carried her head well. She had fair, curling hair, serious blue eyes and a mouth which had been puckered into a kind of sternness.

"So you have come back, Helen," she said. "You should have told me. I have been to the road to look for you. You are very late."

"Yes. I'm sorry. I met Dr. Mackenzie."

"He ought to have brought you home."

"He wanted to. I got turbot for Uncle Alfred. It's on the kitchen table."

"Then I expect the cat has eaten it," said Mrs. Caniper with resignation, but her mouth widened delightfully into what might have been its natural shape. "Miriam, go and put it in the larder."

Surreptitiously and in farewell, Miriam dropped the poker on Helen's toes. "Why can't she send you?" she muttered. "It's your turbot."

"But it's your cat."

Wearing what the Canipers called her deaf expression, their stepmother looked at the closing door. "I did not hear what Miriam said," she remarked blandly.

"She was talking to me."

"Oh!" Mrs. Caniper flushed slowly. "It is discourteous to have private conversations in public, Helen. I have tried to impress that on you—unsuccessfully, it seems; but remember that I have tried."

"Yes, thank you," Helen said, with serious politeness. She made a movement unnatural to her in its violence, because she was forcing herself to speak. "But you don't mind if the boys do things like that." She hesitated and plunged again. "It's Miriam. You're not fair to her. You never have been."

Over Mrs. Caniper's small face there swept changes of expression which Helen was not to forget. Anger and surprise contended together, widening her eyes and lips, and these were both overcome, after a struggle, by a revelation of self-pity not less amazing to the woman than to the girl.

"Has she ever been fair to me?" Mildred Caniper asked stumblingly, before she went in haste, and Helen knew well why she fumbled for the door-handle.

The acute silence of the unhappy filled the room: John rose, collided clumsily with the table and approached the hearth.

"Now, what did you do that for?" he said. "I can't stomach these family affairs."

Helen smoothed her forehead and subdued the tragedy in her eyes. "I had to do it," she breathed. "It was true, wasn't it?" She looked at Rupert, but he was looking at the fire.

"True, yes," said John, "but it does Miriam no harm. A little opposition—"

"No," said Helen, "no. We don't want to drive her to—to

being silly."

"She is silly," John said.

"No," Helen said again. "She ought not to live here, that's all."

"She'll have to learn to. Anyhow"—he put his hands into his pockets—"we can't have Notya looking like that. It's—it won't do."

"It's quite easy not to hurt people," Helen murmured; "but you had to hurt her yourself, John, about your gardening."

"That was different," he said. He was a masculine creature. "I was fighting for existence."

"Miriam has an existence, too, you know," Rupert said.

From the other side of the hall there came a faint chink of plates and Miriam's low voice singing.

"She's all right," John assured himself.

Helen was smiling tenderly at the sound. "But I wonder why Notya is so hard on her," she sighed.

Rupert knocked his pipe against the fender. "I should be very glad to know what our mother was like," he said.

Long ago, out of excess of loyalty, the Canipers had tacitly agreed not to discuss those matters on which their stepmother was determinedly reserved, and now a certain tightening of the atmosphere revealed the fact that John and Helen were controlling their desires to ask Rupert what he meant.

CHAPTER III

The Canipers had lived on the moor for sixteen years, and Rupert was the only one of the children who had more distant memories. These were like flashes of white light on general darkness, for the low house of his memory was white and the broad-leaved trees of the garden cast their shadows on a pale wall: there was a white nursery of unlimited dimensions and a white bath-room with a fluffy mat which comforted the soles of his feet and tickled his toes. Another recollection was of the day when a lady already faintly familiar to him was introduced by an officious nurse as his new mother, and when he looked up at her, with interest in her relationship and admiration for her prettiness, he saw her making herself look very tall and stern as she said clearly, "I am not your mother, Rupert."

"Notya mother," he echoed amiably, and so Mildred Caniper received her name.

As he grew older, he wondered if he really remembered this occasion or whether Notya herself had told him of it, but he knew that the house and the garden wall and the nursery were true. True, too, was a dark man with a pointed beard whom he called his father, who came and went and at last disappeared; and his next remembrance was of the moor, the biggest thing he had ever seen, getting blacker and blacker as the carriage-load of Canipers jogged up the road. The faces of his stepmother, the nursemaid, John and the twins, were like paper lanterns on the background of night, things pale and impermanent, swaying to the movements of the carriage while this black, outspread earth threatened them, and, with the quick sympathy natural to him even then, he knew that Notya was afraid of something too. Then the horse stopped and Rupert climbed stiffly to the ground and heard the welcome of the friend whom he was to know thereafter as Mrs. Brent. Her voice and presence were rich with reassurance: she was fat and hearty, and the threatening earth had spared her, so he took comfort. The laurels by the small iron gate rattled at him as he passed, but Mrs. Brent had each boy by a hand, and no one could be afraid. It was, he remembered, impossible for the three to go through the gate abreast.

"Run in now," said Mrs. Brent, and when he had obeyed he heard a tall grandfather clock ticking in the hall. He could see a staircase running upwards into shadows, and the half-opened doors made him think of the mouths of monsters. It seemed a long time before Mrs. Brent followed him and made a cheerful noise.

With these memories he could always keep the little girls entranced, even when great adventures of their own came to them on the moor, for Notya was a stepmother by her own avowal, and in fairy tales a stepmother was always cruel. They pretended to believe that she had carried them away by force, that some day they would be rescued and taken back to the big white nursery and the fluffy white mat; but Helen at last spoilt the game by asserting that she did not want to be rescued and by refusing to allow Notya to be the villain of the piece.

"She isn't cruel. She's sad," Helen explained.

"Yes, really; but this is pretending," Rupert said.

"It's not pretending. It's true," Miriam said, and she went on with the game though she had to play alone. At the age of twenty she still played it: Notya was still the cruel stepmother and Miriam's eyes were eager on a horizon against which the rescuer should stand. At one time he had been splendid and invincible, a knight to save her, and if his place had now been taken by the unknown Uncle Alfred, it was only that realism had influenced her fiction, and with a due sense of economy she used the materials within her reach.

Domestic being though Helen was, the white nursery had no attraction for her: she was more than satisfied with her many-coloured one; its floor had hills and tiny dales, pools and streams, and it was walled by greater hills and roofed by sky. On it there grew thorn-bushes which thrust out thin hands, begging for food, in winter, and which wore a lady's lovely dress in summertime and a warm red coat for autumn nights. There was bracken, like little walking-sticks in spring, and when the leaves uncurled themselves and spread, they made splendid feathers with which to trim a hat or play at ostrich farms; but, best of all and most fearsome, as the stems shot upwards and overtopped a child, the bracken became a forest through which she hardly dared to walk, so dense and interminable it was. To crawl up and down a fern-covered hillock needed all Helen's resolution and she would emerge panting and wild-eyed, blessing the open country and still watchful for what might follow her. After that experience a mere game of hunters, with John and Rupert roaring like lions and trumpeting like elephants, was a smaller though glorious thing, and for hot and less heroic days there was the game of dairymen, played in the reedy pool or in Halkett's stream with the aid of old milk-cans of many sizes, lent to the Canipers by the lovable Mrs. Brent.

In those days Mrs. Brent furnished them with their ideas of motherhood. She seemed old to them because her husband was long dead and she was stout, but she had a dark-eyed girl no older than John, and her she kissed and nursed, scolded, teased and loved with a joyous confidence which impressed the Canipers. Their stepmother rarely kissed, her reprimands had not the familiarity of scoldings, and though she had a sense of fun which could be reached and used with discretion, there was no feeling of safety in her company. They were too young to realize that this was because she was uncertain of herself, as that puckered mouth revealed. That she loved them they believed; with all the aloofness of their young souls they were thankful that she did not caress them; but they liked to see Lily Brent fondled by her mother, and they themselves suffered Mrs. Brent's endearments with a happy sense of irresponsibility.

It was Mrs. Brent who gave them hot cakes when they went to the dairy to fetch butter or eggs, and who sometimes let them skim the milk and eventually lick the ladle, but she was chiefly wonderful because she could tell them about Mr. Pinderwell. Poor Mr. Pinderwell was the late owner of the Canipers' home. He had lived for more than fifty years in the house chosen and furnished for a bride who had softly fallen ill on the eve of her wedding-day and softly died, and Mr. Pinderwell, distracted by his loss, had come to live in the big, lonely house and had grown old and at last died there, in the hall, with no voice to bewail him but the ticking of the grandfather clock. Going on her daily visit, for she alone was permitted to approach him, Mrs. Brent had found him lying with his face on his outflung arm, "just like a little boy in his bed."

"And were you frightened?" Miriam asked.

"There was nothing to be afraid of, my dear," Mrs. Brent replied. "Death comes to all of us. It's a good thing to get used to the look of him."

Mrs. Brent had been fond of Mr. Pinderwell. He was a gentleman, she said, and though his mind had become more and more bewildered towards the end, he had been unfailingly courteous to her. She would find him wandering up and down the stairs, carrying a small basket of tools in his hand, for he took to wood-carving at the last, as the panels of the bedroom doors were witness, and he would stop to speak about the weather and beg her to allow him to make her some return for all her kindness.

"I used to clean up the place for him," Mrs. Brent would always continue, "and do a little cooking for him, poor old chap! I missed him when he'd gone, and I was glad when your mother came and took the house, just as it stood, with his lady's picture and all, and made the place comfortable again."

Miriam would press against Mrs. Brent's wide knees. "Will you tell us the story again, please, Mrs. Brent?"

"If you're good children, but not today. Run along home."

At that stage of their development they were hardly interested in the portrait of Mr. Pinderwell's bride, hanging above the sofa in the drawing-room. It was the only picture in the house, and from an oval frame of gilt a pretty lady, crowned with a plait of hair, looked mildly on these usurpers of her home. She was not real to them, though for Helen she was to become so, but Mr. Pinderwell, pacing up and down the stairs, carrying a little chisel, was a living friend. On the wide, wind-swept landing, they studied his handiwork on the doors, and they made a discovery which Mrs. Brent had missed. These roughnesses, known to their fingers from their first day in the house, were letters, and made names. Laboriously they spelt them out. Jane, on the door of Helen's room, was easy; Phoebe, on Miriam's, was for a long time called Pehebe; and Christopher, on another, had a familiar and adventurous sound.

"Funny," Rupert said. "What are they?"

Helen spoke with that decision which often annoyed her relatives. "I know. It's the names of the children he was going to have. Jane and Pehebe and Christopher. That's what it is. And these were the rooms he'd settled for them. Jane is a quiet little girl with a fringe and a white pinafore, and Pehebe has a sash and cries about things, and Christopher is a strong boy in socks."

"Stockings," Rupert said. "He's the oldest."

"He isn't. He's the baby. He wears socks. He's not so smooth as the others, and look, poor Mr. Pinderwell hadn't time to put a full stop. I'm glad I sleep in Jane."

"And of course you give me a girl who cries!" Miriam said. But the characters of Mr. Pinderwell's children had been settled, and they were never altered. Jane and Christopher and Phoebe were added to the inhabitants whom Mildred Caniper did not see, but these three did not leave the landing. They lived there quietly in the shadows, speaking only in whispers, while Mr. Pinderwell continued his restless tramping and his lady smiled, unwearied, in the drawing-room.

"He's the only one who can get at her and them," Helen said

in pain. "I don't know how their mother can bear it. I wonder if she'd mind if we hung her on the landing, but then Mr. Pinderwell might miss her. He's so used to her in the drawing-room, and perhaps she doesn't mind about the children."

"I'm sure she doesn't," said John, for he thought she had a silly face.

This was when John and Rupert went to the Grammar School in the town, while the girls did their lessons with Mildred Caniper in the schoolroom of Pinderwell House. Enviously, they watched the boys step across the moor each morning, but their stepmother could not be persuaded to allow them to go too. The distance was so great, she said, and there was no school for girls to which she would entrust them.

"The boys get all the fun," Miriam said. "They see the people in the streets, and get a ride in Mrs. Brent's milk-cart nearly every day, and we sit in the stuffy schoolroom, and Notya's cross."

"You make her cross on purpose," Helen said.

"She shouldn't let me," Miriam answered with perspicuity.

"But it's so silly to make ugliness. It's wicked. Do be good, and let's try to enjoy the lessons and get them over."

But Miriam was not to be influenced by these wise counsels. During lesson hours the strange antipathy between herself and Mildred Caniper often blazed into a storm, and Helen, who loved to keep life smooth and gracious, had the double mortification of seeing Miriam, whom she loved, made naughtier, and Notya, whom she pitied, made more miserable.

"Oh, that we'd had an ignorant stepmother!" Miriam cried. "If stepmothers are not witches they ought to be dunces. Everybody knows that. I'll worry her till she sends us both to boarding-school."

Mildred Caniper was not to be coerced. Her mouth grew more puckered, her eyes more serious, and her tongue sharper; for though anger, as she found, was useless, sarcasm was potent, and in time Miriam gave up the battle. But she did not intend to forgive Mildred Caniper for a single injury, and even now that she was almost woman she refused her own responsibility. Notya had arranged her life, and the evil of it, at least, should be laid at Notya's door.

CHAPTER IV

For Helen, the moor was a personality with moods flecking the solid substance of its character, and even Miriam, who avowed her hatred of its monotony, had to admit an occasional difference. There were days when she thought it was full of secrets and capable of harbouring her own, and there were other days when she forgot its little hills and dales and hiding-places and saw it as a large plain, spread under the glaring eye of the sun, and shelterless, so that when she walked there she believed that her body and, in some mysterious way, her soul, were visible to all men.

Such a day was that on which Uncle Alfred was expected. Miriam went out with a basket on her arm to find flowers for the decoration of his room, and she had no sooner banged the garden door behind her and mounted the first rise than she suffered from this sensation of walking under a spyglass of great size. There was a wonderful clearness everywhere. The grass and young heather were a vivid green, the blue of the sky had a certain harshness and heavily piled clouds rolled across it. Miriam stood on a hillock and gazed at the scene which looked as though something must happen to it under the concentration of the eye behind the glass, but she saw nothing more than the familiar things: the white road cutting the moor, Brent Farm lying placidly against the gentle hillside, the chimneys of Halkett's Farm rising amid trees, and her own home in its walled garden, and, as she looked, a new thought came to her. Perhaps her expectation was born of a familiarity so intense as to be unreal and rarely recognized, and with the thought she shut her eyes tightly and in despair. Nothing would happen. She did not live in a country subject to convulsions, and when she opened her eyes the same things would still be there; yet, to give Providence an opportunity of proving its strength and her folly, she kept her eyelids lowered for a while. This was another pastime of her childhood: she tried to tempt God, failed, and laughed at Him instead of at herself.

She stood there, clad in a colour of rich earth, her head bare and gilded by the sunlight, both hands on the frail basket, and the white eyelids giving the strange air of experience to her face.

"I'm going to look in a minute," she said, and kept her word. Her dark eyes illumined her face, searched the world and found nothing new. There was, indeed, the smallest possible change, but surely it was not one in which God would trouble to take a hand. She could see John's figure moving slowly on the Brent Farm road. A woman's form appeared in the porch and went to meet his: the two stood together in the road.

Miriam made an impatient noise and turned her back on them. She was irritated by the sight of another woman's power, even though John were its sole victim, for she knew that the world of men had only to become aware of her existence and the track to Pinderwell House would be impassable.

"There's no false modesty about me!" she cried to an astonished sheep, and threw a tuft of heather at it.

Suddenly she lifted her chin and began to sing on notes too high for her, and tunelessly, as sign of her defiance, and the words of her song dealt with the dreariness of the moor and her determination to escape from it; but in the midst of them she laughed delightedly.

"I'm an idiot! Uncle Alfred's coming. But if he fails me"—she kicked the basket and ran after it—"I'll do that to him!"

She sang naturally now, in her low, husky voice, as she searched the banks for violets, but once she broke off to murmur, without humour, with serious belief, "He can't fail me. Who could? No one but Notya." Such was her faith in the word's acknowledgement of charm.

She found the violets, but she would not pick them because

they stared at her with a confidence like her own, and with an appealing innocence, and thinking she might get primroses under Halkett's larches she went on swiftly, waving the basket as though it were an Indian club.

She stopped when she met the stream which foamed into the stealthy quiet of the wood, and on a large flat stone she sat and was splashed by the noisy water. The larch-trees were alive with feathery green, and their arms waved with the wind, but when Miriam peered through their trunks, all was grave and secret except the stream which shouted louder than before in proof of courage. She did not like the trees, but the neighbourhood of Halkett's Farm had an attraction for her. Down there, in the hollow, old Halkett was drinking himself to death, after a life which had been sober in no respect. Mrs. Samson, the charwoman, now exerting herself at Pinderwell House, and the wife of one of Halkett's hands, had many tales of the old man's wickedness and many nodded hints that the son was taking after him. The Halketts were all alike, she said. They married young and their wives died early, leaving their men to take comfort, or celebrate relief, in their own way.

"Ah, yes! They're a hearty, jolly lot," she often said, and smacked her lips. She was proud and almost envious of the Halketts' exploits, for her own husband was a meek man who never misused her and seldom drank.

Widely different as Mrs. Samson and Miriam believed themselves to be, they had a common elementary pleasure in things of ill report, a savage excitement in the presence of certain kinds of danger, and Miriam sat half fearfully by the larch-wood and hoped something terrible would happen. If there was a bad old man on the moor it was a pity that she should not benefit by him, yet she dreaded his approach and would have run from him, for he was ugly, with a pendulous nose and a small leering eye. She decided to stay at a safe distance from the house and not to venture among the larches: any primroses growing there should live undisturbed, timid and pale, within earshot of old

Halkett's ragings, and Uncle Alfred must go without his flowers. Helen had said he would not like them, but that was only because Helen did not like the thought of Uncle Alfred. Helen did not want new things: she was content: she was not wearied by the slow hours, the routine of the quiet house with its stately, polished furniture, chosen long ago by Mr. Pinderwell, the rumbling of cart-wheels on the road, and the homely sounds of John working in the garden. She belonged, as she herself averred, to people and to places.

"And I," Miriam called aloud, touching her breast—"I belong to nobody, though everything belongs to me."

In that announcement she outcried the stream, and through the comparative quietness that followed a hideous noise rumbled and shrieked upwards from the hollow. Bestial, but humanly inarticulate, it filled the air and ceased: there was the loud thud of furniture overthrown, a woman's voice, and silence. Then, while Miriam's legs shook and her back was chilled, she heard a sweet, clear whistling and the sound of feet. A minute later George Halkett issued from the trees.

"George!" she said, and half put out her hand.

He stood before her, his mouth still pursed for whistling, and jerked his head over his shoulder.

"You heard that?"

"Yes. Oh, yes!"

"I'm sorry."

"It's my fault for being here. Was it—what was it?"

His eyes narrowed and she could see a blue slit between lashes so thick that they seemed furred.

"My father. He's ill. I'm sorry you heard."

"Will he—do it again?"

"He's quiet now and Mrs. Biggs can manage him."

"Isn't she afraid?"

"Not she." His thoughts plainly left old Halkett and settled themselves on her. "Are you?"

"Yes." She shuddered. "But then, I'm not used to it."

He was beating his leggings with his cane. "There's a lot in use," he said vaguely. He was a tall man, and on his tanned face were no signs of the excesses imputed to him, perhaps out of vainglory, by Mrs. Samson. A brown moustache followed the line of a lip which was sometimes pouted sullenly, yet with a simplicity which could be lovable. The hair was short and crisp on his round head.

Miriam watched his shapely hands playing with the cane, and she looked up to find his eyes attentively on her. She smiled without haste. She had a gift for smiling. Her mouth stretched delicately, her lips parted to show a gleam of teeth, opened widely for a flash, and closed again.

"What are you laughing at?" he asked her, and there was a faint glow in his cheeks.

"That wasn't laughing. That was smiling. When I laugh I say ha, ha!"

"Well, you looked pleased about something," he mumbled.

"No, I was just being friendly to you."

He took a step nearer. "That's all very well. Last time I met you you hadn't a look for me, and you saw me right enough."

"Yes, George, I saw you, but I wasn't in the mood for you."

"And now you are?"

She looked down. "Do you like people always to be the same? I don't." Laughter bubbled in her voice. "I get moments, George, when my thoughts are so—so celestial that though I see earthly things like you, I don't understand them. They're like shadows, like trees walking." She pointed a finger. "Tell me where that comes from!"

He looked about him. "What?"

She addressed the stream. "He doesn't know the foundation of the English language, English morals—I said morals, George—the spiritual food of his fathers. Do you ever go to church?"

He did not answer: he was frowning at his boots.

"Neither do I," she said. "Help me up."

His hand shot out, but she did not take it. She leapt to her feet and jumped the stream, and when he said something in a low voice she put her fingers to her ears and shook her head, pretending that she could not hear and smiling pleasantly. Then she beckoned to him, but it was his turn to shake his head.

"Puss, puss, puss!" she called, twitching her finger at him. "Don't laugh! Well, I'll come to you." At his side, she looked up solemnly. "Let us be sensible and go where we needn't shout at each other. Beside that rock. I want to tell you something."

When they had settled themselves on a cushion of turf, she drew her knees to her chin and clasped her hands round them, and in that position she swayed lightly to and fro.

"I think I am going away," she said, and stared at the horizon. For a space she listened to the chirping of a cheerful insect and the small, regular noise of Halkett's breathing, but as he made no other sound she turned sharply and looked at him.

"All right," he said.

She moved impatiently, for that was not what she wished to hear, and, even if it expressed his feeling, it was the wrong word. He had roughnesses which almost persuaded her to neglect him.

"Aren't you sorry?"

There was courage in his decision to be truthful. He showed her the full blue of his eyes, and said "Yes" so simply that she felt compassionate. "Where?" he added.

"I'm going to be adopted by an uncle," she said boldly.

"You'll like that?"

"I'm tired of the moor."

"You don't fit it. I couldn't tire of it, but it'll be—different when you've gone."

She consoled him. "I may not go at once."

"How soon?"

"I don't know."

"Are you really going?" he asked and his look pleaded with her for honesty.

"I shall have to arrange it all with Uncle Alfred."

He straightened himself against the rock, but he said nothing.

"And we're just beginning to be friends," she added sensibly, with the faintest accent of regret.

At that he stirred again, and "No," he said steadily, "that's not true. We're not friends—couldn't be. You think I'm a fool, but I can see you're despising me all the time. I can see that, and I wonder why."

She caught her lip. "Well, George," she began, and thought quickly. "I have heard dreadful stories about you. You can't expect me to be—not to be careful with you."

"What stories?" he demanded.

"Oh! I couldn't tell you."

"H'm. There never was a Halkett but was painted so black that he got to think it was his natural colour. That doesn't matter. And you don't care about the stories. You've some notion— D'you know that I went to the same school as your brothers?"

"Yes, I know." She swung herself to her knees. "But you're not like them. But that isn't it either. It's because you're a man." She laughed a little as she knelt before him. "I can't help feeling that I can—that men are mine—to play with. There! I've told you a secret."

"I'd guessed it long ago," he muttered. He stood up and turned aside. "You're not going to play with me."

"Just a little bit, George!"

"Not a little bit."

"Very well," she said humbly, and rose too. "I may never see you again, so I'll say good-bye."

"Good-bye," he answered, and held her hand.

"And if I don't go away, and if I feel that I don't want to play with you, but just to—well, really to be friends with you, can I be?"

"I don't know," he said slowly. "I don't trust you."

She nodded, teasing her lip again. "Very well," she repeated. "I shall remember. Yes. You're going to be very unhappy, you know."

"Why?" he asked dully.

"For saying that to me."

"But it's the truth."

She shook her little hands at him and spoke loudly. "You seem to think the truth's excuse enough for anything, but you're wrong, George, and if you were worth it, I should hate you."

Then she turned from him, and as he watched her run towards home he wished he had lied to her and risked bewitchment.

CHAPTER V

The efforts of Mildred Caniper, Helen and Mrs. Samson produced a brighter polish on floors and furniture, a richer brilliance from brass, a whiter gleam from silver, in a house which was already irreproachable, and the smell of cleanliness was overcome by that of wood fires in the sitting-rooms and in Christopher where Uncle Alfred was to sleep. A bowl of primroses, brought by John from Lily Brent's garden and as yellow as her butter, stood on a table near the visitor's bed: the firelight cast shadows on the white counterpane, a new rug was awaiting Uncle Alfred's feet. In the dining-room, the table was spread with the best cloth and the candles were ready to be lighted.

"When we see the trap," Miriam said, "I'll go round with a taper. And we'd better light the lamp in the kitchen passage or Uncle Alfred may trip over something when he hangs up his coat."

"There won't be anything for him to trip over," Helen said.

"How do you know? It's just the sort of accident that happens to families that want to make a good impression. We'd better do it. Where are the steps?"

"The lamp hasn't been trimmed for months, and we can't have a smell of oil. Leave it alone. The hall is so beautifully dim. Rupert must take his coat and hang it up for him."

"Very well," Miriam said resignedly; "but if Notya or John had suggested the lamp, you would have jumped at it."

"No, I should have fetched the steps."

"Oh, funny, funny! Now I'm going to dress."

"There are two hours."

"It will take me as long as that. What shall I wear? Black or red? It's important, Helen. Tell me."

"Black is safer."

"Yes, if only I had pearls. I should look lovely in black and pearls."

"Pearls," Helen said slowly, "would suit me."

"You're better without them."

"I shall never have them."

"When I've a lot of money I'll give you some."

"Thank you," Helen said.

"Because," Miriam called out when she was half way up the stairs, "I'm going to marry a rich man."

"It would be wise," Helen answered, and went to the open door.

She could hear Notya moving in her bedroom, and she wondered how a sister must feel at the approach of a brother she had not seen for many years. She knew that if she should ever be parted from John or Rupert there would be no shyness at their meeting and no effusion: things would be just as they had been, for she was certain of an affection based on understanding, and now the thought of her brothers kept her warm in spite of the daunting coldness of the light lying on the moor and the fact that doors were opening to a stranger.

She checked a little sigh and stepped on to the gravel path, rounded the house and crossed the garden to find John locking up the hen-house for the night. He glanced at her but did not speak, and she stood with her hands clasped before her and watched the swaying of the poplars. The leaves were spreading and soon they would begin their incessant whispering while they peeped through the windows of the house to see what the Canipers were doing.

"They know all our secrets," she said aloud.

John dropped the key into his pocket. "Have we any?"

"Perhaps not. I should have said our fears."

"Our hopes," he said stubbornly.

"I haven't many of those," she told him and, to hide her trouble, she put the fingers of both hands to her forehead.

"What's the matter with you? You sound pretty morbid."

"No, I'm only—careful. John, are you afraid of life?"

His eyes fell on the rows of springing vegetables. "Look at 'em coming up," he murmured. "Rather not. I couldn't grow things." He gathered up his tools and put them in the shed.

"You see," she said, "one never knows what's going to happen, but it's no good worrying, and I suppose one must just go on."

"It's the only thing to do," John assured her gravely. "Have you made yourself beautiful for the uncle?"

She pointed to an upper window smeared with light. "I have left that to Miriam, but I must go and put on my best frock."

"You always look all right," he said. "I suppose it's because your hair's so smooth."

"No," she answered, and laughed with her transforming gaiety, "it's just because I'm mediocre and don't get noticed."

He hesitated and decided to be bold. "I'll tell you something, as you're so down in the mouth. Rupert thinks you're better looking than Miriam. There! Go and look at yourself." He waved her off, and the questions fell from her lips unuttered.

She lighted a candle and went upstairs, but when she had passed into the dark peace of Jane and put the candle on her dressing-table, she found she needed more illumination by which to see this face which Rupert considered fair.

"Miriam will have heaps of them," she said and knocked at Phoebe's door.

"I've come to borrow a candle," she said as she was told to enter, and added, "Oh, what waste! I hope Notya won't come in."

"She can't unless I let her," Miriam answered grimly.

There were lights on the mantelpiece, on the dressing-table, on the washstand, and two in tall sticks burned before the cheval glass as though it had been an altar.

"You can take one of them," Miriam said airily.

The warm whiteness of her skin gleamed against her under-linen like a pale fruit fallen by chance on frozen snow: her hair was held up by the white comb she had been using, and this stood out at an impetuous angle. She went nearer to the mirror.

"I've been thinking," she said, "what a lovely woman my mother must have been. Do you think I look like a Spanish dancer? Now, don't tell me you've never seen one. Take your candle and go away."

Helen obeyed and shut both doors quietly. She put the second candle beside the first and studied her pale face. She was not beautiful, and Rupert was absurd. She was colourless and rather dull, and to compare her with the radiant being in the other room was to hold a stable lantern to a star.

She turned from her contemplation and, changing grey dress for grey dressing-gown, she brushed her long, straight hair. Ten minutes later she left the room and went about the house to see that all was ready for the guest.

She put coal on the fire in Christopher and left the door ajar so that the flames might cast warm light on the landing: she took a towel from the rail and changed it for another finer one; then she went quietly down the stairs, with a smile for Mr. Pinderwell, and fancied she smelt the spring through the open windows. The hall had a dimness which hid and revealed the rich mahogany of the clock and cupboard and the table from which more primroses sent up a memory of moonlight and a fragrance which was no sooner seized than lost. She could hear Mrs. Samson in the kitchen as she watched over the turbot, and from the schoolroom there came the scraping of a chair. John had dressed as quickly as herself.

In the dining-room she found her stepmother standing by the fire.

"Oh, you look sweet!" Helen exclaimed. "I love you in that dark blue."

"I think I'll wait in the drawing-room," Mildred Caniper said, and went away.

Once more, Helen wandered to the doorway; she always sought the open when she was unhappy and, as she looked over the gathering darkness, she tried not to remember the tone of

Notya's words.

"It's like pushing me off a wall I'm trying to climb," she thought, "but I mean to climb it." And for the second time within an hour, she gave tongue to her sustaining maxim: "I must just go on."

She hoped Uncle Alfred was not expectant of affection.

Night was coming down. The road was hardly separable from the moor, and it was the Brent Farm dogs which warned her of the visitor's approach. Two yellow dots slowly swelled into carriage lamps, and the rolling of wheels and the thud of hoofs were faintly heard. She went quickly to the schoolroom.

"John, the trap's coming."

"Well, what d'you want me to do about it? Stop it?"

"I wish you could."

"Now, don't get fussy."

"I'm not."

"Not get fussy?"

"Not getting fussy."

"That's better. If your grammar's all right the nerves must be in order."

"You're stupid, John. I only want some one to support me—on the step."

"Need we stand there? Rupert's with him. Won't that do?"

"No, I think we ought to say how-d'you-do, here, and then pass him on to Notya in the drawing-room."

"Very good. Stand firm. But they'll be hours rolling up the track. What the devil do we want with an uncle? The last time we stood like this was when our revered father paid us a call. Five years ago—six?"

"Six."

"H'm. If I ever have any children—Where's Miriam? I suppose she's going to make a dramatic entry when she's sure she can't be missed."

"I hope so," Helen said. "The first sight of Miriam—"

"You're ridiculous. She's no more attractive than any other

girl, and it's this admiration that's been her undoing."

"Is she undone?"

"She's useless."

"Like a flower."

"No, she has a tongue."

"Oh, John, you're getting bad-tempered."

"I'm getting tired of this damned step."

"You swear rather a lot," she said mildly. "They're on the track. Oh, Rupert's talking. Isn't it a comfortable sound?"

A few minutes later, she held open the gate and, all unaware of the beauty of her manners, she welcomed a small, neat man who wore an eyeglass. John took possession of him and led him into the hall and Helen waited for Rupert, who followed with the bag. She could see that his eyebrows were lifted comically.

"Well?" she asked.

"Awful. I know he isn't dumb because I've heard him speak, nor deaf because he noticed that the horse had a loose shoe, but that's all I can tell you, my dear. I talked—I had to talk. You can't sit in the dark for miles with some one you don't know and say nothing, but I've been sweating blood." He put the bag down and leaned against the gate. "That man," he said emphatically, "is a mining engineer. He—oh, good-night, Gibbons—he's been all over the globe, so Notya tells us. You'd think he might have picked up a little small talk as well as a fortune, but no. If he's picked it up, he's jolly careful with it. I tell you, I've made a fool of myself, and talked to a thing as unresponsive as a stone wall."

"Perhaps you talked too much."

"I know I did, but I've a hopeful disposition, and I've cured hard cases before now. Of course he must have been thinking me an insufferable idiot, but the darkness and his neighbourhood were too much for me. And that horse of Gibbons's! It's only fit for the knacker. Oh, Lord! I believe I told him the population of the town. There's humiliation for you! He grunted now and then. Well, I'll show the man I can keep quiet too. We ought to have sent John to meet him. They'd have been happy enough together."

"You know," Helen said sympathetically, "I don't suppose he heard half you said or was thinking about you at all."

Rupert laughed delightedly and put his arm through hers as he picked up the bag.

"Come in. No doubt you're right."

"I believe he's really afraid of us," she added. "I should be."

As they entered the hall, they saw Miriam floating down the stairs. One hand on the rail kept time with her descent; her black dress, of airy make, fluffed from stair to stair; the white neck holding her little head was as luminous as the pearls she wanted. She paused on one foot with the other pointed.

"Where is he?" she whispered.

"Just coming out of the drawing-room," Rupert answered quickly, encouraging her. "Stay like that. Chin a little higher. Yes. You're like Beatrix Esmond coming down the stairs. Excellent!"

A touch from Helen silenced him as Mildred Caniper and her brother turned the corner of the passage. They both stood still at the sight of this dark-clad vision which rested immobile for an instant before it smiled brilliantly and finished the flight.

"This is Miriam," Mildred Caniper said in hard tones.

Miriam cast a quick, wavering glance at her and returned to meet the gaze of Uncle Alfred, who had not taken her hand. At last, seeing it outstretched, he took it limply.

"Ah—Miriam," he said, with a queer kind of cough.

"She's knocked him all of a heap," Rupert told himself vulgarly as he carried the bag upstairs, and once more he wished he knew what his mother had been like.

CHAPTER VI

At supper, Uncle Alfred was monosyllabic, and the Canipers, realizing that he was much shyer than themselves, became hospitable. Notya made the droll remarks of which she was sometimes capable, and Miriam showed off without fear of a rebuke. It was a comely party, and Mrs. Samson breathed her heavy pleasure in it as she removed the plates. When the meal was over and Uncle Alfred was smoking placidly in the drawing-room, Helen wandered out to the garden gate. There she found John biting an empty pipe.

After their fashion, they kept silence for a time before Helen said, "Would it matter if I went for a walk?"

"I was thinking of having one myself."

"He won't miss you and me," she said. "May I come with you, or were you going to Brent Farm?"

"I'm not going there. Come on."

The wind met them lightly as they headed towards the road. The night was very dark, and the ground seemed to lift itself before them and sink again at their approach.

"It's like butting into a wave," John said. "I keep shutting my eyes, ready for the shock."

"Yes." Helen began to talk as though she were alone. "The moor is always like the sea, when it's green and when it's black. It moves, too, gently. And now the air feels like water, heavy and soft. And yet the wind's far more alive than water. I'd like to have a wind bath every day. Oh, I'm glad we live here."

She stumbled, and John caught her by the elbow.

"Want a hand?"

"No, thank you. It's these slippers."

"High heels?"

"No, a stone. I wonder if the fires are out. It's so long since last night. We'd better not go far, John."

"We'll stop at Halkett's turning."

They took the road, and their pace quickened to the drum beats of their feet.

"It sounds like winter," Helen said.

"But it feels like spring."

She thought she heard resentment for that season in his voice. "Well, why don't you go and tell her?"

"Oh, shut up! What's the use? I've no money. A nice suitor I'd make for a woman like that!"

Helen's voice sang above their footsteps and the swishing of her dress. "Silly, old-fashioned ideas you've got! They're rather insulting to her, I think."

"Perhaps, if she cares; but if she doesn't—She'd send me off like a stray dog."

"That's pride. You shouldn't be proud in love."

"You should be proud in everything, I believe. And what do you know about it?"

"Oh—I think. Can you hear a horse, a long way off? And of course I want to be married, too, but Miriam is sure to be, and then Notya would be left alone. Besides, I couldn't leave the moor, and there's no one but George Halkett here!"

"H'm. You're not going to marry him."

"No, I'm not—but I'm sorry for him."

"You needn't be. He's no good. You must have nothing to do with him. Ask Lily Brent. He tried to kiss her once, the beast, but she nearly broke his nose, and serve him right."

"Oh? Did she mind?"

"Mind!"

"I don't think I should have. He looks clean, and if he really wanted to kiss me very badly, I expect I should let him. It's such a little thing."

"Good heavens, girl!" He stopped in a stride and turned to her. "That kind of charity is very ill-advised."

Her laughter floated over his head with the coolness of the wind. "I hope I shan't have to give way to it."

He continued to be serious. "Well, you're not ignorant. Rupert and I made up our minds to that as soon as we knew anything ourselves; but women are such fools, such fools! Tender-hearted idiots!"

"Is that why you're afraid to go to Lily Brent?" she asked.

"Ah, that's different," he mumbled. "She's more like a man."

Helen was smiling as they walked on. "If you could have Lily Brent and give up your garden, or keep your garden and lose her—"

"I'm not going to talk about it," he said.

"I wanted to know how much love really matters. That horse is much nearer now. We'll see the lights soon. And there's some one by the roadside, smoking. It's George. Good-evening, George."

His deep voice rumbled through the darkness, exchanging salutations. "I'm waiting for the doctor."

"Some one's coming now."

"Yes, it's his old nag. That horse makes you believe in eternity, anyhow."

She felt a sudden, painful anger. "He's a friend of mine—the horse," and quietly, she repeated to herself, "The horse," because he had no name by which she could endear him.

"Is Mr. Halkett worse?" John asked, from the edge of the road.

The red end of Halkett's cigar glowed and faded. "I'm anxious about him."

The yellow lights of the approaching dog-cart swept the borders of the moor and Helen felt herself caught in the illumination. The horse stopped and she heard the doctor's clear-cut voice.

"Is that you, Helen?"

"Yes."

"Anything wrong?"

"No, I'm just here with John," she said and went close to the cart. "And George is waiting for you."

"He'd better hop up, then." He bent towards her. "Did you find the fires?"

She nodded with the vehemence of her gladness that he should remember. "And," she whispered hurriedly, "you were quite right about the doors. Uncle Alfred's going to be a friend."

"That's good. Hullo, Halkett. Get up, will you, and we'll go on. Where's John?"

"Sitting on the bank."

The cart shook under Halkett's added weight, and as he took his seat he bulked enormous in the darkness. Dwarfed by that nearness, the doctor sat with his hat in one hand and gathered the reins up with the other.

"No, just a minute!" Helen cried. "I want to stroke the horse." Her voice had laughter in it.

"There's a patient waiting for me, you know."

"Yes. There! It's done. Go on. Good-night."

The cart took the corner in a blur of lamplight and shadow, tipped over a large stone and disappeared down the high-banked lane, leaving Helen with an impressive, half-alarming memory of the two jolted figures, black, with white ovals for faces, side by side, and Zebedee's spare frame clearing itself, now and then, from the other's breadth.

In the drawing-room, Uncle Alfred sat on one side of the hearth and Miriam on the other. The room was softly lighted by candles and the fire, and at the dimmer end Mr. Pinderwell's bride was smiling. The sound of Mildred Caniper's needle, as she worked at an embroidery frame, was added to the noises of the fire and Uncle Alfred's regular pulling at his pipe. Rupert was proving his capacity for silence on the piano stool.

"And which country," Miriam asked, leaning towards her uncle, "do you like best?"

"Oh—well, I hardly know."

"I never care for the sound of Africa—so hot."

"Hottish," conceded Uncle Alfred.

"Oh, Lord!" Rupert groaned in spirit.

"And South America, full of crocodiles, isn't it?"
"Is it?"
"Haven't you been there?"
"Yes, yes—parts of it."
"Miriam," said Mildred Caniper, "Alfred is not a geography book."
"But he ought to be," she dared.
"And," the cool voice went on, "you never cared for geography, I remember."

Miriam sat back sullenly, stiffening until her prettily shod feet reached an inch further along the fender. Rupert would not relieve the situation and the visitor smoked on, watching Miriam through his tobacco smoke, until a knock came at the door.

"I beg your pardon, M'm—"
"It's Mother Samson," said Rupert. "Shall I look after her?"
"No. I will go." The door closed quietly behind Mrs. Caniper.

Uncle Alfred lowered his pipe. "You are extraordinarily like your mother," he said in quick and agitated tones, and the life of the room was changed amazingly. Rupert turned on his seat, and his elbow scraped the piano notes so that they jangled like a hundred questions. Miriam slipped out of her chair.

"Am I?" she asked from her knees. "I knew I was. Tell me!"

He put his hand to his breast-pocket. "Ah," he said, as a step sounded in the passage, "perhaps tomorrow—"

Miriam lifted the poker. "Because you mustn't poke the fire, Uncle Alfred," she was saying as Mildred Caniper came back. "You haven't known us long enough." She turned to her stepmother. "Did Mrs. Samson want her money? She's saving up. She's going to have a new dress this summer because she hasn't had one since she was married."

"And if she hadn't married," Rupert went on, feeling like a conspirator, "she would have had one every year."

"That gives one something to think about—yes," said Uncle Alfred, doing his share. He was astonished at himself. He had spent the greater part of his life in avoiding relationships which might hamper him and already he was in league with these young people and finding pleasure in the situation.

Miriam was looking at him darkly, mischievously, from the hearthrug. "Tomorrow," she said, resting on the word, "I'll take you for a walk to see the sights. There are rabbits, sheep, new lambs, very white and lively, a hare if we're lucky, ponies, perhaps, if we go far enough. We've all these things on the moor. Oh," her grimace missed foolishness by the hair's breadth which fortune always meted to her, "it's a wonderful place. Will you come with me?"

He nodded with a guilty quickness. "What are these ponies?"

"Little wild ones, with long tails."

"I'm fond of horses," he said and immediately looked ashamed of the confession. "Ha, ha, 'um," he half hummed, trying to cloak embarrassment.

"I'm fond of all animals," Miriam said with loud bitterness, "but we are only allowed to have a cat."

"Hens," Rupert reminded her.

"They're not animals; they're idiots."

"Would you like to keep a cow in the garden?" Mildred Caniper enquired in the pleasantly cold tones which left Miriam powerless.

Uncle Alfred's tuneless humming began again. "Yes, fond of horses," he said vaguely, his eyes quick on woman and girl.

"And can you ride?" Miriam asked politely, implying that it was not necessary for the whole family to be ill-mannered.

"I've had to—yes, but I don't care about it. No, I like to look at them."

"We rode when we were children," his sister said.

"Hung on."

"Well, yes."

Miriam would not encourage these reminiscences, so belated on the part of her stepmother. "We have a neighbour who grows horses," she said. "And he's a wonderful rider. Rupert, don't you think he'd like to show them to Uncle Alfred? On Saturday afternoon, couldn't you take him to the farm?"

"But I'm going on Saturday," Uncle Alfred interposed.

"Saturday! And today's Thursday! Oh!"

"At least I think so," he said weakly.

Secretly she shook her head at him. "No, no," she signed, and said aloud, "A Sunday in the country—"

"No place of worship within four miles," Rupert announced.

"Ah," Uncle Alfred said with a gleam of humour, "that's distinctly cheering."

Miriam beat her hands together softly. "And yet," she said, "I've sometimes been to church for a diversion. Have you?"

"Never," he answered firmly.

"I counted the bald heads," she said mournfully, "but they didn't last out." She looked up and saw that Uncle Alfred was laughing silently: she glanced over her shoulder and saw Mildred Caniper's lips compressed, and she had a double triumph. This was the moment when it would be wise for her to go to bed. Like a dark flower, lifting itself to the sun, she rose from her knees in a single, steady movement.

"Good-night," she said with a little air. "And we'll have our walk tomorrow?"

He was at the door, holding it open. "Yes, but—in the afternoon, if we may. I am not an early riser, and I don't feel very lively in the mornings."

"Ah," she thought as she went upstairs, "he wouldn't have said that to my mother. He's getting old: but never mind, I'm like a lady in a romance! I believe he loved my mother and I'll make him love me."

CHAPTER VII

She was not allowed time for that achievement. On the morning of the day which was to have been productive of so much happiness, the postman brought a letter with a foreign stamp, and Miriam took it to the kitchen where her stepmother and Helen were discussing meals.

"A letter," Miriam said flippantly, "from Italy."

"Thank you, Miriam. Put it on the table." The faint colour our deepened on her cheeks. "I'm afraid one of you will have to go into the town again. I forgot to ask Rupert to order the meat. Miriam—"

"No, I can't go. I'm engaged to Uncle Alfred."

"I think we might easily persuade him to excuse you. He really dislikes walking, though he would not say so."

"Or," Helen said with tact, "we could get chickens from Lily Brent. Wouldn't that be better?"

"Very well. Now, about sweets."

"This letter," Miriam said, bending over it and growing bold in the knowledge that Uncle Alfred was not far off, "this letter looks as if it wants to be opened. All the way from Italy," she mumbled so that Mildred Caniper could not distinguish the words, "and neglected when it gets here. If he took the trouble to write to me, I wouldn't treat him like that. Poor letter! Poor Mr. Caniper! No wonder he went away to Italy." She stood up. "His writing is very straggly," she said clearly.

Mildred Caniper put out a hand which Miriam pretended not to see.

"Shall I order the chickens?" she asked; but no one answered, for her stepmother was reading the letter, and Helen preserved silence as though she were in a church. With care that the dishes should not click against each other, she put the newly washed china on the dresser and laid the silver in its place, and now and then she glanced at Notya, who stood beside the table. It was some time before she folded the letter with a crackle and looked up. Her eyes wandered from Helen to Miriam, and rested there with an unconsciousness so rare as to be startling.

"Philip is ill," she said in a voice carried by her thoughts to a great distance. She corrected herself. "Your father is ill." She picked up the envelope and looked at it. "That's why his writing is so—straggly." She seemed to be thinking not only of Philip Caniper, but of many things besides, so that her words, like her thoughts, came through obstacles.

Intensely interested in a Notya moved to some sign of an emotion which was not annoyance, Miriam stood in the doorway and took care to make no movement which might betray her; but Helen stared at the fire and suffered the pain she had always felt for her stepmother's distresses.

"However—" Mildred Caniper said at last, and set briskly to work, while Miriam disappeared into the shadows of the hall and Helen watched the flames playing round the kettle in which the water for Uncle Alfred's breakfast was bubbling.

"How ill is he?" she asked.

"Are you speaking of your father?"

"Yes—please."

"I wish you would use names instead of pronouns. A good deal worse, I am afraid."

"And there's nobody to look after him—our father?"

"Certainly there is."

"Oh! I'm glad," Helen said, looking candidly at Notya. "We can't pretend to care about him—can we? But I don't like to have a father who is ill."

"If he had known that—" the other began, and stopped the foolish little sarcasm in time. "It is no use discussing things, Helen. We have to do them."

"Well, let us go to Italy," Helen said.

Mildred Caniper did not conceal her surprise. Her lips dropped apart, and she stood, balancing in a spoon the egg she was about to boil for Uncle Alfred, and gazed at Helen, before she recovered herself and said easily, "You are rather absurd, Helen, aren't you?"

But Helen knew that she was not. "I thought that was just what you were wanting to do," she answered.

The egg went into the saucepan and was followed by another.

"We can't," Mildred Caniper said with the admonishing air which sat like an imposition on her; "we cannot always do as we wish."

"Oh, I know that," Helen said. She put on a pair of gloves, armed herself with brooms and dusters, and left the room.

It seemed to her that people wilfully complicated life. She put a just value on the restraint which had been a great part of her training, but a pretence which had the transparency of its weakness moved her to a patient kind of scorn, and in that moment she had a flash of insight which showed her that she had sometimes failed to understand her stepmother because she had not suspected the variability of the elder woman's character. Mildred Caniper produced an impression of strength in which she herself did not believe; she had imprisoned her impulses in coldness, and they only escaped in the sharp utterances of her tongue; she was uncertain of her power, and she insisted on its acceptance.

"And she's miserable, miserable," Helen's heart cried out, and she laughed unhappily herself. "And Miriam's afraid of her! There's nothing to be afraid of. She knows that, and she's afraid we'll find it out all the time. And it might all have been so simple and so—so smooth."

Helen was considered by the other Canipers and herself as the dullest of the family, and this morning she swept, dusted and polished in the old ignorance of her acuteness, nor would the knowledge of it have consoled her. She was puzzling over the cause which kept the man in Italy apart from the woman here, and when she gave that up in weariness, she tried to picture him in a white house beside an eternally blue sea. The windows of the house had jalousies of a purplish red, there were palm-trees in the sloping garden and, at the foot of it, waves rocked a shallow, tethered boat. And her father was in bed, no doubt; the flush redder on his thin cheeks, his pointed black beard jerked over the sheet. She had seen him lying so on his last visit to the moor, and she had an important little feeling of triumph in the memory of that familiarity. She was not sentimental about this distant parent, for he was less real than old Halkett, far less real than Mr. Pinderwell; yet it seemed cruel that he should lie in that warm southern country without a wife or daughter to care for him.

"Helen," Miriam said from Phoebe's door, "do you think he is going to die?"

"How can I tell?"

"And you don't care?"

"Not much, of course, but I'm sorry for him."

"Sweet thing! And if he dies, shall we wear black?"

Helen's pale lips condescended to a rather mocking smile. "I see you mean to."

"Well, if you can do the proper thing and look nice at the same time—" She broke off and fidgeted. "I don't mind his dying if he does it far away, but, oh, wouldn't it be horrible if he did it here? Ill people make me sick."

"Why don't you go and do something yourself? Go and amuse Uncle Alfred."

"No, he's not nice in the mornings. He said so, and I've peeped at him. Liverish."

"Order the chickens, then, but ask Notya first."

"Where is she?"

Together they peeped over the banisters and listened.

"You'd better ask," Miriam said. "I wonder where she is. Call her," she added, daring Helen to break one of the rules of that quiet house; and Helen, who had discovered the truth that day, lifted her voice clearly.

"If she's not cross," Miriam whispered, "we'll know she's worried."

"Oh," Helen said soberly, "how horrid of us! I wish I hadn't."

Miriam's elbow was in her side. "Here she comes, look!"

They could see the crown of Mildred Caniper's fair head, the white blot of her clasped hands.

"What is it?" she asked quietly, turning up her face.

"Shall Miriam order the chickens?" Helen called down.

"Oh, yes—yes," she answered, and went away.

"Ha, ha! Quite successful! Any special kind of chicken? Black legs? Yellow legs?"

"She'll give you the best she has," Helen said.

Miriam popped her head round the door of the dining-room where Uncle Alfred was smoking, waved her hand, and spared him the necessity of speech by running from the house. The sun shone in a callous sky and the wind bit at her playfully as she went down the track, to remind her that though she wore neither hat nor coat, summer was still weeks away. Miriam faced all the seasons now with equanimity, for Uncle Alfred was in the dining-room, and she intended that her future should be bound up with his. Gaily she mounted the Brent Farm road, with a word for a melancholy calf which had lost its way, and a feeling of affection for all she saw and soon meant to leave. She liked the long front of the farmhouse with its windows latticed into diamonds, the porch sentinelled by large white stones, the path outlined with smaller ones and the green gate with its two steps into the field.

The dairy door stood open, and Miriam found both Lily Brent and John within. They stood with the whole space of the floor between them and there was a certain likeness in their attitudes. Each leaned against the stone shelf which jutted, waist high, from the wall, but neither took support from it. Her brown eyes were level with his grey ones; her hands were on her hips, while his arms were folded across his breast.

"Hullo, Napoleon!" Miriam said. "Good-morning, Lily. Is he being tiresome? He looks it."

"We're only arguing," she said. "We often do it."

This was the little girl whom Mrs. Brent, now in her ample grave, had slapped and kissed and teased, to the edification of the Canipers. She had grown tall and very straight; her thick dark hair was twisted tightly round her head; her skirt was short, revealing firm ankles and wooden shoes, and she wore a jersey which fitted her body closely and left her brown neck bare. Her watchful eyes were like those of some shy animal, but her lips had the faculty of repose. Helen had once compared her to a mettlesome young horse and there was about her some quality of the male. She might have been a youth scorning passion because she feared it.

"If it's a very important argument," said Miriam, "I'll retire. There's a sad baby calf down by your gate. I could go and talk to him."

"Silly little beast!" Lily said; "he's always making a fuss. Listen to this, Miriam. John wants to pay me for letting him work a strip of my land that's been lying idle all these years."

"If you won't let me pay rent—"

"He hasn't any money, Lily."

"I can try to pay you by helping on the farm. You can lie in bed and let me do your share of milking."

"He'll do no harm," Miriam asserted.

"I know that. He's been doing odd jobs for us ever since we began carrying his vegetables to town. He likes to pay for all he gets. You're mean-spirited, John."

"All right. I'll be mean-spirited, and I'll be here for this evening's milking."

"That's settled, then," she said, with a great semblance of relief.

"And Mrs. Caniper of Pinderwell House will be very much obliged if you'll let her have two chickens as soon as possible."

"Certainly, miss. I'll go and see about them."

Miriam let out a little scream and put her hands to her ears.

"No, no, don't kill them yet! Not till you're quite sure that I'm safely on the other side of the road. John, stop her!"

"You're a little goose," Lily said. "They're lying quite comfortably dead in the larder."

"Oh, thank Heaven! Shall I tell you a horrible secret of my past life? Once when I was very small, I crept through Halkett's larch-wood just to see what was happening down there, because Mrs. Samson had been hinting things, and what I saw—oh, what do you think I saw?" She shuddered and, covering her face, she let one bright eye peep round the protecting hand. "I saw that idiot boy wringing a hen's neck! And now," she ended, "I simply can't eat chicken."

"Dear, dear!" John said, and clucked his tongue. "Dreadful confession of a young girl!"

Lily Brent was laughing. "And to think I've wrung their necks myself!"

"Have you? Ugh! Nasty!"

"It is, but some one had to do it."

"Don't do it again," said John quickly.

She raised her eyebrows, met his glance, and looked away.

"I can't get on with my work while you two are gossiping here."

"Come home, John. Father's iller. Notya's too much worried to be cross. She had a letter—Aren't you interested?"

He was thinking, "I'll start breaking up that ground tomorrow," and behind that conscious thought there was another: "I shall be able to watch her going in and out."

"John—"

"No, I'm not interested. Go home and look after your uncle. I've a lot to think about."

She left him sitting on a fence and staring creatively at his knees.

CHAPTER VIII

Helen met Miriam in the hall.

"There's been a telegram and Notya's going to Italy."

"Ah!" Miriam said, but her bright looks faded when Helen added, "With Uncle Alfred."

Miriam dropped her head and thrust her doubled fists under her chin, in the angry movement of her childhood. "Oh, isn't that just my luck!" she muttered fiercely. "I—I hadn't done with Uncle Alfred."

"Perhaps father hasn't done with life," Helen remarked.

"Oh, don't be pious! Don't be pious! You're always adorning tales. You're a prig!"

"Well, I haven't time to think about that now," Helen said with the excellent humour which made amends for her many virtues. "I'm helping Notya to pack and I want you to ask George Halkett if he will drive her down. The train goes at a quarter to three."

"I'm sorry," Miriam said, looking like the heroine in a play, "but I can't go there. I—don't approve of George."

"Oh!" Helen cried, screwing up her face. "Has John been telling you about Lily Brent?"

"No. What? Tell me!" Miriam answered with complete forgetfulness of her pose.

"Some nonsense. George tried to kiss her."

"Did he?" There was a flat tone in Miriam's voice.

"And she hit him, and now John thinks he's wicked."

"So he is." She was hardly aware of what she said, for she was hesitating between the immediate establishment of her supremacy and the punishment of George, and having decided that his punishment should include sufficient tribute, she said firmly, "I won't have anything to do with him."

"Then I'll go. Help Notya if you can."

Miriam took a step nearer. "What is she like?"

"Oh—queer."

"Then perhaps I'd rather go to George," she whispered.

"I'm halfway there already," Helen said from the door.

She slipped across the moor with the speed which came so easily to her, and her breathing had hardly quickened when she issued from the larch-wood and stood on the cobble-stones before the low white house. Already the leaves of a rose-tree by the door were budding, for in that sheltered place the sun was gathered warmly. So, too, she thought, darkness would lie closely there and rain would shoot down in thick splinters with intent to hurt. She was oppressed by a sense of concentration in this tree-lined hollow, and before she stepped across the yard she lifted and shook her shoulders to free them of the weight. She remembered one summer day when the air had been clogged by the scent of marigolds, but this was not their season, and the smell of the larches came healthfully on the winds that struggled through the trees.

She had raised her hand to knock on the open door when she heard a step, and turned to see George Halkett.

"George," she said without preamble, "I've come to ask you to do something for us. Our stepmother has unexpectedly to catch a train. Could you, would you, drive her down—and a box, and our uncle, and his bag?"

She found, to her surprise, that John's story had given George a new place in her mind. She had been accustomed to see him as a mere part of the farm which bore his name, and now she looked at him with a different curiosity. She imagined him bending over Lily Brent and, with a strong distaste, she pictured him starting back at her assault. It seemed to her, she could not tell why, that no woman should raise her hand against a man, and that this restraint was less for her dignity than for his.

"I'll do it with pleasure," George was saying.

"Thank you very much," she murmured, and named the time.

"Is Mr. Halkett better?"

"I'm afraid he's never going to get better, Miss Helen," he said, using the title he had given her long ago because of a childish dignity which amused him.

"I'm sorry," she said, and wondered if she spoke the truth.

Her gaze, very wide and serious, affected his, and as they looked at each other she realized that, with those half-closed eyes of his, he was considering her as he had never done before. She became conscious of her physical self at once, and this was an experience strange to her; she remembered the gown she wore, the fashion of her hair, her grey stockings and worn, low shoes; slowly, almost imperceptibly, she shifted a foot which was twisted inwards, and having done this, she found that she did not like George's appraisement. With a broken word of farewell and thanks she quickly left him.

"I didn't like that," she said emphatically to the broad freedom of the moor. George's interest was like the hollow: it hemmed her in and made her hot, but here the wide winds swept over her with a cleansing cold. Nevertheless, when she went to Notya's room, she took the opportunity of scanning herself in the glass.

"You have been running," Mildred Caniper said.

"No, not lately."

"You are very pink."

"Yes."

Mildred Caniper's tone changed suddenly. "And I don't know where you have been. I wish you would not run off without warning. And I could not find Miriam anywhere." From anger she sank back to helplessness. "I don't know what to take," she said, and her hands jerked on her lap.

"Let's see," Helen said cheerfully. "Warm things for the journey, and cooler things for when you get there." She made no show of consulting Notya and, moving with leisurely competence from wardrobe to chest of drawers, she laid little heaps of clothing on the bed.

"Handkerchiefs: one, two, three, four—"

"I shan't need many."

"But you'd better take a lot."

"I shall soon come back."

"Five, six, seven," Helen counted on, and her whispers sounded loudly in the room where Mildred Caniper's thoughts were busy.

"You haven't a very warm coat, so you must take mine," Helen said, and when she looked up she discovered in her stepmother the extraordinary stillness of a being whose soul has gone on a long journey. Her voice came, as before, from that great distance, yet with surprising clearness, as though she spoke through some instrument which reduced the volume and accentuated the peculiarities of her tones.

"One ought never to be afraid of anything," the small voice said—"never." Her lips tightened, and slowly she seemed to return to the body which sat on the sofa by the window. "I don't know what to take," she said again.

"I'm doing it," Helen told her. "You mustn't lose the train."

"No." She stood up, and, going to the dressing-table, she leaned on it as though she searched intently for something lying there. "I expect he will be dead," she said. "It's a long way. All those frontiers—"

Helen looked at the bent back, and her pity shaped itself in eager words. "Shall I come with you? Let me! I can get ready—"

Mildred Caniper straightened herself and turned, and Helen recognized the blue light in her eye.

"Your presence, Helen," she said distinctly, "will not reduce the number of the frontiers." Her manner blamed Helen for her own lack of self-control; but to this her stepchildren were accustomed, and Helen felt no anger.

"Oh, no," she answered pleasantly; "it would not do that."

She packed on methodically, and while she feigned absorption in that business her thoughts were swift and troubled, as they were when she was a little girl and, suffering for Notya's sake, wept in the heather. It was impossible to help this woman whose curling hair mocked her sternness, whose sternness so easily collapsed and as easily recovered at a word; it was, perhaps, intrusive to attempt it, yet the desire was as quick as Helen's blood.

"You are much too helpful, Helen," Mildred Caniper went on, and softened that harshness quickly. "You must learn that no one can help anybody else." She smiled. "You must deny yourself the luxury of trying!"

"I shall remember," Helen said with her quiet acquiescence, "but I must go now and see about your lunch. Would you mind writing the labels? Uncle Alfred will want one for his bag. Oh, I know I'm irritating," she added on a wave of feeling which had to break, "but I can't help it. I—I'm like that." She reflected with humiliation that it was absurd to obtrude herself thus on a scene shadowed by tragedy, yet when she saw a glint of real amusement on Mildred Caniper's face, a new thought came to her. Perhaps reserve was not so great a virtue as she had believed. She must not forget; nor must she forget that Miriam considered her a prig, that Mildred Caniper found her too helpful. She pressed her hands against her forehead and concentrated her energies on the travellers' food.

The minutes, busy as they were, dragged by like hours. Uncle Alfred ate his luncheon with the deliberation of a man who cannot expect to renew his digestive apparatus, and the road remained empty of George Halkett and his trap. Mildred Caniper, calm now, and dressed for her journey, had many instructions for Helen concerning food, the employment of Mrs. Samson, bills to be paid, and other domestic details which at this moment lacked reality.

"And," she ended, "tell Rupert not to be late. The house should be locked up at ten o'clock."

"Yes," Helen answered, but when she looked at her stepmother she could see only the distressed figure which had sat on the sofa, with hands jerking on its knee. Did she love Philip Caniper? Had they quarrelled long ago, and did she now want to make amends? No, no! She shut her eyes. She must not pry.

She felt as though she had caught herself reading a letter which belonged to some one else.

Not deterred by such squeamishness, Miriam watched the luncheon-party with an almost indecent eagerness. Her curiosity about Mildred Caniper was blurred by pleasure in her departure, and each mouthful unwillingly taken by that lady seemed to minister to Miriam's freedom. Now and then she went to the garden gate to look for George, yet with her hurry to drive out her stepmother there was that luckless necessity to let Uncle Alfred go. On him her dark gaze was fastened expectantly. Surely he had something to say to her; doubtless he waited for a fitting opportunity, and she was determined that he should have it, but she realized that he was past the age when he would leap from an unfinished meal to whisper with her. This put a disturbing limit to her power, and with an instinct for preserving her faith in herself she slightly shifted the view from which she looked at him. So she was reassured, and she waited like an affectionate grand-daughter in the dark corner of the passage where his coat and hat were hanging.

"Let me help you on," she said.

"Thank you. Thank you. This is a sad business."

She handed him his hat. She found that, after all, she could say nothing, and though hope was dying in her, she made no effort to revive it.

"Well—good-bye," Uncle Alfred was saying, and holding out his hand.

She gave hers limply. "Good-bye." She hardly looked at him. Uncle Alfred, who had loved her mother, was going without so much as a cheering word. He looked old and rather dull as he went on with his precise small steps into the hall and she walked listlessly behind him.

"He's like a little performing animal," she thought.

Fumbling in his breast pocket, he turned to her. "If you should need me," he said, and produced his card. "I'll write and tell you what happens—er—when we get there."

She thanked and passed him coldly, for she felt that he had broken faith with her.

Outside the gate George Halkett sat in his high dog-cart and idly laid the whip across the horse's back. John stood and talked to him with the courtesy exacted by the circumstances, but George's eye caught the sunlight on Miriam's hair, and sullenly he bowed to her. She smiled back, putting the venom and swiftness of her emotion into that salute. She watched until his head slowly turned towards her again, and then it happened that she was looking far beyond the chimneys of Brent Farm.

"Now he's angry," she told herself, and pleasure went like a creeping thing down her back. She could see by the stubborn set of his head that he would not risk another glance.

Behind her, on the step, Notya was still talking to Helen.

Uncle Alfred stopped swinging his eyeglass and clicked the gold case of his watch. "We must be going," he said, and Miriam's heart cried out, "Yes; go, go, go!"

Lightly and strangely, Mildred Caniper kissed the cheeks of Miriam and Helen and shook John's hand, before she took her place beside George Halkett, with a word of thanks. Uncle Alfred stiffly climbed to his perch at the back, and, incommoded by his sister's box, he sat there, clasping the handrail. A few shufflings of his feet and rearrangements of his body told of his discomfort, and on his face there was the knowledge that this was but the prelude to worse things. Mildred Caniper did not look back nor wave a hand, but Uncle Alfred's unfortunate position necessitated a direct view of his young relatives. Three times he lifted his hat, and at last the cart swung into the road and he need look no more.

Miriam fanned herself with her little apron. "Now, how long can we count on in the most unfavourable circumstances?" she asked, but, to her astonishment, the others walked off without a word. She set her teeth in her under-lip and stared through tears at the lessening cart. She began to sing so that she might keep down the sobs that hurt her throat, and the words told of her satisfaction that Uncle Alfred was perched uncomfortably on the back seat of the cart.

"And I wish he would fall off," she sang. "Oh, dear, oh, dear, oh, dear!"

CHAPTER IX

The three did not meet again until the sun had set and the brilliant sky had taken on the pale, cold colour in which, like a reluctant bride, it waited for the night. Then John put away his tools and Miriam began to stir about the house which was alive with a secret life of stone and woodwork, of footsteps silenced long ago, and thoughts which refused to die: then, too, Helen came back from the moor where she had gone for comfort. Her feet were wet, her hair was for once in disarray, but her eyes shone with a faith restored. Warring in her always were two beliefs, one bright with the beauty and serenity which were her idea of good, the other dark with the necessity of sacrifice and propitiation. She had not the freedom of her youth, and she saw each good day as a thing to be accepted humbly and ultimately to be paid for, yet she would show no sign of fear. She had to go on steadily under the banner of a tranquil face, and now the moor and the winds that played on it had made that going easier.

She passed through the darkening garden, glanced at the poplars, which looked like brooms sweeping away the early stars, and entered the house by the kitchen door. John and Miriam sat by a leaping fire, but the room was littered with unwashed dishes and the remains of meals.

"Well," Miriam said in answer to Helen's swift glance and the immediate upturning of her sleeves, "why should I do it all? Look at her, John, trying to shame me."

"I'm not. I just can't bear it."

"Have some tea first," John said.

"Let me pile up the plates."

"Have some tea," Miriam echoed, "and I'll make toast; but you shouldn't have gone away without telling me. I didn't know where you were, and the house was full of emptiness."

"I found her snivelling about you," John said. "She wanted me to go out and look for you with a lantern! After a day's work!"

"Things," Miriam murmured, "might have got hold of her."

"I shouldn't have minded moor things. Oh, these stained knives! John, did she really cry?"

"Nearly, I did."

"Not she!"

"I did, Helen. I thought the dark would come, and you'd be lost perhaps, out on the moor—O-oh!"

"I think I'd like it—wrapped up in the night."

"But the noises would send you mad. Your eyes are all red. Have you been crying too?"

"It's the wind. Here's the rain coming. And where's my hair?" She smoothed it back and took off her muddy shoes before she sat down in the armchair and looked about her. "Isn't it as if somebody were dead?" she asked. "There are more shadows."

"I'll turn up the lamp," John said.

The tinkle of Helen's cup and saucer had the clearness of a bell in the quiet room, and she moved more stealthily. Miriam paused as she spread butter on the toast.

"This house is full of dead people," she whispered. "If you begin to think about them—John, you're not going, are you?"

"Only to draw the curtains. Yes, here's the rain."

"And soon Notya will be on the sea," Helen said, listening to the sounds of storm.

"And I hope," Miriam added on a rich burst of laughter, "that Uncle Alfred will be sea-sick. Oh, wouldn't he look queer!" She flourished the knife. "Can't we be merry when we have the chance? Now that she's gone, why should the house still feel full of her? It isn't fair!"

"You're dripping butter on the floor," Helen said.

"Make your old toast yourself, then!"

"It's not only Notya," Helen went on, as she picked up the knife. "It's the Pinderwells and their thoughts, and the people who lived here before them. Their thoughts are in the walls and they come out when the house is quiet."

"Then let us make a noise!" Miriam cried. "Tomorrow's Saturday, and Daniel will come up. Shall we ask him to stay? It would make more live people in the house."

"If he stays, I'm not going to have Rupert in my room again. He talks in his sleep."

"It's better than snoring," Helen said.

"Awful to marry a man who snores," Miriam remarked. "Uncle Alfred does. I heard him."

"You're not thinking of marrying him?" John asked.

"No. I don't like the little man," she said incisively. "He gave me his card as though he'd met me in a train. In case we needed him! I've thrown it into Mrs. Pinderwell's desk." She looked frowningly at the fire. "But he liked me," she said, throwing up her head and defying the silent criticism of the company. "Yes, he did, but I hadn't enough time."

"That's better than too much," Helen said shrewdly, and stretched her stockinged feet to the bars. "Thank you for the tea, and now let us wash up."

"You're scorching," Miriam said, and no one moved. The lamplight had driven the shadows further back, and the room was the more peaceful for the cry of the wind and the hissing of the rain.

"Rupert will get wet," Helen said.

"Poor lad!" John mocked drowsily over his pipe.

"And he doesn't know about our father," Miriam said from her little stool. "Our father, who may be in Heaven."

"That's where Notya is afraid he is," Helen sighed remembering her stepmother's lonely figure on the sofa backed by the bare window and the great moor.

"Does she hate him as much as that?"

"Oh, I hate jokes about Heaven and Hell. They're so obvious," Helen said.

"If they weren't, you wouldn't see them, my dear."

Helen let that pass, but trouble looked from her eyes and sounded in her voice. "She wanted to see him and she was afraid, and no one should ever be afraid. It's ugly."

"Perhaps," Miriam said hopefully, "he will be ill for a very long time, and then she'll have to stay with him, and we can have fun. Fun! Where can we get it? What right had she to bring us here?"

"For God's sake," John said, "don't begin that again. We're warm and fed and roofed, and it's raining outside, and we needn't stir. That ought to make you thankful for your mercies. Suppose you were a tramp."

"Yes, suppose I was a tramp." She clasped her knees and forgot her anger in this make-believe. "A young tramp. Just like me, but ragged."

"Cold and wet."

"My hair would still be curly and my face would be very brown."

"You'd be dirty," Helen reminded her, "and your boots would be crumpled and too big and sodden." She looked at her own slim feet. "That is what I should hate."

"Of course there'd be disadvantages, but if I were a tramp and dwelt on my mercies, what would they be? First—freedom!"

"Ha!" John snorted.

"Well?"

"Freedom! Where is it?"

"With the lady tramp."

"And what is it?"

"Being able to do what you like," Miriam said promptly, "and having no Notya."

John was trying to look patient. "Very well. Let us consider that."

"Yes, grandpapa," Miriam answered meekly, and tweaked Helen's toe.

"You think the tramp can do what she likes, but she has no money in her pocket, so she can't buy the comfortable bed and the good meal she is longing for. She can only go to the first workhouse or sell herself for the price of a glass of gin."

"A pretty tramp like me," Miriam began, and stopped at Helen's pleading. "But John and I are facing facts, so you must not be squeamish. When you come to think of it," she went on, "lady tramps generally have gentlemen tramps with them."

"And there's your Notya."

"Ah!"

"And he'd beat you."

"I might like it."

"And he'd be foul-mouthed."

"Horrid!" Helen exclaimed.

"But I should be used to nothing else."

"And if you came down our high road one day and begged at our door, and saw some one like yourself, some one clean and fresh and innocent—"

"So that's what he thinks of me!"

"Hush! I like this," Helen said.

"Even if there were a stern stepmother in the background, you'd be envious of that girl. You might obey no laws, but you'd find yourself the slave of something, your own vice, perhaps, or folly, or the will of that gentleman tramp of yours." He ended with a sharp tap of his emptied pipe, and sank back in a thoughtful silence.

Helen's hands slid down her stockings from knee to ankle and back again: her eyes were on the fire, but they saw the wet high road and the ragged woman with skirt flapping against shapeless boots. The storm's voice rose and fell, and sometimes nothing could be heard but the howling of the wind, and she knew that the poplars were bent under it; but when it rested for a moment the steady falling of the rain had a kind of reassurance. In the room, there were small sounds of shifting coals and breathing people.

Miriam sat on her stool like a bird on a branch. Her head was on one side, the tilted eyebrows gave her face an enquiring look, and she smiled with a light mischief. "You ought to have been a preacher, John dear," she said. "And you took—they always do—rather an unfair case."

"Take any case you like, you can't get freedom. When you're older you won't want it."

"You're very young, John, to have found that out," Helen said. "But you know it."

Miriam clapped her hands in warning. "Don't say," she begged, "that it's because you are a woman!"

"Is that the reason?" Helen asked.

"No, it's because you are a Helen, a silly, a slave! And John makes himself believe it because he's in love with a woman who is going to manage him. Clever me!"

Colour was in John's cheeks. "Clever enough," he said, "but an awful little fool. Let's do something."

"When I have been sitting still for a long time," Helen said, as though she produced wisdom, "I'm afraid to move in case something springs on me. I get stiff-necked. I feel—I feel that we're lost children with no one to take care of us."

"I'm rather glad I'm not that tramp," Miriam owned, and shivered.

"And I do wish Notya were safe at home."

"I don't," said Miriam stubbornly.

The wind whistled with a shrill note like a call, and upstairs a door banged loudly.

"Which room?" Miriam whispered.

"Hers, I think. We left the windows open," John said in a sensible loud voice. "I'll go and shut them."

"Don't go. I won't be left here!" Miriam cried. "This house—this house is too big."

"It's because she isn't here," Helen said.

"John, you're the oldest. Make us happy."

"But I'm feeling scared myself," he said comically. "And the front door's wide open, I'll bet."

"And that swearing tramp could walk in if he liked!"

"But we mustn't be afraid of open doors," Helen said, and

listened to her own words for a moment. Then she smiled, remembering where she had heard them. "We're frightening each other, and we must wash up. Look at the muddle!"

"It will make a clatter," Miriam objected, "and if you hadn't gone for that walk and made the house feel lonely, I shouldn't be like this now. Something's peeping at me!"

"It's only Mr. Pinderwell," Helen said. "Come and dry."

"I shall sleep in your bed tonight."

"Then I shall sleep in yours."

"I wish Rupert would come."

"John, do go and shut the windows."

"But take a light."

"It would be blown out."

Helen lowered the mop she had been wielding. "And Notya—where is she?"

John lifted his shoulders and opened the door. A gust of wind came down the passage, the front door was loudly shut, and Rupert whistled clearly.

"Oh, here he is," Miriam said on a deep breath, and went to meet him.

John pointed towards the hall. "I don't know why he should make us all feel brave."

"There's something—beautiful about him," Helen said.

CHAPTER X

Helen was ironing in the kitchen the next afternoon when Daniel Mackenzie appeared in the doorway. She turned to him with a welcome, but the perfection of her manner was lost on Daniel: for the kitchen was empty of Miriam, and that was all he noticed.

"Hasn't Rupert come with you?" Helen asked.

"I missed him," he said in his melancholy voice. "Perhaps he missed me," he added with resignation. He was a tall young man with large hands and feet, and his eyes were vague behind his spectacles. "I thought he would be here. Is everybody out?"

"Notya's away, you know."

"He told me."

"And John and Miriam—I don't know where they are."

He found it difficult to talk to Helen, and as he sat down in the armchair he searched his mind for a remark. "I thought people always ironed on Tuesdays," he said at last.

"Some people do. These are just odd things."

"Eliza does. She makes us have cold supper. And on Mondays. It's too bad."

"But there can't be much to do for you."

"I don't know. There's washing on Monday, and on Sunday she goes to church—so she says."

Helen changed her iron and worked on. She moved rhythmically and her bare forearms were small and shapely, but Daniel did not look at her. He seemed to be interested in the wrinkled boots he wore, and occasionally he uttered a sad; "Puss, Puss," to the cat sleeping before the fire. A light breeze was blowing outside and Helen sometimes paused to look through the open window.

"Our poplars are getting their leaves," she said. "It's strange that I have never seen your garden. Are there any trees in it?"

He sat like a half-empty sack of grain, and slowly, with an effort, he raised his head. "What did you say?"

"Have you any trees in your garden?"

"There's a holly bush in the front and one of those thin trees that have berries—red berries."

"A rowan! Oh, I'm glad you have a rowan!" She looked as though he had made a gift to her.

He was born to ask questions. "Why?" he said, with his first gleam of interest.

"Oh, I like them. Is there a garden at the back?"

"Apple-trees," he sighed. "No fruit."

"They must want pruning. You know, gardening would do you good."

He shook his head. "Too long in the back."

"And Zebedee hasn't time?"

"No, he hasn't time." Daniel was wondering where Miriam was, and how long Rupert would be, and though Helen knew she wearied him, she went on serenely.

"Is he very busy now?"

"Yes."

"I can't think why people get ill in the spring, just when the lovely summer's coming. Does he get called up at night?"

"I suppose so." He was growing tired of this. "But when I'm in bed, I'm asleep, you know."

"Ah, that's nice for you," Helen said with a touch of irony as she carefully pulled out the lace of a dainty collar. "Isn't he rather lonely when you are up here?"

"Lonely!" Daniel's mouth dropped wider and while he tried to answer this absurd question adequately, Rupert entered the room.

"I told you to meet me outside the Bull, you old idiot."

Like Miriam, Rupert had the effect of fortifying the life of his surroundings, but, unlike her, he had a happy trick of seeming more interested in others than in himself. He saw at once, with something keener than his keen eyes, that Daniel was bored, that Helen was at work on more than ironing, and with his entrance he scattered the vague dissension which was abroad. The kitchen recovered from the gloom with which Daniel had shadowed it and Daniel himself grew brighter.

"I thought you said the Plover."

"You didn't listen. Even you couldn't mistake one for the other, but I've scored off you. Helen, we shall want a good tea. I drove up with Zebedee, and he's coming here when he's finished with old Halkett."

She stood with a cooling iron in her hand. "I'll make some scones. I expect Eliza gives him horrid food. And for supper there's cold chicken and salad and plenty of pudding; but how shall we put up the horse?"

"Don't worry, Martha. He's only coming to tea. He won't stay long."

"Oh, yes, he will." She had no doubt of it. "I want him to. Make up the fire for me, Daniel, please." She folded away the ironing cloth and gathered up the little damp cuffs and collars she had not ironed. A faint smile curved her steady lips, for nothing gave her more happiness than serving those who had a claim on her, and Zebedee's claim was his lack of womankind to care for him and her own gratitude for his existence. He was the one person to whom she could give the name of friend, yet their communion had seldom expressed itself in confidences: the knowledge of it lay snugly and unspoken in her heart.

"He has never had anything to eat in this house before," she said with a solemnity which provoked Rupert to laughter.

"What a sacrament women make of meals!"

"I wish they all did," Daniel said in the bass notes of genuine feeling.

"I don't know why you keep that awful woman," Helen said.

"Don't start him on Eliza," Rupert begged. "Eliza and the intricacies of English law—"

"Have you seen her?" Daniel persisted.

"No, but of course she's awful if she doesn't give you proper food."

His look proclaimed his realization that he had never appreciated Helen before. "I'm not greedy," he said earnestly, "but I've got to be fed." He sent a wavering glance from his chest to his boots. "Bulk is what I need, and fat foods, and it's a continuous fight to get them."

Rupert roared aloud, but there was sympathy in Helen's hidden mirth. "I'll see what I can do for you today," she said, like an attentive landlady. "And you are going to stay the night. I fry bacon—oh, wonderfully, and you shall have some for breakfast. But now," she added, with a little air of dismissal, "I am going to make the scones."

"Let's have a walk," Rupert said.

"I've walked enough." He had an impulse to stay with Helen.

"Then come outside and smoke. It's as warm as June."

Daniel rose slowly, lifting his body piece by piece. "I shouldn't like you to think," he said, "that I care too much for food."

"I don't."

"But I've got to be kept going."

"I quite understand," she answered busily. Her hands were in the flour; a patch of it, on her pale cheek, showed that her skin had a warm, faint colour of its own.

"We'll sit outside and watch for Zebedee," Rupert told her.

She had baked the scones, changed her dress and made the table ready before the guest arrived. From the dining-room she heard his clear voice, broken by Miriam's low gay one, and, looking from the window, she saw them both at the gate. Out of sight, behind the wall, Daniel and Rupert were talking, involved in one of their interminable discussions, and there were sounds made by the horse as he stretched to eat the grass. For an instant, Helen felt old and forgotten; she remembered Notya, who was in trouble, and she herself was shrouded by her own readiness to see misfortune; all her little preparations, the flowers on the table, the scones before the fire, her pretty dress, were gathered into one foolishness when she saw Zebedee pushing open the gate and looking down at Miriam. There was a sudden new pain in Helen's heart, and in a blinding light which dazzled her she saw that the pain was compounded of jealousy because Miriam was beautiful, and of renunciation because it would be impossible to keep anything which Miriam wanted.

But in the hall, these feelings, like a nightmare in their blackness, passed away when Zebedee uttered the cheerful "Hullo!" with which he had so often greeted her. There were comfort and safety in his neighbourhood, in his swift, judging way of looking at people, as though, without curiosity, he wished to assure himself of their well-being and health, and while there was something professional in the glance, it seemed to be a guarantee of his own honesty. His eyes, grey with brown flecks in them, expected people to be reasonable and happy.

Helen said simply, "I am so glad you have come."

"I made him," Miriam said, and put her hand fleetingly on his arm.

"You didn't. Rupert asked him."

"Yes, but I waylaid him. He was sneaking home."

"No, no, I wasn't."

"Somewhere else, then!"

He thrust his gloves into the pocket of his coat.

"You were coming, weren't you?" Helen asked.

"Of course I was."

She smiled with her extraordinary, almost comic, radiance. "I'll go and make the tea."

Because Daniel blundered through the doorway at that moment, Miriam followed Helen to the kitchen.

"He's going to teach me to drive," she said. "But what a horse! It goes on from generation to generation, like the practice!"

George Halkett had laughed at the horse, too, and Helen felt a cold resentment against him and Miriam.

"Your hair is very untidy, and your cheeks are blue," she said.

"Now you're being a cat. We certainly don't miss Notya when you are here. I'm in the delightful position, my dear, of being able to afford blue cheeks and untidy hair. Daniel won't notice them."

"No, he's arguing with Rupert."

"He came into the house after me. I'm going back to tease him."

"Oh, do leave the poor thing alone."

"No, I shan't. He'd be disappointed."

Helen stood by the fire and watched the kettle and listened to the noises in the schoolroom. Then a shuffling step came down the passage and Daniel spoke.

"Can I help you?"

"Thank you very much." She knew that he had come for refuge and she filled the teapot and put it into his hands. "Don't drop it."

"I'll be careful," he said humbly.

Walking in the trail of the tea he spilt, she followed him with the kettle. She had not the heart to scold him, and at the dining-room door he let out a sharp sound.

"Oh, dear, has it gone through your boot?" she asked, checking her laughter.

"I should just think it has!"

Miriam, whose ears were like a hare's, cried from the schoolroom: "Then perhaps he'll have to have his boot cut off, and that would spoil that lovely pair! Whatever you do, Zebedee, try to spare his boot!"

"She never leaves me alone," Daniel muttered to the pot.

"Don't take any notice of her," Helen said.

Daniel looked up mournfully. "Wouldn't you?"

"No. Sit here and talk to me." She called through the open door. "Come in, everybody!" With Daniel on one side of the table and Zebedee on the other, John's absence was the less apparent. Twilight had not yet come, but Helen had lighted candles to give the room a festive look, and there was a feeling of freedom and friendship in the house. They all talked of unimportant things, and there was laughter amid the chinking of the cups. For the young men, the presence of the girls had a potent, hardly admitted charm: for Miriam there was the exciting antagonism of sex: for Helen there was a pleasure which made her want to take deep breaths.

"Oh!" Miriam cried at last, and flung herself back in her chair. "Isn't this good? Why can't it always be like this?"

"Hush!" Helen said.

"You know it's nicer without her."

"I didn't want you to tempt things," Helen explained.

"She's as superstitious as a savage," Rupert said. "Talk to her, Zebedee, man of science."

"Yes, I will." His glance was humorous but not quite untroubled.

"When?" she said, with great willingness.

"After tea."

"We've finished, haven't we?" Miriam asked. "Daniel, be quick and drink that. We're all waiting for you. And don't slop it on your waistcoat. There's a good boy! Very nice. Come into the drawing-room and I'll play to you. I might even sing. Ask Helen if you may get down."

"May I?" he asked, and went after Miriam.

The notes of the old piano tinkled through the hall. Miriam was playing a waltz, lightly and gaily.

"I'll go and make Daniel dance with me," Rupert said.

"Don't tease him any more."

"It'll do him good, and I want Zebedee to have a chance of lecturing you."

"It's not easy to lecture you," Zebedee said.

"Isn't it?"

Above their voices and the tinkling music there now came Daniel's protest, Rupert's persuasions, and Miriam's laughter: then these all died away and the waltz called out plaintively and with desire.

"She is making the piano cry," Helen said.

Zebedee did not speak, for he was listening: the whole house was listening. No other sound came from the drawing-room, and Helen fancied that Mr. Penderwell was standing on the stairs, held by the memory of days when he had taken his lady by her tiny waist and felt the whiff of her muslin skirts against him as they whirled. The children on the landing were wide-eyed and hushed in their quiet play. The sounds grew fainter; they faded away as though the ballroom had grown dark and empty, and for a little space all the listeners seemed to be easing themselves of sighs. Then Miriam's whistle, like a blackbird's, came clearly. She did not know how well she had been playing.

Helen stood up. "I wonder if the horse has walked away. Go into the drawing-room. I'll see."

"No. I'll come with you."

The music had subdued their voices and, because they had heard it together, they seemed to be wrapped round by it in a world unknown to anybody else. Quietly they went out of the house and found the horse, only a few yards distant, with his feet tangled in the reins.

"You ought to have fastened him to the post," Helen said, and together they led him back.

"Shall we take him out of the cart?"

"But I ought to go home."

"No," she said.

"Perhaps not."

The sunshine had gone, and over the moor the light was grey; grey clouds hung low in the sky, and as he looked down at her, it seemed to Zebedee that Helen was some emanation of grey earth and air.

"We'll take him out," she said.

"And then what shall we do with him?"

"I believe he'd be quite happy in the kitchen!"

"Yes, he's a domesticated old boy."

"We can't put him in the hen-house. Just tie him to the post and let him eat."

When that was done, she would have gone into the house, but Zebedee kept her back.

"Mayn't we stay in the garden? Are you warm enough?"

She nodded to both questions. "Let us go round to the back." The path at the side of the house was dark with shrubs. "I don't like this little bit," she said. "I hardly ever walk on it. It's—"

"What?"

"Oh, they don't come out. They stay there and get unhappy."

"The bushes?"

"The spirits in them."

He walked beside her with his hands behind his back and his head bent.

"You're thinking," she said.

"Yes."

"Don't," she begged, "think away from me."

He stopped, surprised. "I'm not doing that—but why?"

"I don't know," she said, looking him in the eyes, "but I should hate it."

"I was wondering how to bring myself to scold you."

They had reached the lawn and, caught by the light from the drawing-room, they stood under the poplars and watched the shadows moving on walls and ceiling. The piano and the people in the room were out of sight, and Miriam's small, husky voice came with a hint of mystery.

"'Drink to me only with thine eyes,'" she sang.

"'And I will pledge with mine,'" Rupert joined in richly.

"'Or leave a kiss within the cup—'"

In silence, under the trees, Helen and Zebedee listened to the singing, to voices wrangling about the words, and when a figure appeared at the window they turned together and retreated beyond the privet hedge, behind John's vegetable garden and through the door on to the moor.

The earth was so black that the rising ground was exaggerated into a hill; against it, Helen's figure was like a wraith, yet Zebedee was acutely conscious of her slim solidity. He was also half afraid of her, and he had an easily controlled desire to run from the delight she gave him, a delight which hurt and reminded him too clearly of past joys.

"Now," she said, and stood before him in her dangerous simplicity. "What are you going to say?"

She seemed to have walked out of the darkness into his life, a few nights ago, an unexpected invasion, but one not to be repelled, nor did he wish to repel it. He was amazed to hear himself uttering his thoughts aloud.

"I always liked you when you were a little girl," he said, as though he accounted for something to himself.

"Better than Miriam?" she asked quickly.

"Of course."

"Oh," she said, and paused. "But I feel as if Miriam—" She stopped again and waited for his next words, but he saw the steepness of the path on which he had set his feet and he would not follow it.

"And I used to think you looked—well, brave."

"Did I? Don't I now?"

"Yes; so you see, you must be."

"I'll try. Three stars," she said, looking up. "But mayn't I— mayn't I say the things I'm thinking?"

"I hope you will," he answered gravely; "but then, you must be careful what you think."

"This is a very gentle lecture," she said. "Four stars, now. Five. When I've counted seven, we'll go back, but I rather hoped you would be a little cross."

Pleased, yet half irritated, by this simplicity, he stood in silence while she counted her seven stars.

CHAPTER XI

It had long been a custom of the Canipers to spend each warm Sunday evening in the heather, and there, if Daniel were not already with them, they would find him waiting, or they would watch for his gaunt, loose figure to come across the moor. This habit had begun when his father was alive, and the stern chapel-goer's anger must be dared before Daniel could appear with the light of a martyr on his brow. In those days, Zebedee, who was working under the old doctor, sometimes arrived with Daniel, and sank with an unexpressed relief into the lair which was a little hollow in the moor, where heather grew thickly on the sides, but permitted pale violets and golden tormentilla to creep about the grassy bottom. Zebedee was more than ten years older than his brother, and he suffered from a loneliness which made their honest welcome of great value to him. He liked to listen to the boys' precocious talk and watch the grace and beauty of the girls before he went back to the ugly house in the town of dreary streets, to the work he liked and wearied himself over, and the father he did not understand. Then he went away, and he never knew how bitterly Helen missed him, how she had recognized the tired look which said he had been working too hard, and the unhappy look which betrayed his quarrels with his father, and how, in her own fashion, she had tried to smooth those looks away, and now he had returned with a new expression on his face. It was that, she thought, of a man who, knowing misery like a great block in his path, had ridden over it and not looked back. She knew what Rupert meant by saying he was different, and again she felt a strong dislike for all his experiences which she had not shared.

On the evening after his visit, the Canipers and Daniel went to the trysting place. Helen wrapped herself in a shawl and lay down with her head on her arms and one eye for the clouds, but she did not listen to the talk, and she had no definite thoughts. The voices of Rupert and Daniel were like the buzzing of bees, a sound of warmth and summer, and the smell of their tobacco came and went on the wind. She was aware that John, having smoked for a time and disagreed with everything that was said, had walked off towards the road, and the succeeding peace was proof that Miriam too, had disappeared.

Helen rolled on her back and went floating with the clouds. While she merely watched them, she thought they kept a level course, but to go with them was like riding on a swollen sea, and as she rose and fell in slow and splendid curves, she discovered differences of colour and quality in a medium which seemed invariable from below. She swooped downwards like a bird on steady wings and saw the moor lifting itself towards her until she anticipated a shock; she was carried upwards through a blue that strained to keep its colour, yet wearied into a pallor which almost let out the stars. She saw the eye of a hawk as its victims knew it, and for a time she kept pace with a lark and saw the music in his throat before he uttered it. Joy escaped her in a little sound, and then she felt that the earth was solid under her.

Daniel and Rupert were still discussing the great things which did not matter, and idly she marvelled at their capacity for argument and quarrel; but she realized that for Rupert, at least, this was a sport equivalent to her game of sailing with the clouds, and when she turned to look at him, she saw him leaning against his heather bush, wearing the expression most annoying to an antagonist, and flicking broken heather stalks at Daniel's angular and monumental knees.

"You talk of the mind," Rupert said, "as though it were the stomach."

"I do," Daniel said heavily.

"And your stomach at that! Bulk and fat foods—"

"This is merely personal," Daniel said, "and a sign that you are being beaten, as usual. I was going to say that in a day of fuller knowledge we shall be able to predict the effect of emotions with the same certainty—"

"With which you now predict the effect of Eliza's diet. God forbid! Anyhow, I shall be dead. Come on."

Daniel stood up obediently, for they had now reached the point where they always rose and walked off side by side, in the silence of amusement and indignation.

There was a rustling in the heather, and she heard no more of them. Then the thud of approaching footsteps ran along the ground, and she sat up to see Miriam with Zebedee.

"I went fishing," Miriam said, "and this is what I caught."

He smiled at Helen a little uncertainly. "I had some time to spare, and I thought you wouldn't mind if I came up here. You used to let me."

"I've always wanted you to come back," she said with her disconcerting frankness.

"You may sit down," Miriam said, "and go on telling us about your childhood. Helen, we'd hardly said how d'you do when he began on that. It's a sure sign of age."

"I am old."

"Oh," Helen murmured. "No." She dropped back into her bed. She could see Zebedee's grey coat sleeve and the movements of his arm as he found and filled his pipe, and by moving her head half an inch she saw his collar and his lean cheek.

"Yes, old," he said, "and the reason I mentioned my unfortunate childhood was to point a moral in content. When I was young I was made to go to chapel twice on Sundays, three times counting Sunday-school, and here I find you all wandering about the moor."

"I'd rather have had the chapel," Miriam said. "One could at least look at people's hats."

"The hats in our particular Bethel were chiefly bonnets. Bonnets with things in them that nodded, and generally black." He stared across the moor. "I don't know that the memory of them is a thing to cherish."

Helen tried to do justice to the absent. "We were never told not to go. We could do what we liked."

"Ah, but we weren't encouraged," Miriam chuckled. "You have to be encouraged, don't you, Zebedee, before you go into places like that?"

"My father had other methods," he said grimly.

The silence tightened on his memories, and no one spoke until Miriam said, almost gently, "Please tell us some more."

"The pews were a bright yellow, and looked sticky. The roof was painted blue, with stars. There was a man in a black gown with special knowledge on the subject of sin."

"That," Miriam said pensively, "must have been amusing."

"No. Only dreary and somehow rather unclean. I liked to go to the surgery afterwards and smell the antiseptics."

"I wish the horrible black-gowned man could know that," Helen said fiercely.

He looked down, smiling tolerantly. "But it doesn't matter now."

"It does. It will always matter. You were little—" She broke off and huddled herself closer in her shawl, as though she held a small thing in its folds.

He found nothing to say; he was swept by gratitude for this tenderness. It was, he knew, what she would have given to anything needing comfort, but it was no less wonderful for that and he was warmed by it and, at the same time, disturbed. She seemed to have her hands near his heart, and they were pressing closer.

"Go on," said Miriam, unconscious of the emotions that lived near her. "I like to hear about other people's miseries. Were you rather a funny little boy?"

"I expect so."

"Pale and plain, I should think," she said consideringly, "with too big a nose. Oh, it's all right now, rather nice, but little boys so often have noses out of proportion. I shall have girls. Did you wear black clothes on Sunday?"

"I'm afraid so."

"Poor little ugly thing! Helen, are you listening? Black clothes! And your hair oiled?"

"No, not so bad as that. My mother was a very particular lady."

"Can you tell us about her?" Helen asked.

"I don't know that I can."

"You oughtn't to have suggested it," Miriam said in a reproof which was ready to turn to mockery at a hint from Zebedee.

"He won't tell us if he doesn't want to. You wouldn't be hurt by anything we said, would you?"

"Of course not. The difficulty is that there seems nothing to tell. She was so quiet, as I remember her, and so meek, and yet one felt quite safe with her. I don't think she was afraid, as I was, but there was something, something that made things uncertain. I can't explain."

"I expect she was too gentle at the beginning," Helen said. "She let him have his own way and then she was never able to catch up, and all the time—all the time she was thinking perhaps you were going to suffer because she had made that mistake. And that would make her so anxious not to make another, wouldn't it? And so—"

"And so it would go on. But how did you discover that?"

"Oh, I know some things," she said, and ended feebly, "about some things."

"She died when I was thirteen and Daniel three, and my father was very unhappy."

"I didn't like your father a bit," Miriam said.

"He was a good man in his way, his uncomfortable way."

"Then I like them wickeder than that."

"It made him uncomfortable too, you know."

"If you're going to preach—"

He laughed. "I didn't mean to. I was only offering you the experience of my maturity!"

"Well, I'm getting stiff and cold. Helen likes that kind of

thing. Give it to her while I get warm. Unless you'll lend me your shawl, Helen?"

"No, I won't."

"I must go too," said Zebedee, but he did not move and Helen did not speak. His thoughts were on her while his eyes were on the dark line of moor touching the sky; yet he thought less of her than of the strange ways of life and the force which drew him to this woman whom he had known a child so short a time ago. He wondered if what he felt were real, if the night and the mystery of the moor had not bewitched him, for she had come to him at night out of the darkness with the wind whistling round her. It was so easy, as he knew, for a solitary being to fasten eagerly on another, like a beaten boat to the safety of a buoy, but while he thus admonished himself, he had no genuine doubt. He knew that she was what he wanted: her youth, her wisdom, her smoothness, her serenity, and the many things which made her, even the stubbornness which underlay her calm.

Into these reflections her voice came loudly, calling him from the heights.

"I do wish you wouldn't keep Eliza. She's a most unsuitable person to look after you."

He laughed so heartily and so long that she sat up to look at him. "I don't know what's amusing you," she said.

"It's so extraordinarily like you!"

"Oh!"

"And why don't you think her suitable?"

"From things Daniel has told me."

"Oh, Daniel is an old maid. She's ugly and disagreeable, but she delivers messages accurately, and that's all I care about. Don't believe all Daniel's stories."

"They worry me," she said.

"Do you worry about every one's affairs?" he asked, and feared she would hear the jealousy in his voice.

"I know so few people, you see. Oughtn't I to?"

"I'm humbly thankful," he said with a light gravity.

"Then I'll go on. Aren't you lonely on Sundays in that house with only the holly bush and the rowan and the apple-trees that bear no fruit? Why don't you come up here?"

"May I?"

"You belong to the moor, too," she said.

He nodded his thanks for that. "Who told you about our trees? Daniel again?"

"Yes; but I asked him."

He stood up. "I must go back. Thank you and good night."

It was getting dark and, with a heavy feeling in her heart, she watched him walk away, while Miriam ran up with a whirl of skirts, crying out, "Is he going? Is he going? Come and see him to the road."

Helen shook her head. She would let Miriam have anything she wanted, but she would not share with her. She turned her back on the thin striding figure and the small running one behind it, and she went into the house. There, the remembrance of Mildred Caniper went with her from room to room, and the house itself seemed to close on Helen and hold her in.

She stood at the schoolroom window and watched the twilight give place to night. In the garden, the laurel bushes were quite black and it seemed to her that the whole world was dead except herself and the lurking shadows that filled the house. Zebedee, who tramped the long road to the town, had become hardly more than a toy which had been wound up and would go on for ever. Then, on the hillside, a spark leapt out, and she knew that John or Lily Brent had lighted the kitchen lamp.

CHAPTER XII

Miriam took Zebedee to the road and, finding him uninteresting, she gave him a scant good-night and left him. She sank into the heather and told herself many times that she did not know what to do. She had wit enough to realize that she was almost ridiculous in her discontent, but for that Notya must be blamed, and her own immediate necessity was to find amusement. In all the vastness of the moor, George Halkett was the only being who could give her a taste of what she wanted, and she had quarrelled with George Halkett. She sat and glowered at the white road cutting the darkness of the moor and she thought it had the cruel look of a sharp and powerful knife. It seemed to threaten her and, though she had all youth's faith in her good fortune, at times she was taken by a panic lest she should turn out to be one of those whom fate left stranded. That fear was on her now, for there were such women, she knew, and sometimes they were beautiful! Perhaps they were often beautiful, and in the long run it might be better to be good, yet she would not have exchanged her looks for all the virtues in the world.

"Nobody would!" she cried aloud, and, seizing two bunches of heather by their stalks, she shook them violently.

Nevertheless, she might grow old on the moor and marry Daniel in despair. She shuddered. No one could love Daniel enough to pardon his appearance, and amusement would soon change to hatred. She tormented herself with pictures of their common life. She saw his shapeless clothes lying about the room she had to share with him; his boots stared up at her from the hall with much of his own expression. She heard him talking legally to her through their meals and saw him gazing at her with his peculiar, timid worship. But if they had children, they would have Daniel's stamp on them, and then he would grow bold and take all she gave for granted. Girls and boys alike, they would be big and gaunt and clumsy, but considerate and good.

She threw her arms across her breast and held herself in a fury of self-possession. Marriage suddenly appeared to her as an ugly thing even if it attained to the ideal. No, no! Men were good to play with, to tease and torture, but she had fixed her limits, and she fixed them with some astonishment for her own reserve. The discovery of this inherent coldness had its effect: it bounded her future in a manner which was too disturbing for much contemplation, but it also gave her a new freedom of action, assuring her that she need have no fears for her own restraint, that when her chance came, she might go into the world like a Helen of Troy who could never be beguiled. In the meantime, though she had quarrelled with George Halkett, she remembered that she had not forsworn his company; she had only sworn to punish him for having told the truth, and she easily pretended not to know that her resentment was no more than an excuse.

She swung herself to her feet, and not without fear, for the moor had never been her friend, she walked quickly towards the patch of darkness made by the larch-trees. "I am being driven to this," she thought dramatically and with the froth of her mind. She went with her head held tragically high, but in her throat, where humour met excitement, there was a little run of laughter.

The trees stood without movement, as though they were weighted by foreknowledge and there was alarm in the voice of the stream. She stopped short of the water and stood by the brown path that led down to the farm, and her feet could feel the softness of many falls of larch needles. She listened and she could hear nothing but the small noises of the wood and all round it the moor was like a circle of enchantment keeping back intruders. There was no wind, but she was cold and her desire for George had changed its quality. She wanted the presence of another human being in this stillness; she would have welcomed

Mrs. Samson with a shout and even Notya with a smile, but she found herself unable to turn and make for home. It would have been like letting danger loose on her.

"George!" she called loudly, before she knew she was going to do it. "George, George, George!" Her voice, shriller than its wont, raged at her predicament.

A dog barked in the hollow and came nearer. She heard George silence him, and she knew that man and dog were approaching through the wood. Then her fears vanished and she strolled a few paces from the trees and stood, an easy mark for George when he appeared.

"Was it you who called?" he asked her from a little distance.

"Me?" Now he was close to her, and she saw his guarded eyes soften unwillingly.

"Somebody called. Didn't you hear the dog barking? Somebody called 'George!'"

"Perhaps," she ventured in the falsely innocent manner which both recognized as foolish and unworthy and in which both took a different delight, "perhaps it was—thought-reading!"

"With the dog?" he sneered.

"You and the dog," she said, joining them deliberately. "It's getting so dark that I can hardly see your cross face. That's a good thing, because I want to say thank you for driving Uncle Alfred and Notya to the station."

"That's all right," he said, and added with a sullen curiosity, "Is he the one who's going to adopt you?"

"Yes."

"He hasn't done it yet?"

"I'm not sure that I want to go. George, shall I tell you something? Something charming, a pillar of cloud by day and of fire by night—I did call you!"

"Well," he said after a pause, "I knew that."

"You weren't certain. Tell the truth! Were you certain?"

"No, I was not," he said with the sulky honesty which should have moved her.

"And had you been thinking of me?"

He would not answer that.

"I shan't be hurt," she said, swaying from foot to foot, "because I know!" Against the invading blackness her face and teeth gleamed clearly.

"You're like a black cat!" he burst out, in forgetfulness of himself.

"A witch's cat!"

"A witch."

"Do you think witches are ever afraid? Only when they see the cross, isn't it? But I was, George, when I called out."

"What of?"

"I—don't know. The quietness and the dark."

He gave a short laugh which tried to conceal his pleasure in her weakness.

"Aren't you ever?"

"Can't remember it."

"Not of anything?"

"No."

"How—stupid of you."

"Stupid?"

"Yes, when the world's full of things you don't understand."

"But nothing happens."

That was her own complaint, but from him the words came in the security of content. "But tonight—" she began, shivered lightly and raised her hand. "What's that?"

He lifted his head; the dog, sitting at his feet, had cocked his ears. "Nothing."

"I heard something."

Hardly heeded, he put his strong fingers on her wrist and grasped it. His voice was rich and soft. "What's the matter with you tonight?"

Unmistakably now, a sound came from the hollow; not, this time, the raging of old Halkett, but a woman's cry for help, clear and insistent.

"It must be my father," he said, and his hand fell away from

Miriam's; but for a few seconds he stared at her as though she could tell him what had happened. Then he went after the dog in his swift passage through the trees, while, urged by an instinct to help and a need for George's solid company, Miriam followed. She was soon outstripped, so that her descent was made alone. Twigs crackled under her feet, the ranks of trees seemed to rush past her as she went, and, with the return of self-remembrance, she knew that this was how she had felt long ago when she read fairy stories about forests and enchanted castles.

Yet she would have been less alarmed at the sight of a moated, loop-holed pile than at this of Halkett's farm, a white-washed homestead, with light beaming from a window on the ground floor, the whole encompassed by a merely mortal possibility of strange events. Her impulse had been to rush into the house, but she stood still, feeling the presence of the trees like a thick curtain shutting away the outer, upper world and, having paused, she found that she could not pursue her course.

"I must go back," she whispered. After all, this was not her affair.

A murmur of voices came from the lighted room; the movement of a horse in the stables was the friendliest sound she had ever heard. Reluctantly, for she was alive with curiosity, she turned to go when a step rang on the flagged passage of the farm and George stood in the doorway. He beckoned and met her half way across the yard.

"He's gone," he said, and he looked dazed. "Can't believe it," he muttered.

"Oh!" she said under her breath. "Oh, dear!" It was her turn to put a hand on him, for she was afraid of death.

"Can't believe it," he said again, and taking her with him, he went as though he were drawn, towards the lighted windows and looked in.

"Yes," he said, assuring himself that this thing really was.

Fascinated by the steadfastness of his gaze, Miriam looked too and drew back with a muffled cry. She had seen the old man rigid on a red velvet sofa, his head on a yellow cushion, his grey hair in some way coarsened by the state of death, his limbs clad in the garments of every day and strangely insulted by them. Near him, with her back to the window and straight and stiff as a sentinel, sat Mrs. Biggs, the housekeeper, the knob of her smooth black hair defying destiny.

Still whispering, Miriam begged, "George, don't look any more." Her horror was as much for the immobile woman as for the dead man. "Come away, before she turns round. I want to go home. George—I'm sorry."

"Yes," he said.

"Good-night."

"Good-night," he answered, and she saw him look through the window again.

Going across the moor, she cried feebly. She wished old Halkett had not been lying on the red sofa. He should have died in the big kitchen of his fathers, or upstairs in a great bed, not in that commonly-furnished little sitting-room where the work-basket of Mrs. Biggs kept company with a cheap china lamp and photographs in frames. She wondered how they would manage to undress him, and for how long Mrs. Biggs would sit beside him like a fate, a fate in a red blouse and a brown skirt. Perhaps even now they were pulling off his clothes. Terrible for George to have to do that, she thought, yet it seemed natural enough work for Mrs. Biggs, with her hard mouth and cold eyes, and no doubt she had often put him to bed in the lusty days of his carousals. Perhaps the dead could really see from under their stiff eyelids, and old Halkett would laugh at the difficulty with which they disrobed him for this last time. Perhaps he had been watching when George and she looked through the window. Until now she had never seen him when he did not leer at her, and she felt that he must still be leering under the mask of death.

The taint of what she had looked on hung heavily about her, and the fresh air of the moor could not clear it away. Crying still, in little whimpers which consoled her, she stole through the garden and the house to the beautiful solitude of Phoebe's room and the cleanliness of linen sheets.

Supperless she lay there, by turn welcoming and rejecting the pictures which appeared on the dark wall of her mind, and when Helen knocked on the door she was not bidden to enter.

"Don't you want anything to eat?" she called.

"No."

"What's the matter?"

"I—feel sick."

"Then mayn't I come in and look after you?" Helen asked in a voice which impelled Miriam to bark an angry negative.

It was Helen, who liked to help people, to whom this thing should have happened, yet Miriam possessed her experience jealously; it had broken into the monotony of life and to that extent she was grateful.

"And I must be very kind to George," she decided before she went to sleep.

She dropped her white eyelids the next morning when John gave the news of the old man's death, for she did not want to betray her knowledge.

"Oh!" Helen said, and Rupert remarked lightly and watchfully that Zebedee would now be less often on the moor.

"There's still the funeral," Helen said oddly.

"And let's hope they'll bury him soon," John added, and so finished with old Halkett.

Helen was still thoughtful. "Perhaps we ought to go and be nice to George. There won't be anything we can do, but we might ask him if there is."

"The less you have to do with George—" John began, and Miriam interrupted him, clicking her tongue.

"Helen, Helen, haven't you heard about George and Lily Brent? A dreadful story. Ask John."

"If you're not careful," he said menacingly, "I'll do what she did to him."

"No, no, you won't, Johnny; for, in spite of everything, you're a little gentleman."

"Oh, do be quiet, you two! Rupert's trying to say something."

"Send a note of condolence to George," he advised, "and I'll go to the funeral. It's no good asking John to do it. He wouldn't shine. Heavens! it's late, and I haven't cleaned the boots!"

The boys went about their business and left the girls to theirs.

"I don't think a note is enough for George," Helen said as she rolled up her sleeves. "A man without a mother or a father, and only a Mrs. Biggs!"

"H'm," Miriam commented. "Except for Mrs. Biggs, I don't know that he's to be pitied. Still, I'm quite willing to be agreeable, unless you mean to go and knock at the farm door?"

"No. Couldn't we catch him somewhere!"

"Yes," Miriam said too promptly. She made a cautious pause. "He won't be riding on the moor today, because there'll be undertakers and things. If we went down the road—or shall I go alone?"

"Both of us—to represent the family. And we can say we're sorry—"

"But we're not."

"Yes, in a way. Sorry he hadn't a nicer father to be sorry for."

"What about ours?" Miriam asked.

"He may be dead, too, by now."

"And that will matter less to us than old Halkett does to George."

"But the great thing," Helen said, "is to have people one can't be ashamed of."

"Oh!"

"I know; but it's true. And our father would always look nice and be polite, even when he was dying. Old Halkett—"

"Don't talk about him! Come along. We'll catch George on his way to that shop with the pictures of hearses in the window. If I die before you, don't put me in one of those black carts."

"I don't think I could put you into anything," Helen said with simple fervour.

"Then you'd have to mummify me and stick me up in the hall beside the grandfather clock, and you'd think the ticking was my heart."

"There are hearts beating all over the house now," Helen said. "But this is not meeting George," she added, and rolled her sleeves down again.

They waylaid him successfully where the road met Halkett's lane, and from his horse he looked down on the two upturned faces.

"We've heard about Mr. Halkett," Helen said, gazing with friendliness and without embarrassment into his eyes. "I suppose there's nothing we can do?"

"Nothing, thanks."

"And Rupert said he would like to go to the funeral, if he may."

"Thank you. I'll let him know about it." He glanced at Miriam and hesitated, yet when he spoke it was in a franker voice than the one she was used to hear. "I'm afraid you were upset last night."

Her answering look made a pact between them. "We didn't hear about it till this morning."

He nodded, watching her through his thick lashes. He gave her a strong impression that he was despising her a little, and she saw him look from her to Helen as though he made comparisons. Indeed, at that moment, he thought that these sisters were like thirst and the means to quench it, like heat and shade; and a sudden restlessness made him shift in his seat.

"I expect you have a lot to do," Helen said. "Good-bye."

"Good-bye. And thank you," he said gruffly, and caught the flash of Miriam's smile as he turned.

Helen stood looking after him. "Poor George!" she said. "I rather like him. I wish he wouldn't drink."

"Exaggerated stories," Miriam remarked neatly.

"Oh, yes, but he looks as if he had never had a chance of being nice."

"I don't believe he has ever wanted one," Miriam said.

CHAPTER XIII

Uncle Alfred wrote a short note from Calais, and on the day when old Halkett was taken to his grave another letter came to say that Philip Caniper was dead before the travellers could reach him.

"Then we're poor little orphans, like George," Miriam said, and, with the peering look which asked how far she might venture, she added, "And, like George, we have our Mrs. Biggs."

If Helen heard those words, she made no sign. "She'll never be happy again," she said.

"Well, she never has been happy, and she has never wanted us to be happy, so nothing's changed."

"What can we do?" Helen went on, and her thoughts alighted on such practical kindnesses as a perfect state of cleanliness in the house to which Notya would return, flowers in her bedroom for a welcome, and a great willingness to do what pleased her. "But we mustn't be too obvious," she murmured to herself.

"And whatever you do, don't slobber."

"Is it likely?" Helen asked superbly.

The firmest intentions in that direction would have been frustrated by the sight of Mildred Caniper's cold face, and Helen saw with surprise that it was almost as it had always been. Her "Well, Helen!" was as calm as her kiss, and only when she raised her veil was her bitter need of sleep revealed. Then, too, Helen saw that her features and her fair, bright colouring had suffered an indefinable blurring, as though, in some spiritual process, their sharpness had been lost, and while she looked at her, Helen felt the full weight of responsibility for this woman settling once more on her own slim shoulders. Yet she noticed that the shadows which had hung so thickly in the house became thinner as soon as Mildred Caniper entered it. No doubt they had slipped into the body which was their home.

"Daniel is here," Helen said, "because it's Saturday and we didn't know you were coming."

"Well?"

"I thought you might be sorry. And we have asked him to stay the night."

"I promise not to turn him out," Mildred Caniper said, with her humorous look, and Helen laughed back with a friendliness for which Miriam, listening in a corner, admired her secretly.

"But I shall want to talk to you this evening when you are all together," Notya said.

For that ceremony, Miriam wore her customary black with an air which at once changed the dress into one of mourning; the fashion of her hair was subdued to match her manners, and Daniel, having a dim notion that he might unknowingly have offended, asked in his clumsy way what troubled her.

She edged closer to him and looked up, and he could see that she was laughing at herself, though that helped him not at all.

"Isn't my father dead? And aren't we going to have a family consultation in the dining-room? Well, here am I."

"I see."

"What do you see?"

He turned away. "I'm not going to tell you."

"Ah, Daniel dear, do! I know I'm horrid and frivolous and vain, and I tease you, but I'm very fond of you and I should love—oh, love—you to tell me something nice. Quick, Daniel! Quick, before the others come in!"

He was red, and his forehead glistened as he said, "You'll only throw it up at me."

"Oh, as if I would! I don't care for that expression, but I won't. Daniel, some one's coming!"

He blew his nose and bent over his book, yet through the trumpeting and the manipulation of his handkerchief, she heard a word.

"Beautiful," he mumbled.

"Always?"

He nodded, and like a delighted child, she clapped her hands.

Rupert, less debonair than usual, opened the door. "Come on," he said. "We're all ready. Daniel, stay where you are. We don't want you tumbling into the conclave."

"All right, all right."

"Got something to keep you quiet?"

"Greek grammar."

"Good man. Now then!" He plunged across the hall as though it were an icy bath.

In the candle-lighted dining-room, Mildred Caniper sat by a wood fire. The table barricaded her from the four Canipers who sat and looked at her with serious eyes, and suddenly she found that she had very little to say. Those eyes and the four mouths curved, in their different ways, for passion and resolve, seemed to be making courteous mock of her; yet three at least of the Canipers were conscious only of pity for her loneliness behind the shining table.

"After all," she said, trying to be at ease, "there is not much to tell you; but I felt that, perhaps, you have never understood your father very well."

"He did not give us the opportunity," Rupert said.

John had his shoulders raised as though he would shield his ears from family discordances, and he swore inwardly at Rupert for answering back. What was the good of that? The man was dead, and he might be allowed to rest. It was strange, he thought, that Rupert, under his charming ways, had a hardness of which he himself was not capable.

"No," Mildred Caniper was saying, and by her tone she shifted the blame from her husband to his children. The word acted as a full stop to her confidences, and there was an uneasy pause.

"But tell us, please," Helen said, leaning forward.

"Oh, please," Rupert added.

Mildred Caniper smiled waveringly, between pride and pain.

"I was only going to tell you a little about him, but now I don't know that I can." She swallowed hard. "I wanted you to know how gifted he was."

"How?" Rupert asked.

"He wrote," she said, defying their criticism of what they had not seen, "but he destroyed all he did because he was never satisfied. I found nothing—anywhere."

Here was a father whom Rupert could understand, and for the first time he regretted not having known him; but to John it was foolishness for a man to set his hand to work which was not good enough to stand. He must content himself with a humbler job.

"He liked only the best," Mildred Caniper said, doing her duty by him, and the next moment she caught the full shaft of Miriam's unwary glance which was bright with the conviction that her father's desertion needed no more explanation.

Mildred Caniper's mind registered the personal affront, and swept on to its implication as rain sweeps up a valley. The result was darkness, and as she sat straight and motionless in her chair, she seemed to herself to struggle, for her soul sighted despair. Long ago, she had taken life into her hands and used it roughly, and life was taking its slow revenge. In the shuttered room by the sea, the dead man, deaf to the words with which she had hurried to him, and here, in this house, the eyes of Miriam announced her failure, yet to that cold clay and to this living flesh she had been, and was, a power.

She dropped her hands limply. She was tired of this fictitious power; she was almost ready to pretend no longer; and with that thought she found herself being observed by Helen with a tenderness she was not willing to endure. She spoke abruptly, resigning the pious task of sweetening Philip Caniper's memory.

"Your father has left you each nearly a hundred pounds a year"—she glanced at Miriam—"to be handed over when you have reached the age of twenty-one."

There was a feeling that some one ought to thank him, but no one spoke, and his children left the room with an unaccountable sense of guilt.

In the safety of the schoolroom Miriam's voice rose bitterly: "Oh, why aren't we an ordinary family? Why can't we cry for a father who leaves us nearly a hundred pounds?"

"Try to," Rupert advised. He was smiling queerly to himself.

"Helen, isn't it horrid?"

"No: I don't like crying."

"John, you look as though you're going to refuse the money. I will if you do. John—"

"Don't be a little fool," he said. "Refuse it! I'm holding on to it with both hands."

She drooped forlornly, but no one seemed to notice her. Daniel was absorbed in the Greek grammar, and the others were thinking their own thoughts.

"I'll go on to the moor," she told herself, and she slipped through the window in search of what adventure she could find. Outside the garden she paused and nodded towards the house.

"I don't care," she said. "It's all their fault. And Helen—oh, I could kill Helen!" Wickedly she tried to mimic Helen's face.

A few minutes later John followed through the window, and he went into the darkness with a strange excitement. For a time he did not think, for he was experiencing all the relief of daring to feel freely, and the effect was at first only a lightening of the heart and feet. Hardly knowing where he wandered, he found himself on the moor behind Brent Farm, and there, in the heather, he sat down to light his pipe. He was puzzled when the match quivered in his hand, and then he became aware that innumerable pulses were beating in his body, and with that realization others rushed on him, and he knew how he had held himself in check for months, and how he desired the touch of Lily Brent's splendid strength and the sight of her drowsy, threatening eyes. Picturing her, he could not rest, and he rose and marched aimlessly to and fro. He had been a fool, he told himself: he had denied his youth and doubted her: proud in poverty, he should have gone to her and offered all he had, the love and labour of his body and brain, honouring her in asking her to take him empty-handed if she would take him at all. Now he must go to her as though she could be bought at the price of a hundred pounds a years and the poor thing he had once called his pride, known now for a mere notion gathered from some source outside himself. He who had scorned convention had been its easy victim, and he bit hard at his pipe stem and grunted in disgust.

"We get half our ideas out of books," he said. "No woman would have been such a fool. They get things at first hand."

He stopped and pointed at the farm. No doubt the woman down there had read his thoughts and laughed at him, yes, loving him or not, she must be laughing at him. He laughed himself, then listened for the chance sound of her distant voice. He could hear footsteps on the cobbled yard, the clattering of a pail, the shrill stave of a song uttered by the maid-servant, but no more; and he paced on until the lights in Brent Farm went out and his own home was darkened.

In the grey of the morning, he went down the track. Mists were lying on the moor; above them, trees showed like things afloat, and when he crossed the road he felt that he was breasting silent floods. Through his thick boots he could feel the cold of ground soaked by a night of unexpected rain, and against his gaiters the long grasses rid themselves of their loads of drops and swung back to their places as he passed. He turned at the sound of footsteps on the road and saw one of Halkett's men walking through that semblance of grey water. The man gave a nod of greeting, John raised a hand, and the peace of the waking day was not shattered by human speech.

In the corner of the meadow near the house, the cows, looming large and mysterious and unfamiliar, were waiting with hanging heads, and John stood and looked at them in a kind of dream before he fetched his pail and stool and settled down to work. His hands were not steady and the cow was restless at his touch, and when he spoke to her the sound of his own voice startled him, for the world was leagued with silence and even the hissing of the milk into the pail had the extravagance of a cascade.

As he worked, he watched the house. No smoke came from its chimneys, but at length he heard the opening of a door and Lily Brent appeared. He thought she was like the morning, fresh and young, with all the promise and danger of a new day, and while he looked at her his hands dropped idle. She stood on the step and nodded to him before she walked across the grass.

"You here alone?" she said, and there was a fine frown on her brow. "Where's the rest of them? If I don't rout them out myself—"

"Don't," he said. "It's early, and it's Sunday morning. They'll come soon enough." He stood up and rested his folded arms on the cow's back and looked at Lily.

"She'll have the pail over," she warned him quickly.

He put it out of danger and returned.

"You haven't fetched my stool," she said.

"I forgot it. Wait a bit. I'll get it soon."

"What's the matter with you this morning? We're wasting time."

"Let's waste time," he said. He looked round at the mists floating off the moor. The light was clearing; the cows had dwindled; the road was no longer a fairy flood but a highway for the feet of men.

"I want you to pretend it's yesterday," he said.

"What's the matter with you, John?"

"I'm going to tell you. Will you pretend it's yesterday?"

"Yes. It's Saturday morning, a busy day for us. We ought to get to work."

"Come a step nearer," he said, and she obeyed.

He clutched the hair on the cow's back and spoke in a harsh voice. "Will you marry me?" he said, frowning and looking her in the eyes. "I've hardly any money, but I love you. I want you. I didn't know what to do. If I'd waited till I had as much as you, I might have lost you. I didn't know what to do, but I thought I'd tell you."

"You needn't explain any more," she said. Her hands, too, fell on the cow's back, and with a little movement she bade him take them. He gathered her fingers into his and turned and twisted them.

"I thought—if you wanted me—why should we live on opposite sides of the way? I can help you—and I love you." He relied on that.

"I love you," he said again.

He heard her ask softly, "Why?"

"Because—because—oh, you're all I want. You're like the earth, like herbs, like fresh green grass. I've got your hands: give me the rest of you!"

Her eyes flashed open, he saw and heard her laugh, and their lips met across the bulky barrier.

"But I want you in my arms," he said, and in the clearing light he held her there, though the sound of an opening window told them that the farm was waking.

CHAPTER XIV

On the night of Mildred Caniper's return, Helen felt that the house had changed. A new emotion was mingling with the rest, and it was as unmistakable as a scent, and like a scent, it would grow fainter, but now it hung in every room and on the stairs. Surely Mr. Pinderwell must be disturbed by it. She fancied his grey old face puckered in bewilderment and his steps going faster up and down the stairs. Helen, too, was restless, and having slept uneasily, she woke in the dark of the night.

Outside her widely-opened windows the poplars were moving gently. They seemed near enough to touch, but she found something formidable in their aspect. Black, tall and bare, they watched her to the accompaniment of their indifferent whispering and swaying, and they warned her that whatever might be her lot, theirs would continue to be this one of lofty swinging. So, aware of all that happened they had always watched and whispered, and only tonight was she resentful in her love for them. Could they not feel a little sorrow for the woman burdened with trouble who had come back to the house? Had not the sense of that trouble stolen through the doors and windows? Beyond the garden walls there was, she knew, immunity from human pain. The moor understood it and therefore remained unmoved. It was the winds that grieved, the grey clouds that mourned and the sunshine that exulted; under all these, and changed only on the surface, the moor spread itself tranquilly, but the poplars were different. For Helen, all trees were people in another shape and she could not remember a time when these had not been her friends, but now they seemed not to care, and she started up in the sudden suspicion that nothing cared, that perhaps the great world of earth and sky and growing things had lives as absorbing and more selfish than her own.

"But only perhaps," she said aloud, asserting her faith in what she loved.

She pushed the pillow behind her back and stared into the clearing darkness of Jane's large bare room. The curved front of her elegant dressing-table with its oval mirror became distinct. Helen's clothes lay like a patch of moonlight on a chair, the tallboy and the little stool by which she reached the topmost drawers changed from their semblances of beasts to sedate and beautiful furniture. By the bedside, soft slippers waited with an invitation, and into them Helen soon slipped her feet, for it seemed to her that the trouble thickened with each minute and that Notya must be in need of help.

Yet, when she had noiselessly opened the door of the room opposite, she found Mildred Caniper sleeping in her narrow bed with the steadiness of complete fatigue, with something, too, touchingly childlike in her pose. She might have been a child who had cried bitterly for hours before she at last found rest, but Notya's grief, Helen divined, had not the simplicity which allowed of tears nor the beauty which was Mr. Pinderwell's consolation. It was not death which had hurt her.

Mildred Caniper's head had slid from the pillow and lay on her outstretched arm; the other arm, slender and round as youth, was thrown outside the bed-clothes, and only when Helen bent quite low could she see the frown of trouble between the brows. Then, feeling like a spy, she returned to the darkness of the landing where Phoebe and Jane and Christopher were wondering what she did.

She might have been a mother who, waking from a bad dream, goes about the house to see that all is safe: she wished she could go into each room to make sure that its occupant was there, but such kindnesses had never been encouraged in a family trained to restraint; moreover, Miriam might wake in fright, Rupert was a light sleeper and John had an uncertain temper. There was nothing to do but to go back to bed, and she did not want to do that. She could not sleep, and she would rather stay on the landing with the Pinderwells, so she leaned against the wall and folded her arms across her breast. She wanted to be allowed to care for people practically and she wished her brothers and sister were small enough to be held in the arms which had to be contented with herself. She had, she complained silently to the Pinderwells, to pretend not to care for the others very much, lest she should weary them. But she had her secret visions of a large house with unencumbered shining floors on which children could slide, with a broad staircase down which they would come heavily, holding to the rails and bringing both feet to each stair. She lived there with them happily, not thwarted by moods and past miseries, and though she had not yet seen the father of those children about the house, tonight, as she stood in the covering darkness, she thought she heard his footsteps in the garden where the children played among the trees.

She moved abruptly, slipped, and sat down with a thud. Her laughter, like a ghost's, trickled through the stillness, and even while she laughed a door was opened and John appeared, holding a lighted candle in his hand.

"It's only me," Helen said.

"What the devil are you up to?"

"I'm not up to anything. I'm on the floor."

"Ill?"

"No."

"I thought I heard some one prowling about."

"Couldn't you sleep either?"

He put his fingers through his hair. "No, I couldn't sleep."

"The house is full of—something, isn't it?"

"Fools, I think," he answered, laughing a little. "Look here, you mustn't sit there. It's cold. Get up."

"Help me."

"Why didn't you put on your dressing-gown?"

"You didn't."

"I don't wear this flimsy rubbish. Go back to bed."

"Yes. What's the time?"

"One o'clock. The longest night I've ever known!"

Rather wistfully she looked at him. "What's the matter, John?"

"I'm waiting for tomorrow," he said almost roughly.

"So am I," she said, surprising herself so that she repeated the words slowly, to know their meaning. "So am I—and it's here."

"Not till the dawn," he said. "Go to sleep."

Together their doors were softly closed and Helen knew now whose footsteps were in the children's garden. She went to the window and nodded to the poplars. "And you knew, I suppose; but so did I, really, all the time."

She slept profoundly and woke to a new wonder for the possibilities of life, a new fear for the dangers which might assail those who had much to cherish; and now she descried dimly the truth she was one day to see in the full light, that there is no gain without loss and no loss without gain, that things are divinely balanced, though man may sometimes throw his clumsy weight into the scale. Yet under these serious thoughts there was a song in her heart and her pleasure in its music shone out of her eyes so brilliantly that Rupert, watching her with tolerant amusement, asked what had befallen her.

"It's only that it's Sunday," the quick-witted Miriam said and Helen replied with the gravity which was more misleading than a lie: "Yes, that's all."

Nevertheless, when Zebedee arrived on the moor, her brightness faded. Already the desire of possession hurt her and Miriam had attached herself to him as though she owned him. She was telling him about Philip Caniper's death, about the money which was to come to them, and asserting that Daniel now wanted to marry her more than ever. Daniel was protesting through his blushes, and Zebedee was laughing. It all seemed very foolish, and she was annoyed with Zebedee for even pretending to be amused.

"Oh, don't," she murmured and lay back.

"Be quiet, prig!"

"She's not that, is she?" Zebedee asked, his strangely flecked eyes twinkling.

"Oh, a bad one. She disapproves of everything she doesn't like herself."

"Helen, wake up! I want to know if this is true."

"Do you think it is?"

"I'm afraid it's very likely."

"Oh, dear!" she sighed, "I don't know what to do about it. A person without opinions is just nothing, and you really were being very silly just now. I hate jokes about marrying."

"H'm, they are rather feeble," Zebedee owned.

"Vulgar, I think," she said, with her little air of Mildred Caniper.

"Ah," said Rupert, tapping Daniel lightly on the head, "a man with a brain like this can't develop a taste for the real thing. I've seen him shaking over jokes that made me want to cry, but you mustn't expect too much of him. He does very well. Come along, my boy, and let's have some reasonable talk."

"He doesn't want to go!" Miriam cried.

"But he must. I know what's good for him."

"He looks just like an overgrown dancing bear," Miriam said as she watched the two figures stepping across the moor.

Helen continued her own gloomy thoughts. "No one can like a prig."

"Oh, yes," Zebedee assured her cheerfully, "I can. Besides, you'll grow out of it."

"She never will! She's getting worse, and it's with living here. As a doctor, I think you might prescribe a change for her—for all of us. What will become of us? I can't," she added bitterly, "be expected to marry a dancing bear!"

"If you're speaking of Daniel—" Zebedee began sharply.

"Oh, don't you be cross, too! I did think I had one friend!"

"Daniel's a good man. He may be queer to look at, but he's sound. You only hurt yourself, you know, when you speak like that."

Miriam pouted and was silent, and Helen was not sure whether to be angry with Zebedee for speaking thus to her who must be spoiled, or glad that he could do it to one so beautiful, while he could preserve friendliness for a prig. But her life-long loyalty refused this incipient rivalry; once more she decided that Miriam must have what she wanted, and she lay with clenched hands and a tranquil brow while she listened to the chatter which proclaimed Miriam's recovery.

Helen could see nothing but a sky which was colourless and unclouded, and she wished she could be like that—vague, immaterial, without form. Perhaps to reach that state was happiness; it might be negation, but it would be peace and she had a young, desperate wish to die and escape the alternations of joy and pain. "And yet this is nothing," she said with foresight, and she stood up. "I'm going home."

"No!" Zebedee exclaimed in the middle of one of Miriam's sentences.

"I must. Notya's all alone. Good-night."

He would not say the word, and he walked beside her. "But I'm your guest," he reminded her.

"I know. But you see, she's lonely."

"And I've been lonely all my life."

She caught her breath. "Have you?" Her hands moved against her skirt and she looked uneasily about her. "Have you?" She was pulled two ways, and with a feeling of escape, she found an answer for him. "But you are you. You're not like her. You're strong. You can manage without any one."

"I've had to."

"Oh," she moaned, "don't make me feel unhappy about going."

"I wouldn't have you unhappy about anything."

"You're a wonderful friend to me. Good-night."

He watched her move away, but when she had gone a few paces she ran back.

"It wasn't quite the truth," she said. "It was only partly Notya."

"You're not angry with me?"

"With you? I couldn't be. It was just my silly self, only I didn't want to be half truthful with you."

Their hands touched and parted, and he waited until she was out of sight before he went back to Miriam.

"You're a little pest," he said, "wasting my time—"

"Ha, ha! I knew. I won't waste any more of it. Wasn't it horrid of me? If you hadn't scolded me I might have been kind; but I always, always pay people out."

"Silly thing to do," he muttered, and went off.

Miriam chuckled under her whistling as she strolled across the moor. She did not whistle a tune, but uttered sweet, plaintive notes like a bird's call, and as she reached the stream a tall figure rose up from the darkness of the ground.

"Oh, are you here, George?" she said. "I'm glad. I'm sick of everything."

"H'm. I'm glad I'm useful. Are the others having their usual prayer-meeting?"

"What do you mean?"

"That Mackenzie of yours and your brother, sitting in the dip and talking. I can't think what on earth they find to say."

"Well, you see, George, they are very clever people. Let us sit down. You can't—I mean you and I can't appreciate them properly."

"The Mackenzie looks a fool."

"He is a great friend of mine. You must not be rude. Manners makyth man. According to that, you are not always a man when you're with me."

He breathed deeply. "There's something about you—"

"Now you're blaming me, and that's not gallant."

"You think I'm not fit to breathe the same air with you, don't you?"

"Yes, sometimes." She sat hugging her knees and swaying to and fro, and with each forward movement her face neared his. "But at others you are quite presentable. Last night you were charming to me, George."

"I can be what I choose. D'you know that I had the same education as your brothers?"

"You're always saying that. But you forget that you didn't have me for a sister."

"No, thank God."

"Now—!"

"That's a compliment."

"Oh! And, George," she peered at him and dared herself to say the words, though old Halkett's ghost might be lurking among the trees: "I don't think your father can have been a ve-ry good influence on a wild young man like you."

"The old man's dead. Leave it at that. And who says I'm wild?"

"Aren't you? Don't disappoint me."

"I'm all right," he said with admirable simplicity, "if I don't drink."

"Then you mustn't, and yet I love to think that you're a bold, bad man."

His eyes, which rarely widened, did so now, and in the gathering dusk she saw a flash of light.

"You see, it makes me feel so brave, George."

"It ought to."

There was danger in his presence and she liked invoking it; but there was a certain coarseness, also invoked by her, from which she shrank, towards which she crept, step by step, again. She made no answer to his words. In her black dress and against the darkness of the wood, she was hardly more than a face and two small hands. There was a gentle movement among the trees; they were singing their welcome of a peaceful night; the running of the stream came loudly, giving itself courage for the plunge into the wood.

Miriam spoke in a low voice. "It's getting late. The others must have gone in. They'll wonder where I am."

"And they'd be horrified, I suppose, if they knew."

She bent towards him so that he might see her reproachful face.

"You've spoilt this lovely night. You don't match the sky and stars. I wish I hadn't met you."

"You needn't have done," he said.

"Are you sorry I did?" she challenged him.

"Oh, I don't know," he muttered almost to himself. "That's it. I never know."

She choked down the lilt of triumph in her voice. "I'll leave you to think, about it," she said and, looking at the high firwood, she added, "But I thought we were going to be such friends, after all."

Halkett stood up, and he said nothing, for his feelings were not to be put into words he could say to her. In her presence he suffered a mingling of pain and pleasure, anger and delight; cruelty strove in him with gentleness, coarseness with courtesy; he wanted to kiss her roughly and cast her off, yet he would have been grateful for the chance of serving her.

"George," she said quietly.

"Yes?"

"When you think of life, what do you see?"

"I—don't know."

"But you must."

He compelled his imagination. "The moor, and the farm, and the folks in the town, standing on the pavement, and Oxford Street in London—and Paris."

"Have you been to Paris?"

"I couldn't think about it if I hadn't."

She gave the laugh which coolly put him from her. "Couldn't you? Poor George!" She balanced from her heels to her toes and back again, with steadying movements of her arms, so that she was like a bird refusing to take flight. "I don't see things plainly like that," she murmured. "It's like a black ball going round and round with sparks inside, and me; and the blackness and the sparks are feelings and thoughts, and things that have happened and are going to happen, all mixing themselves up with the me in the middle. George, do you feel how strange it is? I can't explain, but here we are on the moor, with the sky above us, and the earth underneath—and why? But I'm really rolling over and over in the black ball, and I can't stop and I can't go on. I'm just inside."

"I know," he said. "It's all mixed. It's—" He kicked a heather-bush. "You want a thing and you don't want it—I don't know."

"I always know what I want," she said, and into her thoughtfulness there crept the personal taint. "I want every one to adore me. Good-night, George. I wonder if we shall ever meet again!"

In the garden, with her hands folded on her knee, Helen was sitting meekly on a stool under the poplars and watching the swaying of the tree-tops.

"The young nun at prayer," Miriam said. "I thought you came back to be with Notya."

"She seemed not to want me."

"Then you sacrificed me for nothing. That's just like you."

"How?"

"By throwing me into the alluring company of that young man. If I love him and he doesn't love me, well, you've blighted my life. And if he loves me and I don't love him—"

"You are always talking about love," Helen said with an accent of distaste.

"I know it's not the sort of thing a young virgin should be interested in; but after all, what else can be so interesting to the Y. V.?"

"But you spoil it."

"I don't. Do you mind if I put my head on your knee? No, I'm not comfortable. That's better. It's you who spoil it with being sentimental and one-love-one-life-ish. Now for me it's a game that nymphs and goddesses might play at."

"But you can't play it alone," said Helen, troubled.

"No, that's the fun of it." She smiled against Helen's dress. "I wonder if my young man is at home yet. And there's only a cold supper for him! Dear, dear, dear!"

With her apparent obtuseness, Helen said, "It won't matter so much in the summertime."

"Ah, that's a comfort," Miriam said, and rolled her head luxuriously.

John came through the French window.

"I've been looking for you both," he said. "I want to tell you something."

"Now it's coming," Miriam muttered.

"Sit down, then," Helen said. "We can't see you so high up."

"What! in my best clothes? All right." The light was dim, but they felt the joviality that hung about him and saw his teeth exposed in a smile he could not subdue. "The ground's damp, you know. There's a heavy dew."

There was a silence through which the poplars whispered in excitement.

"Perhaps I am a little deaf," Miriam said politely, "but I haven't heard you telling us anything."

"Yes; he said the ground was damp."

"So he did! Come along, we'll go in."

"No, don't!" he begged. "I know I'm not getting on very fast, but the fact is—I can't bear women to be called after flowers. If it weren't for that I should have told you long ago. And hers is one of the worst," he added sadly.

Miriam and Helen shook each other with their silent laughter.

"You can call her something else," Helen said.

"Mrs. C. would be a jaunty way of addressing her."

"Well, anyway, she's going to marry me, bless her heart. Get up! Notya wants to know why supper isn't ready." He did a clumsy caper on the grass. "Who's glad?"

"I am," Helen said.

"When?" Miriam asked.

"Soon."

"What did Notya say?" was Helen's question.

"Nothing worth repeating. Don't talk of that."

"Well," Miriam remarked, "it will be a very interesting

affair to watch."

"Confound your impudence!"

"You're sure to have heaps of children," she warned him.

"Hope so."

"You'll forget how many there are, and mix them up with the dogs and the cats and the geese. They'll be very dirty."

"And perfectly happy."

"Oh, yes. Now Helen's will always be clean little prigs who couldn't be naughty if they tried. I shall like yours best, John, though they won't be clean enough to kiss."

"Shut up!" he said.

"I shall be a lovely aunt. I shall come from London Town with a cornucopia of presents. We're beginning to go," she went on. "First John, and then me, as soon as I am twenty-one."

"But Rupert will be here," Helen said quickly.

"He'll marry, too, and you'll be left with Notya. Somebody will have to look after her old age. And as you've always been so fond of her—!"

"There would be the moor," Helen said, answering all her unspoken thoughts.

"It wouldn't comfort me!"

"Don't worry, my dear," John said kindly; "the gods are surely tender with the good."

"But she won't grow old," Helen said earnestly. "I don't believe she could grow old. It would be terrible." And it was of Mildred Caniper and not of herself she thought.

CHAPTER XV

Mildred Caniper was wearing her deaf expression when they went into the house, and getting supper ready as a form of reproof. John was another of her failures. He had chosen work she despised for him, and now, though it was impossible to despise Lily Brent, it was impossible not to disapprove of such a marriage for a Caniper. But when she was helpless, Mrs. Caniper had learnt to preserve her pride in suavity, and as they sat down to supper she remarked that she would call on Lily Brent tomorrow.

"How funny!" Helen said at once.

Miriam darted a look meant to warn Helen that Notya was in no mood for controversy, and John frowned in readiness to take offence.

"Why funny?" he growled.

"I was just wondering if Notya would put on a hat and gloves to do it." She turned to Mildred Caniper. "Will you?"

"I'm afraid I have not considered such a detail."

"None of us," Helen went on blandly, "has ever put on a hat to go to the farm. I should hate any of us to do it. Notya, you can't."

"You forget," Mildred Caniper said in her coldest tones, "that I have not been accustomed to going there."

"Well, do notice Lily's primroses," Helen said pleasantly. "They're like sunshine, and she's like—"

"No, please," John begged.

"I wonder why Rupert has not come to supper," Mildred Caniper said, changing the subject, and Helen wondered pityingly why one who had known unhappiness should not be eager to spare others.

"But," Miriam began, her interest overcoming dread of her

stepmother's prejudices, "we shall have to wear hats for John's wedding. I shall have a new one and a new dress, a dusky blue, I think, with a sheen on it."

"Did you mention my wedding?" John asked politely.

"Yes. And a peacock's feather in my hat. No, that's unlucky, but so beautiful."

"Nothing beautiful," Helen said, "can be unlucky."

"I wouldn't risk it. But what can I have?"

"For my wedding," John announced, "you'll have nothing, unless you want to sit alone in the garden in your new clothes. You're not going to be present at the ceremony. Good Lord! I'll have Rupert and Daniel for witnesses, and we'll come home in time to do the milking, but there'll be no show. It would make me sick."

"Not even a party?"

"What the—what on earth should we have a party for?"

"For fun, of course. Daniel and Zebedee and us." She leaned towards him. "And George, John, just to show that all's forgiven!" To see if she had dared too much, she cast a glance at Mildred Caniper, but that lady sat in the stillness of determined indifference.

"Not one of you!" John said. "It's our wedding, and we're going to do what we like with it."

"But when you're going to be happy—as I suppose you think you are—you ought to let other people join in. Here's a chance of a little fun—"

"There's nothing funny about being married," Helen said in her deep tones.

"Depends who—whom—you're marrying, doesn't it?" Miriam asked, and looking at Mildred Caniper once more, she found that she need not be afraid, for though the expression was the same, its effect was different. Notya looked as though she could not rouse her energies to active disapproval; as though she would never say her rare, amusing things again, and Miriam was reminded of the turnip lanterns they had made in their youth—hollowness and flickering light within.

The succeeding days encouraged that reminder, for something had gone from Mildred Caniper and left her stubbornly frail in mind and body. Rupert believed that hope had died in her but the Canipers did not speak of the change which was plain to all of them. She was a presence of flesh and blood, and she would always be a presence, for she had that power, but she approached Mr. Pinderwell in their thoughts, and they began to use towards her the kind of tenderness they felt for him. Sometimes she became aware of it and let out an irony with a sharpness which sent Helen about the house more gaily and persuaded her that Notya would be better when summer came, for surely no one could resist the sun.

John's soft heart forgave his stepmother's coldness towards his marriage and his bride, and prompted him to a generous suggestion. He made it shyly and earnestly one night in the drawing-room where Mildred Caniper sat under the picture of Mr. Pinderwell's lady.

"Notya," he began, "we want you to come to our wedding, too. Just you and Rupert and Daniel. Will you?"

She looked faintly amused, yet, the next moment, he had a fear that she was going to cry. "Thank you, John."

"We both want you," he said awkwardly, and went nearer.

"I'm glad you have asked me, but I won't come. I'm afraid I should only spoil it. I do spoil things." She smiled at him and looked at the hands on her knee. "It seems to me that that's what I do best."

He did not know what to say and, having made inarticulate noises in his throat, he went quickly to the schoolroom.

"Go to Notya, some one, and make her angry. She's being miserable in the drawing-room. Tell her you've broken something!"

"I won't," Miriam said. "I've had too much of that, and I'm going to enjoy the unwonted peace. You go, Helen."

"Leave her alone," Rupert advised. "You won't cure Notya's

unhappiness so easily as that."

"When the summer comes—" Helen began, cheerfully deceiving herself, and John interrupted.

"Summer is here already. It's June next week."

He was married in his own way on the first day of that month, and Miriam uttered no more regrets. She was comparatively contented with the present. Mildred Caniper seldom thwarted her, and she knew that every day George Halkett rode or walked where he might see her, and her memory of that splendid summer was to be one of sunlight blotted with the shapes of man and horse moving across the moor. George was not always successful in his search, for she knew that he would pall as a daily dish, but on Sundays if Daniel would not be beguiled, and if it was not worth while to tease Helen through Zebedee, she seldom failed to make her light secret way to the larch-wood where he waited.

Her excitement, when she felt any, was only sexual because the danger she sought and the power she wielded were of that kind, and she was chiefly conscious of light-hearted enjoyment and the new experience of an understanding with the moor. Secrecy quickened her perceptions and she found that nature deliberately helped her, but whether for its own purposes or hers she could not tell. The earth which had once been her enemy now seemed to be her friend, and where she had seen monotony she discovered delicate differences of hour and mood. If she needed shelter, the hollows deepened themselves at her approach, shadows grew darker and the moor lifted itself to hide her. She seemed to take a friend on all her journeys, but she was not quite happy in its company. It was a silent, scheming friend and she was not sure of it; there were times when she suspected laughter at which she would grow defiant and then, pretending that she went openly in search of pleasure, she sang and whistled loudly on her way.

There was an evening when that sound was answered by the noise of hoofs behind her, the music of a chinking bridle, the creaking of leather and the hard breathing of a horse. She did not turn as George drew rein beside her and said "Good-evening," in his half sulky tones. She had her hands behind her back and she looked at the sky.

"'Sunset and evening star,'" she said solemnly, "'and one clear call for me.' Do you know those beautiful words, George?"

He did not answer. She could hear him fidgeting with whip and reins, but she gazed upward still.

"I'm sorry I can't recite the rest. I have forgotten it, but if you will promise to read it, I'll lend you a copy. On Sunday evenings you ought to sit at home and improve your mind."

He gave a laugh like a cough. "I don't care about my mind," he said, and he touched the horse with his heel so that she had to move aside. He saw warm anger chase the pious expression from her face.

"Ah!" she cried, "that is the kind of thing you do! You're rough! You make me hate you! Why!" her voice fell from its height, "that's a new horse!" Her hands were busy on neck and nose. "I like him. What is he called?"

Halkett was looking at her with an eagerness through which her words could hardly pierce. She was wonderful to watch, soft as a kitten, swift as a bird.

"What do you call him, George?" she said again, and tapped his boot.

"'Charlie'—this one."

She laughed. "You choose dull names. Is he as wicked as Daisy?"

"Nothing like."

"Why did you get him, then?"

"I want him for hard work."

"I believe you're lazy. If you don't walk you'll get fat. You're the kind of man that does."

"Perhaps, but that's a long way off. Riding is hard work enough and my father was a fine man up to sixty."

A thin shock of fear ran through her at the remembrance of

old Halkett's ruined shape. "I was always frightened of him," she said in a small voice, and she looked at George as though she asked for reassurance. There was a cold grey light on the moor; darkness was not far off and it held a chill wind in leash.

"Do you wish he wasn't dead?" she whispered.

He lifted his shoulders and pursed his mouth. "No," he said.

"Are you lonely in that house?"

"There's Mrs. Biggs, you know," he said with a sneer.

"Yes, I know," she murmured doubtfully, and drew closer.

"So you don't think she's enough for me?"

"Of course I don't. That's why I'm so kind to you. She couldn't be listening to us, could she? Everything seems to be listening."

"So you're kind to me, are you?"

"Yes," she said, raising her eyebrows and nodding her head, until she looked like a dark poppy in a wind.

"And when I saw you on the road the other day you wouldn't look at me. That's the second time."

"I did."

"As if I'd been a sheep."

"Oh!" Laughter bubbled in her. "You did look rather like one. I was occupied in thinking deeply, seriously, intently—"

"That's no excuse."

"My good George, I shouldn't think of excusing myself to you. I chose to ignore you and I shall probably ignore you again."

"Two can play at that game."

"Well, dear me, I shan't mind."

He bent in the saddle, and she did not like the polished whiteness of his eyeballs. His voice was very low and heavy. "You think you can go on making a mock of me for ever."

She started back. "No, George, no."

"You do, by God!" He lifted his whip to shake it in the face of heaven.

"Oh, don't, George, please! I can't stay"—she crept nearer—"if you go on like that. What have I done? It's you who treat me badly. Won't you be nice? Tell me about something." She put her face against the horse's neck. "Tell me about riding. It must be beautiful in the dark. Isn't it dangerous? Dare you gallop?"

"Well, we do."

"Such lots of rabbit-holes."

"What does it matter?"

"Oh, dear, you're very cross."

"I can't help it," he said like an unhappy child. "I can't help it." And he put his hand to his head with an uncertain movement.

"Oh." With a practical air she sought for an impersonal topic. "Tell me about Paris."

"Paris." There was no need for him to speak above a murmur. "I want to take you there."

"Do you?"

He leant lower. "Will you come?"

Her eyes moved under his, but they did not turn aside. "I think I'm going there with some one else," she said softly, and before her vision of this eager lover there popped a spruce picture of Uncle Alfred.

"That isn't true," Halkett said, but despair was in his voice.

She was angered instantly. "I beg your pardon?"

"It isn't true," he said again.

"Very well," she said, and she began to walk away, but he called after her vehemently, bitterly, "Because I won't let you go!"

She laughed at that and came back to her place, to say indulgently, "How silly you are! I'm only going with an aged uncle!"

"But he's not the man to take you there."

"No."

"Come with me now."

"Shall I?"

"Get up beside me and I'll carry you away."

She was held by his trouble, but she spoke lightly. "Could he swim with us both across the Channel? No, I don't think I want to come tonight. Some day—"

"When?"

"Oh," she said on a high note, "perhaps when I'm very tired of things."

"You're tired already."

"Not so much as that. And we're talking nonsense, and I must go."

"Not yet."

"I must. It's nearly time for bed, and I'm not sure that it's polite of you to sit on that horse while I stand here."

"Come up and you'll see how well he goes."

"He wouldn't bear us both."

"Pooh! You're a feather."

"Oh, I couldn't. Wouldn't he jump?"

"He'd better try!"

"Now, don't be cruel to him."

"What do you know about it? I've ridden since I could walk."

"Lucky you!"

"I'll teach you."

"Could you?"

"Give me a chance."

"Here's one! No, no, I didn't mean it," she cried as he dismounted and lifted her to the saddle. "Oh, I feel so high up. Don't move him till I get used to it. I'm not safe on this saddle. Put me a little further on, George. That's further forward! I'm nearly on his neck. No, I don't think I like it. Take me down."

"Keep still." The words were almost threatening in the gloom. "Sit steady. I'm coming up."

"No, don't. I shall fall off!"

But already he was behind her, holding her closely with one arm. "There! He's quiet enough. I couldn't do this with Daisy. And he's sure-footed. He was bred on the moor." He set the horse trotting gently. "He goes well, doesn't he?"

"Yes."

"Don't you like it?"

"Ye-es."

"What's the matter?"

"There isn't room enough," she said, and moved her shoulders.

He spoke in her ear. "If I don't hold you, you'll fall off. Here's a smooth bit coming. Now, lad, show us what you can do and remember what you're carrying!"

The saddle creaked and the bit jangled and George's arm tightened round her. Though she did not like his nearness, she leaned closer for safety, and he and the horse seemed to be one animal, strong and swift and merciless. Once or twice she gasped, "Please, George, not quite so fast," but the centaur paid no heed. She shut her eyes because she did not like to see the darkness sliding under them as they passed, and they seemed to be galloping into a blackness that was empty and unending. Her hands clutched the arm that fenced her breasts: her breath came quickly, exhilaration was mixed with fear, and now she was part of the joint body that carried her and held her.

She hardly knew when the pace had slackened; she was benumbed with new sensations, darkness, speed and strength. She had forgotten that this was a man she leaned against. Then the horse stood still and she felt Halkett's face near hers, his breath on her cheeks, a new pressure of his arm and, unable to endure this different nearness, she gave his binding hand a sharp blow with her knuckles, jerked her head backwards against his and escaped his grasp; but she had to fall to do it, and from the ground she heard his chuckle as he looked down at her.

At that moment she would have killed him gladly; she felt her body soiled by his, but her mind was curiously untouched. It knew no disgust for his desire nor for her folly, and while she hated him for sitting there and laughing at her fall, this was still a game she loved and meant to play. In the heather she sat and glowered at him, but now she could hardly see his face.

"That was a silly thing to do," she heard him say. "You might easily have been kicked. What did you do it for?"

She would not own her knowledge of his real offence, and she muttered angrily, "Galloping like that—"

"Didn't you like it? He's as steady as a rock."

"How could I know that?"

"And I thought you had some pluck."

"I have. I sat quite still."

Again he laughed. "I made you."

"Oh," she burst out. "I'll never trust you again."

"You would if you knew—if you knew—but never mind. I wanted to see you on a horse. You shall have him to yourself next time. I'll get a side saddle."

"I don't want one," she said.

"Oh, yes, you do. Let me help you up. Say you forgive me."

With her hand in his she murmured, "But you are always doing something. And my head aches."

"Does it? I'm sorry. What made it ache?"

"It—I—I bumped myself when I fell."

"Poor little head! It was silly of you, wasn't it? Let me put you on his back again, and I'll walk you slowly home."

He was faithful to his word, letting her go without a pressure of the hand, and she crept into the house with the uneasy conviction that Helen was right, that George wanted the chance he had never had, and her own responsibility was black over her bed as she tried to sleep. Turning from side to side and at last sitting up with a jerk, she decided to evade responsibility by evading George, and with that resolution she heaved a deep sigh at the prospect of her young life despoiled by duty.

CHAPTER XVI

Zebedee had the lover's gift of finding time which did not exist for other men, and there were few Sundays when he did not spend some minutes or some hours on the moor. There were blank days when Helen failed him because she thought Mildred Caniper was lonely, others when she ran out for a word and swiftly left him to the memory of her grace and her transforming smile; yet oftenest, she was waiting for him in the little hollow of earth, and those hours were the best he had ever known. It was good to sit and see the sky slowly losing colour and watch the moths flit out, and though neither he nor she was much given to speech, each knew that the other was content.

"Helen," he said one night in late September when they were left alone, "I want to tell you something."

She did not stir, and she answered slowly, softly, in the voice of one who slept, "Tell it."

"It's about beauty. I'd never seen it till you showed it to me."

"Did I? When?"

"I'm not sure. That night—"

"On the moor?"

"Always on the moor! When you had the basket. It was the first time after I came back."

"But you couldn't see me in the darkness."

"Yes, a little. You remember you told me to light the lamps. And I could hear you—your voice running with the wind—And then each day since. I want to thank you."

"Oh—" She made a little sound of depreciation and happiness.

"Those old Sundays—"

"Ah, yes! The shining pews and the painted stars. This is better."

"Yes, this is better. Heather instead of the sticky pews—"

"And real stars," she murmured.

"And you for priestess."

"No, I'm just a worshipper."

"But you show the way. You give light to them that sit in darkness."

"Ah, don't." There was pain in her voice. "Don't give me things. At least, don't give me praise. I'm afraid of having things."

"But why, my dear?" The words dropped away into the gathering dusk, and they both listened to them as they went.

"I'm afraid they will be taken away again."

"Don't have that feeling. It will be hard on those who want to give you—much."

"I hadn't thought of that," she cried, and started up as though she were glad to blame him. "And you never tell me anything. Why don't you? Why don't you tell me about your work? I could have that. There would be no harm in that."

"Harm? No. May I?"

"Why shouldn't you? They all tell me things. Don't you want somebody to talk to?"

"I want you, if you care to hear."

"Oh, Zebedee, yes," she said, and sank into her place.

"Helen," he said unsteadily, "I wish you would grow up, and yet, Helen, what a pity that you should change."

She did not answer; she might have been asleep, and he sat in a stillness born of his disturbance at her nearness, her pale smooth skin, her smooth brown hair, the young curves of her body. If he had moved, it would have been to crush her beautiful, firm mouth, but her youth was a chain wound round him, and though he was in bonds he seemed to be alive for the first time. He and Helen were the sole realities. He could see Miriam's figure, black against the sky as she stood or stooped to pick a flower, but she had no meaning for him, and the voices of the young men, not far off, might have been the droning of some late bee. The world was a cup to hold him and this girl, and over that cup he had a feeling of mastery and yet of helplessness, and all his past days dwindled to a streak of drab existence. Life had begun, and it went at such a pace that he did not know how much of it was already spent when Helen sat up, and looking at him with drowsy eyes, asked, "What is happening?"

"There was magic abroad. The sun has been going down behind the moor, and night is coming on. I must be going home."

"Don't go. Yes, it's getting dark. There will be stars soon. I love the night. Don't go. How low the birds are flying. They are like big moths. The magic hasn't gone."

Grey-gowned, grey-eyed, white-faced, he thought she was like a moth herself, fragile and impalpable in the gloom, a moth motionless on a flower, and when he saw her smile he thought the moth was making ready for flight.

"I want this to go on for ever," she said. "The moor and the night and you. You're such a friend—you and the Pinderwells. I don't know how I should live without you."

"Do you know what you're saying to me?"

"I'm telling you I like you, and it's true. And you like me. It's so comfortable to know that."

"Comfortable!"

"Isn't it?"

"Comfortable?" he said again. "Oh, my love—" He broke off, and looking at each other, both fell dumb.

He got to his feet and looked down with an expression which was strange to her, for into that moment of avowal there had come a fleeting antagonism towards the woman who, in spite of all her gifts to him, had taken his possession of himself: yet through his shamed resentment, he knew that he adored her.

"Zebedee," she said in a broken voice. "Oh, isn't it a funny name! Zebedee, don't look at me like that."

"How shall I look at you?" he asked, not clearly.

"In the old way. But don't say things." She sprang up. "Not tonight."

"When?" he asked sternly.

"I—don't know. Tonight I feel afraid. It's—too much. I shan't be able to keep it, Zebedee. It's too good. And we can't get this for nothing."

"I'm willing to pay for it. I want to pay for it, in the pain of parting from you now, in the work of all my days—" He stopped in his realization of how little he had to give. "I can't tell you," he added simply.

"Will it hurt you to leave me tonight?" she whispered.

"Yes."

She touched his sleeve. "I don't like you to be hurt, yet I like that. Will you come next Sunday?"

"Not if you're afraid. I can't come to see you if you won't let me say things."

"I'll try not to be afraid; only, only, say them very softly so that nothing else can hear."

He laughed and caught her hand and kissed it. "I shall do exactly what I like," he said; but as he strode away without another word he knew from something in the way she stood and looked at him, something of patience and resolve, that their future was not in his hands alone.

When he was out of sight and hearing, Helen moved stiffly, as though she waked from a long sleep and was uncertain where she was. The familiar light shone in the kitchen of Brent Farm, yet the house seemed unreal and remote, marooned in the high heather. The heather was thick and rich that year, and the flowers touched her hands. The smell of honey was heavy in the air, and thousands of small, pale moths made a honey-coloured cloud between the purple moor and the night blue of the sky. If she strained her ears, Helen could hear the singing of Halkett's stream and it said things she had not heard before. A sound of voices came from the road and she knew that some faithful Christians of the moor were returning from their worship in the town: she remembered them crude and ugly in their Sunday clothes, but they gathered mystery from distance and the night. Perhaps they came from that chapel where Zebedee had spent his unhappy hours. She turned and her hands swept the heather flowers. This was now his praying place, as it had always been hers, and when the Easter fires came again they would pray to them together.

At the garden door her hand fell from the latch and she faced the moor. She lifted her arms and dropped them in a kind of pleading for mercy from those whom she had served faithfully; then she smoothed her face and went into the house.

In the drawing-room, Mildred Caniper was sitting on the sofa, and near her John and Lily had disposed themselves like guests.

Helen stopped in the doorway. "Then the light in your house meant nothing," she said reproachfully.

"What should it mean?" John asked.

"Happiness and peace—somewhere," she said.

"It does mean that," and turning to Lily, he asked, "Doesn't it?"

"Yes, yes, but don't brag about it."

They laughed together, and they sat with an alert tranquillity of health which made Mildred Caniper look very small and frail. She was listening courteously to the simple things John told her about animals and crops and butter-sales, but Helen knew that she was almost too tired to understand, and she felt trouble sweeping over her own happiness.

To hide that trouble, she asked quickly, "Where are the others?" and an invisible Rupert answered her.

"You're the last in." He sat outside the window, and as she approached, he added, "And I hope you have had a happy time."

"Yes." She looked back into the room.

"Daniel wouldn't stay," Rupert went on, smoking his pipe placidly. "If it hadn't been for my good offices, my dear, he'd have hauled Zebedee off long ago. He suddenly thought of a plan for getting rid of Eliza. Why aren't you thanking me?"

"He wouldn't have gone."

"Oh, ho!"

"But they ought to get rid of Eliza. I've told Zebedee."

"Quite right," Rupert said solemnly. His dark eyes twinkled at the answering stars. "When I have lunch with Daniel, I'm afraid of being poisoned, though she rather likes me, and she's offensively ugly—ugh! Yet I like to think that even Eliza has had her little story. Are you listening, Helen? I'm being pastoral and kind. I'm going to tell you how Eliza fell in love with a travelling tinker."

"Is it true?"

"As true as anything else."

"Go on."

"It happened when Eliza was quite young, not beautiful, but fresh and ruddy. She walked out one summer night to meet the farm hand who was courting her, but he was not at the appointed place, so Eliza walked on, and she had a sore heart because she thought her lover was unfaithful. She was walking over high downs with hollows in them and the grass cropped close by sheep, and there was a breeze blowing the smell of clover from some field, and suddenly she stood on the edge of a hollow in which a fire was burning, and by the fire there sat a man. He looked big as he sat there, but when he stood up he was a giant, in corduroys, and a check cap over his black eyes. Picturesque beggar. And the farm hand had deserted her, and there was a smell of burning wood, and the sky was like a velvet curtain. What would you? Eliza did not go home that night, nor the next, nor the next. She stayed with the travelling tinker until he tired of her, and that was very soon. For him, she was no more than the fly that happened to get into his web, but for Eliza, the tinker—the tinker was beauty and romance. The tinker was life. And he sent her back to the ways of virtue permanently soured, yet proud. Thus, my dear young friend, we see—"

"Don't!" Helen cried. "You're making me sorry for Eliza. I don't want to be sorry for her. And you're making me like the tinker. He's attractive. How horrid that he should be attractive." She shuddered and shook her head. "Your story is too full of firelight—and the night. I'll go and get supper ready."

"Miriam's doing it. Stay here and I'll tell you some more."

But she slipped past him and reached the kitchen from the garden.

"Rupert has been telling me a story," she said a little breathlessly to Miriam who was filling a tray with the noisy indifference of a careless maid-servant.

"Hang the plates! Hang the dishes! What story?"

"It's rather wonderful, I think. It's about the Mackenzies' Eliza."

"Then of course it's wonderful. And hang the knives and forks!" She threw them on the tray.

"And there's a travelling tinker in it." With her hands at her throat, she looked into the fire and Miriam looked at her.

"I'll ask him to tell it to me," she said, but very soon she returned to the kitchen, grumbling. "What nonsense! It's not respectable, and it isn't even true."

"It's as true as anything else," Helen said.

"Oh, you're mad. And so is Rupert. Let's have supper and go to bed. Why can't we have a servant to do all this? Why don't we pay for one ourselves?"

"I don't want one."

"But I do, and my hands are ruined."

"Upstairs in Jane," Helen said, "in the small right-hand drawer of my chest of drawers, there's the lotion—"

"It's not only my hands! It's my whole life! Your lotion isn't going to cure my life!" She sat on the edge of a chair and drooped there.

"No," Helen said. "But what's the matter with your life?"

Miriam flapped her hands. "I'm so tired of being good. I want—I want—"

Helen knelt beside her. "Is it Zebedee you want?" Her voice and her body shook with self-sacrifice and love and when Miriam's head dropped to her shoulder Helen was willing to give her all she had.

"I'm not crying," Miriam said, after an agitated pause. "I'm not overcome. I'm only laughing so much that I can't make a sound! Zebedee! Oh! No! That's very funny." She straightened herself. "Helen dear, did you think you'd discovered my little secret, my maidenly little secret? I only want Uncle Alfred to come and take me away. This is a dreadful family to belong to, but there are humorous moments. It's almost worth while. John, here's Helen suggesting that I'm in love with Zebedee!"

"Well, why not?" he asked, but he was hardly thinking of what he said. "I've left Lily on guard in there. Notya has gone to sleep."

"But she can't have," Helen said.

"She has, my child."

"Are you sure she's not—are you sure she is asleep?"

"Like a baby."

"Then we shall have to make a noise and wake her. She would never forgive us if she found out that we knew, so tell Lily to come out and then we must all burst in."

CHAPTER XVII

Lily and John went down the track: Mildred Caniper climbed slowly, but with dignity, up the stairs; Miriam was heard to bang her bedroom door and Rupert and Helen were left together in the schoolroom.

"I can't get the tinker out of my head," she told him.

"I must have done it very well."

"Miriam didn't like it. She thought it silly."

"So it is."

"No, it's real, so real that he has been sitting in our hollow," she complained.

"That won't do. Turn him out. He doesn't belong to our moor."

"No. I think I'll go for a walk and forget him."

"I should," he said, in his sympathetic way. "I won't go to bed till you come back." He pulled his chair nearer to the lamp, opened a book and contentedly heard Helen leave the house, for though he was fond of her there were times when her forebodings and her conscience became wearisome. Let the moor be her confessor tonight!

Helen dropped into the darkness like a swimmer taking deep water quietly and at once she was immersed in happiness. She forgot her stepmother sitting so stiffly on the sofa and for a little while she forgot that the future which held her and Zebedee in its embrace held a solitary Mildred Caniper less warmly. In the scented night, Helen allowed herself to taste joy without misgiving.

She walked slowly because she was hemmed in by feelings which were blissful and undefined: she knew only that the world smelt sweeter than it had ever done, that the stars shone with amazing brightness. Through the darkness she could see the splendid curves of the moor and the shapes of thorn bushes thick with leaves. The familiar friends of other days seemed to wait upon her happiness, but the stars laughed at her as they had always done. She looked up and saw a host of them, clear and distant, shining in a sky so blue and vast that to see it was like flight. They were secure in their high places, and with the smiling benignity of gods they assured her of her littleness, and gladly she accepted that assurance, for she shared her littleness with Zebedee, and now she understood that her happiness was made of small great things, of the hope of caring for him, of keeping that shining house in order, of cradling children in wide, airy rooms. She had a sudden desire to mend Zebedee's clothes and put them neatly in their places, to feel the smoothness of his freshly-laundered collars in her hand.

She sat down in the heather and it was her turn to laugh up at the stars who could do none of these things and lived in isolated grandeur. The earth was nearer to her finite mind. It was warm with the sunshine of many days and trodden by human, beloved feet; it offered up food and drink and consolation. Darker than the sky, it had no colour but its own, yet Helen sat among pale spikes of blossom.

It was a night when even those beings who could not wander in the daytime must be content to lie and listen to the silence, when evil must run from the face of beauty and hide itself in streets. All round her, Helen fancied shapes without substance, lying in worship of the night which was their element, and when she rose from her bed at last she moved with quietness lest she should disturb them.

She had not gone far before she was aware that some one else was walking on the moor. For a moment she thought it must be Rupert in search of her, but Rupert would have called out, and this person, while he rustled through the heather, let forth a low whistled note, and though he went with care, it was for some purpose of his own and not for courtesy towards the mystery of the night.

She could not decide from what direction the sounds came; she stopped and they stopped; then she heard the whistle again, but nearer now, and with a sudden realization of loneliness and of the womanhood which had seldom troubled her, she ran with all her strength and speed for home.

Memories ran with her strangely, and brought back that day when she had been hotly chased by Mrs. Brent's big bull, and she remembered how, through all his fears for her, Rupert had laughed as though he would never stop. She laughed in recollection, but more in fear. The bull had snorted, his hoofs had thundered after her, as these feet were thundering now.

"But this is the tinker, the tinker!" her mind cried in terror, and overcome by her quickened breathing, by some sense of the inevitable in this affair, she stumbled as she ran. She saved herself, but a hand caught at her wrist and some one uttered a sound of satisfaction.

She did not struggle, but she wondered why God had made woman's strength so disproportionate to man's, and looking up, she saw that it was George Halkett who held her. At the same moment he would have loosed her hand, but she clung to his because she was trembling fiercely.

"Oh, George," she said, "it's you! And I thought it was some one horrid!"

She could not see him blush. "I'm sorry," he mumbled. She gleamed, in the starlight, as he had seen pale rocks gleaming on such a night, but she felt like the warm flesh she was, and the oval of her face was plain to him; he thought he could see the fear leaving her widely-opened eyes. "I'm sorry," he said again, and made an awkward movement. "I thought—I—Wouldn't you like to sit down? There's a stone here."

"It's the one I fell against!" She dropped on to it and laughed. "You weren't there, were you, years and years ago, when the bull chased me? That red bull of Mrs. Brent's? He was old and cross. No, of course you weren't."

"I remember the beast. He had a broken horn."

"Yes. Just a stump. It made him frightful. I dream about him now. And when you were running after me—"

He broke in with a muffled exclamation and shifted from one foot to the other like a chidden child. "I'm sorry," he said again, and muttered, "Fool!" as he bent towards her. "Did you hurt yourself against that stone? Are you all right? You've only slippers on."

"I've nearly stopped shaking," she said practically. "And it doesn't matter. You didn't mean to do it. I must go home. Rupert is waiting for me."

His voice was humble. "I don't believe I've spoken to you since that day in the hollow."

She remembered that occasion and the curious moment when she felt his eyes on her, and she was reminded that though he had not been running after her, he had certainly been running after somebody. She glanced at him and he looked very tall as he stood there, as tall as the tinker.

"Why don't you sit down?" she asked quickly, and as he did so she added, on a new thought, "But perhaps I'm keeping you. Perhaps—Don't wait for me."

"I've nothing else to do," he told her.

"I spoke to you," she said, "the day after your father died."

"I meant alone," he answered.

They sat in silence after that, and for Helen the smell of heather was the speech of those immaterial ones who lay about her. Some change had taken place among the stars: they were paler, nearer, as though they had grown tired of eminence and wanted commerce with the earth. The great quiet had failed before the encroachment of little sounds as of burrowing, nocturnal hunting, and the struggles of a breeze that was always foiled.

"Do you know what time it is?" Helen asked in a small voice.

He held his watch sideways, but he had to strike a match, and its light drew all the eyes of the moor.

"Quick!" Helen said.

He was not to be hurried. "Not far off midnight."

"And Rupert's waiting! Good-night, George."

"And you've forgiven me?" he asked as they parted at the gate.

"No." She laughed almost as Miriam might have done, and startled him. "I'll forgive you," she said, "I'll forgive you when you really hurt me." She gave him her cool hand and, holding it, he half asked, half told her, "That's a promise."

"Yes. Good-night."

Slowly she walked through the dark hall, hesitated at the schoolroom door and opened it.

"I've come back," she said, and disappeared before Rupert could reply, for she was afraid he would make some allusion to the tinker.

It was characteristic of her that, as she undressed, carefully laying her clothes aside, her concern was for George's moral welfare rather than for the safety of the person for whom he had mistaken her, and this was because she happened to know George, had known him nearly all her life, while the identity of the other was a blank to her, because she had no peculiar feeling for her sex; men and women were separated or united only by their claim on her.

Mildred Caniper, whose claim was great, came down to breakfast the next morning with a return of energy that gladdened Helen and set Miriam thinking swiftly of all the things she had left undone. But Mildred Caniper was fair, and where she no longer ruled, she would not criticize. She condescended, however, to ask one question.

"Who was on the moor last night?"

"Daniel," Helen said.

"Zebedee," said Miriam.

"Zebedee?" she said, pretending not to know to whom that name belonged.

"Dr. Mackenzie."

"Oh."

"The father of James and John," Miriam murmured.

"So he has children?" Mrs. Caniper went on with her superb assumption that no one joked in conversation with her.

"Oh, I don't think so," Helen said earnestly. "He isn't married! Miriam meant the gentleman in the Bible."

"I see." Her glance pitied Miriam. "But this was early in the evening. Some one came in very late. Rupert, perhaps."

"No, it was me," Helen said.

"I," Mildred Caniper corrected.

"Yes. I."

"Did I hear voices?"

"Did you?" Helen returned in another tone and with an innocence that surprised herself and revealed the deceit latent in the mouth of the most truthful. It was long since she had been so near a lie and lying was ugly: it made smudges on the world; but disloyalty was no better, and though she could not have explained the debt, she felt that she owed George silence. She had to choose. He had been like a child as he fumbled over his apologies and she could not but be tender with a child. Yet only a few seconds earlier she had thought he was the tinker. Oh, why had Rupert ever told her of the tinker?

"I would rather you did not wander on the moor so late at night," Mildred Caniper said.

"But it's the best time of all."

"I would rather you did not."

"Very well. I'll try to remember."

A sign from Miriam drew Helen into the garden.

"Silly of you to come in by the front way. Of course she heard. If the garden door is locked, you can climb the wall and get on to the scullery roof. Then there's my window."

Helen measured the distance with her eye. "It's too high up."

"Throw up a shoe and I'll lower a chair for you."

"But—this is horrid," Helen said. "Why should I?"

Miriam's thin shoulders went up and down. "You never know, you never know," she chanted. "You never know what you may come to."

"Don't!" Helen begged. She leaned against a poplar and looked mournfully from the window to Miriam's face.

"No," Miriam said, "I've never done it. I only planned it in case of need. It would be a way of escape, too, if she ever locked me up. She's capable of that. Helen, I don't like this rejuvenation!"

"Don't," Helen said again.

"I haven't mended the sheets she gave me weeks ago."

"I'll help you with them."

"Good, kind, Christian girl! There's nothing like having a reputation to keep up. That's why I told you about my secret road."

"You're—vulgar."

"No, I'm human, and very young, and rather beautiful. And quite intelligent." There came on her face the look which made her seem old and tired with her own knowledge. "Was it Zebedee last night?"

Heat ran over Helen's body like a living thing.

"You're hateful," she stammered. "As though Zebedee and I— as though Zebedee and I would meet by stealth!"

"Honestly, I can't see why you shouldn't. Why shouldn't you?"

Helen smoothed her forehead with both hands. "It was the way you said it," she murmured painfully and then straightened herself. "Of course nothing Zebedee would do could be anything but good. I beg his pardon." And in a failing voice, she explained again, "It was the way you said it."

"I suppose I'm not really a nice person," Miriam replied.

CHAPTER XVIII

During the week that followed, a remembrance of her responsibilities came back to Helen and when she looked at Mildred Caniper, alternating between energy and lassitude, the shining house seemed wearily far off, or, at the best, Notya was in it, bringing her own shadows. Helen had been too happy, she told herself. She must not be greedy, she must hold very lightly to her desires lest they should turn and hurt her, yet with all her heart she wanted to see Zebedee, who was a surety for everything that was good.

By Rupert he sent letters which delighted her and gave her a sense of safety by their restraint, and on Sunday another letter was delivered by Daniel because Zebedee was kept in town by a serious case.

"So there will be no fear of my saying all those things that were ready on my tongue," he wrote, to tease, perhaps to test her, and she cried out to herself, "Oh, I'd let him say anything in the whole world if only he would come!" And she added, on her own broken laughter, "At least, I think so."

She felt the need to prove her courage, but she also wanted an excuse fit to offer to the fates, and when she had examined the larder and the store cupboard she found that the household was in immediate need of things which must be brought from the town. She laughed at her own quibble, but it satisfied her and, refusing Miriam's company, she set off on Monday afternoon.

It was a soft day and the air, moist on her cheek, smelt of damp, black earth. The moor would be in its gorgeous autumn dress for some months yet and the distances were cloaked in blue, promising the wayfarer a heaven which receded with every step.

With a destination of her own, Helen was not daunted.

Walking with her light long stride, she passed the side road leading to Halkett's farm and remembered how George and Zebedee, seated side by side, something like figures on a frieze, had swung down that road to tend old Halkett. Beyond the high fir-wood she came upon the fields where old Halkett had grown his crops: here and there were the cottages of his hands, with dahlias and staring children in the gardens, and before long other houses edged the road and she saw the thronging roofs of the town.

It was Zebedee who chanced to open to her when she knocked and she saw a grave face change to one of youth as he took her by the wrist to draw her in.

"Do you always look like that when I'm not here?" she asked anxiously, quickly, but he did not answer.

"It's you!" he said. "You!"

In the darkness of the passage they could hardly see each other, but he had not loosed his grasp and with a deft turn of the wrist she thrust her whole hand into his.

"I was tired of waiting for you," she said. "A whole week! I was afraid you were never coming back!"

"You know I'd come back to you if I were dead."

"Yes, I know." She leaned towards him and laughed and, wrenching himself free from the contemplation of her, he led her to his room. There he shut the door and stood against it.

"I want to look at you. No, I don't think I'd better look at you." He spoke in his quick usual way. "Come and sit down. Is that chair all right? And here's a cushion for you, but I don't believe it's clean. Everything looks dirty now that you are in the room. Helen, are you sure it's you?"

"Yes. Are you sure you're glad? I want to sit and laugh and laugh, do all the laughing I've never had. And I want to cry—with loud noises. Which shall I do? Oh—I can't do either!"

"I've hardly ever seen you in a hat before. You must take it off. No, let me find the pins. Now you're my Helen again. Sit there. Don't move. Don't run away. I'm going to tell Eliza about tea."

She heard a murmur in the passage, the jingle of money, the front door opened and shut and she knew the Eliza had been sent out to buy cakes.

"I had to get rid of her," Zebedee said. "I had to have you to myself." He knelt before her. "I'm going to take off your gloves. What do you wear them for? So that I can take them off?"

He did it slowly. Each hand was like a flower unsheathed, and when he had kissed her fingers and her palms he looked up and saw a face made tragic by sudden knowledge of passion. Her eyes were dark with it and her mouth had shaped itself for his.

"Helen—!"

"I know—I know—"

"And there's nothing to say."

"It doesn't matter—doesn't matter—" His head was on her knees and her hands stroked his hair. He heard her whispering: "What soft hair! It's like a baby's." She laughed. "So soft! No, no. Stay there. I want to stroke it."

"But I want to see you. I haven't seen you since I kissed you. And you're more beautiful. I love you more—" He rose, and would not see the persuasion of her arms. "Ah, dear, dearest one, forget I love you. You are too young and too beautiful for me, Desire."

"But I shall soon be old. You don't want to wait until I'm old."

"I don't want to wait at all."

"And I'm twenty, Zebedee."

"Twenty! Well, Heaven bless you for it," he said and swung the hand she held out to him.

"And this is true," she said.

"It is."

"And I never thought it would be. I was afraid Miriam was loving you."

"But," he said, still swinging, "I was never in any danger of loving Miriam."

She shook her head. "I couldn't have let her be unhappy."

"And me?"

She gave him an illuminating smile. "You're just myself. It doesn't matter if one hurts oneself."

"Ah!" He bent her fingers and straightened them. "How small they are. I could break them—funny things. So you'd marry me to Miriam if she wanted me. That isn't altogether satisfactory, my dear. To be you—that's perfect, but treat me more kindly than you treat yourself."

"Just the same—it must be. Swing my hand again. I like it." She went on in a low voice. "All the time, I've been thinking she would come between."

"She can't now."

She looked up, troubled, and begged, "Don't say so. Sometimes she's just like a bat, flying into one's face. Only more lovely, and I can't be angry with her."

"I could. But let's talk about you and me, how much we love each other, and how nice we are."

"We do, don't we?"

"We are, aren't we?"

"Oh, how silly!"

"Let's be sillier than any one has ever been before."

"Listen!" Helen said and Zebedee stopped on his way to her.

"It's that woman. Why didn't something run over her? Is my hair ruffled?"

"Come quickly and let me smooth it. Nice hair."

"Yours is always smooth, but do you know, it curls a little."

"Oh, no."

"It does, really, on the temples. Come and look. No, stay there. She'll be in soon, confound her."

"We ought to be talking sensibly."

"Can we?"

"I can. Shall I put my hat on?"

"No, no, not for one greater than Eliza. I'm afraid of you in a hat. Now I'll sit here and you can begin your sensible conversation."

"I'm serious, truly. It's about Notya. She's funny, Zebedee. At night I can hear her walking about her room and she's hardly ever strict. She doesn't care. I wish you would make her well."

"Will she let me try?"

"I couldn't ask her that because I pretend not to notice. We all do. She's like a person who—who can't forget. I—don't know."

"I'm sorry, darling."

"Don't be. I'm always afraid of being sorry or glad because you don't know what will happen. Father leaving us like that, making her miserable—it's given you to me." She looked up at him. "The world's difficult."

"Always; but there are times when it is good. Helen—"

Eliza entered, walking heavily in creaking boots, and when Helen looked at her, she wondered at the tinker. Eliza was hard-featured: she had not much hair, and on it a cap hung precariously. Spreading a cloth on a small table, she went about her business slowly, carrying one thing at a time and leaving the door open as a protest against Helen's presence.

"Who'll pour?" she asked.

"You can leave the table there."

"They were out of sugar cakes. I got buns."

He looked at them. "If that's the best they can do, they ought to be ashamed of themselves."

"If you want cakes you should get them in the morning. I've kept the change to pay the milkman."

With a flourish of the cosy Zebedee turned to Helen as the door was shut.

"Isn't she dreadful?"

"She wants a new pair of boots."

"And a new face."

"I know she doesn't clean the house properly. How often does she sweep this carpet? It isn't clean, but I wouldn't mind that if she took care of you."

"Daniel beat her on the supper question. He thought she'd leave rather than give in, and he was hopeful, but she saw through that. She stuck."

"Isn't she fond of you?" Helen asked wistfully.

"No, darling, we detest each other. Do I put the milk in first?"

"Bring the table to me and I'll do it. Is she honest?"

"Rigidly. I notice that the dishonest are generally pleasing. No, you can't have the table. It would hide a lot of you. I want to talk to you, Helen. Have one of these stale buns. What a meal for you! We've got to settle this affair."

"But it is settled."

"Eat your bun and listen, and don't be forward."

She laughed at him. "It was forward to come here, wasn't it?"

"It was adorable. But since last Sunday, I have been thinking. What do you know about life, about men? I'm just the one who has chanced across your path. It's like stealing you. It isn't fair."

"There's Daniel," she said solemnly. "And the dentist. And your father when we had measles. And George Halkett—"

"Be serious."

"There's the tinker."

"Who on earth is he?"

"A man Rupert told me about, a made-up man, but he has come alive in my mind. I wish he hadn't. I might meet him. Once I nearly did, and if I met him, Zebedee—"

"Darling, I wish you'd listen. Suppose you married me—"

"You want me to marry you?"

"My dear, precious child—"

"I wasn't sure. Go on."

"If you married me, and afterwards you found some one you liked better, as well you might, what would happen then?"

"I should make the best of you."

"You wouldn't run away?"

"If I went, I should walk, but I shouldn't go. I'm like that. I belong to people and to places."

"You belong to me."

"Not yet. Not quite. I wish I did, because then I should feel safe, but now I belong to the one who needs me most. Notya, perhaps."

"And if we were married?"

"Then I should just be yours."

"But we are married."

"No," she said.

"I don't see the distinction."

"But it's there," she said, and once more he felt the iron under her grace.

"This isn't modern, Helen."

"No, I'm simple."

"And I don't like it." He was grave; the muscles in his cheek were twitching and the brown flecks in his eyes moved quickly. "Marry me at once."

"You said I was too young!"

"I say it still." He paced the room. "It's true, but neither your youth nor anything else shall take you from me, and, oh, my little heart, be good to me."

"I can't be good enough and I'll marry you when you want me."

"This week?"

She caught his hand and laid her cheek against it. "Oh, I would, I would, if Notya didn't need me."

"No one," he said, "needs you as I do. We'll be married in the spring."

Her hand and her smile acknowledged what he said while her eyes were busy on his thin face, his worn, well-brushed clothes, the books and papers on his desk, the arrangements of the room.

"I don't like any of your furniture," she said suddenly. "And those ornaments are ugly."

He took them from the mantelpiece and threw them into the waste-paper basket.

"Anything else? It won't hold the furniture."

"Ah, you're nice," she said, and, going to the window, she looked out on the garden, where the apple-trees twisted themselves out of a rough lawn.

"When you marry me," Zebedee said, standing beside her and speaking quietly, "we'll leave this house to Daniel and Eliza.

There's one outside the town, on the moor road, but set back in a big garden, a square house. Shall we—shall we go and look at it?"

"Shall we?" she repeated, and they faced each other unsmiling.

"It's an old house, with big square windows, and there's a rising copse behind it."

"I know," Helen said.

"There's a little stream that falls into the road."

"Does it run inside the garden?"

"That's what I'm not sure about."

"It must."

He put his hand on her shoulder. "We could peep through the windows. Are you coming?"

"I don't know," she said and there was a fluttering movement in her throat. "Don't you think it's rather dangerously near the road?"

"We could lock the gate," he said.

She dropped her face into her hands. "No, I can't come. I'm afraid. It's tempting things to happen."

"It has been empty for a long time," he went on in the same quiet tones. "I should think we could get it cheap."

She looked up again. "And I shall have a hundred pounds a year. That would pay the rent and keep the garden tidy."

He turned on her sharply. "Mind, I'm going to buy your clothes!"

"I can make them all," she said serenely. She leaned against him. "We love each other—and we know so little about each other. I don't even know how old you are!"

"I'm nearly thirty-one."

"That's rather old. You must know more than I do."

"I expect I do."

A faint line came between her eyebrows. "Perhaps you have been in love before."

"I have." His lips tightened at the memory.

"Very much in love?"

"Pretty badly."

"Then I hope she's dead!"

"I don't know."

"I can't bear her to be alive. Oh, Zebedee, why didn't you wait for me?"

"I should have loved you less, child."

"Would you? You never loved her like this?"

"She wasn't you."

In a little while she said, "I don't understand love. Why should we matter so much to each other? So much that we're afraid? Or do we only think we do? Perhaps that's it. It can't matter so much as we make out, because we die and it's all over, and no one cares any more about our little lives." On a sigh he heard her last words. "We mustn't struggle."

"Struggle?"

"For what we want."

To this he made no answer, but he had a strange feeling that the firm, fine body he held was something more perishable than glass and might be broken with a word.

He took her to the moor, but when they passed the empty house she would not look at it.

"The stream does run through the garden," he said. "We could sail boats on it." And he added thoughtfully, "We should have to dam it up somewhere to make a harbour."

CHAPTER XIX

Disease fell heavily on the town that autumn and Zebedee and Helen had to snatch their meetings hurriedly on the moor. She found that Miriam was right and she had no difficulty and no shame in running out into the darkness for a clasp of hands, a few words, a shadowy glimpse of Zebedee by the light of the carriage lamps, while the old horse stood patiently between the shafts and breathed visibly against the frosty night. Over the sodden or frozen ground, the peat squelching or the heather stalks snapping under her feet, she would make her way to that place where she hoped to find her lover with his quick words and his scarce caresses and, returning with the wind of the moor on her and eyes wide with wonder and the night, she would get a paternal smile from Rupert and a gibing word from Miriam, and be almost unaware of both. For weeks, her days were only preludes to the short perfection of his presence and her nights were filled with happy dreams: the eyes which had once been so watchful over Mildred Caniper were now turned inwards or levelled on the road; she went under a spell which shut out fear.

In December she was brought back to a normal world by the illness of Mildred Caniper. One morning, without a word of explanation or complaint, she went back to her bed, and Helen found her there, lying inert and staring at the ceiling. She had not taken down her hair and under the crown of it her face looked small and pinched, her eyes were like blue pools threatening to over-run their banks.

"Is your head aching?" Helen said.

"I—don't think so."

"What is it, then?"

"I was afraid I could not—go on," she said carefully. "I was afraid of doing something silly and I was giddy."

"Are you better now?"

"Yes. I want to rest."

"Try to sleep."

"It isn't sleep I want. It's rest, rest."

Helen went away, but before long she came back with a dark curtain to shroud the window.

"No, no! I want light, not shadows," Mildred cried in a shrill voice. "A dark room—" Her voice fell away in the track of her troubled memories, and when she spoke again it was in her ordinary tones. "I beg your pardon, Helen. You startled me. I think I must have dozed and dreamed."

"And you won't have the curtain?"

"No. Let there be light." She lay there helpless, while thoughts preyed on her, as vultures might prey on something moribund.

At dinner-time she refused to help herself to food, though she ate if Helen fed her. "The spoon is heavy," she complained.

Miriam was white and nervous. "She ought to have Zebedee," she said. "She looks funny. She frightens me."

"We could wait until tomorrow," Helen said. "He is so busy and I don't want to bring him up for nothing. He's being overworked."

"But for Notya!" Miriam exclaimed. "And don't you want to see him?" She could not keep still. "I can't bear people to be ill. He ought to come."

"Go and ask John."

"What does he know about it?" she whispered. "I keep thinking perhaps she will go mad."

"That's silly."

"It isn't. She looks—queer. If she does, I shall run away. I'm going to George. He'll drive into the town. You mustn't sacrifice Notya to Zebedee, you know."

Helen let out an ugly, scornful sound that angered Miriam.

"Old sheep!" she said, and Helen had to spare a smile, but she was thoughtful.

"Perhaps John would go."

"But why not George?"

"We're always asking favours."

"Pooh! He likes them and I don't mind asking."

"Well, then, it would be rather a relief. I don't know what to do with her."

The sense of responsibility towards George which had once kept Miriam awake had also kept her from him in a great effort of self-denial, and it was many days since she had done more than wave a greeting or give him a few light words.

"I believe I've offended you," he had told her not long ago, but she assured him that it was not so.

"Then I can't make you out," he muttered.

She shut her eyes and showed him her long lashes. "No, I'm a mystery. Think about me, George." And before he had time to utter his genuine, clumsy speech, she ran away.

"But I can't avoid temptation much longer," she told herself. "Life's too dull."

And now this illness which alarmed her was like a door opening slowly.

"And it's the hand of God that left it ajar," she said as she sped across the moor.

Her steps slackened as she neared the larch-wood, for she had not ventured into it since the night of old Halkett's death; but it was possible that George would be working in the yard and, tiptoeing down the soft path, she issued on the cobble-stones.

George was not there, nor could she hear him, and she was constrained to knock on the closed door, but the face of Mrs. Biggs, who appeared after a stealthy pause, was not encouraging to the visitor. She looked at Miriam and her thin lips parted and joined again without speech.

"I want Mr. Halkett," Miriam said, straightening herself and speaking haughtily because she guessed that Mrs. Biggs was suspicious of her friendliness with George.

"He's out. You'll have to wait," she said and shut the door.

A cold wind was swooping into the hollow, but Miriam was hot with a gathering anger that rushed into words as Halkett appeared.

"George!" She ran to him. "I hate that woman. I always did. I wish you wouldn't keep her. Oh, I hate her!"

"But you didn't come here to tell me that," he said. In her haste she had allowed him to take her hand and the touch of her softened his resentment at her neglect; amusement narrowed his eyes until she could not see their blue.

"She's horrid, she's rude; she left me on the step. I didn't want to go in, but she oughtn't to have left me standing there."

"She ought not. I'll tell her."

"Dare you?"

"Dare I!" he repeated boastfully.

"But you mustn't! Don't, George, please don't. Promise you won't. Promise, George."

"All right."

"Thank you." She drew her hand away.

"The fact is, she's always pretty hard on you."

Miriam's flame went out. "You don't mean," she said coldly, "that you discuss me with her?"

"No, I do not."

"You swear you never have?"

He had a pleasing and indulgent smile. "Yes, I swear it, but she dislikes the whole lot of you, and you can't always stop a woman's talk."

"You should be able to," she said. She wished she had not come for George did not realize what was due to her. She would go to John and she nodded a cold good-bye.

Her hands were in the pockets of her brown woollen coat, her shoulders were lifted towards her ears; she was less beautiful than he had ever seen her, yet in her kindest moments she had not seemed so near to him. He was elated by this discovery; he did not seek its cause and, had he done so, he was not acute enough to see that hitherto the feelings she had shown him had been chiefly feigned, and that this real resentment, marking her face with petulance, revealed her nature to be common with his own.

"But you've not told me what you came for," he said.

She was reluctant, but she spoke. "To ask you to do something for us."

"You know I'll do it."

Still sulky, she took a few steps and leaned against the house wall; she had the look of a boy caught in a fault.

"We want the doctor."

"Who's ill?"

"It's Notya."

"What's the matter?"

"I don't know." She forgot her grievance. "I don't like thinking of it. It makes me sick."

"Is she very bad?"

"No, but I think he ought to come."

"Must I bring him back?"

"Just leave a message, please, if it doesn't put you out."

In the pause before he spoke, he studied the dark head against the white-washed wall, the slim body, the little feet crossed on the cobbles, and then he stammered:

"You—you're like a rose-tree growing up."

She spread her arms and turned and drooped her head to encourage the resemblance. "Like that?"

He nodded, with the clumsiness of his emotions. "Look here—"

"Now, don't be tiresome. Oh, you can tell me what you were going to say."

"All these weeks—"

"I know, but it was for your sake, George."

"How?"

"It's difficult to explain, but one night my good angel bent over my bed, like a mother—or was it your good angel?"

He grinned. "I don't believe you'd know one if you saw one."

"I'm afraid I shouldn't," she admitted, with a laugh. "Would you?"

"I fancy I've seen one."

"Mrs. Biggs?" she dared. "Me?"

"I'm not going to tell you."

"I expect it's me. But run away and bring the doctor."

"I say—will you wait till I get back?"

"I couldn't. Think of Mrs. Biggs!"

"Not here. Up in the wood. But never mind. Come and see me saddle the little mare."

She liked the smell of the long, dim stable, the sound of the horses moving in their stalls, the regular crunching as they ate their hay. Years ago, she had been in this place with John and Rupert and she had forgotten nothing. There were the corn-bins under the windows and the pieces of old harness still hanging on big nails; above, there was the loft that looked as vast as ever in the shadowy gloom, and again it invited her ascent by the iron steps between the stalls.

From the harness-room Halkett fetched a saddle, and as he put it on the mare's back, he said, "Come and say how d'you do to her."

"It's Daisy. She'll go fast. Isn't she beautiful! She's rubbing her nose on me. I wish I could ride her."

"She might let you—for half a minute. Charlie's the boy for you. Come and see what's in the harness-room."

"Not now. There isn't time."

"Wait for me then." There was pleading in his voice. "Wait in the wood. I've something to show you. Will you do that for me?"

He was standing close to her, and she did not look up. "I ought to go back, but I don't want to. I don't like ill people. They sicken me."

"Don't go, then."

Now she looked at him in search of the assurance she wanted. "I needn't, need I? Helen can manage, can't she?"

He forgot to answer because she was like a flower suddenly

brought to life in Daisy's stall, a flower for grace and beauty, but a woman for something that made him deaf to what she said.

"She can manage, can't she?"

"Of course." He snatched an armful of hay from a rack and led her to the larch trees and there he scraped together the fallen needles and laid the hay on them to make a bed for her.

"Rest there. Go to sleep and I'll be back before you wake."

She lay curled on her side until all sounds of him had passed and then she rolled on to her back and drew up her knees. It was dark and warm in the little wood; the straight trunks of the larches were as menacing as spears and the sky looked like a great banner tattered by their points. Though she lay still, she seemed to be marching with a host, and the light wind in the trees was the music of its going, the riven banner was a trophy carried proudly and, at a little distance, the rushing of the brook was the sound of feet following behind. For a long time she went with that triumphant army, but at length there came other sounds that forced themselves on her hearing and changed her from a gallant soldier to a girl half frightened in a wood.

She sat up and listened to the galloping of a horse and a voice singing in gay snatches. The sounds rose and sank and died away and came forth lustily again, and in the singing there was something full-blooded and urgent, as though the singer came from some danger joyfully escaped or hurried to some tryst. She stood up and, holding to a tree, she leaned sideways to listen. She heard Halkett speaking jovially to the mare as he pulled her up on the cobbles and gave her a parting smack of his open hand: then there began a sweet whistling invaded by other sounds, by Daisy's stamping in her stall, a corn-bin opened and shut, and Halkett's footsteps in the yard. Soon they were lost in the softness of the larch needles, but the whistling warned her of his coming and alarmed her with its pulsing lilt, and as she moved away and tried to make no noise, a dry branch snapped under her feet.

"Where are you?" he called out.

"Here," she answered, and awaited him. She could see the light gleaming in his eyes.

"Were you running off?"

"I didn't run."

He wound his arm about a tree and said, "We came at a pace, the mare and I."

"I heard you. Is Dr. Mackenzie coming?"

"Yes—fast as that old nag of his will bring him."

She slipped limply to the ground for she was chilled. She had braced herself for danger and it had turned aside, and she felt no thankfulness: she merely found George Halkett dull.

"Thank you for going," she said in cool tones. "Now I must go back and see how Notya is."

"No. I want to show you the side saddle."

"Which?"

"The one for you."

Adventure was hovering again. "For me? Are you really going to teach me to ride?"

"Didn't I say so?"

"But when?"

"When the rest of the world's in their beds."

"Oh. Won't it be too dark?"

"We'll manage. We'll try it first in daylight, right over the moor where no one goes. Most nights are not much darker than it is now, though. I can see you easily."

"Can you?" She was rocking herself in the way to which she had accustomed him. "What can you see?"

"Black hair and black eyes. Come here."

"I'm quite comfortable and you should never tell a lady to come to you, George."

"Are you asking me to come to you?"

"Don't be silly. Aren't you going to show me the saddle?"

"Yes. Where's your hand? I'll help you up. There you are! No, I'll keep your hand. The ground's steep and you might fall."

"No. Let me have it, George."

Her resistance broke the bonds he had laid on himself, and over her there fell a kind of wavering darkness in which she was drawn to him and held against his breast. His coat smelt of peat and tobacco; she felt his strength and the tense muscles under his clothes, and she did not struggle to get free of him. Ages of warm, dark time seemed to have passed over her before she realized that he was doing something to her hair. He was kissing it and, without any thought, obedient to the hour, she turned up her face to share those kisses. He uttered a low sound and put a hand to either of her cheeks, marking her mouth for his, and it was then she pushed him from her, stepped back, and shook herself and cried, "Oh, oh, you have been drinking!"

As she retreated, he advanced, but she fenced him off with outstretched hands.

"Go away. You have been drinking."

"I swear I haven't. I had one glass down there. I was thirsty—and no wonder. I swear I had no more. It's you, you that's sent it to my head."

At that, half was forgiven, but she said, "Anyhow, it's horrid and it makes me hate you. Go away. Don't touch me. Don't come near." In her retreat she stumbled against a tree and felt a bitterness of reproach because he did not ask if she were hurt.

"I'll show you I'm sober," he grumbled. "What do you know about it? You're a schoolgirl."

"Then if you think that you should be still more ashamed."

"Well, I'm not. You made me mad and—you didn't seem to mind it."

"I didn't, but I do now, and I'm going."

He followed her to the wood's edge and there she turned.

"If your head is so weak you ought never to take spirits."

"My head isn't weak, and I'm not a drunkard. Ask any one. It's you that are—"

She offered the word—"Intoxicating?" And she let a smile break through her lips before she ran away.

She felt no mental revulsion against his embrace; the physical one was only against the smell of spirits which she disliked, and she was the richer for an experience she did not want to repeat. She saw no reason, however, why he should not be tempted to offer it. She had tasted of the fruit, and now she desired no more than the delight of seeing it held out to her and refusing it.

The moor was friendly to her as she crossed it and if she had suffered from any sense of guilt, it would have reassured her. Spread under the pale colour of the declining sun, she thought it was a big eye that twinkled at her. She looked at the walls of her home and felt unwilling to be enclosed by them; she looked towards the road, and seeing the doctor's trap, she decided to stay on the moor until he had been and gone, and when at last she entered she found the house ominously dark and quiet. The familiar scent of the hall was a chiding in itself and she went nervously to the schoolroom, where a line of light marked its meeting with the floor.

Helen sat by the table, mending linen in the lamplight. She gave one upward glance and went on working.

"Well?" Miriam said.

"Well?"

"Did he come?"

"Yes."

"What did he say?"

"He called it collapse."

"How clever of him!"

"I have left the tea-things for you to wash, and will you please get supper?"

"You needn't talk like that. I'm willing to do my share."

"You shirked it today, and though I know you're frightened of her, that's no excuse for leaving me alone."

Miriam leaned on the table and asked in a gentler voice, "Is she likely to be ill long?"

"It's very likely."

"Well, we shan't miss her while you are with us, but it's a pity, when we might have peace. You're just like her. I hope you'll never have any children, for they'd be as miserable as I am, only there wouldn't be one like me. How could there be? One only has to think of Zebedee."

Helen stood up and brought her hand so heavily to the table that the lamplight flared.

"Go!" she said, "go—" Her voice and body shook, her arms slid limply over her mending, and she tumbled into her chair, crying with sobs that seemed to quaver for a long time in her breast. Miriam could not have imagined such a weeping, and it frightened her. With one finger she touched Helen's shoulder, and over and over again she said, "I'm sorry, Helen. I'm sorry. Don't cry. I'm sorry—" until she heard Rupert whistling on the track. At that Helen stirred and wiped her eyes, but Miriam darted from the room, shouted cheerfully to Rupert and, keeping him in talk, led him to the dining-room, while Helen sat staring with blurred eyes at the linen pile, and seeing the misery in Mildred Caniper's face.

CHAPTER XX

It was a bitter winter, with more rain than snow, more snow than sunshine, and it seemed to Helen that half her life was spent in watching for Zebedee's figure bent against the storm as he drove up the road, while Mildred Caniper lay slackly in her bed. She no longer stared at the ceiling, for though her body had collapsed, her will had only wavered, and it was righting itself slowly, and the old thoughts which had been hunting her for years had not yet overcome her. Like hounds, they bayed behind, and some day their breath would be on her neck, their teeth in her flesh, and she would fall to them. This was the threat in the sound which reached her, soft or loud, as bells are heard in the wind, and in the meantime she steadied herself with varying arguments. Said one of these, "The past is over," yet she saw the whole future of these Canipers as the product of her acts. Reason, unsubdued, refused to allow her so much power, and she gave in; but she knew that if good befell the children she could claim no credit; if evil, she would take all the blame. There remained the comfortable assurance that she had done her best, and then Miriam's face mocked her as it peeped furtively round the bedroom door. Thus she was brought back to her starting place, and finding the circle a giddy one, she determined to travel on it no more, and with her old rigidity, she kept this resolve. It was, however, less difficult than it would once have been, for her mind was weary and glad of an excuse to take the easiest path. She lay in bed according to Zebedee's bidding, hardly moving under the clothes, and listening to the noises in the house. She was astonished by their number and significance. All through the night, cooling coals ticked in the grate or dropped on to the hearth; sometimes a mouse scratched or cheeped in the walls, and on the landing there were movements for which Helen could have accounted: Mr. Pinderwell, more conscious of his loss in the darkness, and unaware that his children had taken form, was moving from door to door and scraping his hands across the panels. Often the wind howled dolorously round the house while rain slashed furiously at the windows, and there were stealthy nights when snow wound a white muffler against the noises of the world. The clock in the hall sent out clear messages as to the passing of man's division of time, and at length there came the dawn, aged and eternally young, certain of itself, with a grey amusement for man's devices. Before that, Helen had opened her door and gone in soft slippers to light the kitchen fire, and presently Rupert was heard to whistle as he dressed. Meanwhile, as though it looked for something, the light spread itself in Mildred Caniper's room and she attuned her ears for the different noises of the day. There was Miriam's laughter, more frequent than it had been before her stepmother was tied to bed, and provocative of a wry smile from the invalid; there was her farewell shout to Rupert when he took the road, her husky singing as she worked about the house. Occasionally Mildred heard the stormy sound of Mrs. Samson's breathing as she polished the landing floor, or her voice raised in an anecdote too good to keep. Brooms knocked against the woodwork or swished on the bare floors, and still the clock, hardly noticed now, let out its warning that human life is short, or as it might be, over long. Later, but not on every day of the week, the jingle of a bit, the turning of wheels, rose to Mildred's window, telling her that the doctor had arrived, and though she had a grudge against all who saw her incapacitated, she found herself looking forward to his visits. He did not smile too much, nor stay too long, though it was remarkable that his leave-taking of her was not immediately followed by the renewed jingling of the bit. She was sure her condition did not call for prolonged discussion and, as she remembered Miriam who was free to come and go unchecked, to laugh away a man's wits, as her mother had done before her, Mildred Caniper grew hot and restless: she felt that she must get up and resume control, yet she knew that it would never be hers in full measure again, and while, in a rare, false moment, she pretended that the protection of Zebedee was her aim, truth stared at her with the reminder that the legacy of her old envy of the mother was this desire to thwart the daughter.

After that, her thoughts were long and bitter, and their signs were on her face when Helen returned.

"What have you been doing?" Helen demanded, for she no longer had any awe of Mildred Caniper, a woman who had been helpless in her hands.

"Please don't be ridiculous, Helen."

"I'm not."

"This absurd air of authority—"

"But you look—"

"We won't discuss how I look. Where is Miriam?"

"I don't know. Yes, I do. She went to Brent Farm to get some cream. Zeb—He says you're to have cream."

Mildred made a movement which was meant to express baffled patience. "I have tried to persuade you not to use pronouns instead of proper names. Can't you hear how vulgar it is?"

"Dr. Mackenzie wishes you to have cream," Helen said meekly.

"I do not need cream, and his visits are becoming quite unnecessary."

"So he said today."

"Oh."

"But I," Helen said, smiling to herself, "wish him to come."

"And no doubt the discussion of what primarily concerns me is what kept Dr. Mackenzie so long this afternoon."

"How did you know he stayed?"

"My good Helen, though I am in bed, I am neither deaf nor an imbecile."

"Oh, I know," Helen said with a seriousness which might as well have been mockery as stupidity. "I gave him—I gave Dr. Mackenzie tea. He was driving further, and it's such a stormy day."

"Quite right. He looks overworked—ill. I don't suppose he is properly cared for."

"He has a cough. He says he often gets one," Helen almost pleaded, and she went, at the first opportunity, from the room.

She encountered Jane's solemn and sympathetic stare. "I can't have neglected him, can I?" she asked of the little girl in the pinafore, and the shadows on the landing once more became alive with the unknown. "He does cough a lot, Jane, but he says it's nothing, and he tells the truth." She added involuntarily and with her hand at her throat, "I've been so happy," and immediately the words buzzed round her with menace. She should not have said that; it was a thing hardly to be thought, and she had betrayed her secret, but it comforted her to remember that this was nearly the end of January, and before long the Easter fires would burn again and she could pray.

Between the present and that one hour in the year when she might ask for help, Zebedee's cough persisted and grew worse. He had to own to a weakness of the lungs; he suffered every winter, more or less, and there had been one which had driven him to warmer climes.

"And you never told me that before!" she cried, with her hand in that tell-tale position at her throat.

"My dear, there has been no time to tell you anything. There hasn't been one day when we could be lavish. We've counted seconds. Would I talk about my lungs?"

"Perhaps we don't really know each other," Helen said, hoping he would not intercept this hostage she was offering to fortune, and she looked at him under her raised brows, and smiled a little, tempting him.

"We don't," he said firmly, and she drew a breath. "We only know we want each other, and all the rest of our lives is to be the adventure of finding each other out."

"But I'm not adventurous," she said.

"Oh, you'll like it," he assured her, smiling with his

wonderfully white teeth and still more with the little lines round his eyes. He looked at her with that practical air of adoration which was as precious to her as his rare caress; she felt doubly honoured because, in his love-making, he preserved a humour which did not disguise his worship of her. "You'll like it," he said cheerfully. "Why don't you marry me now and take care of me?"

She made a gesture towards the upper room. "How can I?"

"No, you can't. Not," he added, "so much on that account, as simply because you can't. I'd rather wait a few months more—"

"You must," she said, and faintly irritated him. She looked at her clasped hands. "Zebedee, do you feel you want to be taken care of?" Her voice was anxious and, though he divined how much was balanced on his answer, he would not adjust it nicely.

"Not exactly," he said honestly, and he saw a light of relief and a shadow of disappointment chase each other on her face.

"After all, I think I do know you rather well," he murmured, as he took her by the shoulders. "Do you understand what I am doing?"

"You're telling me the truth."

"And at what a cost?"

She nodded. "But you couldn't help telling me the truth."

"And if I bemoaned my loneliness, how my collars get lost in the wash, how tired I am of Eliza's cooking and her face, how bad my cough is, then you'd let me carry you away?"

"I might. Zebedee—are those things true, too?"

"Not particularly."

"And your cough isn't bad?"

He hesitated. "It is rather bad."

"And you're a doctor!"

"But my dear, darling, love—I've no control over the weather."

"You ought to go away," she said in a low voice.

"I hope it won't come to that," he said.

It was Rupert who asked her a week later if she had jilted Zebedee.

"Why?" she asked quickly.

"He's ill, woman."

"I know."

"But really ill. You ought to send him away until the spring."

Her lips moved for a few seconds before she uttered "Yes," and after that sound she was mute under the double fear of keeping him and parting from him, but, since to let him go would give her the greater pain, it was the lesser fear, and it might be that the powers who were always waiting near to demand a price would, in this manner, let her get her paying done. She welcomed the chance of paying in advance and she kept silence while she strengthened herself to do it bravely.

Because she did not speak, Rupert elaborated. "When Zebedee loses his temper, there's something wrong."

"Has he done that?"

"Daniel daren't speak to him."

"He never speaks to people: he expounds."

"True; but your young man was distinctly short with me, even me, yesterday. Listen to your worldly brother, Helen. Why don't you marry him and take him into the sun? It's shining somewhere, one supposes."

"I can't."

"Why not? There's Miriam."

"What good is she?"

"You never give her a chance. You're one of those self-sacrificing, selfish people who stunt other people's growth. It's like not letting a baby learn to walk for fear it falls and hurts itself, or tumbles into the best flower-beds and ruins 'em. Have you ever thought of that?"

"But she's happier than she used to be," Helen said and smiled as though nothing more were needed. "And soon she will be going away. She won't stay after she is twenty-one."

"D'you think that fairy-tale is going to come true?"

"Oh, yes. She always does what she wants, you know. And she is counting on Uncle Alfred, though she says she isn't. She had a letter from him the other day."

"And when she has gone, what are you going to do?"

"I don't know what I'm going to do."

"Things won't be easier for you then. You'd better face that."

"But she'll be better—Notya will be better."

"And you'll marry Zebedee."

"I don't like saying what I'm going to do."

Rupert's dark eyes had a hard, bright light. "Are you supposed to love that unfortunate man? Look here, you're not going to be tied to Notya all her life. Zebedee and I won't have it."

"What's going to happen to her, then?"

"Bless the child! She's grown up. She can look after herself."

"But I can't leave just you and her in this house together."

He said in rather a strained voice, "I shan't be here. The bank's sending me to the new branch."

"Oh!" Helen said.

"I'm sorry about it. I tried not to seem efficient, but there's something about me—charm, I think. They must have noticed how I talk to the old ladies who don't know how to make out their cheques. So they're sending me, but I don't know that I ought to leave you all."

"Of course you must."

"I can come home on Saturdays."

"Yes. And Notya's better, and John is near. Why shouldn't you go?"

"Because your face fell."

"It's only that everybody's going. It seems like the end of things." She pictured the house without Rupert and she had a sense of desolation, for no one would whistle on the track at night and make the house warmer and more beautiful with his entrance; there would be no one to look up from his book with unfailing readiness to listen to everything and understand it; no one to say pleasant things which made her happy.

"Why," she said, plumbing the depths of loss, "there'll be no one to get up early for!"

"Ah, it's Miriam who'll feel that!" he said.

"And even Daniel won't come any more. He's tired of Miriam's foolishness."

"To tell you a secret, he's in love with some one else. But he has no luck. No wonder! If you could be married to him for ten years before you married him at all—"

"I don't know," Helen said thoughtfully. "Those funny men—" She did not finish her thought. "It will be queer without you," and after a pause she added the one word, "lonely."

It was strange that Miriam, whom she loved best, should never present herself to Helen's mind as a companion: the sisters, indeed, rarely spoke together except to argue some domestic point, to scold each other, or to tease, yet each was conscious of the other's admiration, though Helen looked on Miriam as a pretty ornament or toy, and Miriam gazed dubiously at what she called the piety of the other.

"Yes, lonely," she said, but in her heart she was glad that her payment should be great, and she said loudly, as though she recited her creed: "I wouldn't change anything. I believe in the things that happen."

"May they reward you!" he said solemnly.

"When will you have to go?"

"I'm not sure. Pretty soon. Look here, my dear, you three lone women ought to have a dog to take man's place as your natural protector—and so on."

"Have you told Zebedee you are going?"

"Yesterday."

"Then he will be getting one."

"H'm. He seems to be a satisfactory lover."

"He is, you know."

"Thank God for him."

"Would you?" Helen said. She had a practical as well as a superstitious distaste for offering thanks for benefits not actually received, and also a disbelief in the present certainty of her possession, but she took hope. John had gone, Rupert was going, of her own will she would send Zebedee away, and then surely the powers would be appeased, and if she suffered enough from loneliness, from dread of seeing Mildred Caniper ill again, of never getting her lover back, the rulers of her life might be willing, at the end, to let her have Zebedee and the shining house—the shining house which lately had taken firmer shape, and stood squarely back from the road, with a little copse of trees rising behind.

CHAPTER XXI

She cried out when next she saw him, for between this and their next meeting he had grown gaunter, more nervous, sharper in voice and gesture.

"Oh, you're ill!" she said, and stepped back as though she did not know him.

"Yes, I'm ill." He held to a chair and tipped it back and forth. "For goodness' sake, don't talk about it any more. I'm ill. That's settled. Now let's get on to something else."

He saw her lip quiver and, uttering a desperate, "I'm sorry," he turned from her to the window.

The wisdom she could use so well with others was of no avail with him: he was too much herself to be treated cunningly. She felt that she floated on a sea vastly bigger than she had ever known, and its waves were love and fear and cruelty and fate, but in a moment he turned and she saw a raft on which she might sail for ever.

"Forgive me."

"You've made me love you more."

"With being a brute to you?"

"Were you one? But—don't often be angry. I might get used to it!"

He laughed. "Oh, Helen, you wonder! But I've spoilt our memories."

"With such a little thing? And when I liked it?"

"You nearly cried. I don't want to remember that."

"But I shall like to because we're nearer than we were," she said, and to that he solemnly agreed. "And I am going to talk about it."

"Anything, of course."

"You look tired and hungry and sleepy, and I'm going to send you away."

"My dear," he said with a grimace, "I've got to go."

"Give me the credit of sending you."

"I don't want it. Ah! you've no idea what leaving you is like."

"But I know—"

"That's not the same thing."

"It's worse, I believe. Darling one, go away and come back to me, but don't come back until you're well. I want—I want to do without you now—and get it over." Her eyes, close to his, were bright with the vision of things he could not see. "Get it over," she said again, "and then, perhaps, we shall be safe."

He had it in him at that moment to say he would not go because of his own fear for her, but he only took her on his knee and rocked her as though she were a baby on the point of sleep and he proved that, after all, he knew her very well, for when he spoke he said, "I don't think I can go."

She started up. "Have you thought of something?"

"Yes."

"What is it?"

"You."

"Me?" she asked on a long note.

"I don't know whether I can trust you."

"Me?" she said again.

"Don't you remember how I asked you to be brave?"

"I tried, but it was easier then because I hadn't you." Her arm tightened round his neck. "Now you're another to look after."

He held her off from him. "What am I to do with you? What am I to do with you? How can I leave this funny little creature who is afraid of shadows?"

"That night," she said in a small voice, "you told me I looked brave."

"Yes, brave and sane. And I have often thought—don't laugh at me—I have thought that was how Joan of Arc must have looked."

"And now?"

"Now you are like a Joan who does not hear her voices any more."

She slipped from his knee to hers. "You're disappointed then?"

"No."

"You ought to be."

"Perhaps."

"Would you love me more if I were brave?"

"I don't believe I could."

She laughed, and with her head aslant, she asked, "Then what's the good of trying?"

"Just to make it easier for me," he said.

She uttered a little sound like one who stands in mountain mists and through a rent in the grey curtain sees a light shining in the valley.

"Would it do that for you? Oh, if it's going to help you, I'm afraid no longer." She reached out and held his face between the finger-tips of her two hands. "I promise not to be afraid. Already"—she looked about her—"I am not afraid. How wonderful you are! And what a wise physician! Physician, heal thyself. You'll go away?"

"Yes, I can go now."

"Where?"

"For a voyage. The Mediterranean. Not a liner—on some slow-going boat."

"Not a leaky one," she begged.

"Ah, I'd come back if she had no bottom to her. Nothing is going to hurt me or keep me from you!"

She did not protest against his boasting, but smiled because she knew he meant to test her.

"You'll be away a long time," she said.

"And you'll marry me when I come back?"

"Yes. If I can."

"Why not? In April? May? June? In June—a lovely month. It has a sound of marriage in it. But after all," he said thoughtfully, "it seems a pity to go. And I wouldn't," he added with defiance, "if I were not afraid of being ill on your hands."

"My hands would like it rather."

"Bless them!"

"Oh—what silly things we say—and do—and you haven't seen Notya yet."

"Come along then," he said, and as they went up the stairs together Helen thought Mr. Pinderwell smiled.

It was after this visit that Mildred Caniper coolly asked Helen if Dr. Mackenzie were in the habit of using endearments towards her.

"Not often," Helen said. Slightly flushed and trying not to laugh, she stood at the bed-foot and faced Mildred Caniper fairly.

"You allow it?"

"I—like it."

Mildred Caniper closed her eyes. "Please ask him not to do it in my presence."

"I'll tell him when he comes again," Helen answered agreeably, and her stepmother realized that the only weapons to which this girl was vulnerable were ones not willingly used: such foolish things as tears or sickness; she seemed impervious to finer tools. Helen's looks at the moment were unabashed: she was trying to remember what Zebedee had said, both for its own sake and to gauge its effect on Notya to whose memory it was clear enough, and its naturalness, the slight and unmistakable change in his voice as he spoke to Helen, hurt her so much with their reminder of what she had missed that pain made her strike once more.

"This is what I might have expected from Miriam."

"But," said Helen, all innocence, "she doesn't care for him."

"And you do."

She did not wish to say yes; she could not say no; she kept her half-smiling silence.

"How long has this been going on?" The tones were sharp with impotence.

"Oh—well—since you went to Italy. At least," she murmured vaguely, "that was when he came to tea."

But Mildred did not hear the last homely sentence, and Helen's next words came from a great distance, even from the shuttered room in Italy.

"And why should you mind? Why shouldn't we—like each other?"

Mildred Caniper opened her remarkably blue eyes, and said, almost in triumph, "You'll be disappointed."

At that Helen laughed with a security which was pathetic and annoying to the woman in the bed.

"Life—" Mildred Caniper began, and stopped. She had not yet reached the stage, she reflected, when she must utter platitudes about the common lot. She looked at Helen with unusual candour. "I have never spoken to you of these things," she said.

"Oh, I shouldn't like you to!" Helen cried, and her hands were near her ears.

Mildred allowed her lips to curve. "I am not referring to the facts of generation," she said drily, and her smile broadened, her eyebrows lifted humorously. "I am quite aware that the—the advantages of a country life include an early arrival at that kind of knowledge. Besides, you were fortunate in your brothers. And then there were all the books."

"The books?"

"The ones Rupert used to bring you."

"So you knew about them."

"I have had to remind you before, Helen, that I am not out of my mind."

"What else do you know?" Helen asked with interest, and sat down on the bed.

This was Miriam's inquiry when the conversation was reported to her.

"She didn't tell me anything else. I think she had said more than she meant. She is like that sometimes, now. It's because she hasn't so much strength."

"I expect she knows everything we ever did."

"Well, we never did much."

"No. And everything we do now."

"She didn't know about Zebedee."

"Oh, she wouldn't suspect you."

"Then don't do anything you shouldn't," Helen said mildly.

"Her 'should' and my 'should' are very different members of the same family, my dear." She peered into Helen's face and squeaked, "And what the devil is there to do?"

"Don't use words like that."

"Wow! Wow! This is the devil's St. Helena, I imagine. There's nothing to be done in it. I believe she has eyes all round her head."

"He's a gentleman always, in pictures."

"Are you really stupid?"

"I think so."

"I was talking about Notya."

"Oh."

"And I believe she can see with her ears and hear with her eyes. Helen—Helen, you don't think she gets up sometimes in the night, and prowls about, do you?"

"I should hear her."

"Oh. Are you sure?"

"I sleep so lightly. The other night—"

"Yes?"

"I was waked by a sheep coughing outside the garden."

Miriam burst out laughing. "Did you think it was Zebedee?" She laughed a great deal more than was necessary. "Now she's putting on her never-smiled-again expression! Will he be back before I go away?"

Helen looked at her dumbly. She heard the garden gate shutting behind John and Zebedee, Rupert and Miriam, with a clang which seemed to forbid return, and her dread of Zebedee's going became sharper, though beneath her dread there lay the courage she had promised him.

"And there will be the dog," she found herself saying aloud.

The animal, when he arrived, leapt from the dog-cart in which he had been unwillingly conveyed and proved to be an

Airedale, guaranteed to be a perfect watch-dog and suspicious of all strangers.

Proudly, Zebedee delivered himself of these recommendations. "He's trained, thoroughly trained to bite. And he's enormously strong. Just look at his neck! Look at his teeth—get through anything."

Helen was kneeling to the dog and asking, "Are you sure he'll bite people? He seems to like me very much."

"I've been telling him about you. My precious child, you can't have a dog who leaps at people unprovoked. He'd be a public danger. You must say 'Rats!' or something like that when you want him to attack."

"Well—I love him," she said.

"And I've something else for you."

"Oh, no!"

"Shut your eyes—"

"And open my mouth?"

"No, give me your hand. There! Will you wear that for me?"

"Oh! Oh! It's the loveliest thing I've ever seen in my life! Much! Oh, it's perfect. It's so white."

"Tell me I'm rather a success today."

"You're one all the time. Did you have it made for me?"

"D'you think I'd get you something out of a shop window? I made it up. And there's another thing—"

"But you won't have any money left!" she cried.

"Then I won't tell you about the third thing."

She said solemnly, "You ought to have no secrets from me."

"Have you none from me?"

"Not one. Except—but that's so silly—except the tinker."

"Tell me that one."

She obeyed him, and she frowned a little, because she could not understand why the thing should need telling. "And then I went on to the moor, and George Halkett ran after me, and I thought it was the tinker."

"Why," Zebedee asked, "did he run after you?"

"He must have thought I was some one else."

"Why does he run after anybody?"

"Because he's George, I think, and if John were here he would tell you the story of how he tried to kiss Lily Brent!"

"That sort of animal oughtn't to be let loose."

"I like him," Helen said. "I'm sorry for him."

"H'm," said Zebedee. "Well, you have the dog."

"Oh," she said, "he isn't like that with me. We've known each other all our lives. And you don't mind about the tinker?"

"I don't think so."

"It's not nearly so bad," she persuaded him, "as the real woman you once liked."

He did not contradict her. "We're not going to argue about dreams and the past. We haven't time for that."

"And I haven't begun to thank you! I knew you were going to bring a dog!"

"Who told you?"

"I just knew you'd think of it. But two lovely presents in one day, and both from you! But I feel—I feel—"

"I know. You want to drown the dog and throw the ring away as hostages for my safety."

"Yes, don't laugh."

"My dear," he said wearily, "there are moments when one can do nothing else."

"I'm sorry. And don't be angry with me in case you make me love you too much to let you go! And I'm brave, really. I promise to be good."

He nodded in his quick way while he looked at her as though, in spite of all he said, he feared he might never look at her again, and she was proud of his firm lips and steady eyes in the moment of the passionate admiration which lived with her like a presence while he was away.

CHAPTER XXII

Helen passed into a pale windy world one February morning and walked slowly down the track. There was no sharpness in the air and the colours of approaching spring seemed to hover between earth and heaven, though they promised soon to lay themselves down to make new green and splendid purple and misty blue. Slow-moving clouds paced across the sky, and as she looked at them Helen thought of Zebedee sailing under richer colour and with white canvas in the place of clouds. She wondered if time crept with him as slowly as it did with her; if he had as much faith in her courage as she had in his return. She knew he would come back, and she had trained herself to patience: indeed, it was no hard matter, for hers had always been a world in which there was no haste. The seasons had their leisured way; the people moved with heavy feet; the moor lay in its wisdom, suffering decay and growth. Even the Brent Farm cattle made bright but stationary patches in the field before the house, and as she drew nearer she came upon John and Lily leaning on a fence. Their elbows touched; their faces were content, as slowly they discussed the fate of the cow they contemplated, and Helen sat down to await their leisure.

Before her, the moor sloped to the road and rose again, lifting Pinderwell House on its bosom, and to her right, from the hidden chimneys of Halkett's Farm, she could see smoke rising as though it were the easy breath of some monster lying snug among the trees. There was no other movement, though the sober front of Pinderwell House was animated for an instant by the shaking of some white substance from a window. Miriam was at her household tasks, and Helen waved a hand to the dark being who had made life smoother for her since her night of stormy weeping. She waved a hand of gratitude and friendship, but the signal was not noticed, the house returned to its discretion, John and Lily talked sparsely but with complete understanding, and Helen grew drowsy in the sunshine. She was happier than she had ever been, for Zebedee had laid peace on her, like a spell, and the warmth of that happiness stole up from her feet and spread over her breast; it curled the corners of her mouth so that John, turning to look at her, asked her why she smiled.

"I'm comfortable," she said.

"Never been comfortable before?"

She gave him the clear depths of her eyes. "Not often."

He went away, driving the cow before him, and Lily stood looking after him.

"He's wonderful," she said. "He comes along and takes hold of things and begins to teach me my own business."

"So you're pleased with him?" Helen said demurely.

"Yes," the other answered with twitching lips, "he's doing very well." Her laughter faded, and she said softly, "I wonder if they often happen—marriages like ours."

"Tell me about it."

"Nothing to tell. It's just as if it's always been, and every minute it seems fresh."

"No," Helen said consideringly, "I shouldn't think it often happens. I've come for a pound of butter, please."

"How's Mrs. Caniper?"

"She's better, but I think she would be rather glad to die. I let her make a cake yesterday, and it did her good. Come and see her soon."

"I will. Let's go to the dairy. Will you have it in halves or quarters? Look at my new stamp!"

"What is it meant to be?"

"Well! It's a Shetland pony, of course."

"I like the pineapple better. I don't think a pony seems right on butter. I'll have the pineapple."

"John says there's as much sense in one as in the other, because we don't get butter from either of them."

"The pineapple is food, though."

"So's the pony, by some accounts!" She leaned in her old attitude against a shelf, and eyed Helen nervously. "Talking of ponies, have you seen anything of these ghostly riders?"

"I don't know what they are."

"That's what my—our—shepherd calls them. He saw them late one night, a while back. One was a woman, he said, and the air was cold with them and set him sneezing. That's what he says."

"It was some of the wild ponies, I suppose."

"Maybe."

"You don't think it was really ghosts?"

"No, for I've seen them myself." She paused. "I haven't said anything to John, but I'm wondering if I ought."

"Why not?"

Lily's gaze widened in her attempt to see what Helen's point of view would be and she spoke slowly, that, if possible, she might not offend.

"It was George Halkett I saw. There was no woman, but he was leading one horse and riding another. It was one night when John was late on the moor and I went to look for him. George didn't see me. I kept quiet till he'd gone by. There was a side saddle on the led horse."

"Well?" Helen said.

"That's all. I thought you ought to know."

In that moment Helen hated Lily. "Is it Miriam you're hinting at?" she asked on a high note.

"Yes, it is. You're making me feel mean, but I'm glad I've told you. It's worried me, and John—I didn't like to tell John, for he has a grudge against the man, and he might have made trouble before he need."

"I think that's what you're doing," Helen said.

"That may be. I took the risk. I know George Halkett. Miriam, having a bit of fun, might find herself landed in a mess. I'm sorry, Helen. I hope I'm wrong."

Helen was half ashamed to hear herself asking, "How late was it?"

"About twelve."

"But I'm awake half the night. I should have heard. Besides—would there be any harm?"

"Just as much as there is in playing with fire," Lily said.

"'Behold how great a matter a little fire kindleth,'" Helen said, looking at the ground.

"Yes, but there's more than a little fire in Miriam, and George Halkett's a man, you know."

Helen raised her head and said, "We've lived here all our lives, and we have been very lonely, but I have hardly spoken to a man who was not gentle. John and Rupert and Zebedee and Daniel, all these—no one has spoken roughly to us. It makes one trustful. And George is always kind, Lily."

"Yes, but Miriam—she's not like you."

"She's much more beautiful."

Lily's laughter was half a groan. "That won't make George any gentler, my dear."

"Won't it?"

Lily shook her head. "But perhaps there's nothing in it. I'm sorry to have added to your worries, but Miriam's so restless and discontented, and I thought—"

"Ah," Helen interrupted gladly, "but lately she has been different. Lately she has been happier. Oh!" She saw where her words had led her, and with a little gesture of bewilderment she turned and walked away.

Perhaps, after all, the things that happened were not necessarily best, and for the first time Helen felt a blind anger against the unknown. In a moment of sharp vision, she saw what this vaguely concentrated life had done for her and Miriam, and she wondered by whose law it had been decreed that no human being could have a destiny unconditioned by some one else, and though she also saw that this law was the glory as well as the tragedy of life, she rebelled against it now, lest the radiant being whom she loved should be dishonoured or disillusioned.

Helen's firm curved lips took a harder line as she went slowly home, for it seemed to her that in an active world the principle of just going on left all the foes unconquered and ready for the next victim who should pass that way.

She slept fitfully that night, and once she woke to a sound of galloping on the moor. She knew it was made by more animals than two, yet her heart beat quickly, and her thoughts sprang together to make a picture of George Halkett leading a horse without a rider through the night, waiting in the darkness with his ears stretched for the sound of one coming through the heather.

She started up in bed, for the mysterious allurement of George's image was strong enough to make her understand what it might be for Miriam, and she held herself to the bed lest she should be tempted to play the spy; yet, had she brought herself to open her sister's door, she would have been shamed and gladdened by the sight of that pretty sleeper lying athwart her bed in profound unconsciousness.

Miriam, whose heart was still untouched by God or man, could lie and sleep soundly, though she knew George waited for her on the moor. The restlessness that had first driven her there had sent her home again, that, by a timely abstention, she might recover the full taste of adventure, and that, by the same means, George might learn her worth. She was a little puzzled by his behaviour, and she began to find monotony in its decorum. According to his promise, he had taught her to ride, and while all her faculties were bent on that business, she hardly noticed him, but with confidence in her own seat and Charlie's steadiness, there came freedom to look at George, and with it the desire to rule the expression of his face and the modulations of his voice.

He would not be beguiled. "I'm teaching you to ride," he said, and though she mocked him he was not stirred to quarrel. She was temporarily incapable of realizing that while she learnt to ride, he learnt to honour her, and found safety for himself and her in silence; nor, had she realized it, would she have welcomed it. What she wanted was the pleasure of being hunted and seeing the hunter discomfited, and though she could not get that from him, she had a new joy when Charlie carried her strongly and safely across the moor; again she knew the feeling of passing through a void, of sailing on a thunder-cloud without hope of rescue and careless of it, and she paid a heavy price when she decided that it would do George good to wait in vain for her. She would not have him disrespectful, but she desired him ardent; she wished to see that stubbornly set mouth open to utter longings, and, when she went to bed after a dull day, she laughed to think of how he waited and stared into the gloom.

A fortnight passed before she stole out on a misty night and at the appointed place found him like a grey carved figure on a grey carved horse. Only his lips moved when she peered at him through the mist. He said, "This is the fifteenth night. If you'd waited till tomorrow, you wouldn't have found me here."

"George," she said, with her face close to his knee, "how unkind you are to me. And, oh, George, do you really think I should have cared?"

In the mist, she, too, had the look of one not made of flesh and blood, but she had no likeness to some figure carved: she was the spirit of the mist with its drops on her hair, a thing intangible, yet dowered with power to make herself a torment. So she looked, but Halkett had felt the touch of her, and taking her by the wrist, he dragged her upwards while he bent down to her.

"You—you—!" he panted.

"You're hurting, George!"

"What do I care? I haven't seen you for two weeks. I've been—been starving for you."

She spoke coolly, with a ringing quality in her tones. "You would see me better if you didn't come so near."

Immediately he loosened her without looking at her, and she

stood chafing her hands, hating his indifference, though she knew it was assumed, uncertain how to regain her supremacy. Then she let instinct guide her, and she looked a little piteous.

"Don't be rough with me. I didn't mean—I don't like you to be rough with me."

He was off his horse and standing by her at those words, and, still watchful for rebuffs, he took her hand and stroked it gently.

"Did I hurt you, then?" he said.

"Yes. Why are you like that?" She lifted her head and gave him the oval face, the dark, reproachful eyes like night.

"Because I'm mad for you—mad for you. Little one—you make me mad. And you'll never marry me. I know that. And I'm a fool to let you play the devil with me. I know that, too. A mad fool. But you—you're in my blood."

Softly she said, "You never told me that before. You needn't scold me so. How should I know you wanted that?"

"You knew I loved you."

"No. I knew you liked me and I hoped—"

He bent his head to listen.

"I hoped you loved me."

His words came thickly, a muddy torrent. "Then marry me, marry me, Miriam. Marry me. I want—I can't—You must say you'll marry me."

Keeping her eyes on him, she moved slowly away, and from behind Charlie's back she laughed with a genuine merriment that wounded inexpressibly.

"You're funny, George," she said. "Very funny. At present I have no intention of doing anything but riding Charlie."

Through a mist doubled and coloured by his red rage, he watched her climb into the saddle and, before she was fairly settled in it, he gave the horse a blow that sent him galloping indignantly out of sight.

Halkett did not care if she were thrown, for his anger and his passion were confounded into one emotion, and he would have rejoiced to see her on the ground, her little figure twisted with her fall, but he did not follow her. He went home in the rain that was now falling fast, and when the mare was stabled he brewed himself a drink that brought oblivion.

CHAPTER XXIII

Helen waked, that night, from a short deep sleep, to hear the falling of heavy rain and sharp gusts of wind that bowed the poplars. As the storm strengthened, raindrops were blown on to her pillow, and she could hear the wind gathering itself up before it swept moaning across the moor and broke with a miserable cry against the walls. She hoped Mildred Caniper slept through a wailing that might have a personal note for her, and as she prepared to leave the room and listen on the landing, she thought she heard a new sound cutting through the swish of the rainfall and the shriek of wind. It was a smaller sound, as though a child were alone and crying in the night, and she leaned from her window to look into the garden. The rain wetted her hair and hands and neck, while she stared into varying depths of blackness—the poplars against the sky, the lawn, like water, the close trees by the wall—and as she told herself that the wind had many voices, she heard a loud, unwary sob and the impact of one hard substance on another.

Some one was climbing the garden wall, and a minute later a head rose above the scullery roof. It was Miriam, crying, with wet clothes clinging to her, and Helen called out softly.

"Oh, is that you?" she answered, and laughed through a tangled breath. "I'm drenched."

"Wait! I'll go into Phoebe and help you through."

"There's a chair here. I left it. I'm afraid it's ruined!"

Helen entered the other room as Miriam dropped from the window-ledge to the floor.

"Don't make a noise. We mustn't wake her. Oh, oh, you look—you look like rags!"

Miriam sat limply; she shook with cold and sobs and laughter.

Water dripped from every part of her, and when Helen helped her up, all the streams became one river.

Helen let go of the cold hands and sank to the bed. "There must be gallons of it! And you—!"

"I'm frozen. Mop it up. Towels—anything. I'll fling my clothes out of the window. They are quite used to the scullery roof."

"Speak quietly. Whisper. She may hear you!"

"That would be—the devil, wouldn't it? Good thing Rupert isn't here! Put something at the bottom of the door. Lock it. My fingers are numb. Oh, dear, oh, dear, I can't undo my things."

"Let me. You ought to have hot water, and there's no fire. I'll rub you down. And your hair! Wring it out, child. What were you doing on the moor?"

"Just amusing myself."

"With George Halkett?"

"We-ell, I was with him in the spirit, oh, yes, I was; but in the flesh, only for a very little while. What made you think I was with him?"

"Something I heard. Are you warmer now?"

"Much warmer. Give me my nightgown, please. Oh, it's comfortable, and out there I was so cold, so cold. Oh," she cried out, "I should love to set his farm on fire!"

"Hush!"

"But I would! If I'd had matches, and if it hadn't been raining, and if I'd thought about it, I would have done it then."

"But what did he do to you?" Helen's eyes were sombre. "He surely didn't touch you?"

Miriam's arrested laughter marked their differences. She remembered George Halkett's hand on hers and the wilder, more distant passion of his arms clasping her among the larches.

"It wasn't that," she said. "He asked me to marry him—and it wasn't that. I met him to go riding, and I think I must have teased him. Yes, I did, because he hit my horse, and I couldn't hold him, and I fell off at last. I lay in the heather for a long time. It was wet, Helen, and I was all alone. I cried at first. I would have killed him if he had come near. I would, somehow, but he never came. He didn't care, and I might have been killed, just because I teased him. Then I cried again. Would you mind coming into bed with me to keep me warm? I'm glad I'm here. I lost my way. I thought I should be out there all night. It was dark, and the wind howled like demons, and the rain, the rain—! Closer, Helen."

"Did he frighten you?"

"Of course he didn't. I was angry. Oh"—the small teeth gritted on each other—"angry! But I'll pay him out. I swear I will."

"Don't swear it. Don't do it. I wish Rupert were here. I'm glad Zebedee gave me Jim."

"Pooh! Do you think George will break into the house? Jim would fly at him. I'd like that. He's got to be paid out."

Helen moved in the bed. "What's the good of doing that?"

"The good! He made me bite the earth. I joggled and joggled, and at last I went over with a bump, and when I bumped I vowed I'd hurt him."

"You needn't keep that kind of vow."

"Then what was the good of making it? We always keep our promises."

"Promise not to see him any more."

"Don't worry. I've finished with him—very nearly. Will you stay with me all night? There's not much room, but I want you to keep hold of me. I'm warm now, and so beautifully sleepy."

Her breathing became even, but once it halted to let her say, "He's a beast, but I can't help rather liking him."

She slept soon afterwards, but Helen lay awake with her arm growing stiff under Miriam's body, and her mind wondering if that pain were symbolic of what wild folly might inflict.

It was noticeable that Miriam did not venture on the moor in the days that followed, but every day Helen went there with Jim, who needed exercise and was only restrained from chasing sheep by timely employment of his energy, and every day Halkett, watching the house, saw these two sally forth together. They went at an easy pace, the woman with her skirt outblown, her breast fronting the wind, her head thrown back, her hands behind her, the dog marching by her side, and in their clearness of cut, their pale colour, for which the moor was dado and the sky frieze, he found some memory of sculptures he had seen and hardly heeded, ancient things with the eternity of youth on them, the captured splendour of moving limb and passionate brain. Then he was aware of fresh wind and fruitful earth, but as she passed out of sight, he was imprisoned again by stifling furies. He had begun to love Miriam with a sincerity that wished to win and not to force her; he had controlled the wild heritage of his fathers and tried to forget the sweetness of her body in the larch-wood; he was determined not to take what she would not give him gladly; and now, by her own act, she had changed his striving love into desire—desire to hurt, to feel her struggling in his arms, hating his kisses, paying a bitter price for her misuse of him. He had a vicious pleasure in waiting for the hour when he should feel her body straining away from his, and each night, as he sat drinking, he lived through that ecstasy; each day, as he went about his work, he kept an eye on the comings and goings of the Canipers, waiting for his chance. Miriam did not appear, and that sign of fear inflamed him; but on Sunday morning she walked on the moor with Rupert, holding him by the arm and making a parade of happiness, and in the afternoon, Daniel was added to the train.

Monday came, and no small, black-haired figure darted from the house: only Helen and the majestic dog walked together like some memory of a younger world.

His mind held two pictures as he sat alone at night, and, corresponding to them, two natures had command of him. He saw Helen like dawn and Miriam like night, and as one irritated him with her calm, the other roused him with her fire, and he came to watch for Helen that he might sneer inwardly at her, with almost as much eagerness as he watched for Miriam that he might mutter foul language, like loathed caresses.

Drink and desire and craving for peace were all at work in

him. The dreams he had been building were broken by a callous hand, and he sat among the ruins. He could laugh, now, at his fair hopes, but they had had their part in him, and he could never go back to the days when he rode and drank and loved promiscuously, with a light heart. She had robbed, too, when she cast down his house, but there was no end to her offence, for when, out of coarser things, this timid love had begun to creep, it had been thrown back at him with a gibe.

He was in a state when the strongest suggestion would have its way with him. He wanted to make Miriam suffer; he wanted to be dealt with kindly, and he had a pitiful and unconscious willingness to take another's mould. So, when he saw Helen on the moor, the sneering born of her distance from him changed slowly to a desire for nearness, and he remembered with what friendliness they had sat together in the heather one autumn night, and how peace had seemed to lie upon them both. A woman like that might keep a man straight, he thought, and when she stopped to speak to him one morning, her smile was balm to his hurts.

She looked at him in her frank way. "You don't look well, George."

"Oh—I'm all right," he said, hitting his gaiters with his stick.

"It's a lovely day," she said, "and you have some lambs already. I hope the snow won't come and kill them."

"Hope not. We're bound to lose some of them, though."

Why, he asked himself angrily, was she not afraid of him who was planning injury to her sister? She made him feel as though he could never injure any one.

"You haven't noticed my dog," she said.

"Yes—" he began. He had been noticing him for days, marching beside her against the sky. "He's a fine beast."

"Isn't he?" Her finger-tips were on Jim's head.

"You want a dog now there's no man in your house."

She laughed a little as she said, "And he feels his responsibility, don't you, Jim?"

"Come here, lad," Halkett called to him. "Come on. That's right!"

"He seems to like you."

"I never knew the dog that didn't; but don't make him too soft, or he'll be no good to you."

"Well," she said gaily, "you are not likely to break into our house!"

His flush alarmed her, for it told her that she had happened on the neighbourhood of his thoughts, and her mind was in a flurry to assert her innocence and engender his, but no words came to her, and her hand joined his in fondling the dog's head.

"Well, I must be going on," George said, and after an uncertain instant he walked away, impoverished and enriched.

Helen sat down heavily, as though one of her own heartbeats had pushed her there, and putting her arm round Jim's neck, she leaned her head on him.

"Jim," she said, "don't you wish Zebedee would come back? If I hadn't promised—" She looked about her. George had disappeared, and near by grey sheep were eating with a concentration that disdained her and the dog. It was a peaceful scene, and a few early lambs dotted it with white. "It's silly to feel like this," she said. "Let's go and find Miriam."

She was discovered in the garden, digging.

"But why?" Helen asked.

"I must have exercise." Her hair was loosened, her teeth worked on her under-lip as her foot worked on the spade. "You don't know how I miss my riding!"

"I've just seen George."

"Have you?"

"I spoke to him."

"How brave! How did he look?"

"Horrid. His eyes were bloodshot."

"Ah! He has been drinking. That's despair. Perhaps it's time I tried to cheer him up."

"Don't make him angry."

"I'm not going to. I'm not vindictive. I'm rather nice. I've recovered from my rage, and now I wouldn't set his farm on fire for worlds. Why, if I saw it blazing, I should run to help! But I'd like to tease him just a little bit."

"I wish you wouldn't. I think it's rather mean, he looks so miserable. And I'm sure it isn't safe. Please, Miriam."

"I can take care of myself, my dear."

"I'm not so sure."

"Oh, yes, I can. I'm going to make it up with him. I must, or I shall never be able to walk about the moor again."

"I wish you didn't live here," Helen said.

"Well, so do I. But it's not for long." She was working vigorously, and, with her peculiar faculty for fitting her surroundings, she looked as though she had been begotten of sun and rain and soil. Helen took delight in her bright colour, strong hands and ready foot.

"I wonder," Helen said thoughtfully, "if Uncle Alfred would take you now."

"Do you want to save me from George's clutches?"

"Yes, I do."

Miriam threw back her head and laughed. "You funny little thing! You're rather sweet. George hasn't a clutch strong enough to hold me. You can be sure of that."

She was herself so certain that she waylaid him on the moor next day, but to her amazement he did not answer her smile of greeting and passed on without a word.

"George!" she called after him.

"Well?" He looked beyond her at the place where green moor met blue sky: he felt he had done with her, and Helen's trust had taken all the sweetness from revenge.

"Aren't you going to say good-morning? I came on purpose to see you."

"You needn't trouble," he said and, stealing a look at her, he weakened.

"But I need." He was wavering, she knew, and her mouth and

eyes promised laughter, her body seemed to sway towards him.

"I want—I want to forgive you, George."

"Well, I'm—"

"Yes, you are, no doubt, but I don't want to be, so I forgive my trespassers, and I've come to make friends."

"You've said that before."

"I've always meant it. Must I hold out my arm any longer?"

"No." She was too tempting for his strength. He took her by the shoulders, looked greedily at her, saw the shrinking he had longed for and pressed his mouth on hers. She gave a cry that made a bird start from the heather, but he held her to him and felt her struggling with a force that could not last, and in a minute she dropped against him as helplessly as if she had been broken.

He turned her over on his arm. "You little devil!" he said, and kissed her lips again.

Her face was white and still: she did not move and he could not guess that behind the brows gathered as if she were in pain, her mind ransacked her home for a weapon that might kill him, and saw the carving-knife worn to a slip of steel that would glide into a man's body without a sound. She meant to use it: she was kept quiet by that determination, by the intensity of her horror for caresses that, unlike those first ones in the larch-wood, marked her as a thing to be used and thrown away.

She knew his thoughts of her, but she had her own amid a delirium of hate, and when he released her, she was shaking from the effort of her control.

"Now I've done with you," he said, and she heard him laugh as he went away.

She longed to scream until the sky cracked with the noise, and she had no knowledge of her journey home. She found herself sitting at the dinner-table with Helen, and heard her ask, "Don't you feel well?"

"No. I'm—rather giddy."

She watched the knife as Helen carved, and the beauty of its slimness gave her joy; but suddenly the blade slipped, and she saw blood on Helen's hand and, rushing from the table to the garden, she stood there panting.

"It's nothing," Helen shouted through the window. "Just a scratch."

"Oh, blood! It's awful!" She leaned on the gate and sobbed feebly, expecting to be sick. She could not make anybody bleed: it was terrible to see red blood.

Trembling and holding to the banisters, she went upstairs and lay down on her bed, and presently, through her subsiding sobs, there came a trickle of laughter born of the elfish humour which would not be suppressed. She could not kill George, but she must pay him out, and she was laughing at herself because she had discovered his real offence. It was not his kisses, not even his disdain of what he took, though that enraged her: it was his words as he cast her off and left her. She sat up on the bed, clenching her small hands. How dared he? How dared he? She could not ignore those words and she would let him know that he had been her plaything all the time.

"All the time, George, my dear," she muttered, nodding her black head. "I'll just write you a little letter, telling you!"

Kneeling before the table by her window, she wrote her foolish message and slipped it inside her dress: then, with a satisfaction which brought peace, she lay down again and slept.

She waked to find Helen at her bedside, a cup of tea in her hand.

"Oh—I've been to sleep?"

"Yes. It's four o'clock. Are you better?"

"Yes."

"Lily is here. John's gone to town. It's market-day."

"Market-day!" She laughed. "George will get drunk. Perhaps he'll fall off his horse and be killed. But I'd rather he was killed tomorrow. Perhaps a wild bull will gore him—right horn, left horn, right horn—Oh, my head aches!"

"Don't waggle it about."

"I was just showing you what the bull would do to George."

"Leave the poor man alone."

But that was what Miriam could not do, and she waited eagerly for the dark.

The new green of the larches was absorbed into the blackness of night when she went through them silently. She had no fear of meeting George, but she must wait an opportunity of stealing across the courtyard and throwing the letter through the open door, so she paused cautiously at the edge of the wood and saw the parlour lights turning the cobbles of the yard to lumps of gold. There was no sign of Mrs. Biggs, but about the place there was a vague stir made up of the small movements and breathings of the horses in the stable, the hens shut up for the night, the cows in their distant byres. Branches of trees fretted against each other and the stream sang, out of sight.

The parlour light burned steadily, no figure came into view, and, lifting her feet from her slippers, Miriam went silently towards the door.

She had thrown in the letter and was turning back, when she heard nailed boots on the stones, a voice singing, a little thickly, in an undertone. She caught her breath and ran, but as she fumbled for her slippers in the dark, she knew she was discovered. He had uttered a loud, "Ha!" of triumph, his feet were after her, and she squealed like a hunted rabbit when he pounced on her.

It was very dark within the wood. His face was no more than a blur, and her unseen beauty was powerless to help her. She was desperate, and she laughed.

"George, you'll spoil my little joke. I've left a letter for you. It's a shame to spoil it, Georgie, Porgie."

His grasp was hurting her. "Where is the letter?" he asked in a curious, restrained voice.

"In the doorway. Let me go, George. I'll see you tomorrow. George—please!"

"No," he said thoughtfully, carefully, "I don't think I shall let you go. Come with me—come with me, pretty one, and we'll read your love-letter together."

CHAPTER XXIV

While these things happened at Halkett's Farm, Helen sat sewing in the schoolroom. Mildred Caniper had been in bed all day, as often happened now, and there Miriam was supposed to be, on account of that strange giddiness of hers.

Helen worked at the fashioning of a dress in which Zebedee should think her fair and the lamplight shone on the pale grey stuff strewing the table and brought sparks from the diamonds on her hand: the clipping of the scissors made a cheerful sound, and Jim, as he sat before the fire, looked up at her sometimes with wise and friendly eyes.

It was late when she began to be oppressed by the quiet of the house. It was as though some one had just stopped whispering and would begin again. She felt that she was watched by the unseen, and the loudness of her own movements shocked her, but she worked on, using the scissors stealthily and starting if a coal fell in the grate.

Surely there was some one standing outside the door? She changed her seat to face it. Surely eyes were peering through the window? She rose and drew the curtains with a suddenness that made Jim growl.

"Be quiet, dog!" She stood and listened. The night held its breath, the stored impressions of the old house took shape and drew close and, though they did not speak, their silent pressure was full of urging, ominous and discreet.

She folded her work and put out the light, told Jim to follow her up the stairs, and trod them quietly. It was comforting to see the Pinderwells on the landing, but she had no time for speech with them. She was wondering if death had come and filled the house with this sense of presences, but when she bent over

Mildred Caniper's bed she found her sleeping steadily.

On the landing, she let out a long breath. "Oh, Jane, I'm thankful."

She went into Miriam's room and saw that the bed was empty and the window wide. She looked out, and there was a chair on the scullery roof and, as she leant, trembling, against the sill, she heard the note of the hall clock striking eleven. That was a late hour for the people of the moor, and she must hasten. She was sure that the house had warned her, and, gathering her wits, she posted Jim at the bottom of the stairs and ran out, calling as she ran. She had no answer. The lights of Brent Farm were all out and she went in a dark, immobile world. There was no wind to stir the branches of the thorn-bushes, the heather did not move unless she pressed it, and her voice floated to the sky where there were no stars. Then the heavier shade of the larches closed on her, and when she left them and fronted Halkett's Farm, there was one square of light, high up, at the further end, to splash a drop of gold into the hollow.

Towards that light Helen moved as through thick black water. She carried her slippers in her hand and felt her feet moulded to the cobbles as she crossed the yard and stood below the open window. She listened there, and for a little while she thought her fears were foolish: she heard no more than slight human stirrings and the sound of liquid falling into a glass. Then there came Miriam's voice, loud and high, cutting the stillness.

"I'll never promise!"

There was another silence that held hours in its black hands.

"No? Well, I don't know that I care. But you're not going home. When the morning comes perhaps it'll be you begging me for a promise! Think it over. No hurry. There's all night." George was speaking slowly, saying each word as if he loved it. "And you're going to sit on my knee, now, and read this letter to me. Come."

Helen heard no more. She rushed to the front door and found it locked, and wasted precious seconds in shaking it before she abandoned caution and rushed noisily round the house where the kitchen door luckily yielded to her hand. Through a narrow passage and up narrow stairs she blundered, involved in ignorance and darkness, until a streak of light ran across her path and she almost fell into a room where Miriam stood with her back against the wall. She had the look of one who has been tortured without uttering a sound and, in the strain of her dark head against the flowered wall, there was a determination not to plead.

Her face crumpled like paper at the sight of Helen.

"Oh," she said, smiling foolishly, "what—a good thing—you came."

She slipped as a picture falls, close to the wall, and there was hardly a thud as her body met the floor.

Helen did not stir: she looked at Miriam and at Halkett, who was sitting on the bed, and on him her gaze rested. His answered it, and while, for a moment, she saw the man beyond the beast, his life was enlightened by what was rare in her, and his mind, softened by passion to the consistency of clay, was stamped with the picture of her as she stood and looked at him. Vaguely, with uneasiness and dislike, he understood her value; it was something remote as heaven and less desired, yet it strengthened his sensual scorn of Miriam, and rising, he went and made a hateful gesture over her. Some exclamation came from him, and he stooped to pick her up and slake his thirst for kisses. He wanted to beat her about the face before he cast her out.

"Don't touch her!" Helen said in tones so quiet that he hesitated. "She has only fainted."

He laughed at that. "Don't think I'm worrying, but she's mine, and I'll do what I like with her."

He drew up her limp body and held it until it seemed to be merged into his own, and though his mouth was close on hers, he did not kiss it. His lips moved fast, but no words came, and he lowered her slowly and shakily to the floor. He turned to Helen, and she saw that all the colour had left his face.

"Go out!" he said, and pointed.

The clasp of her hands tightened, and while she looked up at him, she prayed vehemently. "O God, God," she thought, "let me save her. O God, what shall I do? O God, God, God!"

"Go out," he said. "I'm going to keep her here till she'll be glad to be my wife, and then it'll be my turn to laugh. She can go home in the morning."

"I want to sit down," Helen said.

She looked for a chair and sat on it, and he dropped to the bed, which gave out a loud groaning sound. He hid his face in his hands and rocked himself to and fro.

"She's tortured me," he muttered, and glared angrily at Helen.

She rose and went to him, saying, "Yes, but she's only a little girl. You must remember that. And you're a man."

"Yes, by God!" he swore.

He raised both hands. "Get out of this!" he shouted. "She shall stay here tonight." The hands went to Helen's shoulders and forced her to her knees. "D'ye hear? I tell you she's made me mad!"

Helen was more pitiful than afraid. She hardly knew what she did, but she thought God was in the room.

"George, I'll do anything in the world for you if you'll give her up. Anything. You couldn't be so wicked. George, be quick. Before she wakes. Shan't we carry her out now? Shan't we?" She forgot his manhood, and saw him only as a big animal that might spring and must be soothed. "Let us do that before she knows. George—"

He looked half stupefied as he said childishly, "But I swore I'd have her, and I want her."

"But you don't love her. No, no, you don't." She laid a hand on his knee. "Why, you've known us all our lives."

"Ah!" He sprang up and past her and the spell of the soft hands and voice was broken. He sneered at her. "You thought you'd done it that time!"

"Yes," she said sadly, and put herself between him and Miriam. With her chin on her clasped hands, and her steady eyes, she seemed to be the thing he had always wanted, for the lack of which he had suffered, been tormented.

"George," she said, "I'll give you everything I have—"

He caught his breath. "Yourself?" he asked on an inspiration that held him astonished, eager and translated.

She looked up as if she had been blinded, then stiffly she moved her head. "What do you mean?"

"Give me yourself. Oh, I've been mad tonight—for days—she made me." He pointed to the limp and gracious figure on the floor and leaned against the bed-rail. "Mad! And you, all the time, out there on the moor against the sky. Helen, promise!"

Her voice had no expression when she said, "I promised anything you asked for. Bring some water."

But he still stood, dazed and trembling.

"Bring some water," she said again.

He spilt it as he carried it. "Why didn't I see before? I did see before. On the moor, I watched for you You're beautiful." His voice sank. "You're good."

She was not listening to him. She dabbled water on Miriam's brow and lips and chafed her hands, but still she lay as if she were glad to sleep.

"Poor little thing!" Helen said deeply and half turned her head. "Some of your brandy," she commanded. "She is so cold."

"I'll take her to the kitchen."

"Is that woman in the house?" she asked sharply.

"She's in bed, I suppose."

"She must have heard—she must have known—and she didn't help!"

He put a hand to his forehead. "No, she didn't help. I'd meant to give her up, and then—I found her here, and I'd been drinking."

"Don't tell me! Don't tell me!" She twisted her hands together. "George, don't make me hate you."

"No," he said with a strange meekness. "Shall I take her to the kitchen? It'll be warm there, and the fire won't be out. I'll carry her."

"But I don't like you to touch her," Helen stated with a simplicity that had its fierceness.

"It's just as if she's dead," he said in a low voice, and at Helen's frightened gasp, he added—"I mean for me."

"Take her," she said, and when he had obeyed she sat on her heels and stared at nothing. For her, a mist was in the room, but through it there loomed the horrid familiarity of Halkett's bed, his washstand and a row of boots. Why was she here? What had she done? She heard him asking gently, "Aren't you coming?" and she remembered. She had promised to marry George because Miriam had been lying on the floor, because, years ago, the woman lying alone in Pinderwell House had brought the Canipers to the moor where George lived and was brutal and was going to marry her. But it could not be true, for, in some golden past, before this ugliness fell between her and beauty, she had promised to marry Zebedee. She held her head to think. No, of course she had given him no promise. They had come together like birds, like bees to flowers—

"Aren't you coming?" Halkett asked again.

She rose. Yes, here was her promised man. She had bought Miriam with a price. She stumbled after him down the stairs.

In the warmth of the kitchen, by the light of a glowing fire and a single candle, Miriam's eyelids fluttered and lay back.

"It's all right, darling," Helen said. "You're quite safe. You're with Helen, with Helen, dear."

Behind Miriam's eyes, thoughts like butterflies with wet wings were struggling to be free.

"Something happened. It was George. Has he gone away?"

"He isn't going to hurt you. He wants to take you home."

"Don't let him. We'll go together, Helen. Soon. Not yet. Take care of me. Don't leave me." She started up. "Helen! I didn't say I'd marry him. I wouldn't. Helen, I know I didn't!"

"You didn't, you didn't. He knows. He frightened you because you teased him so. He just frightened you. He's here—not angry. Look!"

He nodded at her clumsily.

"You see?"

"Yes. I'm glad. I'm sorry, George."

"It doesn't matter," he said.

He looked at Helen and she looked full at him and she knew, when he turned to Miriam, that he still watched over herself. She could recognize the tenderness and wonder in his eyes, but she could not understand how they had found a place there, ousting greed and anger for her sake, how his molten senses had taken an imprint of her to instruct his mind.

"Can you come now?" she said.

"Yes." Miriam stood up and laughed unsteadily. "How queer I feel! George—"

"It's all right," he said. "I'll take you home."

"But we're not afraid," Helen said. "There's nothing to be afraid of on the moor." All possibility of fear had gone: her dread had been for some uncertain thing that was to come, and now she knew the evil and found in it something almost as still as rest.

In the passage, he separated her from Miriam. "I want to speak to you."

"Yes. Be careful."

"Tonight. In your garden. I'll wait there. Come to me. Promise that, too."

"Oh, yes, yes," she said. "That, too."

He watched them go across the yard, their heads bent towards each other, and Helen's pale arm like a streak on Miriam's dress. He heard their footsteps and the shifting of a horse in the stables, and a mingled smell of manure and early flowers crept up to him. The slim figures were now hardly separable from the wood, and they were frail and young and touching. He looked at them, and he was sorry for all the unworthy things he had ever done. It was Helen who made him feel like that, Helen who shone like a star, very far off, but not quite out of reach. She was the only star that night. Not one showed its face among the clouds, and there was no moon to wrinkle her droll features at the little men on earth. Helen was the star, shining in the larch-wood. He called her name, but she did not hear, and he seemed to be caught up by the sound and to float among the clouds.

"It's like being converted," he told himself, and he followed slowly across the moor.

CHAPTER XXV

As the girls passed under the trees, Miriam began to cry.

"Helen, if you hadn't come!"

"But I did."

"Yes, yes. To see you there! It was—oh! And then I fainted. What did you do to him?"

"We needn't talk about it. And don't cry." She was afraid of having to hate this daring, helpless being who clung to her; yet she could hate no one who needed her, and she said tenderly, "Don't cry. It's over now."

"Yes. I've lost my handkerchief."

"Here's mine."

"You're not angry with me, are you? How did you know I'd gone?"

"I think the house told me. Oh, here's the moor. How good to get to it out of that pit. Come quickly. Notya—"

"I can't come faster. Tell me what you said to him. Nothing I said was any good."

"I managed him."

"And I couldn't. Suppose he catches me again."

"He won't. Can't you understand that he may not want you any more? Let us get home."

"I'm doing my best. I wish I were a man. A woman can't have fun."

"Fun!"

"Oh, you're so good! I meant it for fun, and now he'll come after me again. Of course he wants me. He's in love with me."

"There's love and love," Helen said.

"And if you subtract one from the other—I don't know what I'm saying—there may be nothing left. If George does that little sum in the morning—"

"I think it's done already."

"I hope so. I'm miserable. I wish the sea would come up and wash me and make me forget. You're not holding me so lovingly as you did. In the kitchen you were sweet."

"Is that better? I think the moor is like the sea. It's a great, clean bath to plunge into. And here's the garden. That's another bath, a little one, so dark and cold and peaceful. And the poplars. Soon there will be leaves on them." She stopped with a thin cry. "What has happened? I left the house in darkness, and look now!" Every window gave out light that fell in differing patterns on the grass. "Oh! what is it?" For an instant she thought the whole night's work must be some evil fancy, this brilliance as well as the sordid horror at the farm, and then, as Miriam cried, "Is it the house on fire?" the other rushed across the lawn, leaping the golden patches as though, indeed, they might have burned her.

Miriam tried to follow, but, weakness overcoming her, she sat down on the lawn. Half drowsily, she was interested in the windows, for their brightness promised gaiety within the house and she bent her ear expectantly for music. There ought to have been music, sweet and tinkling, and people dancing delicately, but the lights were not darkened by moving figures, and the only sound was Helen's voice anxiously calling her in.

Miriam was indifferent to the anxiety, and she did not want to rise: she was comfortable on the soft, damp earth, and the night had been so long that the morning must be near. If she stayed there, she would be spared the trouble of going to bed and getting up again, and when Helen called once more, she heard the voice as from a great way off, and answered sleepily, "Yes, I'm coming," but the next minute she was annoyed to find Helen standing over her.

"Why didn't you come in? It's Notya. She has put lights in every room. She was afraid of the dark, she says. She couldn't find us. She has been talking—oh, talking. Come and let her see you."

"I wish things wouldn't go round and round."

"You must go to bed, but first you must let her see you. She thinks you are not coming back."

"And I nearly didn't. I won't see her if she's ill."

"You must. She isn't—green, or anything."

"I'm ill, too. I'm giddy."

"Oh, can't you do this to help me? Haven't I helped you?"

"Oh, yes, you have! I'll come, but help me up." Her laughter bubbled out. "I'm afraid you're having rather a busy night!"

Mildred Caniper was sitting on the edge of the bed. Swinging a foot, and with her curly hair hanging to her shoulders, she had a very youthful look.

"So she has come back," she said. Her voice was small and secret. "I thought she wouldn't. She is like Edith. Edith went. And I was glad. Yes, for a little while." Her tones grew mournful and she looked at the floor. "But it hasn't been a happy thing for me. No. I have been very unhappy."

Miriam stood at the door and, holding on to it, she stared with fear and fascination at the strange woman on the bed, and from her throat there came a tiny sound, like the beating of a little animal's heart. "Oh, oh, oh! Oh, oh, oh!"

Helen was murmuring to her stepmother: "Yes, dear, yes. Get into bed. It's late, and we are all going to bed. You are getting cold, you know. Let me lift your feet up. There! That's better."

"Yes." Mildred lay passive. She seemed to think and, in the pause, Miriam's ejaculations changed to sighs that ceased as Mildred said in the sharp tones they welcomed now, "What are you both doing here? Go to bed. Helen, don't fuss. And let us have no more of this wandering about at night."

They left the room like threatened children, and on the landing they took each other's hands.

"Is she mad?" Miriam whispered. "Are we all mad? What's happening to us all?"

"I think she was just—dazed. Come to bed. I'll help you to undress."

"Once before you did. That night it rained—"

"Yes. Don't talk."

"But if she goes out of her mind, will it be my fault? Because of not finding us, and the house all dark? Will that be my fault, too?"

Helen was busy with strings and buttons. "How can we tell who does things?"

"She was talking about Mother. I wish I had a real, comfortable mother now. It was horrible, but I wanted to hear more. I did, Helen. Didn't you?"

"No. I don't like seeing souls if there are spots on them. Shall I put out the light?"

"Yes. Now the darkness is going round. It will whirl me to sleep. I want to go away. Do you think Uncle Alfred—? I'm frightened of this house. And there's George. I think I'd better go away in case he comes after me again."

A whistle like the awakening chirrup of a bird sounded from the garden, and Helen's voice quavered as she said, "We'll talk about it in the morning."

Quietly she shut the door and went downstairs. She had a lighted candle in one hand, and a great shadow moved beside her—went with her to the drawing-room, and stayed there while she wrote a letter to the accompaniment of George's persistent whistling. She hardly needed it, and it stopped abruptly as she passed through the long window to the garden.

Among the poplars she found him waiting and at once she was aware of some change in him. His head was thrust forward from his shoulders, and he searched greedily for her face.

"I thought you'd given me the slip," he muttered.

She frowned a little at his use of words, yet what had he to do with her? She looked up at the bare branches and thought of Zebedee and the masts of ships.

"This must be a secret," she said through stiffening lips. "Come further from the house." She led him to the garden door and opened it. "Out here," she whispered.

The moor was like a tired, simple man asleep, yet it still kept its quality of water, buoyant, moving and impetuous, and she felt that it had swung her here and there amid its waves for many hours, and now had left her on a little shore, battered and bereft, but safe.

"I can't stay," she said softly.

"I thought you wouldn't come," he answered. He did not understand her: she gave no sign of pleading or withdrawal: he was sure she had no fear, and another certainty was born in him.

"I can trust you," he said with a sigh of peace.

"Yes."

"I thought you wouldn't come," he said again.

"But I'm here, you see."

His voice rose. "I'd have got in."

"It would have been quite easy."

"Weren't you afraid?" he asked, and he found a memory of Miriam in her laughter. "No, I wasn't afraid."

"But you're going to marry me."

"That was the bargain."

Her passivity angered him. This dignity of submission put him in the wrong. She seemed to be waiting patiently and without anxiety for her release. Why should he give it? How could he give it? Would he deny God in God's own presence?

He turned to look at her, and as they stood side by side, a foot of earth between them, he could almost hear her breathing. Her smoothly-banded hair and the clear line of brow and nose and chin mocked him with their calm. He spoke loudly, but his voice dropped as the star to which he likened her might shoot across the heavens and disappear.

"You make me think—of stars," he said.

Again she looked upward, and her tilted face was like a waning moon. "There are no stars tonight. I must go in."

"But—tomorrow?" he said.

"Tomorrow?"

"I shall see you tomorrow?"

The repetition of the word gave her its meaning. She took the letter from her belt and held it out to him.

"No, no," he said.

"Won't you have it posted for me?"

"I—I thought it was for me," he stammered. "Yes, I'll have it posted."

"Will it go early?" she asked earnestly.

"I'll take it down tonight."

"Oh, there's no need of that."

"I'd like to do it," and touching his forehead with a childish gesture, he added, "I couldn't sleep."

"It's morning already," Helen said.

He looked eastward. "Hours of darkness yet."

"And you'll go down the road and back, before it's light. You needn't, George."

"I want to think of you," he answered simply, turning the letter in his hands.

She moved to the door and stood against it. "George—" she said. She had an impulse to tell him that his bargain was useless to him because she was a woman no longer. She had been changed from living flesh and blood to something more impalpable than air. She had promised to marry him, and she remained indifferent because, being no woman, she could not suffer a woman's pain; because, by her metamorphosis, there was no fear of that promise's fulfilment. It seemed only fair to tell him, but when he came to her, she shook her head.

"It was nothing," she murmured. Bulky of body, virile of sense, he was immature in mind, and she knew he would not understand.

"I must go now. Good-night."

"Don't go," he muttered.

She stood still, waiting for the words that laboured in him.

"I was mad," he said at last. "She makes me feel like that. You—you're different."

He wanted help from her, but she gave him none, and again

there was a silence in which Jim came through the door and put his head into Helen's hand.

"Jim!" she said, "Jim!" Her thoughts went across a continent to blue water.

"I'd begun to love her," he explained, and moved from one foot to the other.

"George, I must go in."

"But I don't love her now," he added fiercely, with pride, almost with reassurance.

She would have laughed if she had heard him, but her numbness had passed by and all her powers were given to resisting the conviction that she was indeed Helen Caniper, born, to die, a woman; that Zebedee was on the sea, and had not ceased to love her, that she would have a tale to tell him on his return, and a dishonoured body to elude his arms, but she could not resist the knowledge, and under its gathering strength she cried out in a fury of pain that drove Halkett back a step.

"What is it?" he asked.

She did not answer. Her rage and misery left her weak and hopeless and though for a bright, flaming instant she had loathed him, she was now careless of him and of herself because nothing mattered any more.

She drooped against the door, and he approached her nervously, saying as he went, "You're tired. You ought to go to bed. I'll take you to the house."

That roused her and she looked at him. "No. Some one might hear."

"I can tread softly."

"Very well." She halted him among the poplars. "No further."

"I'll come tomorrow," he whispered.

"No, not tomorrow. Not until I tell you. I don't want any one to know. Don't come tomorrow."

"Then come to me," he said. "I wish you'd come to me. I'd like to see you coming through our wood and across the cobbles. And in the morning, the sun's on that side of the house. Helen," he pleaded, "will you come?" It was Miriam who had come before, a dark sprite, making and loving mischief, lowering him in his own regard until he had a longing to touch bottom and make her touch it, too; but if Helen came in her grey frock, slipping among the trees like silver light, he knew she would bring healing to his home and to his heart.

"Will you?" he begged. "Will you, Miss Helen? D'you remember how I used to call you that? Will you?"

"I don't know."

"But I want you so," he said; and when he would have touched her he found her gone.

CHAPTER XXVI

Her bargain had been made and must be kept and Zebedee would understand. He would not be angry with her: he had only been angry with her once, and he had always understood. He would feel her agony in that room at Halkett's Farm, with Miriam, white and stricken, on the floor, and George Halkett, hot and maddened, on the bed, and he would know that hers had been the only way.

These were her thoughts as she went about the house, hasping windows and bolting doors, with a dreary sense of the futility of caution.

"For you see, Jim, the horse is stolen already," she said.

She did not forget to bid Jane good-night; she undressed and laid her clothes neatly in their place, and without difficulty she dropped into a sleep as deep as her own trouble.

She had the virtues of her defects, a stoicism to match her resolutions, and she was angered when she rose and saw the reflection of eyes that had looked on sorrow. She shook her head at the person in the glass and, leaning from the window and finding the garden no less lovely for the traffic of the night, she was enspirited by that example, and ran downstairs to open the front door and let in the morning. Then she turned to face the business of another day.

She was amazed to find her stepmother in the kitchen, making pastry by the window, to see the fire burning heartily and the breakfast-things ready on a tray.

"What are you doing?" she demanded from the doorway.

Mildred Caniper looked round. Her eyes were very bright and Helen waited in dread of the garrulousness of last night, but Mildred spoke with the old incisive tongue, though it moved slowly.

"You can see what I am doing."

"But you ought not to do it."

"I refuse to be an invalid any longer."

"And all yesterday you were in bed."

"Yesterday is not today, and you may consider yourself second in command again. It is time I was about the house when you and Miriam choose to spend half the night on the moor. I was left in bed with a house unlocked."

"But Jim was there."

"Jim! Although Dr. Mackenzie gave you the dog, Helen, I have not all that faith in his invincibility."

Helen smiled her appreciation of that sentence, though she did not like her stepmother's looks.

"I would rather trust Jim's teeth than our bolts and locks, and I told him to take care of you."

"That was thoughtful of you!" Mildred said. She rolled her pastry, but it did not please her, and she squeezed the dough into a ball as she turned with unusual haste to Helen.

"You must not wander about at night alone."

"But on the moor—!" Helen protested.

"It's Miriam—Miriam—" the word came vaguely. "You must look after her."

"I do try," Helen said, and hearing the strangeness of her own voice she coughed and choked to cover it.

"What does that mean?"

"What?" Helen's hand was at her throat.

"You are trying to deceive me. Something has happened. Tell me at once!"

"I swallowed the wrong way," Helen said. "It's hurting still."

"I do not believe you."

"Oh, but, Notya, you must. You know I don't tell lies. Why should you be so much afraid for Miriam?"

"Because—Did I say anything? My head aches a little. In fact, I don't feel well." The rolling-pin fell noisily to the floor.

"Tiresome!" she said, and sank into a chair.

When Helen returned with the medicine which Zebedee had left for such emergencies, she found her stepmother beside the rolling-pin. Her mouth was open and a little twisted, and she was heavy and unwieldy when Helen raised her body and made it lean against the wall.

"But she won't stay there," Helen murmured, looking at her. She was like a great doll with a distorted face, and while Helen watched her she slipped to the floor with the obstinacy of the inanimate.

Some one would have to go to Halkett's Farm. Helen stared at the rolling-pin and she thought her whole life had passed in tending Mildred Caniper and sending some one to Halkett's Farm. Yesterday she had done it, and the day before; today and tomorrow and all the days to come she would find her stepmother with this open, twisted mouth.

She forced her way out of this maze of thought and rushed out to see if George, by chance, were already on the moor, but he was not in sight, and she ran back again, through the kitchen, with a shirked glance for Mildred Caniper, and up the stairs to Miriam.

"I can't go!" Miriam cried. "I'll go for John, but I daren't go to Halkett's."

"John and Lily went with the milk this morning. You'll have to go for George. Be quick! She's lying there—"

"Nothing will make me go! How can you ask it?"

Helen longed to strike her. "Then I shall go, and you must stay with Notya," she said and, half-dressed, Miriam was hurried down the stairs. "And if you dare to leave her—!"

"I won't leave her," Miriam moaned, and sat with averted face.

Thus it was that George Halkett had his wish as the sun cleared blue mist from the larches, but Helen did not come stealing, shy and virginal, as he had pictured her; she bounded towards him like a hunted thing and stood and panted, struggling for her words.

He steadied himself against attack. No persuasion and no

abuse would make him let her go. The road he had trodden in the night knew his great need of her and now she caught his senses, for her eyes had darkened, colour was in her cheeks, and she glowed as woman where she had shone as saint.

She did not see his offered hands. "It's Notya, again, George, please." She had a glimpse of Mrs. Biggs peering between window curtains, and her tongue tripped over the next words. "S-so will you—can you be very quick?"

"The doctor?"

"Yes. Dr. Mackenzie is away, but there's another there, and he must come."

He nodded, and he did not see her go, for he was in the stable harnessing the horse and shouting to a man to get the cart.

"You've got to drive to town like hell, William, and the sooner you bring the doctor the better for you."

"I'll have to change my clothes."

"You'll go as you are, God damn you, and you'll go now."

He waited until the cart was bowling towards the road before he followed Helen so swiftly that he saw her dress whisk through the garden door. He used no ceremony and he found her in the kitchen, where Miriam was sitting stiffly on a chair, her feet on one of its rungs, her neck and shoulders cream-coloured above the whiteness of her under-linen. He hardly looked at her and he did not know whether she went or stayed. He spoke to Helen:

"Do you want me to carry her upstairs? William's gone to town. I've come to help you."

"Then you've spoilt the game, George. It's always you who go to town and bring the doctor. Never mind. Yes. Carry her up. Don't step on the rolling-pin." She looked at it again. "She's not dead, is she?"

"No."

"What is it, then?"

He stooped to lift the heavy burden, and she heard him say a word mumblingly, as though ashamed of it.

She moved about the room, crying, "A stroke! It's ugly. It's horrid. A stroke! Why can't they say a blow?"

He could not bear the bitterness of her distress. "Don't, don't, my dear," he said, and startled her into quiet.

* * * * *

The doctor came and went, promising to return, and a nurse with large crowded teeth assumed control over the sick-room. There was little to be done; she sat on a chair by the window and, because of those excessive teeth, she seemed to smile continually at Mildred Caniper's mockery of death.

Outside, a cold rain was falling: it splashed on the laurel leaves by the gate and threw a shifting curtain across the moor. The fire in the room made small noises, as though it tried to talk; the nurse bent over her patient now and then, but Mildred Caniper did not move.

Downstairs, in the kitchen, Miriam sat on her feet in the big armchair: she was almost motionless, like one who has been startled into a posture and dare not move lest her fear should take shape. The rain darkened the room and filled it with a sound of hissing; a kettle whistled on the fire, and there was a smell of airing linen.

Helen turned a sheet. "The nurse must have Christopher's bed," she said at last. "We must carry it in."

"Who?"

"You and I."

"I can't! I can't go in. I should—I should be sick! I can't. Helen, after last night—"

"Very well. Can you manage to go to Brent Farm and tell John? They ought to be at home now."

"But there's George."

"He won't hurt you."

"He'd speak to me if he saw me."

"No. He took no notice of you this morning."

"That was because I wasn't dressed."

Helen laughed rather weakly and for a long time.

"You're not really laughing!" Miriam cried. "This house is horrible. You making that noise, and Notya upstairs, and that hideous nurse grinning, and George prowling about outside. I can't stay here."

"Go to Brent Farm, then. You can tell John and stay there. Lily won't mind."

"Shall I? John would be angry."

Helen made no reply as she moved quietly and efficiently about the kitchen, preparing food, setting things on a tray, turning the linen, working quickly but with no sign of haste. The rain splattered on the gravel path outside and clicked sharply into some vessel which stood by the scullery door.

A voice came unhappily from the pale face blotted against the chair.

"Helen, what are you going to do about me?"

She turned in astonishment and stared at Miriam.

"You said we were to talk about it."

"I know." What held her silent was the realization that while she felt herself helpless, under the control of some omnipotent will, here was one who cried out to her as arbiter. It was strange and she wanted to laugh again but, refusing that easy comment, she came upon a thought which terrified and comforted her together. She was responsible for what she had done; Zebedee would know that, and he would have the right, if he had the heart, to blame her. A faint sound was caught in her throat and driven back. She had to be prepared for blame and for the anger which so endeared him, but the belief that she was not the plaything of malevolence gave her the dignity of courage.

"Helen," said the voice again.

"Yes. I wrote to Uncle Alfred yesterday—this morning. I shouldn't think he could be here tomorrow, but the next day, if he comes—"

But blame or anger, how small they were in the face of this common gash—this hurt! She shut a door in her brain, the one which led into that chamber where all lovely things bloomed among the horrors. And Zebedee, as she had always told him, was just herself: they shared.

"Oh, you've done that? How wonderful! But—it's like running away."

"I don't want you here."

There was an exclamation and a protest.

"Only because I couldn't be happy about you."

"Because of George? No, I don't see how I can stay here, but there's Notya."

"You're no use, you see."

"Oh—"

"If you can't even carry in that bed."

"I'll try to go in," she said, in a muffled voice.

"I can ask the nurse. I don't want you to stay, but try," she went on dispassionately, "try not to be silly any more. I shan't always be there to—save you."

"It was very dramatic."

"Yes; just like a story, wasn't it?"

"Don't be so unpleasant. I still feel ill. It was horrid to faint. I can't make out why Mrs. Biggs didn't stop you."

"Do you want to talk about it?"

"N-no—"

"Neither do I."

"But I can't make out—"

"Never mind. What does it matter? It's over. For you it's over. But don't play with people's lives any more, and ruin them."

There was a pause, in which the room grew darker.

"Do you think," Miriam asked in an awed voice, "he minds so much?"

Helen moved the little clothes-horse and knelt before the fire and its heat burnt her face while her body shivered under a sudden cold. She thought of George, but not as an actor in last night's scenes; her memory swung back, as his had often done, to the autumn night when they sat together in the heather, and his figure and hers became huge with portent. She had thought he was the tinker, and so, indeed, he was, and he no doubt had mistaken her for Miriam, as latterly he had mistaken his own needs. No, she was not altogether responsible. And why had Rupert told her that tale? And why, if she must have a tinker, could she not desire him as Eliza had desired hers?

"Oh, no, no!" she said aloud and very quickly, and she folded her arms across her breast and held her shoulders, shrinking.

"I don't think so either," Miriam said.

CHAPTER XXVII

Uncle Alfred in a trap and Rupert on foot arrived at the same moment on Saturday, and while Rupert asked quick questions about Mildred Caniper, the other listened in alarm.

He was astonished to feel Helen's light touch leading him to the corner where the hats were hanging, to hear her low voice in his ear.

"Pretend that's why you've come!"

He whispered back, "Where is she?"

"In bed."

"Miriam?"

"No, no. Dressing up for you!"

"Ah," he said, relieved, but he felt he was plunged into melodrama. Nothing else could be expected of a family which had exiled itself mysteriously in such a wilderness, but he felt himself uncomfortably out of place and he straightened his tie and gave his coat a correcting pull before he went into the schoolroom, where John and Lily were sitting by the fire.

"We're all waiting for the doctor," Helen explained.

"Ah!" Uncle Alfred said again, on a different note. He clasped his hands behind his back and nodded, and in spite of this inadequate contribution he conveyed an impression of stiff sympathy, and gave the youthful gathering the reassurance of his age as they made a place for him by the fire.

"I'm jolly glad you're here," Rupert said cordially, and Uncle Alfred, not used to a conspirator's part, stole a glance at Helen. She was standing near him; her stillness was broken by constant tiny movements, like ripples on a lake; she looked from one face to another as though she anticipated and watched the thoughts behind, and was prepared to combat them.

"I wish you'd sit down," Lily said, as Helen went to the window and looked out.

"Yes, sit down, sit down," said Uncle Alfred, and he stood up, pointing to his chair.

"No; I'm listening, thank you," Helen said.

The nurse's heavy tramp thudded across the room above, and her steps had something in them of finality, of the closing of doors, the shutting down of lids, the impenetrability of earth.

Sitting next to John, with her arm in his, Lily moved a little. Her eyes were full of pity, not so much for the woman upstairs, or for the Canipers, as because the emotions of these people were not the heartily unmixed ones which she had suffered when her own mother died.

"He's a long time," Helen said. She went into the hall and passed Miriam, in a black dress, with her hair piled high and a flush of colour on her cheeks.

"He's in there," Helen said with a wave of her hand, and speaking this time of Uncle Alfred.

The front door stood open, and she passed through it, but she did not go beyond the gate. The moor was changelessly her friend, yet George was on it, and perhaps he, too, called it by that name. She was jealous that he should, and she did not like to think that the earth under her feet stretched to the earth under his, that the same sky covered them, that they were fed by the same air; yet this was not on account of any enmity, but because the immaterial distance between them was so great that a material union mocked it.

Evening was slipping into night: there was no more rain, but the ground smelt richly damp, and seemed to heave a little with life eager to be free; a cloud, paler than the night, dipped upon the moor above Brent Farm and rose again, like the sail of a ship seen on a dark sea. Then a light moving on the road caught back Helen's thoughts and she went into the house.

"He's coming," she said listlessly, careless of the use of pronouns. There was a pronoun on a ship, one on the moor, another driving up the road, and each had an importance and a supremacy that derided a mere name.

She shut the schoolroom door and waited in the hall, but half an hour later, she opened the door again.

"It's good news," she said breathlessly. "Do you want to speak to him, Rupert? She's going to live!"

She could not see her own happiness reflected.

"Like that?" John asked roughly.

"No, better, better. Always in bed, perhaps, but able to speak and understand."

He lifted his big shoulders; Uncle Alfred flicked something from his knee and, in the silence, Helen felt forlorn; her brightness faded.

"And you'll be left here with her, alone!" Miriam wailed, at last.

"Alone?" asked John.

"Uncle Alfred's going to take me away," Miriam said, yet she was not sure of that, and she looked curiously at him.

"I want her to go," Helen said quickly.

John was still glowering at Miriam. "Take you away! You talk as if you were a parcel!"

"I knew you would be angry," she said. "You've always been hard on me, and you don't understand."

"Well, it's Helen's affair."

"You don't understand," Miriam said again. She sat close to Uncle Alfred, and he patted her.

"Helen knows best," Lily said cheerfully, for she suspected what she did not know. "And we'll look after her. Come along, John. It's time we all went to bed."

"He'll grumble all the way home," Miriam said with a pout.

Rupert was still talking to the doctor: they had found some subject to their taste, and their voices sounded loudly in the quiet house. Helen had gone out to speak to Zebedee's old horse.

"Now, tell me what's the matter," Uncle Alfred said.

"Didn't Helen tell you?"

"No."

"Well," she swayed towards him, "the fact is, I'm too fascinating, Uncle Alfred. It's only fair to warn you."

All the strain had left her face, and she was more beautiful than he had remembered, but he now looked at her with the practical as well as the romantic eye, for his middle-aged happiness was to depend largely on this capricious creature, and for an instant he wondered if he had not endangered it.

"Probably," he said aloud.

"Aren't you sure of it?"

"Er—I was thinking of something else."

"That," she said emphatically, "is what I don't allow."

He looked at her rather sternly, bending his head so that the eye behind the monocle was full on her. She would never be as charming as her mother, he reflected, and with a start, he straightened himself on the thought, for he seemed to hear that remark being uttered by dull old gentlemen at their clubs. It was a thing not to be said: it dated one unmistakably, though in this case it was true.

"We must have a talk."

"A serious one?"

"Yes."

She looked at him nervously, regardless of her effect. "Will you mind taking care of me?" she asked in a low voice.

"My dear child—no."

"What is it, then?"

"I am trying to frame a piece of good advice. Well—er—this is the kind of thing." He was swinging the eyeglass by its string. "Don't go out into the world thinking you can conquer it: go out meaning to learn."

"Oh," Miriam said drearily. This meant that he was not entirely pleased with her. She wondered which of them had changed during these months, and characteristically she decided that it was he.

"Are you certain you want me?" she asked sadly.

"Quite certain, but you're not going to object to criticism, are you?" he asked.

She shook her head.

"Well then—" he began and they both smiled, simultaneously reassured about each other.

"And will you take me with you when you go back? Perhaps on Monday?"

"If the mistress of the house approves." This was addressed to Helen, who had entered.

"On Monday, Helen, may I go?"

"Yes. But then we ought to have told the trap to come for you."

"There's always George," Miriam said with innocence.

"Yes, he's always there. That's quite true," Helen said, and she spoke hollowly, as though she were indeed the shell she felt herself to be.

"But," Miriam went on, "it would be unkind to ask him."

To Uncle Alfred's concern, Helen leaned towards her sister, and spoke rapidly, in a hard, angry voice.

"Stop saying things like that! They're not funny. They make you ridiculous. And they're cruel. You've no respect—no respect for people. And George is better than you. He's sorry. That's something—a great deal. I'm not going to have him laughed at."

"Now, now," Uncle Alfred said feebly, but Helen had stopped, amazed at herself and at the loyalty which George evoked already. She knew, unwillingly, that it was a loyalty of more than words, for in her heart she felt that, in truth, she could not have him mocked. She stared before her, realizing herself and looking into a future blocked by George's bulk. She could not remember what she had been saying to Miriam; she looked at her, huddled in her chair against the storm, and at Uncle Alfred, standing with his back to the fire, jauntily swinging his eyeglass to seem at ease.

"Was I rude?" she asked.

"No, just horrid."

She went from the room slowly, through the passage and the kitchen into the garden, and George's figure went before her.

She looked up at the poplars and saw that they would soon have their leaves to peep into the windows and whisper secrets of the Canipers.

"They knew," she said solemnly, "they always knew what was to happen."

Beyond the garden door she walked into a dark, damp world: mist was settling on the moor; drops spangled her dress and rested softly on her face and hands. She shut her eyes and seemed to be walking through emptiness, a place unencumbered by thoughts and people; yet she was not surprised when she was caught and held.

"Let go!" she said, without opening her eyes, and she was obeyed.

"I've been waiting for you," George said in a husky whisper.

"But I didn't say I would come."

She could hear him breathing close to her. "I can't see your eyes. You've got them shut. What's the matter? You're not crying?"

She opened them, and they were the colour of the night, grey and yet black, but they were not wet.

"I've been waiting for you," he said again, and once more she answered, "I didn't say I would come."

"I was coming to the door to ask about Mrs. Caniper," he went on, still speaking huskily and very low.

"Were you?"

"You wouldn't have liked that!"

"She is better." Emptiness was becoming peopled, and she remembered Mildred Caniper in bed, and the nurse smiling when she meant to be sympathetically sad, and Miriam, pitiful under scolding, but George was only the large figure that blocked the future: he was not real, though he talked and must be answered.

"I was coming to ask: do you hear?"

"You know now."

"But there's more. Who's the old chap who drove up tonight?

Your uncle, isn't it?"

Her mind, which had lain securely in her body out of reach of hurt, was slowly being drawn into full consciousness; but he had to repeat his words before she answered them, and then she spoke with a haughtiness to which Miriam had accustomed him.

"So you have been watching?"

"Why not?" he asked defiantly. "I've got to watch. Besides," he became clumsy, shy, and humble, "I was waiting to see you."

"I'm here."

"But you're—you're like a dead thing. That night, in my room, you were alive enough. You sat there, with your mouth open, a little—I could see your teeth, and your eyes—they shone."

His words were like touches, and they distressed her into movement, into a desire to run from him.

"I'm going in," she said.

"Not yet."

"I must."

He was hovering on the edge of sentences which had their risk: she could feel that he wished to claim her but dared not, lest she should refuse his claim. He found a miserable kind of safety in staying on the brink, yet he made one venture.

"There are things we've got to talk about."

"But not tonight."

"You'll say that every night."

"There's never really any need to talk about anything," she said.

He stammered, "But—you're going to marry me. I must make—make arrangements."

She had her first real scorn of him. He was afraid of her, and she despised him for it, yet she saw that she must keep him so. She could hardly bring herself to say, "Do what you like," but having said it, she could add, with vehemence, "Don't bother me! I'm busy."

"But—" he said, and looked down: and now she seemed to be caught in his shame, a partner, and she had to wait for what he tried to say.

He looked up, saying, "You promised."

"Oh, I know."

She did not go. Perhaps people lying side by side in their graves would talk to each other like this, in voices muffled by their coffins and inarticulate because of fleshless lips, with words that had no meaning now that life, which made them, was done. And again she felt that she and George were moles, burrowing in the earth, scratching, groping for something blindly.

She brought her hands together and shook them.

"If only one could see!" she said aloud.

"What is it?"

"I feel as if I'm in a dark room."

"It's a dark night," he said, and touched her wrist. "When shall I see you again? Tomorrow?"

"You can't see me now."

"I can. Your hair has drops on it, and your face—"

"No!" she cried. "Don't tell me. Don't come with me."

She ran from him at last, and he did not follow her. Like her, he was bewildered, but for him she was a light he could not put out: for her he was the symbol of that darkness which had fallen on life.

CHAPTER XXVIII

The next day had its own bewilderment and confusion, and Helen learnt that high tragedy is not blackest gloom but a thing patched and streaked with painful brightness, and she found herself capable of a gaiety which made Miriam doubly reproachful.

"You've never been like this before," she said, "and we might have had such fun. And you shouldn't be like it now, when I'm going away tomorrow." She sat in her empty box, with her legs dangling over the side. "I'm not sure that I shall go."

"You've only two pairs of stockings without holes in them," Helen said. She was kneeling before Miriam's chest of drawers.

"Doesn't matter. I shall have to buy heaps of things. D'you know, I'm afraid he's going to be strict."

"Poor little man!"

"And when one begins to think about it seriously, Helen, will one like it very much? Who's going to play with me? There'll be Uncle Alfred and a housekeeper woman. And do you know what he said?" She struggled from the box, shut down the lid and sat on it. "He said I must think I'm going into the world to learn. Learn!"

"I expect you'll want to. You won't like yourself so much when you meet other people."

"And shan't I hate my clothes! And I have visions, sister Helen, of four elderly gentlemen sitting round a whist-table, and me reading a book in a corner. So you see—no, I don't want to take that: give it to Samson—so you see, I'm a little damped. Well, if I don't like it, I shall come back. After all, there's Daniel."

"He's tired of you."

She showed her bright, sharp teeth, and said, "He'll recover after a rest. Oh, dear! I find I'm not so young and trustful as I was, and I'm expecting to be disappointed."

"The best thing," Helen said slowly, sitting down with a lapful of clothes, "is for the worst to happen. Then you needn't be troubled any more." She took a breath. "It's almost a relief."

"Oh, I don't feel so bad as that," Miriam explained, and Helen fell back laughing loudly.

"You've spilt all my clothes," Miriam said, and began to pick them up. "And don't make such a noise. Remember Notya!"

Helen was on her side, her head rested on her outstretched arm, and her face was puckered, her mouth widened with the noise she made.

"Oh," she said, "you always think of Notya at such funny times."

"Somebody has to," Miriam replied severely, and Helen laughed again, and beat her toes against the ground. Over her, Miriam stood, stern and disgusted, clasping linen to her breast.

"You're hysterical. Nurse will come in. In fact, I'll go and fetch her. She'll grin at you!"

"Is this hysterical? It's rather nice," Helen giggled. "Let me laugh while I can. There'll be no one to say such things when you are gone." She sat up with a start, and seemed to instruct herself. "You're going," she said, and faced the fact.

Miriam threw her bundle on the bed and stood irresolute. For once, the thoughts of the two had kinship, and they saw the days before them deprived of the companionship which had been, as it were, abortive, yet dear to both; necessary, it seemed now; but the future had new things in it for Miriam, and for Helen it had fear. Nevertheless, it was Miriam who cried through quivering lips, "Helen, I won't go!"

"You must," she said practically.

"Because of George?"

She nodded: it was indeed because of George, for how could she keep her promise with Miriam in the house?

"And, after all," Miriam said brightly, "there's Zebedee. I'm not leaving you quite alone. He'll be back soon. But—it's that I don't want to do without you. I can't think how to do it."

"I know," Helen said, and added, "but you'll find out."

"And John—"

"Never mind. John doesn't know about—things. Let's pack."

And while Mildred Caniper lay on one side of the landing where the Pinderwells were playing quietly, Helen and Miriam, on the other, laughed at the prospect before them and made foolish jokes as they filled the trunk.

It was harder, next day, than Helen had guessed to hold Miriam's hand in good-bye, to kiss her with a fragile, short-lived kiss, to watch her climb into the trap and to hear her box banged into its place by the driver's seat, with an emphatic noise that settled the question of her going.

It was a cold morning and the wind bustled as though it had an interest in this affair; it caught Miriam's skirt as she stood on the trap step, and lifted the veil floating from her hat, fluttered the horse's mane and disordered Helen's hair. It was like a great cold broom trying to sweep these aliens off the moor, and, for a moment, Helen had more pity for Miriam than for herself. Miriam was exiled, while she stayed at home.

She looked up at the house front and heard the laurels rattling, and round her she saw the moor spread clear-coloured under the east wind. Halkett's high wood stood up like ranks of giants set to guard her and, though she saw them now as George's men, she had no fear of them.

"Helen!" Miriam called to her.

She went forward and stood at the carriage door. "Yes?"

"Helen—we're going. Do you remember the first time we bathed in the sea? The wind was so cold, like this, before we went into the water. We nearly ran back. That's how I feel now."

"But we didn't go back."

"Oh! here's Uncle Alfred."

"And we learnt to swim."

"Yes. Good-bye. Kiss me again."

Helen stood quite still with her hands by her sides, while the carriage bumped over the track, stopped on the road that John and Lily might say their farewells, and slowly went on again until it was out of sight and she saw the road left empty. It looked callous, too, as though it did not care what came or went on it, and as she looked about her, Helen discovered that she was in a desert world, a wilderness of wind and dead, rustling heather and angry laurel leaves, of empty houses and women whose breath whistled through their distorted mouths. And the giants, standing so great and black against the sky, were less to guard her than to keep a friend from attempted rescue.

She raised her arms and opened her hands in a gesture of avowal. No one would ever rescue her, for, by her own act, she would be chained more firmly than Andromeda when Zebedee next came up the road.

"I must get it over," she whispered quickly, and she sat down where she had stood. She had to keep her promise, and now that there was no one in the way, the thing must be done before Zebedee could come and fight for her, lest people should be hurt and precious things broken: her word, and peace, and the beauty of the moor. Yet things were broken already: life limped; it would never go quite smoothly again.

She wondered what God was doing in His own place; it seemed that He had too much to do, or had He been careless at the beginning of things and let them get out of hand? She was sorry for Him. It must be dreary to look down on His work and see it going wrong. He was probably looking at her now and clicking His tongue in vexation. "There's Helen Caniper. She ought to have married the doctor. That's what I meant her to do. What's gone wrong? Miriam? I ought to have watched her. Dear, dear, dear! I oughtn't to have set them going at all if I couldn't keep them straight." So her thoughts ran as she sat with her head bowed to her knees, but she remembered how, in George's room that night, with Miriam on the floor, she had called to God without premeditation, with the naturalness of any cry for help, and in a fashion, He had heard her. No one had taught her to pray and until then she had called on no god but the one behind the smoke. Perhaps this other one had a power which she could not understand.

She looked up, and saw a sky miraculously arched and stretching beyond sight and imagination, and she thought, simply enough, that, having made the sky, God might be tired. And surely He had proved Himself: a being who had created this did not make small mistakes with men. It was some human creature who had failed, and though it seemed like Miriam, might it not be herself? Or Mildred Caniper, or some cause beyond Mildred Caniper, going back and back, like the waves of the sea? It was impossible to fix the blame, foolish to try, unnecessary to know it. The thing had happened: it might be good, yet when she heard Halkett's voice behind her, she was only conscious of bitter evil.

"I want to talk to you," he said.

"Yes?"

He came into her view and looked down scowlingly. "I don't know what you've been up to, but I'd better tell you to begin with that I'm not a fool."

She frowned at his manner, but she said patiently, "I don't know what you mean."

"You're clever."

"No."

"Then why have you got rid of her like that?"

"Are you speaking of my sister?"

"Yes, I am. I want to know why you've sent her off."

"I don't think it's your affair, but I will tell you. She was not happy here. If she had been happy, she would not have behaved foolishly with you."

"Ah! I thought you'd come to that. I see."

"What do you see?"

"Why you've got rid of her."

"I suppose you are hinting something," she said wearily.

"Please don't do it. I cannot—I cannot possibly be polite, if you are not straightforward. And please be quick, because I have a lot to do."

He flushed at this gentle hectoring, but he could not still his curiosity.

"I want to know," he said slowly, "what your little idea is about me—about me—and you. Are you going to try backing out of it, now that you have her safe?"

She had not thought of it; her face showed that, and he did not need the assurance of her quiet words.

"I was afraid," he muttered, half abashed. "I thought you'd take a chance."

"I couldn't take one unless you offered it," she said.

There were thoughts behind his eyes; he seemed to waver, and she steadied her own face for fear of doing the one thing that would not move him. Now she did not pray: she had a dread of asking for herself, lest God, in punishment, should grant the prayer and let worse follow. Escape was only to be made through a door of George's opening, and she knew he would never let her through, but she looked at the clouds and waited for him to speak.

His words were heralded by guttural noises in his throat.

"I want you," he said at last, with the simplicity of a desire for bread. "And there isn't any need to wait. I'm going to town today. I'll see about it. In three weeks—"

She said nothing; she was still watching the clouds; they were like baskets overbrimming with heaped snow.

He came nearer. "I'm going to get a ring. And, after all, we needn't wait three weeks. I'll get a licence. What kind of ring?"

Zebedee's ring was hanging on a ribbon round her neck, and she put a hand to her throat and pressed the hard stones against her skin.

"I suppose one has to have a wedding ring."

"I meant—another kind," he said.

"Is it worth while for such a little time?" she asked and did not look at him.

"There's afterwards."

"Yes. There's afterwards." She might have been lingering on the words with love, but suddenly she rose and stamped a foot as though to crush them, and cried out, "I will have no ring at all! Neither one nor the other!"

"You can't get married without a ring," he said stupidly. It pleased him to see her thus: she was less distant from him.

"Very well. Marry me with one. I will not wear it afterwards."

"I don't care about that," he muttered. He was looking at her, peering in the half-blind fashion he used towards her. "Helen—I was awake half the night."

She stared at him. It would not have troubled her if he had never slept again. It was absurd of him to think she cared whether he slept or waked.

"Thinking of you—" he added, and seemed to wait for some reward.

"I am going in," was all she said.

"Not yet. That's all you ever say to me. I wish you'd have a ring."

"But I will not!"

"Something, then," he begged.

"What do such things matter?" she cried, and hated her ungraciousness as she heard it. "If it will make you happy," she conceded. "Good-bye, George. The doctor will soon be here, and there is everything to do."

"Aren't you going to let me in?"

"Oh, yes." She passed into the house and up the stairs, and she did not look back to see if he had followed.

He found himself at a loss in the big house which seemed very empty. There was not a sound in it but the ticking of the clock and, upstairs, Helen's movements, which were few and quiet. He realized that he was practically alone with her, and though he listened earnestly, he could not tell exactly where she was, and at any moment she might come slipping down the stairs before he knew she was at the head of them. The fancy pleased him; it kept him poised for her; it would be fine, he thought, to play at hide-and-seek with her, to search the old house while she ran from him, to hear the clicking of a door or an unwary step, and at last to catch her in his arms, in the dark of a winter night.

He waited, but she did not come, and, understanding that his presence in the hall might well keep her upstairs, he wandered into the kitchen.

The room was neat, but a pile of dirty plates and dishes awaited washing, and having looked at them thoughtfully, he took off his coat, and he was working in the scullery when Helen appeared. Already he had filled the scuttles and the kettles.

"Thank you very much," she said, in a kind of wonder. He was a different person now, and she was touched by the sight of this careful dealing with mop and plates, by his puckered brow and lips. He was like a child, and she did not wish to see him so. If he continued simple, she might grow fond of him, and that, she thought, would be disloyalty to Zebedee. To marry George without love, affection, friendship or respect was only to pay the price he had demanded; but to feel kindness for him, even that human kindness she could seldom refuse to any one, was to make the sacrifice less complete, to cloud, in some way, the honesty of the eyes which would have to look at Zebedee when he learnt what she had done.

"It's kind, George, but don't do it."

"I'm slow, but I can manage."

"Splendidly, but I can do it."

"You can't do everything."

Her face was pinched as she said, "I'm glad to do it."

He straightened the big back he was bending in her service. "Let me help. I'll be here to light the kitchen fire tomorrow."

"There's no need: Mrs. Samson is coming, I've promised to have her every day."

"Samson is my man."

"I know." Lines were beginning to show between her brows. "George, nobody need be told."

Again he straightened himself, but now he seemed to threaten with his bulk. "I'd feel safer if you weren't so secret."

"Can't you trust me?" she said. "How often must I ask you that?"

He had a slow way of flushing to the eyes. "I'm sorry," he said humbly, as he used his thumb nail on a plate.

She was irritated by his meekness, for now he was not childlike. She felt his thoughts circling round her in a stubborn determination to possess, even, if it must be, through his own submission, but she hated him less for that than for his looks, which, at that moment, were without definite sex. He looked neither man nor woman: his knees were slightly bent; his face was red, and his nail still scraped patiently on the plate. Since she must marry him, she would have him as masculine as he could be, so that therein she might find shelter from the shame of being yoked to him.

Her cheeks grew cold in amazement at her own thought, and her mind shrank from it. She felt that all the blood in her body was dropping to her feet, and they were heavy as she moved towards the door.

"Are you going?" he asked her.

"I must watch for the doctor."

She had the mind of a slave, she told herself, the mind of a slave, and she deserved no better than to be one.

She wrapped a grey cape about her and sat outside the garden gate. The wind was strong enough to lean against, stronger than man or anything he had made. Its freshness seemed to get beneath her skin, into her mind, to clean every part of her. Its action had a swiftness that prevented thought, and she was content to sit there till the doctor came, though the nurse had gone to bed in Christopher, and Mildred Caniper was alone. If she could see through those closed lids, she would not mind: she must know how terrible it was to sit and watch her immobility.

The postman came before the doctor and brought a letter with a foreign stamp, and for a long time she held the envelope unopened between her palms. Her body felt like a great heart beating, and she was afraid to read what Zebedee had written, but at last she split the envelope and spread the sheets, and forgot George Halkett in the scullery and Mildred Caniper in bed: she did not hear the calling of the peewits or the melancholy of the sheep; she heard Zebedee's voice, clear-cut and quick, saying perfect things in ordinary tones. He told her of the sea that sometimes seemed to change into the moor, and of the sails that swelled into the big clouds they knew; he told her that though there was never any one who could claim likeness to her, it did not matter because she never left him, and that, in spite of her continuing presence, and because he was well again, he thought he would come home by land to reach her sooner.

She spoke aloud, but her forehead was on the letter on her knee.

"No, don't, Zebedee—darling—dearest—lover. Don't come any sooner. I don't want you to have more days of knowing than you need."

CHAPTER XXIX

The days of that week were marked by little changes for the better in Mildred Caniper's condition, by little scenes with George. Helen never went on to the moor without finding him in wait for her, and always she went as to some unworthy tryst, despising herself for the appeasement she meted out to him, daring to do nothing else. Once more, she saw him as some animal that might be soothed with petting, but, thwarted, would turn fierce and do as he would with her. Her dignity and friendship kept him off; he did not know how to pass the barrier, and to lock material doors against him would have been to tempt him to force the house. She knew that in this matter cowardice was safety, but as the days crept forward, she wondered how long the weapon would serve her.

Rupert came on Saturday and brought sanity into a disordered world, and when he entered the house she caught his arm and held to it.

"Have you been as lonely as all that?" he asked.

"Not a bit lonely, but you're so nice-looking," she explained, "and so alive. And Notya is only coming alive slowly. It's like watching something being born. You're whole."

"And you're rather embarrassing."

"I want you to talk to me all the time you're here. Tell me things that have nothing to do with us. Rupert, I'm sick of us." She dropped on to a chair and whispered, "It's an enchanted house!"

"Are you the princess?"

"Yes. Be careful! I don't want Jane to know."

He glanced up the stairs. "The prince is coming soon."

She ignored that and went on: "Nurse is an ogress."

"By Jove, yes! Why couldn't they send some one who looks

like a Christian?"

"I believe she'll eat me. But I shouldn't see that, and I can't bear to see her eating anything else. D'you know?"

"Rather. That kind of thing oughtn't to be allowed."

"She's very kind. She calls me 'dear' all the time, but Notya will hate her when she notices the teeth. Will you go up to her now? I have to—I want to go out for a little while. Then we can have the rest of the day to ourselves."

He lifted his eyebrows oddly. "Why not?"

"I mean I needn't go out again."

"Where are you going now?"

"Just for a walk. I must have a walk."

"Good girl. I'll look after the family."

She took her cloak from its peg and slipped through the garden. "I don't tell the truth. I'm deceitful," she said to herself, and when she saw George, she hated him.

"I've been here for hours," he said as she approached.

"There was no need to wait."

"I'm not grudging the time."

"Why speak of it then?"

"I was afraid you wouldn't come. I brought a coat for you to sit on. The ground's wet."

"I don't want to sit. I want to walk and walk into something soft—soft and oblivious."

"But sit down, just a minute. I want to show you something." His hand shook as he put something into hers and, clearing his throat, said shyly, "It's a swallow."

"A swallow?"

"A brooch."

"It's pretty."

"Let me pin it on for you."

"No, no, I can't—it's much too good for this plain frock, and I might lose it. Haven't you a case for it? There. Put it in your pocket, please. Thank you very much."

"I don't believe you like it."

"Yes, I do."

"Then let me put it on. I'd like to see you wearing it."

"Oh, if you must," she said.

He took it from its place; his fingers were slow and clumsy, his face close to hers, and with the brooch pinned to her, she hated him more than she had done when he held Miriam in his mad arms.

"I've the ring in my pocket, too," he said. "Next week—Did you hear me? Sometimes—sometimes you look deaf."

"Yes, I did hear."

She shook herself and rose, but he caught a hand. "I want to take you right away. You look so tired."

"I am not tired."

"I shall take care of you."

The limp hand stiffened. "You know, don't you, that I'm not going to leave my stepmother? You are not thinking—?"

"No, no," he said gently, but the mildness in his voice promised himself possession of her, and she snatched away her hand.

"I must have exercise. I'm going to run."

"Give me your hand again."

"There is no need."

"You'll stumble." He did not wait for her assent, and for that and for the strength of his hold she liked him, and, as she ran, and her blood quickened, she liked him better. She did not understand herself, for she had imagined horror at his nearness, but not horror pierced through with a delight that shrank. She thought there must be something vile in her, and while she ran she felt, in her desperate youth, that she was altogether worthless since she could not control her pleasure to this swift movement supported by his hand. She ran, leaping over stones and heather and, for a short time that seemed endless, her senses had their way. She was a woman, young and full of life, and the moor was wide and dark, great-bosomed, and beside her there ran a man who held her firmly and tightened, ever and again, his grasp of her slipping fingers. Soon it was no effort not to think and to feel recklessly was to escape. Their going made a wind to fan their faces; there was a smell of damp earth and dusty heather, of Halkett's tweeds and his tobacco; the wind had a faint smell of frost; there was one star in a greenish sky.

She stopped when she could go no further, and she heard his hurried breathing and her own.

"How you can run!" he said. "Like a hare! And jump!"

"No! Don't!" She could not bear his personalities: she wished she were still running, free and careless, running from the shame that now came creeping on her. "No, no!" she cried again, but this time it was to her own thoughts.

"What have I done?" he asked.

"Nothing. I was speaking to myself."

He never could be sure of her, and he searched for words while he watched the face she had turned skywards.

"Helen, you're different now."

"And you like me less."

"I always love you."

She looked at him and smiled, and very slowly shook her head.

"Oh, no," she said pleasantly. "Oh, no, George."

"What do you mean by that?"

"Perhaps it's a riddle. You can think about it."

"Ah—you—you make me want to shake you!" He gripped her shoulders and saw her firm lips loosened, a pale colour in her cheeks, but something in her look forced him to let her go.

"I can't hurt you," he said.

She smiled again, in a queer way, he thought, but she was always queer: she looked as if she knew a joke she would not tell him, and, in revenge, he had a quick impulse to remind her of his rights.

"Next week," he said, and saw the pretty colour fading.

No one could save the captive princess now. Sunday came and Rupert went; Monday came and Mildred Caniper spoke to Helen; Tuesday was Helen's birthday: she was twenty-one. No one could save her now. On Wednesday she was to meet George in the town.

She had asked Lily to stay with Mildred Caniper.

"I have some shopping to do," she said, and though her words were true, she frowned at them.

Lily came, and her skirts were blown about as she ran up the track.

"It's a bitter wind," she said. "We've had a bad winter, and we're going to have a wicked spring."

"I think we are," Helen said as she fastened on her hat.

"You'll be fighting the wind all the way into town. Need you go today?"

"I'm afraid I must," Helen said gravely.

"Well, perhaps the change will do you good," Lily said, and Helen smiled at her reflection in the mirror. "Don't hurry back."

The smile stayed on Helen's lips, and it was frozen there when, having forced her way against a wind that had no pity and no scorn, she did her shopping methodically and met George Halkett at the appointed place.

"You've come!" he said, and seized her hand. "You're late."

"I had to do some shopping," she said, putting back a blown strand of hair.

"You're tired. You should have let me drive you down." In the shadows of the doorway, his eyes were quick on every part of her. "I wish I'd made you. And you're late. Shall we—hadn't we better go upstairs?"

"There's nothing to wait for, is there?"

Their footsteps made a loud noise on the stairs, and in a few minutes Helen found herself on them again. George had her by the arm, but he loosed her when she put the ring into his hand.

"Helen—" He checked himself, accepting her decree with a patience that made her sorry for him.

"You're going to drive back with me?" His anxiety to please her controlled his eagerness: his wish to tend her was like a warm but stifling cloak, and she could not refuse him.

"They'll think we've met by chance," he said.

"Who will?"

"Any one that sees us."

"I'm not concerned with what people think."

"That's all right then. Nor am I. Will you wait here or come with me to the stable?"

"I'll wait," she said.

People with blue faces and red-rimmed eyes went past her, and there was not one of them she did not envy, for of all the people in that town, she alone was waiting for George Halkett. He came too soon, and held out a helping hand which she disdained.

"My word!" he said, "the wind is cold. Keep the rug round you."

"No, I don't like it." She pushed it off. "I can't bear the smell of it."

"I'm sorry," he said. "It's clean enough."

"I didn't think it was dirty," she explained, and a few minutes afterwards, she added, "I'm sorry I was rude, George."

"You're tired," he said again.

"Drive quickly, won't you?"

He whipped up the horse, and the wind roared behind them; they passed men and women staggering against it.

"Will there be snow?" she asked him.

He bent his ear to her, and again she shouted, "Will there be snow?"

"Feels—rather like it," he boomed back. "I never knew such a year. And they'd begun burning the heather!"

"Had they? Did you say burning heather? Then the fires will be put out. George, they'll be put out!"

He nodded, thinking this a small thing to shout about, in such a wind.

She had forgotten about the fires, but now she looked at the grey sky and hoped the snow would come. She imagined the first flake hissing on the fire, and more flakes, and more and more, until there was no smoke to veil the god, only a thick wet blanket for his burial. She had loved his moor, yet he had forsaken her; she had been afraid to hope, she had gone humbly and she had prayed, but now she need pay him no more homage, for she had nothing more to fear, and she whispered to the snow to hurry and avenge her.

When they were nearly home, George spoke again. "Are you very cold?"

"I'm warmer now."

"I'll drive you up the track."

"I'd rather get out here. Stop, George, please."

"Wait till I help you down," he said, and jumped off on the other side.

"My feet are numb," she said, looking at the arms he held for her.

"I'll catch you."

"I'm not so bad as that." She climbed down stiffly while he watched her, and in some way she felt herself more injured by the quality of his gaze than she would have been by his clasp. Without looking at him, she said good-bye and made a step or two.

"But I shall see you again."

"One—one supposes so!"

"I mean tonight."

"I—don't know."

"Leave the blind up so that I can see if you're alone."

She made no answer, and when she had run lamely up the track, she turned at the door to see her husband still standing in the road.

Lily met her in the hall and said, "Mrs. Caniper's asleep, and she's better, my dear. She seems happier, somehow. So George Halkett brought you home. A good thing, too. Come into the kitchen and get warm. I'll make some tea and toast for you. You're frozen. Here, let me take off your boots. Sit down."

"I can do it, thank you."

"But you're going to let me, just to please me."

Helen submitted and lay back. "You look nice with the firelight on you."

"Hadn't that man a rug?"

"What? Oh, yes, yes." The warmth and peace of the kitchen were almost stupefying. She shut her eyes and felt soft slippers being pushed on to her feet; the singing of the kettle became one sound with the howling of the wind, and Lily's voice dragged her from the very brim of sleep.

"Here's a slice, and the kettle's boiling. A good thing John isn't here! He says it's the water, not the kettle."

"How fussy of him!"

"But he's right."

"Always?"

"Not a bit of it."

"I'm glad of that. Would it have made much difference to you if you hadn't married him?"

"D'you think I don't care enough for him?"

"Of course I don't."

"Now look, you've made me burn the toast."

"Scrape it. I wanted to know—how much he filled of you."

"I don't know. I never thought about it. I wouldn't have been lovesick, anyway. I had my work to do."

"I expect that's how men feel. I sometimes think nothing's worth struggling for."

"Oh, but it is. I'm always fighting. I saved two lambs last week."

"That's different. I meant—for happiness. People struggle and get nothing. It's such a little life. Seventy years, perhaps. They pass—somehow."

"But if you've ever had the toothache, you know how long an hour can be. What's the matter with you?"

"I'm just thinking."

"Unhappy?"

"No."

"When will Zebedee be back?"

"In about ten days."

"Are you feeling he'll never come?"

"I'm sure he'll come."

"Well then—"

"Perhaps it's the wind," Helen said. "You're very good to me."

"Oh, I'm fond of you," Lily said.

"Are you fond enough to kiss me?" Helen asked. She wanted a touch at which she need not shudder, and surely it was fitting that some one should kiss her on her wedding-day.

CHAPTER XXX

Soon after nine o'clock, Helen bade Mildred Caniper and the nurse good-night and went downstairs with Jim close at her heels.

"We're going to sit in the kitchen, James. I'll get my sewing."

She hesitated at the window: the night was very dark, but she could see the violent swaying of the poplars, and she thought the thickening of their twigs was plain and, though it was April already, it was going to snow. She touched the tassel of the blind, but she did not pull on it, for she would not anger George with little things, and she left the window bare for his eyes and the night's.

"Keep close to me, Jim," she said as she sat and sewed, and she stroked him with a foot. She could hear no sound but the raging wind, and when the back door was opened she was startled.

"It's me," George said as he entered.

"I didn't hear you coming."

"I've been looking through the window for a long time." He went to the fireside. "Didn't you know? I hoped you'd be looking out for me, but you weren't anxious enough for that."

"Anxious?"

"Well—eager."

"Of course I wasn't. Why should I be?"

"You're my wife—and wives—"

"You know why I married you, George."

"You're married, none the less."

"I'm not disputing that."

"I suppose you despise me for—getting what I wanted."

"I only wonder if it was worth while."

"I'll make it that."

"But you won't know until your life is over, until lots of lives are over."

"I'll get what I can now."

She nodded lightly, and her coolness warmed him.

"Helen—"

"Why don't you sit down?"

"I don't know. I wish you wouldn't sew."

Without a word, she folded her work and gave it to him, and when he had put it down he knelt beside her, holding the arms of the chair so that he fenced her in.

"You don't understand, you can't understand that night's work," he said. "I want to tell you. You—you were like an angel coming down into the racket. You took away my strength. I wanted you. I forgot about Miriam. If I'd only known it, I'd been forgetting her every day when I saw you walking with the dog. You think I was just a beast, but I tell you—"

"I don't think that. I can't explain unless you give me room. Thank you. You were a beast with Miriam, not with me."

He sat stiffly on his chair and murmured, "That's just it. And now, you see—"

"Yes, I do."

"But you don't like me."

"I might."

"You shall, by God!" He seemed to smoulder.

"I hope so," she said quietly, and damped the glow.

"You'll let me come here every night and sit with you?"

"Yes."

"And Mrs. Caniper, can she hear?"

"No, she is in the front of the house."

"And Jim won't mind?"

"Oh, no, Jim won't."

"Nor you?"

"You can get the big old chair from the schoolroom and bring it here. That shall be yours."

He sat there for an hour, and while he smoked she was idle.

His eyes hardly left her face, but hers were for the fire, though sometimes she looked at him, and then she saw him behind tobacco smoke, and once she smiled.

"What's that for?" he asked.

"I was thinking of the fires on the moor—the heather burning."

"What made you think of that?"

"You—behind the smoke. If the snow comes, the fires will be put out, but there will still be your smoke."

"I don't know what you're talking about," he said.

"I like to see you—behind the smoke."

"I'm glad you're pleased with something."

"I like a fair exchange," she said, and laughed at him, "but I shall offer up no more prayers."

"I don't understand this joke, but I like to see you laugh." Possession had emboldened him. "Helen, you're pretty."

"I'm sleepy. It's after ten. Good-night."

"I'll come tomorrow."

"But not on Saturday. Rupert comes home then."

"He goes on Sunday night?"

"Yes." She locked the door on him, blew out the light, and ran upstairs. She thought Mr. Pinderwell passed her with no new sorrow on his face. "It's worse for me," she said to him. "Jane, it's worse for me."

She went cautiously to her window and peeped through. She saw George standing on the lawn, and tremblingly she undressed in darkness.

The next day, Mildred Caniper called Helen to her side.

"I feel—rested," she said. Her voice had for ever lost its crispness, and she spoke with a slovenly tongue. "I don't like strangers—looking at me. And she—she—"

"I know. She shall go. Tomorrow I'll sleep with you."

Her heart lightened a little, and through the day she thought of Mildred Caniper's room as of a hermitage, but without the nurse the house was so much emptier of human life that it became peopled with the thoughts of all who had lived in it; and while Helen waited for George's coming, she felt them moving round her.

There were the thoughts of the people who had lived in the house before Mr. Pinderwell, and these were massed and indistinct, yet the more troubled; they were too old for form, too young for indifference, and they thronged about her, asking for deliverance. She could not give it, and she was jostled by a crowd that came closer than any one of flesh and blood: it got inside her brain and frightened her. The thoughts of Mr. Pinderwell were familiar, but now she could better understand his wild young despair, the pain of his lonely manhood, the madness of his old age. Yet, when she thought of him, she said again, "It's worse for me." Mr. Pinderwell had not been obliged to marry some one else, and, though he did not know it, his children lived. Nearer than his thoughts, but less insistent than the formless ones that pressed about her, begging shamelessly, were those of Mildred Caniper. Helen saw them in the dining-room where they had been made, and they were rigid under suffering, dignified, but not quite lost to humour, and because she did not know their cause, because their creator lay upstairs, dead to such activities, Helen had a horror of them that made her watch the clock for George's hour. She was less afraid of George than of these shapeless, powerful things, this accumulated evidence of what life did with its own; and until he came she talked to Jim, quickly and incessantly, careless of what she said, if words could calm her.

"Jim, Jim, Jim! I must say something, so I'll say your name, and then other things will come. I do not intend to be silly. I won't let you be silly, Helen. You mustn't spoil things. It's absurd—and wicked! And there's snow outside. It's so deep that I shan't hear him come. And I wish he'd come, Jim. Funny to wish that. Jim, I'm afraid to turn my head. It feels stiff. And I ought to go upstairs and look at Notya's fire, but I don't like the hall. That's where they all meet. And I don't know how I dare say these things aloud. I'll talk about something else. Suppose

I hadn't you? What shall we have for dinner tomorrow? There's a bone for you, and the jelly for Notya, and for me—an egg, perhaps. Boiled, baked, fried, poached, scrambled, omeletted? Somehow, somehow. What shall I say next? Hey diddle diddle, the cat and the fiddle, and all that kind of thing. That will take a long time. I know I sound mad, but I'm not. And this isn't me: not our me, James. Dickory, dickory, dock—But this is worse than before. I wonder why God thought of men and women— and snow—and sheep—and dogs. Dogs—" Her words stopped; she heard the little noises of the fire. She found that this was not the way in which to combat terrors. She knew how Zebedee would look if he saw her now, and she stood up slowly. The muscles in his cheek would twitch, and the queer flecks in his eyes would chase each other as he watched her anxiously and sadly. She could not let him look like that.

She walked into the middle of the room and looked about her. She opened the door and stood in the dark hall and refused the company of the thronging thoughts. Up the stairs she went, seeing nothing more alarming than poor Mr. Pinderwell, and on the landing she found the friendly children whom she loved. Jim followed her, and he seemed to share her views; he paused when she did and stood, sturdily defying the unknown; and so they went together into every room, and mended Mildred Caniper's fire, and returned freely to the kitchen.

"We've conquered that," Helen said. "We'll conquer everything. Fear is—terrible. It's ugly. I think only the beautiful can be good."

She held to the high mantelshelf and looked at the fire from between her arms. A few minutes ago, life had been some mighty and incalculable force which flung its victims where it chose, and now she found it could be tamed by so slight a thing as a human girl. She had been blinded, deafened, half stupefied, tossed in the whirlpool, and behold, with the remembrance that Zebedee believed in her, she was able to steer her course and guide her craft through shallows and over rapids with a steady hand.

"There now!" she exclaimed aloud, and turned a radiant face as Halkett entered.

For an instant, he thought it was his welcome, and his glow answered hers before both faded.

"Good-evening, George."

"Good-evening, Helen," he answered, and there was a little mockery in his tone.

He stood close to her, and the frosty air was still about him. A fine mist and a smell of peat came from his clothes as the fire warmed them. She did not look at him, and when she would have done so, his gaze weighted her eyelids so that she could not lift them; and again, as on that first occasion in the hollow, but ten times more strongly, she was conscious of his appreciation and her sex. There was peril here, and with shame she liked it, while, mentally at first, and then physically, she shrank from it. She dropped into the chair beside her, and with an artifice of which she was no mistress, she yawned, laughed in apology, and looked at him.

"I believe you were awake half the night," he grumbled. "I won't have you tired. You shouldn't have sent the nurse away." He sat down and pulled out his pipe, and filled it while he watched her. "But I'm glad she's gone," he said softly.

She did not answer. She had a gripping hand on each arm of the chair: she wanted to run away, and she hated George; she wanted to stay, and then she hated herself.

"I shan't get tired," she said weakly. "Mrs. Samson stays till six o'clock. I only look after Notya."

"And you sleep with her?"

"Yes," she said and, picking a spill of paper from the hearth, she lighted it and held it out to him. He put his hand round hers and did not let it go until his pipe was lit, and then he puffed thoughtfully for a time.

"I've never been up your stairs except when I carried her to bed," he said, and every muscle in her body contracted sharply. She flogged her mind to start her tongue on a light word.

"Not—not when you were little? Before we came here?"

He laughed. "I wouldn't go near the place. We were all scared of old Pinderwell. They used to say he walked. I was on the moor the night you came, I remember, and saw the house all lighted up, and I ran home, saying he'd set the place on fire. I was supposed to be in my bed, and I had my ears well boxed."

"Who boxed them?"

"Mrs. Biggs, of course. She has hands like flails. I—What's the matter?"

"Is she at the farm still?"

"Mrs. Biggs?"

"Yes."

"D'you want her to go?"

"I should have thought you did."

"Well—" He spoke awkwardly. "She's been there nearly all my life. You can't turn people off like that, but if you want it, she shall go."

"No, it's not my affair," she told him.

"It will be," he said sharply.

"Of course," she said in a high voice, "I should never dream of living in the same house with her, but then," she went on, and her tones loosened, there was an irritating kind of humour in them, "I don't suppose I shall ever live there at all."

She did not know why she spoke so; her wish to hurt him was hardly recognizable by herself, but when she saw him stung, she was delighted.

The colour rushed up to his eyes. "What d'you mean by that? What d'you think you're going to do?"

She raised her eyebrows, and answered lightly, "I'm sure I don't know."

He put a heavy hand on her knee. "But I do," he said, and her mouth drooped and quivered. She knew she had laid herself open to an attack she could not repel.

"He'll get me this way," she found herself almost whispering, and aloud she said, "George, let's wait and see. Tell me some more about when you were little."

Things went smoothly after that, and when she went to bed, she talked to Jane.

"We mustn't have any pauses," she said. "We can feel each other then. We must talk all the time, and, oh, Jane, I'm so fond of silence!"

That night a voice waked her from a dreamless sleep.

"Helen, are you there?"

"Yes. Do you want something?"

"I have been thinking." Her tongue seemed too thick for her mouth. "Is the dog on the landing?"

"Yes. He's always there. You haven't been afraid?"

"No. It's a big house for two women."

Helen sat up and, putting her feet into her slippers, she opened the door. Jim was sleeping in the darkness: he woke, looked up and slept again. It was a quiet night and not a door or window shook.

"I didn't say I heard anything. Go back to bed."

Helen obeyed, and she was falling softly into sleep when the voice, like a plucked wire, snatched her back.

"Helen! I want to tell you something."

"I'm listening." She stared at the corner whence the voice was struggling, and gradually the bed and Mildred's body freed themselves from the gloom.

By a supreme effort, the next words were uttered without a blur and with a loudness that chased itself about the room.

"I am to blame."

"To blame?" Helen questioned softly.

"It was my fault, not Edith's—not your mother's."

"I don't know what you're talking about, Notya dear."

"Your mother." The voice was querulous. "I was—unkind to your mother. Oh—worse than that!" The bed creaked, and a long sigh gave place to the halting speech in which the sibilants were thickened into lisping sounds.

"She was my friend. She was beautiful. You are all like her.

Miriam and Rupert—" The voice dropped like a stone falling into a well without a bottom, and Helen, listening for the sound of it, seemed to hear only the echoes of Mildred Caniper's memory, coming fainter and fainter from the past where the other woman made a gleam.

"Miriam—" she began again. "I haven't seen her."

"No. Uncle Alfred has taken her away."

"Ah!" Mildred said, and there was a silence.

After a time, her voice came back, thin and vague, a ghostly voice, speaking the thoughts of a mind that had lost its vigour.

"Alfred was in love with Edith. They all were. She was so pretty and so gay. But she was not unfaithful. No. I knew that. She told me and she trusted me, but I said nothing. That's what has worried me—all the time." Heavily she sighed again, and Helen drew herself to a sitting posture in her bed. She dared not ask the questions which tramped over each other in her mind; she hardly drew a breath lest the sound should change the current of the other's thought.

"She did silly things. They vexed me. I was jealous, I suppose. Take care of Miriam. Oh—but she's gone. Edith—she made men love her, and she couldn't help it, and then one night—but it's too long to tell. Philip thought she wasn't faithful, but I knew. She wouldn't tell him. She was angry, she wouldn't say a word, but she trusted me to tell him. And you see, I—didn't. He wouldn't go and see her. If he had seen her he would have found out. And soon she died—of measles." The woman in the bed laughed softly.

"That was so foolish! And then I married him. I got w-what I wanted. But there's a verse about leanness in the soul, isn't there? That's what I had. He wanted some one to look after the children, and I looked after you—no more. The struggling hasn't been worth while."

"No." The word came from Helen like a lost puff of wind.

"And then Philip went away, and I came here. That's all. I wanted to tell somebody. Now perhaps I can have peace. I meant to tell him, too, but I was too late. That worried me. All these years—"

Leaning on her elbow, Helen looked at the narrow bed. It had some aspect of a coffin, and the strangely indifferent voice was still. She felt an intolerable pity for the woman, and the pain overcame her bewilderment and surprise, yet she knew she need not suffer, for Mildred Caniper had slipped her burden of confession and lay at rest.

Beyond the relief of tears, Helen slid into her place. The dead, distant mother was not real to her: she was like the gay shadow of a butterfly that must soon die, and Philip Caniper was no more than a name. Their fate could hardly stir her, and their personal tragedy was done; but now she thought she could interpret the thoughts which clustered in the dining-room. This was Mildred Caniper's secret, and it had been told without shame. The irony of that made her laugh silently to the shaking of her bed. She had no words with which to clothe her feelings, the sense of her own smallness, of unhappiness so much the common lot that it could almost pass unheeded. There was some comfort in the mingling of her own misery with all that had been and was to be, but she felt herself in the very presence of disintegration: the room was stirring with fragments of the life which Mildred Caniper could not hold together: mind and matter, they floated from the tired body in the corner and came between Helen and the sleep that would have kept her from thinking of the morrow, from her nightly vision of Zebedee's face changing from that of happy lover to poor, stricken man. Turning in the bed, she left him for the past of which Mildred Caniper had told her, yet that past, as parent of the present, looked anxiously and not without malice towards its grandchildren. What further tragedy would the present procreate?

Answers to that question were still trooping past Helen when dawn came through the windows, and some of them had the faces of children born to an unwilling mother. Her mind cried out in protest: she could not be held responsible; and because she felt the pull of future generations that might blame her, she released the past from any responsibility towards herself. No, she would not be held responsible: she had bought Miriam, and the price must be paid: she and Miriam and all mankind were bound by shackles forged unskilfully long ago, and the moor, understanding them, had warned her. She could remember no day when the moor had not foretold her suffering.

CHAPTER XXXI

A person less simple than Helen would have readjusted her conception of herself, her character and circumstances, in the light of her new knowledge; but with the passionate assertion that she could not be held altogether responsible for what her own children might have to suffer, Helen had made her final personal comment. For a day, her thoughts hovered about the distant drama of which Mildred Caniper was the memento, like a dusty programme found when the play itself is half forgotten, and Helen's love grew with her added pity; but more urgent matters were knocking at her mind, and every morning, when she woke, two facts had forced an entrance. She was nearer to Zebedee by a night, and only the daylight separated her from George and what he might demand and, outside, the moor was covered with thick snow, as cold as her own mind.

A great fire burned in Mildred Caniper's room, another in the kitchen; the only buds on the poplars were frozen white ones, and the whiteness of the lawn was pitted with Halkett's footsteps. Since the first day of snow he had climbed the garden wall close to the kitchen door so that he should not make another trail, but the original one still gaped there, and Helen wished more snow would fall and hide the tracks. She saw them every morning when she went into her own room to dress, and they were deep and black, like open mouths begging the clouds for food.

One day, John, looking from the kitchen window, asked who had been tramping about the garden.

"Doesn't it look ugly?" Helen said. "I can't bear snow when it's blotched with black. Is there going to be more of it?"

"I think so."

"Are your lambs all right?"

"We haven't lost one. Lily's a wonder with them. We've a nursery in our kitchen. Come and see it." He went out, and she heard him on the crisp snow.

"Now he'll mix the trail," she thought happily. "And I might have done it myself. I think I'm growing stupid. But it will be John and George when I get up in the morning: that's better than George and me."

John came back and spoke gravely. "I find those footsteps go right across the moor towards Halkett's Farm."

"Of course! George made them."

"Oh, you knew?"

"Yes. I couldn't imagine Jim had done it, could I?"

"What did he come for?"

"He sat by the fire and smoked."

"You'd better not encourage him."

"I don't."

"Be careful!—What are you laughing at?"

"That old story of the kiss!"

"It makes me mad."

"He doesn't try to kiss me, John. I shouldn't be horrified if he did. You needn't be afraid for me."

"All right. It's your affair. Want any wood chopped?"

"Rupert did a stack for me."

"This is pretty dull for you, isn't it? When does—"

She interrupted. "At the end of next week, I think." She was somewhat tired of answering the question.

That night, as she sat with George, he said, "When we're like this, I wish you'd wear your wedding-ring."

"I said I wouldn't."

"It couldn't do any harm."

"It could—to me."

"You talk as if it's dirt," he said.

"Oh, no, I know it's gold! Let's keep our bargains and talk of something else. Tell me what you have been doing today."

His face reddened to a colour that obscured his comeliness.

"You can't get round me like that."

"What do you mean?" She lifted her head so that he saw her round white throat. "Why should I condescend to get round you, as you call it?"

"That's it!" he shouted angrily. "That's the word!" He rose and knocked his pipe against the stove. "You're too damned free with your condescension, and I'm sick of it." He left the kitchen angrily, and two minutes later she heard the distant banging of the garden door.

She wanted to run after him, for she was afraid of the impulses of his anger. She felt a dreadful need to conciliate, for no other reason than his body's greater strength, but she let him go, and though for several days she did not see him, she had no sense of liberty. He would come back, she knew, and she found herself planning unworthy little shifts, arranging how she would manage him if he did this or that, losing her birthright of belief that man and woman could meet and traffic honestly together. They could not do it, she found, when either used base weapons: she, her guile, or he, his strength; but if he used his strength, how could she save herself from using guile? She had to use it, and she clung fiercely to it, though she knew that, at last, it would be wrested from her.

In these days of his absence, there were hours when she wandered ceaselessly through the house, urged by the pride which refused allegiance to this man, tortured by her love for Zebedee and the pain she had to give him, hunted by the thought that George was making for himself a place in the circle where she kept her pensioners. Each time that he looked at her with longing, though she shrank, she gave her ready pity, and when he walked away into the night, her heart went after him unwillingly. Worse than all, she knew she would not always see him as a pensioner. Far off and indistinct, like a gallows seen on a distant hill, she spied the day when she might own a kind of need of him; she had to love those who loved her enough, and his strength, the very limits of his mind, would some day hold her. But she would not let these thoughts properly take shape: they were vague menaces, and they chased her through Mr. Pinderwell's sparsely-furnished rooms. She was glad that Zebedee had never been a pensioner; he had always given more than he had asked. His had not been an attitude of pleading, and she could not remember once seeing an appeal in his eyes. They had always been quick on her face and busy with herself, and her pride in him was mixed with anger that he had not bound her to him by his need. He would manage without her very well, she thought, and hardened herself a little; but hard or soft, the result of her fierce thinking was the same. She had the picture of Miriam like a broken flower, lying limp and crumpled on the floor, and she believed she had done well in selling herself to save that beauty. It was the only thing to do, and Zebedee would know. These words she repeated many times.

But she went beyond that conclusion on her own path. She had married George, and that was ugly, but life had to be lived and it must be beautiful; it could not be so long that she should fail to make it beautiful: fifty years, perhaps. She beat her hands together. She could surely make it beautiful for fifty years.

But at night, when she waited for George, she trembled, for she knew that her determination meant ultimate surrender.

He came on the fourth night. She gave him half a smile, and with a thin foot she pushed his chair into its place, but he did not sit down. He stood with his hands clasped behind him, his head thrust forward, and having glanced at him in that somewhat sulky pose, she was shaken by inward laughter. Men and women, she reflected, were such foolish things: they troubled over the little matters of a day, a year, or a decade, and could not see how small a mark their happiness or sorrow made in the history of a world that went on marching.

She bent over her sewing while she thought, and she might have forgotten his presence if a movement had not blocked the light.

"George, please, I can't see."

"I beg your pardon."

"I wish you would sit down. It isn't comfortable like this."

"All right." He sank down heavily and sighed.

She lifted her head quickly and showed him her puckered face. "Are you still so cross?"

"I—don't know. I've been miserable enough," he said, but he had to smile on her.

She was astonished that he should have no difficulty in speaking of himself, and she looked at him in this surprised consideration before she tempted him to say more.

"Why?" she asked.

"You wouldn't understand."

"I might."

"How much I wanted you."

She tapped her thimble against her teeth. "It's so absurd," she said softly.

"Eh?"

She hated him to say that, and she frowned a little as he asked, "Why is it absurd?"

"Because you don't know me at all."

"That's nothing to do with it." He stood up and kicked a protruding coal. "Nothing to do with it. I know I—want you." He turned sharply towards her. "I was half drunk that night."

"I wish you wouldn't talk about it."

He added abruptly, "I've had nothing since."

Her silence implied that this was only what she had expected and, feeling baulked of his effect, he sighed again.

"Oh, you are so pathetic! Why don't you smile?" He did it, and she nodded her applause, while he, appeased and daring, asked her, "Well, did you miss me?"

"Yes. A little."

"Are you glad I'm here?"

"I think so."

"When will you be sure?"

"Ah, that depends on you. I hate you to be rough."

"God knows I've had enough to make me. You wear me out, you're so damned superior."

"I'm afraid that's not my fault!"

He swore under his breath. "At it again!"

"Oh, dear!" she cried, "that was meant to be a joke! I thought it rather good! Shall I make some coffee? They say a wise woman always has good things for her—for a man to eat and drink. I'm going to try it."

They drank in silence, but as he put down his cup, she said, twinkling over hers, "Was I a wise woman?" and suddenly she felt the great loneliness of the house, and remembered that she was a woman, and this man's wife. She looked down that he might see no change. He did not answer, and the coals, dropping in the grate, were like little tongues clicking in distress. She wondered if he were ever going to speak.

"Give me your cup," she heard him say, and his voice was confident. She felt a hand put firmly on her shoulder, and she saw him bending over her.

"Good-night," he said, "I'm going," and still with that hand on her, he kissed her mouth.

She did not move when the door was shut behind him: she leaned back in the chair, pressed there by his kiss, her hands limp in her lap. She respected him at last. There had been dignity in that kiss, and she thought it better that he should take what he desired than sit too humble under her gaze, but she knew she was no longer what she had been. He had, in some manner, made her partly his: not by the spirit, not by her will, but by taking something from her: there was more to take, and she was sure now that he would take it. She was not angry, but for a long time she cried quietly in her chair.

CHAPTER XXXII

Snow was falling when Zebedee at last drove up the road, and from the window of Mildred Caniper's bedroom Helen watched his huddled figure and the striving horse. She saw him look for the obliterated track and then turn towards the shelter of Brent Farm.

"Is he coming?" Mildred asked. She was childishly interested in his return.

"Yes. He has gone to put the horse up at the farm."

"He will be cold."

"Yes." Helen was cold, too.

"It is a dreadful day for driving."

"I don't think he minds that," she said in a dead voice.

"No. You had better go downstairs."

"When I see him starting back. He'll have to talk to Lily. No, he's coming now."

She stood at the window while she slowly counted twenty, and then she warmed her hands before she went.

She was irritated by the memory of him running across the road with his hands in his pockets, his head butting against the storm, his eager feet sinking into the snow and dragging themselves out again. She had a crazy wish that he would fall. Why could he not walk? she asked herself. It was absurd to be in such a hurry. There was plenty of time, more than enough, if he but knew it! She laughed, and hated the false, cruel sound, and looked round the hall to see if there were any one to hear; but in the snow, as she opened the gate to him, there was a moment in which she knew nothing but joy.

He had come back, he was close to her, and evil had passed away.

"Oh, my darling—" he said. "Let me get off my coat!"

He took her hands, and unsmilingly he scanned her, from her smooth hair to her mouth, from her hands to her feet.

"What is it?" he asked.

She gave him her clear regard. "All the things that have mattered most to me have been comings and goings through this gate and the garden door."

"Well, dearest one—"

"You've come again."

"And I shall come tomorrow."

"Will you?" She closed her eyelids on what he might see, and he kissed her between the eyes. "I have stayed away too long," he said.

"Yes. I want to talk to you. Come and see Notya first."

"Things have been happening, Daniel tells me."

"Oh, yes, they have."

"And if your letters had shown me your face, I shouldn't have stayed away another day."

"Isn't it so nice, Zebedee?"

"It's lovelier than it ever was, but there's a line here, and here, and here. And your eyes—"

Again she shut them, but she held up her face. "I want you to kiss my mouth."

"Helen," he said, when he had slowly done her bidding, "let us sit on the stairs and think about each other. Yes, there's room for Jim, but, oh, my blessed one, he ought to have a bath. No, you can stay down there, my boy. Are you comfortable, little heart? Let me look at you again. You are just like a pale flower in a wood. Here, in the darkness, there might be trees and you gleaming up, a flower—"

She dropped her forehead to his knees. "I wish—I were—that flower."

She felt his body tighten. "What has happened?"

"I'll tell you soon."

"No, now."

"When you have seen Notya. She might notice if we looked—queer."

"Then let us go to her at once."

* * * * *

Mildred Caniper cut short the interview, saying, "Take him away, Helen. I'm tired. I'm always tired now."

"Come into Jane," Helen said when they were on the landing. "No one will disturb us there. Let Jim come, too."

"He isn't fit to be in your bedroom, dear. Neither am I. And how like you it is!"

"It's cold," she said. Through the window she saw that the new snow had covered George's tracks. "Cold—cold."

He put his arms round her. "I'm back again, and I can only believe it when I'm holding you. Now tell me what's the matter."

"Shall I? Shall I? Don't hold me, or I can't. It's—oh, you have to know. I'm married, Zebedee."

Plainly he did not think her sane. "This can't be true," he said in a voice that seemed to drop from a great height.

"Yes, it's true. I can show you the thing—the paper. Here it is. Do you want to read it? Oh, yes, it's true."

"But it can't be! I don't understand! I don't understand it. Who—For God's sake, tell me the whole tale."

She told it quickly, in dull tones, and as she watched his face she saw a sickly grey colour invade his tan.

"Don't, don't look like that!" she cried.

"Are you quite sure you're married?" he asked in his new voice. "Let me look at this thing."

Outside, the snow fell thicker, darkening the room, and as she took a step nearer, she saw the muscles twitching in his cheeks. He laid the paper on her dressing-table.

"May his soul rot!" he whispered. He did not look at her. Darkness and distance lay between them, but fearfully she crept up to him and touched his arm.

"Zebedee—"

He turned swiftly, and his face made her shrink back.

"You—you dare to tell me this! And you said you loved me. I thought you loved me."

"I did. I do," she moaned, and her hands fluttered. "Zebedee," she begged.

"Oh—did you think I was going to wish you happiness? I'd rather see you dead. I could have gone on loving you if you were dead, believing you had loved me."

"And do you think I want to be alive?" she asked him, and slipped to her knees beside the bed. "I didn't want to die until just now. All the time, I said, Zebedee will understand. He'll know I did my best. He'll be so sorry for me—"

"So sorry for you that he couldn't think about himself! Sorry for you—yes! But can't you see what you have done for me? You never thought of that! It's like a woman. If you'd killed me—but you have killed me. And you did it lightly. You let me come here, you gave me your mouth to kiss, and then you tell me this! This! Oh, it's nothing! You've married some one else! You couldn't help it! Ah—!" He shook with a rage that terrified her, and having held out disregarded arms to him, she let her trembling mouth droop shapelessly, and made no effort to control her heavy tears, the sobs rushing up and out with ugly, tortured sounds. She spoke between them.

"I never thought you would be angry. But I dreamt about you angry. Oh"—she spoke now only to herself—"he doesn't understand. If I hadn't loved him truly, I needn't have kept my word, but I had to be honest, or I wouldn't have been worthy." She dropped her face against the bed and mumbled there. "Nothing matters, then. Not even being honest. I—I—Oh! Angry—Zebedee darling, I can't bear it. Tell me you won't be angry any more."

"Dearest—" He sat on the bed and pulled her wet face to his knee. "Dearest—"

She took his hands and pressed them against her eyes.

"Forgive me, Zebedee."

"I can't forgive you. I can only love you. For ever and ever—I want to think, Helen."

"You're shaking so."

"And you are shivering. Come downstairs beside a fire."

"No; we are safer here." Her arms went round him, beneath his coat, and she leaned her head against his breast. "I wish we could go to sleep and never wake."

"I ought never to have left you."

She looked up. "Zebedee, he hasn't worried me. He kissed me once. That's all. That's why I made you kiss my mouth."

"He shall never worry you. I'm going to see him now, and I shall come back soon. Let me go, sweetheart."

"No, I can't let you go. It isn't that I'm afraid for you. I—I don't mind if you hurt each other, but if you killed him—if he killed you—! But you won't do that. You'll just say dreadful things, and then he'll come to me and take me all. Don't you see? He could. He would. In my own way, I can—I can keep him off, but if you went to him and claimed me—No, Zebedee, there would be no hope for me."

"I'll shoot him, if you like, without giving him a chance. The man ought to be shot. He takes advantage of his own beastliness—" He broke off. "If I talk about it I shall choke."

"But he doesn't know about you."

"You didn't tell him that?"

"I couldn't. I couldn't beg. I didn't want to say your name to him, to bring you into it."

"Yes, I was left out of your calculations pretty thoroughly."

"Zebedee—!"

"Ah, but you expect me to take this very calmly. You keep your promise to a drunken brute, but what of one to me?"

"There wasn't one between us two. We just belonged, as we do now and always shall. You're me and I am you. When I was thinking of myself, I was thinking of you, too. And all the time I thought you'd understand."

"I do—begin to understand. But what about Miriam? Little fool, little fool! Does she know what she's done?"

"No one knows but you. You see, she fainted. I always thought she'd come between us, but what queer things God does!"

His voice rose suddenly, saying, "Helen, it's unbearable. But you shall not stay here. I shall take you away."

"There's Notya."

"Yes."

"Do you mean—Is she going to die?"

"I don't know. She may not live for long. And if she dies, you shall come away with me. We can go together anywhere in the world. There's no morality and no sense and no justice in such a sacrifice."

"Oh," she sighed, "what peace, if I could go with you!"

"You shall go with me."

She felt his heart ticking away the seconds. "But I can't," she said softly. "You see, I've married him."

"Great God—!"

"I know. But I can't help it. I knew what I was doing. And he needs me."

"Ah! If he's going to need you—And again, what of my need of you?"

"You're a better man than he is."

He pushed her from him and went to the window, and she dared not ask him for his thoughts. Perhaps he had none: perhaps, in the waste of snow from which the black trunks of trees stood up, he saw a likeness to his life.

He turned to ask, "How often does that beast get washed?"

She looked at him vaguely. "Who?"

"That dog."

"Oh—once a fortnight."

"Who does it?"

"John or I."

"You let him sleep with you?"

"Outside my door."

"I think he ought to be inside. I'm going over to see John. You can't live here alone. And, Helen, I've not given up my right to you. You shall come to me when Mrs. Caniper sets you free."

She was standing now, and she answered through stiff lips, "You mustn't hope for that. You know I told you long ago the kind of woman I am."

"And you can't change yourself for my sake?"

She moved uneasily. "I would, so gladly, if I could," she said, and he shook his head as though he did not believe her.

"But I will not have you and John trying to arrange my life. I choose to be alone. If you interfere—" His look reproached her. "I'm sorry, Zebedee, but I'm suffering, too, and I know best about George, about myself. After all"—her voice rose and broke—"after all, I've married him! Oh, what a fuss, what a fuss! We make too much of it. We have to bear it. We are not willing to bear anything. Other women, other men, have lost what they loved best. We want too much. We were not meant for happiness."

His hand was on the door, but he came back and stood close to her. "Do you think you have been talking to a stone? What do you expect of me? I"—he held his head—"I am trying to keep sane. To you, this may be a small thing among greater ones, but to me—it's the only one."

"To me, too. But if I made a mistake in promising, I should make another in running away now. One has to do one's best."

"And this is a woman's best!" he said in a voice she did not know.

"Is that so bad?" She was looking at a stranger: she was in an empty world, a black, wild place, and in it she could not find Zebedee.

"There is no logic in it," she heard him say, and she was in her room once more, holding to the bed-rail, standing near this haggard travesty of her man.

"Oh! What have I done to you?" she cried out.

He followed his own thought. "If your sense of duty is greater towards him than towards me, why don't you go to him and give him all he wants?"

"He has not asked for it."

"And I do. If he has no rights, remember mine; but if he has them—"

"Yes, it may come to that," she said, and he saw her lined, white face.

"No, no, Helen! Not for my sake this time, but for yours! No! I didn't mean it. Believe me, I could be glad if you were happy."

"I shan't be happy without you, but if I can't have you, why shouldn't I do my best for him?"

He looked at the floor and said, "Helen, I can't let him touch you." He looked up. "Have you thought of everything?"

"There have been days and days to think in."

"My dear, it isn't possible! To give you into his hands!"

"I shall keep out of them if I can, and no one else can do it for me. Remember that, or you will push me into them. But I'm trying to make my body a little thing. It's only a body, after all. Zebedee, will you let me sit on your knee? Just this once more. Oh, how your arms know how to hold me! I hope—I hope you'll never have to marry any one for Daniel's sake."

He rested his cheek on hers. "Daniel will have to look after himself. Men don't hurt the people they love best for the sake of some one else. That's a woman's trick."

"You never talked like this before."

"Because, you see, no woman had ever hurt me so much."

"And now she has."

"Oh, yes, she has."

"And you love me less?"

"Come with me and see! Helen, Helen, darling, come with me. I want you so. We'll make life beautiful together. Sweetheart, if you needn't suffer, I could bear it for myself, I could manage to bear it for myself."

"I should suffer if I came with you. I should always feel George wanting me."

"And you won't feel me?"

"You are just like myself. You will always be there. No one can come between. George can't."

"But his children will." He set her on her feet and began to walk up and down the room. "Had you thought of that?"

She covered her face and whispered, "I can't talk about it yet. And, oh!" she went on, "I wanted ours. Did you?"

"You know I did."

"And even if I went with you, we couldn't have them. That's gone—just slipped away. They were so clear to me, so beautiful."

"In that house of ours," he said. "Helen, I bought that house before I went away."

"Our house?"

"Our square house—with the trees."

She broke into another storm of sobbing, and he took her on his knee again. He knew that Halkett's children would come and stifle pain and, as he tried to think he would not hate them, her voice came softly through those thoughts.

"Zebedee, I want to tell you something."

"Go on, dear."

"I want to tell you—I—He's not repellent. Don't think that. I didn't want you to think that. I suppose one can forget. And I shall always think, 'It's Zebedee who has the rest, who has all the best of me.'"

"I know you, dear. You'll be giving him all you have."

"Oughtn't I to?"

"Oh, my darling, God only knows. Don't ask me. To me there seems only one thing to do—to smite him in the mouth—and you whom I worship have tied my hands. And I sit here! What do you think is happening to me inside? I'm mad! I can promise nothing. I need time to think. Helen, if you would hate him always, I could bear it better. But you won't, you'll grow fond of him—and I suppose I should be glad; but I can't stand that." He put her down roughly and stood over her. "I can't endure this any longer," he said under his breath, and went.

Then she realized what she had done to him, and with how much gentleness he had used her. She ran after him and called from the stairhead:

"Zebedee! Wait for me. Kiss me once more. I'll never ask again. It isn't easy for me, either, Zebedee."

He stood, helpless, enraged at destiny, aware that any weapon he might lift in her defence would fall on her and wound her. He could do nothing but swear his lasting love, his ready service.

CHAPTER XXXIII

She thought Zebedee would come to her on the next day, or the next, but she watched in vain for him. Though she had sent him from her, she longed for him to be back, and at night, when George entered the kitchen, she hardly looked up to welcome him. Her mind was more concerned with Zebedee's absence than with George's presence, but in her white face and tired eyes he fancied resentment for the kiss that still burned on his own mouth.

"You haven't much to say," he told her, after an hour of silence. He did not know if he most hated or adored the smooth head turned sideways, the small ear and the fine eyebrow, the aloofness that kept him off and drew him on; but he knew he was the victim of a glorious kind of torment of which she was the pain and the delight.

"I have been thinking," she explained.

"Then why don't you tell me what you think about?"

"Would you be interested?" She smiled at the thought of telling him with what anxiety she looked for Zebedee, with what anger she blamed him for neglect, with what increase she loved him.

"Yes, I would. Now you're laughing. D'you think it funny? D'you think I can't read or write, or understand the way you speak?"

"George," she said, "I wish you wouldn't get so cross. I don't think any of those things."

"Never think about me at all, I suppose. Not worth it."

She answered slowly, "Yes, you are," and he grunted a mockery of thanks.

It was some time before he threw out two words of accusation. "You're different."

"Different?"

"That's what I said. You never answer straight."

"Don't I?"

"There you are again!"

"What do you want me to say? Shall I ask you how I'm different? Well, I've asked, George. Won't you answer?"

"I can't. I can't explain. But a few nights back—well—all tonight you've been sitting as if I wasn't here. I don't know why I stand it. Look here! You married me."

"So you are always telling me; but no one can buy the things you want."

"I'll get them somehow." He used the tones that made her shrink, but tonight she was unmoved, and he saw that her womanhood was crushed by the heaviness of her fatigue, and she was no more than a human being who needed rest.

"I think you ought to go to bed," he said. "I'm going. Good-night." He kissed her hand, but he did not let it fall. "You're not to look so white tomorrow night," he said.

She did not know why she went to the kitchen door and stood by it while he climbed the wall and dropped to the crisp snow on the further side. He called out another low good-night and had her answer before she heard his boots crunching the frozen crust. No stars and no moon shone on the white garden, and to her it was like a place of death. The deep black of the trees against the wall made a mourning border, and the poplars lifted their heads in questioning of fate, but they had no leaves to make the question audible, and no wind stirred their branches. Everything was silent; it seemed as if everything had died, and Helen was envious of the dead. She wished she might curl herself up at a poplar's foot and sleep there until the frost tightened on her heart and stopped its beating.

"It is so hard," she said aloud, and shut the door and locked it with limp hands.

The kitchen's warmth gave back her sanity and humour, and she laughed as she sat before the fire again, but when she spoke to Jim, it was in whispers, because of the emptiness of the old house.

"We shall manage if only we can see Zebedee sometimes. Other women have worse things to bear. And George likes me. I can't help liking people when they like me. And there'll be Zebedee sometimes. We'll try to keep things beautiful, and we'll be strong and very courageous, and now we'll go to bed."

The next morning Zebedee appeared, and in the hall of their many greetings, she slipped her hand into his.

"What have you been doing, Zebedee?"

"Working."

"Is that all?"

He laughed, and asked, "Isn't that enough?"

"No; not enough to keep you from me. I thought you would come yesterday and the day before."

He looked at her with an astonishment that was near scorn, for she had driven him from her and now reproached him when he did not run back. She put her hand on his and looked at him with shadowless grey eyes, and showed him a mouth that tempted, as she had done before she married this other man to whom she was determined to be faithful. His thoughts were momentarily bitter, but his words were gentle.

"I told you I wanted time to think." He pressed her hand and gave it back to her. "And I have thought, and, since you are what you are, I see, at present, no other way but yours."

"Oh." She was daunted by his formality.

"Shall I go up to Mrs. Caniper?"

"Yes," she said, puzzled. "But aren't you cold? Come into the kitchen and you shall have some coffee. I had it ready in case you came. Your hands—your cheeks—" She touched him lightly and led him to the kitchen fire.

"I think we shall have more snow," he said, and his manner was snow against her heart.

"Do you?" she said politely, but her anger dropped away as she saw his face more clearly and knew he had not slept. She knew, too, that his mind was as firmly fixed as hers, and she felt as if the whole world were sliding from her, for this was not her lover: this was some ascetic who had not yet forgotten his desires. He looked haggard, fierce with renunciation and restraint, and she cried out, "Zebedee, darling, don't look like that!"

He laughed a little, moved, and passed his hands over his face. "No," he said sensibly.

He killed the words she had ready for him: she felt them fall, dead things, into her throat, and hang helplessly in her breast. She handed him the cup, and while he drank she stood beside the table and watched him with despair and indignation. She had not imagined him thus changed: she had expected the old adoring looks, the loving words, everything but his caresses and his claims, and he treated her as though she were no more to him than any other woman. She knew him to be just and honest, but she thought him cruel and, aghast at the prospect of endless days wherein he would not smile at her nor praise her, she doubted her ability to live without him. She caught her breath in fear that his habit of indifference would change to indifference indeed; and without shame, she confessed that she would rather have him suffering through love of her than living happily through lack of it.

Mechanically, she moved after him up the stairs, played her part, and followed him down again; but when next he came, she had stiffened in emulation of him, and they talked together like people who had known each other for many years, but never known each other well.

Once he trespassed, but that was not to please himself.

"If you need me, you'll still use me?" he said hurriedly, and she answered, "Yes, of course."

He added, "I can't keep it from Daniel for ever."

"No. It need not be a secret now, except from Notya. And if she lives—"

"She may live for a long time if she has no shock."

"Ah, then," Helen said calmly, "she must not know."

He found her more beautiful than she had been, for now her serenity was by conquest, not by nature, and her head was carried with a freer grace. It might have been the freedom of one who had gained through loss and had the less weight to carry, but he tortured himself with wondering what fuller knowledge had given her maturer grace. Of this he gave no sign, and the attitude he maintained had its merciful result on Helen, for if he pretended not to need her, she had a nightly visitor who told her dumbly of his longing. Love bred liking, as she had prophesied, and, because life was lonely, she came to listen for his step. She was born to minister to people, and the more securely Zebedee shut her out, the more she was inclined to slip into the place that George had ready for her. And with George the spring was in conspiracy. The thaw came in a night, and the next morning's sun began its work of changing a white country into one of wet and glistening green. Snow lingered and grew dirty in the hollows, and became marked with the tiny feet of sheep, but elsewhere the brilliance of the moor was like a cry. It was spring shouting its release from bonds. Buds leapt on the trees, the melted snow flooded the streams, tributary ones bubbled and tinkled in unexpected places.

"Now," Helen said, leaning from the window of Mildred Caniper's room, "you can't help getting well. Oh, how it smells and looks and feels! When the ground is drier, you shall go for a walk, but you must practise up here first. Then John shall carry you downstairs."

But Mildred Caniper did not want to be energetic: she sat by the fire in a cushioned wicker chair, and when Helen looked at the lax figure and the loosened lines of the face she recognized the woman who had made confession to relieve a mind that had finished with all struggling. It was not the real Mildred Caniper who had told that story in the night; it was the one who, weakened by illness, was content to sit with folded hands by the fireside.

She dimmed the sun for Helen and robbed the spring of hope.

This glory would not last: colours would fade and flowers die, and so human life itself would slip into a mingling of light and shadow, a pale confluence of the two by which a man could see to dig a grave.

Helen leaned out again, trying to recover the sense of youth, of boundless possibilities of happiness that should have been her sure possession.

"Are you looking for Zebedee?" Mildred asked. "He doesn't come so often."

"You don't need him. And he is busy. He isn't likely to come today."

Yet she wished ardently that he might, for though he would have no tenderness to give her, he would revivify her by the vigour of his being: she would see a man who had refused to let one misfortune cripple him, and as though he had divined her need, he came.

"I had to go to Halkett's Farm," he explained.

"Who's ill there?" she asked sharply.

"The housekeeper."

"I hadn't heard. Is she very ill?"

"She may be."

"Then I hope she'll die," she said in a low voice.

"My dear!" He was startled into the words, and they made her laugh openly for joy of knowing they were ready on his tongue. Lightly she swayed towards him, but he held her off.

"No, no, my heart." He turned deliberately from her. "Why do you wish that?"

"Because of Miriam. She ought to die."

"I'm afraid she won't. She's pretty tough."

"Is there anybody to look after her? I could go sometimes, if you like."

He smiled at this confusion of ministering and avenging angel.

"There's a servant there who seems capable enough."

"I wonder why George didn't tell me."

"She was all right yesterday."

"You'll have to see her tomorrow. Then you'll come here, too."

"There isn't any need."

"But Notya likes to see you. Come and see her now."

She sighed when they walked downstairs together as though things had never changed. "Oh, Zebedee, I wanted you to come today. You have made me feel clean again. Notya—oh—!" She shuddered. "She looks like some fruit just hanging to a tree. Soon she will slip, and she doesn't care. She doesn't think. And once she was like a blade, so bright and edged. And when I looked at her this morning, I felt as if I were fattening and rotting, too, and it wasn't spring any longer. It was autumn, and everything was over-ripe."

"You don't take enough exercise," he said briskly. "Walk on the moor every day. It's only fair to Jim. Read something stiff—philosophy, for instance. It doesn't matter whether you understand it or not, so long as you try. Promise you'll do that. I'll bring some books tomorrow. Take them as medicine and you'll find they're food. And, Helen"—he was at the gate and he looked back at her—"you are rather like a blade yourself."

He knew the curing properties of praise.

CHAPTER XXXIV

When evening came, the blue colour of the sky had changed to one that was a memory of the earth's new green. Helen went through the garden to the moor and sat there on a grey rock out of which her own grey figure might have been carved. She watched the stars blink forth and stare; she saw the gradual darkening of the world, and then Halkett's moving shape came towards her. Out here, he was in his proper place: the kitchen made him clumsy, but wide places set him off, and she felt a kind of pride in his quickness and his strength.

"George," she said softly as he would have passed her, and he swung round and bent and took her in his arms, without hesitation or mistake.

"Were you waiting for me?" he whispered, and felt her nod against his coat. She freed herself very gently. "Shall we stay out here?" he said.

"No. I have left Notya long enough."

"What made you wait for me?"

"I—don't know," she said. She had not asked herself the question, and now the unspoken answer shocked her with its significance. She had gone to wait for him without any thought. It might have been the night that drew her out, but she knew it was not that. Once before, she had called herself a slave, and so she labelled herself again, but now she did it tremulously, without fierceness, aware that it was her own nature to which she was chiefly bound.

"Are you going to wait for me every night?" she heard him say. "Give me your hand, Helen. It is so small. Will you go over the wall or through the door? I'd like to lift you over."

"No. I want to go through the garden. There are primroses

there. Big ones, like stars."

"It's you that are a star."

"I think they liked the snow. And the poplars are all buds. I wish I could sit in the tree-tops and look right across the moor."

"And wait for me. And when I came I'd hold my arms out and you'd jump into them."

"If I didn't fly away."

"Ay, I expect you would do that."

They did not speak again until they reached the house, and when she had lighted the kitchen lamp she saw him looking moodily into the fire.

"Is Mrs. Biggs better?" she asked smoothly.

"What do you know about her?"

"I heard she was ill."

"Who told you?"

"Dr. Mackenzie."

"Oh, he's been again, has he?"

"Yes." Her voice had a ring in it. "And he will come tomorrow."

"And the next day, I suppose, and the next. I should have thought he'd spare that old nag of his; but no, up he comes, and I want to know why."

She did not answer immediately because she feared to betray the indignation that moved in her like a living thing. She found her sewing and signed to him to put her chair into its place, and when she had stitched steadily for a time she said in pleasant tones, "George, you are like a bad person in a book."

"I'm not up to this kind of talk. You told me yourself that Mrs. Caniper hardly needs a doctor. What does he come for, then? Is it for you?"

"No, it is not."

"Do you like the man?"

She opened her lips and shut them several times before she spoke. "I'm very fond of him—and of Daniel."

"Oh, leave Daniel alone. No woman would look at him."

She gave him a considering gaze for which he could have

struck her, because it put him further from her than he had ever been.

"It's no good staring at me like that. I've seen you with him before now."

"Everybody on the moor must have seen me with him."

"Yes, and walking pretty close. I remember that."

"Very likely you will see me walking with him again."

"No, by God!"

"Oh," she said, wearily, "how often you call on God's name."

"No wife of mine—"

She laughed. "You talk like Bluebeard. How many wives have you?"

"I've none," he cried in an extremity of bitterness. "But I'll have one yet, and I'll keep her fast!"

She lifted her head in the haughty way he dreaded. "I will not endure suspicions," she said clearly, but she flushed at her own words, for she remembered that she had been willing to give Zebedee the lesser tokens of her love, and it was only by his sternness that she could look George in the eyes. Zebedee would have taken her boldly and completely, believing his action justified, but he would have no little secret dealings, and she was abashed by the realization of her willingness to deceive. She was the nearer to George by that discovery, and the one shame made her readier to suffer more.

"It's because I want you," he said, shading his eyes; and for the first time she had no resentment for his desires.

"Oh, George, don't you think you had better go home?" she said.

"Why?" he asked her.

"Because—because I want to read."

"Well, I can watch you."

"And you won't think it rude?"

He shook his head. There was a rare joy in sitting within reach of her and honouring her with his restraint.

Her slim feet were crossed on the dog's back, and she hardly stirred except to turn a page: the firelight threw colours on her dress, behind her there was a dark dresser where china gleamed, and sitting there, she made a little picture of home for a man who could remember none but hired women in his house.

"I wish you'd talk to me," he said, and at once she shut her book with a charming air of willingness.

"Do you know what you've been reading about?" he dared to ask her slyly, for surely she had been conscious of his thoughts of her.

She would not be fluttered. "Yes. Shall I tell you?"

"No," he said.

Her voice was influenced by the quick beating of her heart.

"Do you never read anything?"

"I gave it up long ago."

"Why? What did you do at night before you—"

"Before I married you? I used to smoke and wish it was time to go to bed, and look at the newspaper sometimes."

"That must have been very dull."

"I used to watch the clock," he said. He leaned towards her and spoke quickly, softly. "And I watch it still! From waking till dusk I watch it and think of you, sitting and waiting for me. Oh, what's the good of talking to me of books? You're here—and you're my wife, and I'll talk to you of nothing but yourself." He knelt, and his hands were on her waist. "Yourself—my beauty—my little saint—your little hands and feet—your cheeks I want to kiss—your hair—" He drew her to his breast and whispered, "How long is it—your hair?"

There was no resistance in her, and her neck could not hold up the head that drooped over his shoulder when he kissed her ear and spoke in it.

"Helen—Helen—I love you. Tell me you love me. You've got to kiss me—Yes—"

She answered in a quiet voice, but she stopped for breath between the words. "I think—there's some one—in the hall. It must be John."

Reluctantly he loosed her, and she left him quickly for the dark passage which covered and yet cooled her as she called out, "John! Is that you?"

"Both of us," Rupert answered.

"But it's Friday."

"Yes. Won't you let me have a whole holiday tomorrow?"

She looked back into the kitchen and saw George prepared to meet her brothers. Never before had she seen him with so fine a manner, and, smiling at him, she felt like a conspirator, leagued with this man who was liberated by possession of her, against the two who would feel horror when they learnt she was possessed.

John's jaw tightened as he saw George and nodded to him, but Rupert's greeting had its usual friendliness.

"Hullo, here's George!" They shook hands. "I've not seen you for months. What's the weather going to be tomorrow? It's starlight tonight."

"It'll be fine, I think."

"That's good. Helen, you've hidden my slippers again, and I told you not to. What a fiend for tidiness you are!"

"I couldn't leave them in the dust." She was half enjoying her self-consciousness. "They're in the cupboard."

"Find them, there's a dear."

She brought the slippers and went back to her chair. The three men seemed to fill the kitchen. John was silent and, leaning against the table, he filled his pipe and looked up sometimes as the others talked. Rupert, slim against Halkett's bulk, alert and straight, was thinking faster than he spoke, and while he reminded George of this and that, how they had gone ratting once together, how George had let him try a colt that he was breaking, Helen knew there were subtle questions in his brain, but if George suspected them, he gave no sign. He was at his ease, for with men he had neither diffidence nor surliness, and Helen remembered that she had hardly seen him except in the presence of Miriam or herself, two women who, in different ways, had teased him into sulkiness.

Her heart lightened and, when he chanced to look at her, she smiled again. A few seconds later, Rupert followed Helen's glance and learnt what had caused the slight confusion of George's speech. She was looking at him with an absorbed and hopeful interest. She was like a child attracted by some new and changeful thing, and her beauty had an animation it often lacked.

"Can't we all sit down?" Rupert said. He promised himself a pleasant evening of speculation.

John handed his tobacco pouch to George and, having exchanged a few remarks about the frost, the snow, the lambing season, they seemed to consider that courtesy's demands had been fulfilled; but Rupert talked to hide the curiosity which could have little satisfaction until Halkett took his leave.

When he rose to go, he stood before Helen's chair and looked down at her. He was so near that she had to throw back her head before she could see his face.

"Good-night, George."

"Good-night." He took her hand and kissed it, nodded to the others, and went out.

Imperceptibly, Helen straightened herself and took a breath. There was a vague stir in the room.

"Well! I've never been more damned," John said.

"Why?" Helen asked.

"That salute. Is it his usual manner?"

"He has done it before. I liked it."

"He did it very well," said Rupert. "Inspired, I should think. Will you have a cigarette?"

"Will it make me sick?"

"Try it. But why do we find you entertaining the moorland rake?"

She was absurd with the cigarette between her lips, and she asked mumblingly as Rupert held the match, "Why do you call him that?"

Rupert spread his hands. "He has a reputation."

"And he deserves it," said John.

She took the cigarette and many little pieces of tobacco from her mouth. "Before you go any further, I think I had better tell you that I am married to him."

"Good God!" John said, in a conversational tone.

There was a pause that threatened to be everlasting.

"Helen, dear, did you say 'married to him'?"

"Yes, I did."

Rupert lighted one cigarette from another and carefully threw the old one into the fire.

"When?" John asked. He was still staring at her.

"I forget the date."

"Won't you tell us about it?" Rupert said. He leaned against the mantelpiece and puffed quickly.

"There's nothing more to tell."

"But when was it?" John persisted.

"Oh—about a month, six weeks, ago. The paper is upstairs, but one forgets."

"Wants to?"

"I didn't say so, did I? Notya is not to know."

"And Zebedee?"

"Of course he knows."

Rupert was frowning on her with a troubled look, and she knew he was trying to understand, that he was anxious not to hurt her.

"I'm damned if I understand it," John muttered.

Her lips had a set smile. "I'm sure," she said lightly, "you'll never be damned for that. I'm afraid I can't explain, but Zebedee knows everything."

They found nothing else to say: John turned away, at last, and busied himself uneasily with his pipe: Rupert's cigarette became distasteful, and, throwing it after the other, he drove his hands into his pockets and watched it burn.

"I suppose we ought to have congratulated George," he said, and looked grieved at the omission.

Helen laughed on a high note, and though she knew she was disclosing her own trouble by that laughter, she could not stay it.

"Oh, Rupert, don't!"

"My dear, I know it's funny, but I meant it. I wish I could marry you myself."

She laughed again and waved them both away. "Go and see Notya. She may not be asleep."

When John came downstairs, he looked through the kitchen door and said good-night; then he advanced and kissed her. She could not remember when he had last done that, and it was, she thought, as though he kissed the dead. He patted her arm awkwardly.

"Good-night, child."

"Don't worry," she said, steadying her lips.

"Is there anything we can do?"

"Be nice to George."

"Oh, I've got to be."

"John, I wish you wouldn't talk as if he's—bad."

"I didn't mean to set myself up as judge, but I never liked him."

"But I like him," she said. "Go home and tell Lily. I'm afraid she'll lie awake all night!"

"What a family this is!"

"Once, I might have said that to you. I didn't, John."

"But we are a success."

"And why should we not be? We shall be! We—we are. Go home. Good-night."

She waited for Rupert, dreading his quick eyes.

"Notya seems better," he said easily. "Well, did you finish the cigarette?"

"I didn't like it."

"And it looked wrong. A piece of fine sewing suits you better."

She smiled. "Does it? Have you had supper?"

"Lily fed me. I like that girl. The only people I ever want to marry are the ones that some one else has chosen. It's contrariness, I suppose." He looked round. "Two arm-chairs? Do you always sit here?"

"Yes. Notya can't hear us."

"I see."

"And you want to see the rest?"

"I do."

"I shall show you nothing."

"I'd rather find it out."

"Tomorrow," she said, "you will see Daniel and Zebedee. I know you'll be curious about him. I don't mind, but don't let him notice it, please, Rupert."

He marked her little tremor. "Trust me. I'm wasted on the bank."

"You and Daniel will have a fine talk, I suppose. The walls of that house are very thin. Be careful."

"Yes, my dear. I can't help wishing I had not left home."

She stood up. "I don't wish anything undone. If you begin undoing, you find yourself in a worse tangle."

"You're not unhappy?"

"Do I look it?"

"You always answer one question with another. You didn't look it. You do now."

She sighed. "I almost wish you hadn't come, Rupert. You made beauty seem so near."

CHAPTER XXXV

She had another reason for her wish. She knew that Rupert had but delayed what was inevitable, and when it came one night, a few weeks later, she had no feeling beyond relief that the fight was over, that she need no longer scheme to outwit George with her advances and retreats. Afterwards, she suffered from a black anger that she must serve the man she did not love, a dull despair from the knowledge that, while both lived, the tie would hold. Her mind tried, and failed, to make nothing of it; by nature she was bound to him who took most from her, and when George had played the husband, he left her destitute. That Zebedee would always have the best of her had been her boast, but for a time, there was nothing he could have. She was George Halkett's woman. The day was fogged with memories of the night, yet through that fog she looked for his return. She was glad when she heard his step outside and, going to the kitchen door, felt herself lifted off her feet. She did not try to analyze the strange mingling of willingness and shrinking that made up her feeling for him, but she found mental safety in abandoning herself to what must be, a primitive pleasure in the fact of being possessed, a shameful happiness in submission.

Nevertheless, it was only in his presence that she lost her red sense of shame, and though she still walked nobly, looked with clear eyes, and carried a high head, she fancied herself bent by broken pride, blinded and dusty-haired. Zebedee's books helped her to blot out that vision of herself and the other of Mildred Caniper still sitting by the fire and refusing the fulness of the sun. What she read amazed her with its profundity and amused her with its inconclusiveness. She had an awed pity for men whose lives were occupied in these endless questionings, and while Mildred idly turned the pages of periodicals she once had scorned, Helen frowned and bit her lips over the problems of the ages.

They gave her and Zebedee something impersonal to talk of when he came on his weekly visit.

"It's no good telling me," she warned him firmly, "that my poplars are not really there. I can feel them and see them and hear them—always hear them. If they weren't there, they would be! If I exist, so do they."

"Quite so. You're doing very well. I told you the medicine would turn to food."

"It's not food. What is it that nasty people chew? Gum? Yes, chewing-gum. It keeps me going. I mean—"

He helped her over that abyss. "It's a most improper name for wisdom."

"This isn't wisdom. Wisdom is just going on—and—keeping the world clean."

"Then," he said slowly, "you may count among the sages."

They stood together by the schoolroom window and watched the windy sunshine darting among the laurel bushes and brightening the brass on the harness of the patient horse outside the gate.

"I wonder," Helen said, speaking as if she were not quite awake, "whether Mr. Pinderwell ever read philosophy."

"No," Zebedee answered in the same tones; "he took to wood-carving."

This time she leapt the abyss unaided and with a laugh.

"But then, he never had a stepmother nodding beside the fire. What is going to happen to her?"

"She has very little strength."

"But she isn't going to die?"

"Not yet, I think, dear." The word slipped from him, and they both listened to its echoes.

"I wish you'd go," she whispered.

"I'm going." He did not hesitate at the door or he would have seen her drop into a chair and let her limp arms slide across the table as she let out a noisy sob of happiness because his friendliness was still only a cloak that could sometimes be lifted to show the man beneath.

Almost gaily, she went to Mildred Caniper's room.
"Zebedee stayed a long time today. I could hear you talking."
"Yes."
"Isn't he busy now?"
"He works all day and half the night."
"Oh." Mildred's twisted face regained a semblance of its old expression and her voice some of its precision. "Then you ought to be looking after him."
"I can't manage both of you."
"No, but Mrs. Samson could look after me." The words were slovenly again; the face changed subtly as sand changes under water. It became soft and indefinite and yielding, betraying the slackening of the mind.

"Mrs. Samson is a nice woman—very kind. She knows what I want. I must have a good fire. I don't need very much. She doesn't bother me—or talk. I don't want to be bothered—about anything. I'm still—rather tired. I like to sit here and be warm. Give me that magazine, Helen. There's a story—" She found the place and seemed to forget all she had said.

Helen left the room and, as she sat on the topmost stair, she wished Mr. Pinderwell would stop and speak to her, but he hurried up and down as he had always done, intent on his own sad business of seeking what he had lost. It was strange that he could not see the children who were so plain to Helen. She turned to speak to them, but she had outgrown them in these days, and even Jane was puzzled by her grief that Mildred Caniper wanted to be kept warm, and, with some lingering faculty, wished Helen to be happy, but needed her no longer.

Helen whispered into the dimness because her thoughts were unwholesome and must be cast forth.

"She only wants to be kept warm! It was sweet of her to try

to think of me, but she couldn't go on thinking. Oh, Jane, Mrs. Samson and I are just the same. She doesn't mind who puts coals on the fire. I wish she'd die. I always loved her very much, and she loved me, but now she doesn't. She's just a—bundle. It's ugly. If I stay here and look at her, I shall get like her. Oh—she wants me to go and live with Zebedee. Zebedee! He wouldn't like me to go on like this. The philosophers—but that old bishop can't make me think that Notya isn't dying. That's what she's doing, Jane—dying. But no, dying is good and death is splendid. This is decay." She stood up and shuddered. "I mustn't stay here," she murmured sensibly.

She called to Jim in a loud voice that attempted cheerfulness and alarmed her with its noise in the silent house of sorrow and disease.

"The moor, Jim!" she said, and when she had passed through the garden with the dog leaping round her, she shook her skirts and held up her palms to get the freshness of the wind on them.

"We'll find water," she said, but she would not go to the stream that ran into the larch-wood. Today, the taint of evil was about Halkett's Farm, as that of decay was in Mildred Caniper's room.

"We'll go to the pool where the rushes are, Jim, and wash our hands and face."

They ran fleetly, and as they went she saw George at a distance on his horse. He waved his hat, and, before she knew what she was doing, she answered with a grimace that mocked him viciously and horrified her with its spontaneity. She cried aloud, and, sinking to the ground, she hid her dishonoured face.

"No, no," she moaned. She hated that action like an obscenity. Surely she was tainted, too.

Jim licked her covering hands, and whined when she paid no heed.

"Hateful! hateful!" were the words he heard and tried to understand. He sat, alert and troubled, while clouds rolled across the sky, and dark reflections of them made stately progress on the moor. Sheep, absorbed in feeding, drew near, looked up and darted off with foolish, warning bleats, but still his mistress kept her face hidden, and did not move until he barked loudly at the sight of Halkett riding towards them.

"I couldn't keep away," the man said, bending from his saddle.

She rose and leaned against his knee. "George, what do I look like?"

His fervent answer was not the one she wanted.

"But do I look the same?"

He held her by the chin. "Have you been crying?"

"No."

"What is it then?"

She looked beyond him at the magnificence of the clouds and her troubles dwindled. "I felt miserable. I was worried."

"And you're happier now?"

She nodded.

"Then give me a kiss."

She turned her cheek to him.

"No. I said, give me one."

"I can't reach you."

"You don't want to."

"I never want to kiss people."

"People! Then do it to please me."

His cheek hardly felt her pressure.

"It's the way a ghost would kiss," he said.

"That's how I shall haunt you when I'm dead."

"Nay, we'll have to die together."

She wrinkled her face. "But we can't do that without a lot of practice."

"What? Oh!" Her jokes made him uneasy. "I must go on. Helen, I'll see you tonight."

"Yes, you'll see the ghost who gives the little kisses."

"Don't say it!"

"But it's nice to be a ghost, you feel so light and free. There isn't any flesh to be corrupted. I'm glad I thought of that, George. Good-bye."

"No. Come here again. Stand on my foot." He clinched her waist and kissed her on the mouth and let her drop. "You are no ghost," he said, and rode away.

She was indeed no ghost. Some instinct told him how to deal with her, and when he insisted on her humanity, her body thrilled in answer and agreement, and with each kiss and each insistence she became more his own; yet she was thrall less to the impulses of her youth than to some age-old willingness to serve him who possessed her. But her life had mental complications, for she dreaded in Zebedee the disloyalty which she reluctantly meted out to him when George had her in his arms. She would not have Zebedee love another woman, and she longed for assurance of his devotion, but she could not pass the barrier he had set up; she could not try to pass it without another and crueller disloyalty to both men. Her body was faithful to George and her mind to Zebedee, and the two fought against each other and wearied her.

The signs of strain were only in her eyes; her body had grown more beautiful, and when Miriam arrived on a short visit to the moor, she stopped in the doorway to exclaim, "But you're different! Why are you different?"

"It is a long time since you went away," Helen said slowly. "Centuries."

"Not to me! The time has flown." She laughed at her recollections. "And, anyhow, it's only a few months, and you have changed."

"I expect it is my clothes," Helen said calmly. "They must look queer to you."

"They do. But nice. I've brought some new ones for you. I think you'll soon be prettier than I am. Think of that!"

They had each other by the hand and looked admiringly in each other's face, remembering small peculiarities they had half forgotten: there was the soft hair on Helen's temples, trying, as Zebedee said, to curl; there was the little tilt to Miriam's eyebrows, giving her that look of some one not quite human, more readily moved to mischief than to kindness, and never to be held at fault.

"Yes, it's centuries," Helen said.

"It's only a day!"

"Then you have been happy," Helen said, letting out a light sigh of content.

"Yes, but I'm glad to be here again, so long as I needn't stay. I've heaps to tell you." She stretched herself, like a cat. "I knew there was fun in the world. I had faith, my dear, and I found it."

Helen was looking at her with her usual confusion of feelings: she wanted to shake off Miriam's complacence roughly, while she was fondly glad that she should have it, but this remark would not pass without a word, and Helen shook her head.

"No; you didn't find it. Uncle Alfred gave it to you—he and I."

"You? Oh—yes, I suppose you did. Well—thank you very much, and don't let us talk about it any more. You're like a drag-net, bringing up the unpleasant. Don't let us quarrel."

"Quarrel! I couldn't," Helen said simply.

"Are you so pleased to see me?"

Helen's reluctant smile expanded. "I suppose it's that."

"Aha! It's lovely to be me! People go down like ninepins! Why?" Piously, she appealed to Heaven. "Why?"

"They get up again, though," Helen said with a chuckle.

"For instance?" Miriam demanded truculently.

"Oh, I'm not going to be hard on you," Helen said, and though she spoke with genuine amusement, she felt a little seed of anger germinating in her breast. That was what George had done to her: he had made her heart a fertile place for passions which her mind disdained.

"And I'm so glad to have you here," she added, defying harsh emotions.

"Ah! You're rather nice—and, yes, you are much prettier. How have you done it? I should like to kiss you."

"Well, you may." She put her face close to Miriam's, and enjoyed the coolness of that sisterly salute.

"But," Miriam said, startled by a thought, "need I kiss—her?"
"No. You won't want to do that. She isn't very nice to look at."
Miriam shrank against the wall. "Not ugly?"
"You must come and see," Helen said. She was shaken again by a moment's anger as she looked on Miriam's lovely elegance and remembered the price that had been paid for it. "You must come and see her," she repeated. "Do you think you are the only one who hates deformity?"
"Deformity?" Miriam whispered.
"Her face is twisted. Oh—I see it every day!"
"Helen, don't! I'll go, but don't make me stay long. I'll go now," she said, and went on timid feet.

Helen stayed outside the door, for she could not bring herself to witness Mildred Caniper's betrayal of her decay to one who had never loved her: there was an indecency in allowing Miriam to see it. Helen leaned against the door and heard faint sounds of voices, and in imagination she saw the scene. Mildred Caniper sat in her comfortable chair by a bright fire, though it was now late June of a triumphant summer, and Miriam stood near, answering questions quickly, her feet light on the ground and ready to bear her off.

Very soon the door was opened and Miriam caught Helen's arm.

"I didn't think she would be like that," she whispered. "Helen, she's—she's—"

"I know she is," Helen said deeply.

"But I can't bear it!"

"You don't have to."

They went into Phoebe's room and shut the door, and it was a comfort to Miriam to have two solid blocks of wood between her and the deterioration in the chair.

"I know I ought to stay with you—all alone in this house—no one to talk to—and at night—Are you afraid? Do you have to sleep with her?"

"Sometimes," Helen said, and drew both hands down her face.

"She might get up and walk about and say things. It isn't right for you, or for me and you, to have to live here. Why doesn't Zebedee do something? Why doesn't he take you away?"

"And leave her? I wouldn't go. The moor has hold of me, and it will keep me always. I'm rooted here, and I shall tell George to bury me on a dark night in some marshy place that's always green. And I shall make it greener. You're frightened of me! Don't be silly! I'm saner than most people, I think, but living alone makes one different, perhaps. Don't look like that. I'm the same Helen."

"Yes. I won't be frightened. But why did you say 'George'?"

Helen took a breath as though she lifted something heavy.

"Because he is my husband," she said clearly. She had never used the word before, and she enjoyed the pain it gave her.

There were no merciful shadows in the room: daylight poured in at the windows and revealed Helen standing with hands clasped before her and gazing with wide eyes at Miriam's pale face, her parted lips, her horrified amazement.

"George?" she asked huskily.

"Yes."

"But why?"

"Why does one marry?"

"Oh, tell me, Helen! You can't have loved him."

"Perhaps he loved me."

"But—that night! Have you forgotten it?"

"No. I remember."

"So do I! I dream about it! Helen, tell me. What was it? There's Zebedee. And it was me that George loved."

Helen spoke sharply. "He didn't love you. You bewitched him. He loves me."

"You haven't told me everything."

"There is no reason why I should."

Miriam spoke on a sob. "You needn't be unkind. And where's your ring? You haven't said you love him. You're not really married, are you?"

"Yes, I am."

Crying without stint, Miriam went blindly to the window.

"I wish I hadn't come—!"

"You mustn't be unhappy. I'm not. It isn't very polite to George—or me."

"But when—when you think of that night—Oh! You must be miserable."

"Then you should be."

"I?"

"It was your doing. You tormented him. You played with him. You liked to draw him on and push him back. You turned a man into a—into what we saw that night. George isn't the only man who can be changed into a beast when—when he meets Circe! With me—" Her voice broke with her quickened breathing. Her indignation was no longer for her own maimed life: it was for George, who had been used lightly as a plaything, broken, and given to her for mending.

For a long time Miriam cried, and did not speak, and when she turned to ask a question Helen had almost forgotten her; for all her pity had gone out to George and beautified him and made him dear.

"Tell me one thing," Miriam said earnestly. "It hadn't anything to do with me?"

"What?"

"Marrying him. You see, I fainted, didn't I?"

"Yes."

"Something might have happened then."

"It did."

"What was it?"

"He fell in love with me!" She laughed. "It's possible, because it happened! Otherwise, of course, neither of us could believe it! Oh, don't be silly. Don't look miserable."

"I can't help it. It's my fault. It's my fault if Zebedee is unhappy and if you are. Yes, it is, because if I hadn't—Still, I don't know why you married him."

"I think it was meant to be. If we look back it seems as if it must have been." It was not Helen who looked through the window. "Yes," she said softly, "it is all working to one end. It had to be. Don't talk about it any more."

Wide-eyed above her tear-stained cheeks, her throat working piteously, Miriam stared at this strange sister. "But tell me if you are happy," she said in a breaking voice.

"Yes, I am. I love him," she said softly. Now, she did not lie. The pity that had taught her to love Mildred Caniper had the same lesson in regard to George, and that night, when she looked into the garden and saw him standing there, because he had been forbidden the house, she leaned from her bedroom window and held out her hands and ran downstairs to speak to him.

"You looked so lonely," she told him.

"Didn't you want me a little?" he asked. He looked down, big and gentle, and she felt her heart flutter as with wings. She nodded, and leaned against him. It was the truth: she did want him a little.

CHAPTER XXXVI

Miriam had the evidence of her own eyes to assure her that Helen was not unhappy. The strangely united bride and bridegroom were seen on the moor together, and they looked like lovers. Moreover, Helen stole out to meet him at odd hours, and, on the day before Miriam went away, she surprised them in a heathery dip of ground where Helen sewed and George read monotonously from a book.

"I—didn't know you were here," Miriam stammered.

"Well, we're not conspirators," Helen said. "Come and sit down. George is reading to me."

"No, I don't think I will, thank you." Until now, she had succeeded in avoiding George, but there was no escape from his courteous greeting and outstretched hand. His manners had improved, she thought: he had no trace of awkwardness; he was cool and friendly, and, with the folly of the enamoured, he could no longer find her beautiful. She was at once aware of that, and she knew the meaning of his glance at Helen, who bent over her work and did not look at them.

"How are you?" Halkett said.

She found it difficult to answer him, and while she told herself she did not want his admiration, she felt that some show of embarrassment was her due.

"I'm very well. No; I won't stay. Helen, may I take Jim?"

"If he will go with you."

Jim refused to stir, and with the burden of that added insult, Miriam went on her way. It seemed to her that, in the end, Helen had everything.

Helen believed that the wisdom of her childhood had returned to her to teach her the true cause of happiness. For her it was born of the act of giving, and her knowledge of George's need was changed into a feeling that, in its turn, transformed existence. Her mental confusion cleared itself and, concentrating her powers on him, she tried not to think of Zebedee. She would not dwell on the little, familiar things she loved in him, nor would she speculate on his faithfulness or his pain, for his exile was the one means of George's homecoming. And, though she did not know it, Zebedee, loving her truly, understood the workings of her mind, and his double misery lessened to a single one when he saw her growing more content.

He went to Pinderwell House one fine evening, for there were few days when he could find time to drive up the long road, and though Mildred Caniper did not need his care, she looked for his coming every week.

It was a placid evening after a day of heat, and he could see the smoke from the kitchen chimney going straight and delicately towards the sky. The moor was one sheet of purple at this season, and it had a look of fulfilment and of peace. It had brought forth life and had yet to see it die, and it seemed to lie with its hands folded on its broad breast and to wait tranquilly for what might come.

Zebedee tried to imitate that tranquillity as the old horse jogged up the road, but he had not yet arrived at such perfection of control that his heart did not beat faster as he knocked at Helen's door.

Tonight there was no answer, and having knocked three times he went into the hall, looked into each room and found all empty. He called her name and had silence for response. He went through the kitchen to seek her in the garden, and there, under the poplars, he saw her sitting and looking at the treetops, while George smoked beside her and Jim lay at her feet.

It was a scene to stamp itself on the mind of a discarded lover, and while he took the impress he stood stonily in the doorway. He saw Halkett say a word to Helen, and she sprang up and ran across the lawn.

"I never thought you'd come," she said, breathing quickly.

He moved aside so that her body should not hide him from Halkett's careful eyes.

"Has something happened?" she asked. "You look so white."

"The day has been very hot."

"Yes; up here, even, and in that dreadful little town—Are you working hard?"

"I think so."

"And getting rich?"

"Not a bit."

"I don't suppose you charge them half enough," she said, and made him laugh. "Come and see Notya before she goes to sleep."

"Mayn't I speak to Mr. Halkett?" he asked.

She did not look at the two men as they stood together. Again she watched the twinkling poplar leaves and listened to their voices rustling between the human ones, and when she seemed to have been listening for hours, she said, "Zebedee, you ought to come. It's time Notya went to sleep."

She led him through the house, and neither spoke as they went upstairs and down again, but at the door, she said, "I'll see you drive away," and followed him to the gate.

She stood there until he was out of sight, and then she went slowly to the kitchen where George was waiting for her.

"You've been a long time."

"Have I? I mean, yes, I have."

"What have you been doing?"

"Standing at the gate."

"Talking?"

"Thinking."

"Was he thinking too?"

"I expect so."

"H'm. Do you like him to come marching through your house?"

"Why not? He's an old friend of ours."

"He seems to be! You were in a hurry to get away from me, I

noticed, and then you have to waste time mooning with him in the twilight."

"He wasn't there, George." She laid the back of her hand against her forehead. "I watched him out of sight."

"What for?"

"He looked so lonely, going home to—that. Are you always going to be jealous of any one who speaks to me? It's rather tiring."

"Are you tired?"

"Yes," she said with a jerk, and pressed her lips together. He pulled her to his knee, and she put her face against his strong, tanned neck.

"Well," he said, "what's this for?"

"Don't tease me."

"I'm not so bad, then, am I?"

"Not so bad," she answered. "You have been smoking one of those cigars."

"Yes. D'you mind?"

"I love the smell of them," she said, and he laid his cheek heavily on hers.

"George!"

"U-um?" he said, drowsing over her.

"I think the rest of the summer is going to be happy."

"Yes, but how long's this to last? I want you in my house."

"I wish it wasn't in a hollow."

"What difference does that make? We're sheltered from the wind. We lie snug on winter nights."

"I don't want to. I like to hear the wind come howling across the moor and beat against the walls as if it had great wings. It does one's crying for one."

"Do you want to cry?"

"Yes."

"Now?"

"No."

"When, then?"

"Don't you?"

"Of course not. I swear instead." He shook her gently. "Tell me when you want to cry."

"Oh, just when the wind does it for me," she said sleepily.

"I'll never understand you."

"Yes, you will. I'm very simple, and now I'm half asleep."

"Shall I carry you upstairs?"

She shook her head.

"Helen, come to my house. Bring Mrs. Caniper. I want you. And the whole moor's talking about the way we live."

"Oh, let the moor talk! Don't you love to hear it? It's the voice I love best. I shan't like living in your house while this one stands."

"But you'll have to."

She put up a finger. "I didn't say I wouldn't. Will you never learn to trust me?"

"I am learning," he said.

"And you must be patient. Most people are engaged before they marry. You married me at once."

"Hush!" he said. "I don't like thinking about that."

After this confession, her mind crept a step forward, and she dared to look towards a time when Mildred Caniper would be dead and she at Halkett's Farm. The larch-lined hollow would half suffocate her, she believed, but she would grow accustomed to its closeness as she would grow used to George and George to her. Soon he would completely trust her. He would learn to ask her counsel, and, at night, she would sit and sew and listen to his talk of crops and cattle, and the doings and misdoings of his men. He would have no more shyness of her, but sometimes she would startle him into a memory of how he had wooed her in the kitchen and seen her as a star. And she would have children: not those shining ones who were to have lived in the beautiful bare house with her and Zebedee, but sturdy creatures with George's mark on them. She would become middle-aged and lose her slenderness, and half forget she had ever been Helen Caniper; yet George and the children would always be a little strange to her, and only when she was alone and on the moor would she renew her sense of self and be afraid of it.

The prospect did not daunt her, for she had faith in her capacity to bear anything except the love of Zebedee for another woman. She ignored her selfishness towards him because the need to keep him was as strong as any other instinct: he was hers, and she had the right to make him suffer, and, though she honestly tried to shut her thoughts against him, when she did think of him it was to own him, to feel a dangerous joy in the memory of his thin face and tightened lips.

On the moor, harvests were always late, and George was gathering hay in August when richer country was ready to deliver up its corn, and one afternoon when he was carting hay from the fields beyond the farm, Helen walked into the town, leaving Lily Brent in charge of Mildred Caniper.

Helen had seldom been into the town since the day when she had married George, and the wind, trying to force her back, had beaten the body that was of no more value to her. Things were better now, and she had avenged herself gaily on the god behind the smoke. He had heard few sounds of weeping and he had not driven her from the moor: he had merely lost a suppliant and changed a girl into a woman, and today, in her independence of fate, she would walk down the long road and plant a pleasant thought at every step, and she need not look at the square house which Zebedee had bought for her.

She had told George to meet her at the side road if he had any errands for her in the town, and though he had none, he was there before her. Watching her approach, he thought he had never seen her lovelier. She wore a dress and hat of Miriam's choosing, the one of cream colour and the other black, and the beauty of their simple lines added to the grace that could still awe him.

"You look—like a swan," he said.

"Oh, George, a horrid bird!" She came close and looked up, for she liked to see him puzzled and adoring.

"It's the way you walk—and the white. And that little black hat for a beak."

"Well, swan or not," she said, and laughed, "you think I look nice, don't you?"

"I should think I do!" He stepped back to gaze at her. "You must always have clothes like that. There's no need for you to make your own."

"But I like my funny little dresses! Don't I generally please you? Have you been thinking me ugly all this time?"

He did not answer that. "I wish I was coming with you."

"You mustn't. There are hay-seeds on you everywhere. Is the field nearly finished? George, you are not answering questions!"

"I'm thinking about you. Helen, you needn't go just yet. Sit down under this tree. You're lovely. And I love you. Helen, you love me! You're different now. Will you wear that ring?"

Her mind could not refuse it; she was willing to wear the badge of her submission and so make it complete, and she gave a shuddering sigh. "Oh, George—"

"Yes, yes, you will. Look, here it is. I always have it with me. Give me your little hand. Isn't it bright and heavy? Do you like it?" He held her closely. "And my working clothes against your pretty frock! D'you mind?"

"No." She was looking at the gold band on her finger. "It's heavy, George."

"I chose a heavy one."

"Have you had it in your pocket all the time?"

"All the time."

He and she had been alike in cherishing a ring, but when she reached home she would take Zebedee's from its place and hide it safely. She could not give it back to him: she could not wear it now.

"I must go," she said, and freed herself.

He kissed the banded finger. "Be quick and come back and let me see you wearing it again."

It weighted her, and she went more slowly down the road,

feeling that the new weight was a symbol, and when she looked back and saw George standing where she had left him, she uttered a small cry he could not hear and ran to him.

"George, you must always love me now. You—I—"

"What is it, love?"

"Nothing. Let me go. Good-bye," she said, and walked on at her slow pace. Light winds brought summer smells to her, clouds made lakes of shadow on the moor, and here, where few trees grew and little traffic passed, there were no dusty leaves to tell of summer's age; yet, in the air, there was a smell of flowers changing to fruit.

She passed the gorse bushes in their second blossoming, and the moor, stretched before her, was as her life promised to be: it was monotonous in its bright colouring, quiet and serene, broad-bosomed for its children. Old sheep looked up at her as she went by, and she saw herself in some relationship to them. They were the sport of men, and so was she, yet perhaps God had some care of them and her. It was she and the great God of whose existence she was dimly sure who had to contrive honourable life for her, and the one to whom she had yearly prayed must remain in his own place, veiled by the smoke of the red fires, a survival and a link like the remembrance of her virginity.

So young in years, so wise in experience of the soul, she thought there was little more for her to learn, but acquaintance with birth and death awaited her: they were like beacons to be lighted on her path, and she had no fear of them.

CHAPTER XXXVII

She did her shopping in her unhurried, careful way, and went on to the outfitter who made John's corduroy trousers. Clothes that looked as if they were made of cardboard hung outside the shop; unyielding coats, waistcoats and trousers seemed to be glued against the door: stockings, suspended by their gaudy tops, flaunted stiff toes in the breeze, and piles of more manageable garments were massed on chairs inside, and Helen was aghast at the presence of so many semblances of man.

It was dark in the shop, and the smell of fustian absorbed the air. The owner, who wore an intricately-patterned tie, stood on the pavement and talked to a friend, while a youth, pale through living in obscurity, lured Helen in.

She gave her order: two pairs of corduroy trousers to be made for Mr. Caniper of Brent Farm, to the same measurements as before: she wished to see the stuff.

"If you'll take a seat, miss—"

She would rather stand outside the door, she said, and he agreed that the day was warm.

The narrow street was thronged with people who were neither of the town nor of the country, and suffered the disabilities of the hybrid. There were few keen or beautiful faces, and if there were fine bodies they were hidden under clumsy clothes. Helen wanted to strip them all, and straighten them, and force them into health and comeliness, and though she would not have her moor peopled by them, she wished they might all have moors of their own.

The young man was very slow. She could hear him struggling with bales of cloth and breathing heavily. It was much hotter here than on the moor, and she supposed that human beings could grow accustomed to any smell, but she stepped further towards the kerbstone and drew in what air the street could spare to her.

Quite unconscious of her fairness against the dingy background, she watched the moving people and heard the talk of the two men near her. They spoke of the hay crop, the price of bacon, the mismanagement of the gas company, and the words fell among the footsteps of the passers-by, and the noise of wheels, and became one dull confusion of sound to her; but all sounds fainted and most sights grew misty when she saw Zebedee walking on the other side of the street, looking down as he went, but bending an ear to the girl beside him.

Men and women flitted like shadows between him and Helen, but she saw plainly enough. Zebedee was interested: he nodded twice, looked at the girl and laughed, while she walked sideways in her eagerness. She was young and pretty: no one, Helen thought, had ever married her.

The noise of the street rushed on her again, and she heard the shopman say, "That's a case, I think. I've seen that couple about before. Time he was married, too."

Slowly Helen turned a head, which felt stiff and swollen, to look at the person who could say so. She restrained a desire to hold it, and, stepping to the threshold of the shop, she called into the depths that she would soon return.

Without any attempt at secrecy she followed that pair absorbed in one another. She went because there was no choice, she was impelled by her necessity to know and unhindered by any scruples, and when she had seen the two pass down the quiet road leading to his house, with his hand on her elbow and her face turned to his, Helen went back to the young man and the bales of cloth.

She chose the corduroy and left the shop, and it was not long before she found herself outside the town, but she could remember nothing of her passage. She came to a standstill where the moor road stretched before her, and there she suffered realization to fall on her with the weight of many waters. She cried out under the shock, and, turning, she ran without stopping until she came to Zebedee's door.

An astonished maid tried not to stare at this flushed and elegant lady.

"The doctor is engaged, miss," she said.

"I shall wait. Please tell him that I must see him."

"What name shall I say?"

"Miss Caniper. Miss Helen Caniper." She had no memory of any other.

She sat on one of the hard leather chairs and looked at a fern that died reluctantly in the middle of the table. Her eyes burned and would not be eased by tears, her heart leapt erratically in her breast, yet the one grievance of which she was exactly conscious was that Zebedee had a new servant and had not told her. If she had to have her tinker, surely Zebedee might have kept Eliza. She was invaded by a cruel feeling of his injustice; but her thoughts grew vague as she sat there, and her dry lips parted and closed, as though they tried to frame words and could not. For what seemed a long, long time, she could hear the sound of voices through the wall: then the study door was opened, a girl laughed, Zebedee spoke; another door was opened, there were steps on the path and the gate clicked. She sat motionless, still staring at the fern, but when Zebedee entered she looked up at him and spoke.

"Zebedee," she said miserably.

"Come into my room," he said.

The door was shut on them, and she dropped against it.

"Zebedee, I can't bear it."

"My little life!"

"I was so happy," she said piteously, "and, in the street, I saw you with that girl. You held her arm, and I had to come to you. I had, Zebedee."

"Had you, dear?" he said. He was pulling off her gloves, gently and quickly, holding each wrist in turn, and together they looked at the broad band of gold. Their eyes met in a pain beyond the reach of words.

She bowed her head, but not in shame.

"My hat, too," she said, and he found the pins and took it from her.

"Your ring is here," she said, and touched herself. Her lips trembled. "I can't go back."

"You need not, dearest one. Sit down. I must go and speak to Mary."

"She is better than Eliza," Helen said when he returned.

"Yes, better than Eliza." He spoke soothingly. "Are you comfortable there? Tell me about it, dear." He folded his arms and leaned against his desk, and as he watched her he saw the look of strain pass from her face.

She smiled at him. "Your cheeks are twitching."

"Are they?"

"They always do when you think hard."

"You are sitting where you sat when you first came here."

"And there were no cakes."

"Only buns."

"And they were stale."

"You said you liked them."

"I liked—everything—that day."

"I think," he said, jerking his chin upwards, "we won't have any reminiscences."

"Why not?" she asked softly. She went to him and put her arms round his neck. "It's no good, Zebedee. I've tried. I really loved him—but it's you—I belong to you." He could hardly hear what she said. "Can you love me any longer? I've been—his. I've liked it. I was ready to do anything—like that—for him."

"Speak a little louder, dear."

"You see, one could forget. And I did think about children, Zebedee, I couldn't help it."

"Precious, of course you couldn't."

"But you were always mine. And when I saw you this

afternoon, there was no one else. And no one else can have you. You don't love any one but me. How could you? She can't have you. I want you. And you're mine. Your hands—and eyes—and face—this cheek—You—you—I can't—I don't know what I'm saying. I can't go back! He'll—he put this ring on me today. I let him. I was glad—somehow. Glad!" She broke away from him and burst into a fit of weeping.

He knew the properties of her tears, and he had no hope of any gain but what could come to him by way of her renewed serenity; he made shift to be content with that, and though the sound of her crying hurt him violently, he smiled at her insistence on possessing him. She had married another man, but she would not resign her rights to the one she had deserted, though he, poor soul, must claim none. It was one of the inconsistencies he loved in her, and he was still smiling when she raised her head from the arm of the chair where she had laid it.

"I'm sorry, Zebedee. I'm better now. I'm—all right."

"Wipe your eyes, Best of all. We're going to have some tea. Can you look like some one with a—with a nervous breakdown?"

"Quite easily. Isn't that just what I have had?"

Mary was defter than Eliza and apparently less curious, and while she came and went they talked, like the outfitter and his friend, about the crops; but when she had gone Zebedee moved the table to the side of Helen's chair, so that, as long ago, no part of her should be concealed.

"Yes," he said, looking down, "but I like you better in your grey frocks."

"Do you? Do you? I'm glad," she said, but she did not tell him why. Her eyes were shining, and he found her no less beautiful for their reddened rims. "You are the most wonderful person in the world," she said. "It was unkind of me to come, wasn't it?"

"No, dear. Nothing is unkind when you do it."

"But it was, Zebedee. Because I'm going back, after all."

"I knew you would."

"Did you? I must, you know."

"Yes," he said, "I know. Helen, that girl—Daniel's in love with her."

"Oh, poor Miriam! Another renegade! But I'm not jealous any more, so don't explain."

"But I want to tell you about her. He pursues and she wearies of him. I'm afraid he's a dreadful bore."

"But that's no reason why you should take her arm."

"Did I take it? I like her. I wish she would marry Daniel, but he is instructive in his love-making. He has no perceptions. I'm doing my best for him, but he won't take my advice. Yes, I like her, but I shall never love any one but you."

"Oh, no, you couldn't really. But see what I have had to do!" Her eyes were tired with crying. "And have to do," she added in a lower tone. "It makes one think anything might happen. One loses faith. But now, here with you, I could laugh at having doubted. Yes, I can laugh at that, and more. That's the best of crying. It makes one laugh afterwards and see clearly. I can be amused at my struggles now and see how small they were."

"But what of mine?" he asked.

"I meant yours, too. We are not separate. No. Even now that I—that I have a little love for George. He's rather like a baby, Zebedee. And he doesn't come between. Be sure of that; always, always!"

"Dearest, Loveliest, if you will stay with me—Well, I'm here when you need me, and you know that."

"Yes." She looked beyond him. "Coming here, this afternoon, I saw the way. I made it beautiful. And then I saw you, and the mists came down and I saw nothing else. But now I see everything by the light of you." There was a pause. "I've never loved you more," she said. "And I want to tell you something." She spoke on a rising note. "To me you are everything that is good and true—and kind and loving. There is no limit to your goodness. You never scold me, you don't complain, you still wait in case I need you. I ought not to allow you to do that, but some day, some day, perhaps I'll be as good as you are. I want you to remember that you have been perfect to me." She said the word again and lingered on it. "Perfect. If I have a son, I hope he'll be like you. I'll try to make him."

"Helen—"

"Wait a minute. I want to say some more. I'm not going back because I am afraid of breaking rules. I don't know anything about them, but I know about myself, and I'm going back because, for me, it's the only thing to do; and you see," she looked imploringly at him, "George needs me now more than he did before. He trusts to me."

"It is for you to choose, Beloved."

"Yes," she said. "There's nothing splendid about me. I'm just—tame. I wish I were different, Zebedee."

"Then you are the only one who wishes it."

She laughed a little and stood close to him.

"Bless me before I go, for now I have to learn it all again."

CHAPTER XXXVIII

Helen had a greeting ready for each turn of the road, but George did not appear. She looked for him at the side road to the farm, and she waited there for a while. She had thought he would be on the watch for her, and she had hoped for him. Since they had to meet, let it be soon: let her heart learn to beat submissively again, and the mouth kissed by Zebedee to take kisses from another. But he did not come, and later, when she had helped Mildred Caniper to bed, Helen sat on the moor to waylay and welcome him, and make amends for her unfaithfulness.

The night was beautiful; the light wind had dropped, the sky was set with stars, and small, pale moths made clouds above the heather. When she shook a tuft of it, there came forth a sweet, dry smell. She looked in wonder on the beauty of the world. Here, on the moor, there were such things to see and hear and smell that it would be strange if she could not find peace. In the town, it would be harder: it would be harder for Zebedee, though he had his work and loved it as she loved the moor, and she caught her breath sharply as she remembered his white face. There were matters of which it was not wise to think too much, and what need was there when he wanted her to be content, when the stars and a slip of a new moon shone in a tender sky, and birds made stealthy noises, not to wake the world?

Once more it seemed to her that men and women saw happiness and sorrow in a view too personal, and each individual too much isolated from the rest. Here she sat, a tiny creature on the greatness of the moor, a mere heartbeat in a vast life. If the heart missed a beat, the life would still go on, yet it was her part to make the beat a strong and steady one.

She wanted George to come, but she had a new fear of him.

She might have lived a thousand years since she had parted from him a few hours back, and her instinct was to run away as from a stranger, but she would sit there until he was quite close, and then she would call his name and put out her hand, the one that wore his ring, and he would pull her up and take her home. She bowed her head to her knees. Well, already she had much that other people missed: that young man in the shop had not these little moths and the springing heather with purple flowers and the star that shone like a friend above her home.

The night grew darker: colour was sucked from the moor, and it lay as black as deep lake water, blacker than the sky. It was time that country folks were in their beds, and the Brent Farm lights went out as at a signal.

Helen went slowly through the garden and up the stairs, and when she had undressed she sat beside her window, wondering why George had not come. Surely she would have heard if any accident had befallen him?

The quiet of the night assured her that all was well: the poplars were concerned with their enduring effort to reach the sky; a cat went like a moving drop of ink across the lawn. She stretched out for her dressing gown and put it round her shoulders, and she sat there, leaning on the window ledge and looking into the garden until her eyelids dropped and resisted when she tried to raise them.

She had almost fallen asleep when she heard a familiar noise outside her door. She stood up and met George as he entered.

"I'm glad you've come." She put out a timid hand to touch him and had it brushed aside.

"Out of my way!" he said, pushing past her.

She saw he had been drinking though he was not drunk. His eyes were red, and he looked at her as though he priced her, with such an expression of disdaining a cheap thing that she learnt, in that moment, the pain of all poor women dishonoured. Yet she followed him and made him turn to her.

"What have you been doing?" she said. "I have been waiting

for so long."

There came on his face the sneering look she had not lately seen, and in his throat he made noises that for a little while did not come to words.

"Ah! I've been into town, too; you little devil, pranking yourself out, coming to me so soft and gentle—kissing—Here!" He took her by the wrist and dragged the ring from her and made to throw it into the night. "But no," he said slowly. "No. I think not. Come here again. You shall wear it; you shall wear it to your dying day."

"I'm willing to," she said. His arm was round her, hurting her. "Tell me what's the matter, George."

He gripped her fiercely and let her go so that she staggered.

"Get back! I don't want to touch you!" Then he mimicked her. "'Won't you ever learn to trust me?' I'd learnt. I'd have given you my soul to care for. I—I'd done it—and you took it to the doctor!"

"No," she said. "I took my own." She was shaking; her bare feet were ice cold. "George—"

"You lied about him! Yes, you did! You who are forever talking about honesty!"

"I didn't lie. I didn't tell you the whole truth, but now I will, though I've never asked for any of your confessions. I shouldn't like to hear them. I suppose you saw me this afternoon?"

"Ay, I did. I saw you turn and run like a rabbit to that man's house. I'd come to meet you, my God! I was happy. You'd my ring at last. I followed you. I waited. I saw you come out, white, shaking, the way you're shaking now." He dropped into a chair. "Dirt! Dirt!" he moaned.

She made a sad little gesture at that word and began to walk up and down the room. The grey dressing gown was slung about her shoulders like a shawl, and he watched the moving feet.

"And then you went and had a drink," she said. "Yes. I don't blame you. That's what I was having, too. And my thirst is quenched. I'm not going to be thirsty any more. I had a long drink of the freshest, loveliest water, but I'll never taste it again.

I'll never forget it either." For a time there was no sound but that of her bare feet on the bare floor. "What did you think I was doing there?" she whispered, and her pace grew faster.

His tone insulted her. "God knows!"

"Oh, yes."

"Kissing—I don't know. I don't know what you're equal to, with that smooth face of yours."

She halted in her march and stood before him. "I did kiss him. I'm glad. There is no one so good in the whole world."

She pressed her clasped hands against her throat. "I love him. I loved him before I promised to marry you. I love him still. No one could help doing that, I think. But it's different now. It has to be. I'm not his wife. I went to say—I went there, and I said goodbye to all that. I came back to you. You needn't be afraid—or jealous any more. I'm your wife, George, and I'll do my share. I promise." She started on her walk again, and still he watched the small, white feet.

"And I'm not outraged by what you've said," she went on in a voice he had not heard so coldly clear. "Men like you are so ready with abuse. Have you always been virtuous? You ask what you would never allow me to claim."

He looked up. "Since I married you—since I loved you—And I never will."

She laughed a little. "And I won't either. That's another bargain, but I know—I know too much about temptation, about love, to call lovers by bad names. And if you don't, it's your misfortune, George. I think you'd better go home and think about it."

He made an uncertain movement. He was like a child, she thought; he had to be commanded or cajoled, and her heart softened towards him because he was dumb and helpless.

"Let us be honest friends," she pleaded. "Yes, honest, George. I know I've talked a lot of honesty, and I had no right; but now I think I have, because I've told you everything and we can start afresh. I thought I was better than you, but now I know I'm not, and I'm sorry, George."

He looked up. "Helen—"

"Well?" She was on her knees before him, and her hands were persuading his to hold them.

He muttered something.

"I didn't hear."

"I beg your pardon," he said again, and, as she heard the words, she laughed and cried out, "No, no! I don't want you to say that! You've to possess me. Honour me, too, but always possess me!" She leaned back to look at him. "That's what you must do. You are that kind of man, so big and strong and—and stupid, George! Love me enough, and it will be like being buried in good earth. Can't you love me enough?" Her eyes were luminous and tender. She was fighting for two lives, for more that might be born.

"Buried? I don't know what you mean," he said; "but come you here!"

Her face was crushed against him, and it was indeed as though she were covered by something dark and warm and heavy. She might hear beloved footsteps, now and then, but they would not trouble her. Down there, she knew too much to be disturbed, too much to be hurt for ever by her lover's pain: he, too, would know a blessed burying.

It was not she who heard the opening of the bedroom door, but she felt herself being gently pushed from George's breast, and she had a strange feeling that some one was shovelling away the earth which she had found so merciful.

"No," she said. "Don't. I like it."

"Helen!" she heard George say, and she turned to see Mildred Caniper on the threshold.

"I heard voices," she said, looking a little dazed, but standing with her old straightness. "Who is here? It's Helen! It's—Helen! Oh, Helen—you!" Her face hardened, and her voice was the one of Helen's childhood. "I am afraid I must ask for an explanation of this extraordinary conduct."

The words were hardly done before she fell heavily to the floor.

CHAPTER XXXIX

Mildred Caniper died two days afterwards, without opening her eyes. Day and night, Helen watched and wondered whether, behind that mask, the mind was moving to acquaintance with the truth. Between life and death, she imagined a grey land where things were naked, neither clothed in disguising garments nor in glory. It might be that, for the first time, Mildred saw herself, looked into her own life and all the lives she knew, and gained a wider knowledge for the next. Nevertheless, it was horrible to Helen that Mildred Caniper had finally shut her eyes on the scene that killed her, and, for her last impression, had one of falsity and licence. Helen prayed that it might be removed, and, as she kept watch that first night, she told her all. There might be a little cranny through which the words could go, and she longed for a look or touch of forgiveness and farewell. She loved this woman whom she had served, but there were to be no more messages between them, and Mildred Caniper died with no other sound than the lessening of the sighing breaths she drew.

Zebedee guessed the nature of the shock that killed her, but only George and Helen knew, and for them it was another bond; they saw each other now with the eyes of those who have looked together on something never to be spoken of and never to be forgotten. She liked to have him with her, and he was dumb with pity for her and with regrets. To Miriam, when she arrived, it was an astonishment to find them sitting in the schoolroom, hand in hand, so much absorbed in their common knowledge that they did not loose their grasp at her approach, but sat on like lost, bewildered children in a wood.

Wherever Helen went, he followed, clumsy but protective, peering at her anxiously as though he feared something terrible would happen to her, too.

"You don't mind, do you?" he asked her.

"What?"

"Having me."

"I like it—but there's your hay."

"There's hay every year," he answered.

* * * * *

Uncle Alfred moved quietly about the house, stood uneasily at a window, or drifted into the garden, swinging his eyeglass, his expression troubled, his whole being puzzled by the capacity of his relatives to be dramatic, without apparent realization of their gift. Here was a sister suddenly dead, a niece wandering hand in hand with the man from whom another niece had fled, while the discarded lover acted the part of family friend; and that family preserved its admirable trick of asking no question, of accepting each member's right to its own actions. Only Miriam, now and then catching his eye in the friendly understanding they had established, seemed to make a criticism without a comment, and to promise him that, foolish as she was, he need not fear results on Helen's colossal scale.

It was Rupert who could best appreciate Helen's attitude, and when he was not thinking of the things he might have done for a woman he could help no longer, he was watching his sister and her impassivity, her unfailing gentleness to George, the perfection of her manner to Zebedee. She satisfied his sense of what was fitting, and gave him the kind of pleasure to be derived from the simple and candid handiwork of a master.

"If tragedy produces this kind of thing," he said to John with a gesture, "the suffering is much more than worth while—from the spectator's point of view."

"I don't know what you are talking about," John said.

"The way she manages those two."

"Who? And which?"

"Good Lord, man! Haven't you seen it? Helen and the two suitors."

John grunted. "Oh—that!" He had not yet learnt to speak of the affair with any patience.

* * * * * *

Mildred Caniper had left the house and all it held to Helen.

"I suppose you'll try to let it," Rupert said. "I don't like to think of that, though. Helen, I wish she hadn't died. Do you think we were more unpleasant than we need have been?"

"Not much. She was unpleasanter than we were, really, but then—"

"Heavens, yes. What a life!"

Her lips framed the words in echo, but she did not utter them, though she alone had the right.

"So perhaps I am not sorry she is dead," Rupert said.

Helen's lips tilted in a smile. "I don't think you need ever be sorry that any one is dead," she said, and before she could hear what her words told him, he spoke quickly.

"Well, what about this house?"

"I shan't let it."

"Will you live here?"

"No. I'm going to George, but no one else shall have it. I don't think the Pinderwells would be happy. Is there any furniture you want? You can have anything except what's in the dining-room. That's for Zebedee. His own is hideous."

To Zebedee she said, "You'll take it, won't you?"

"I've always taken everything you've given me," he said, and with the words they seemed to look at each other fairly for the last time.

"And don't have any more dead ferns," she told him. "There was one in the dining-room the other day. You must keep fresh flowers on Mr. Pinderwell's table."

"I shall remember."

Nothing was left in the house except the picture of Mr. Pinderwell's bride, who smiled as prettily on the empty room as on the furnished one.

"She must stay with Mr. Pinderwell," Helen said. "What would he do if he found her gone? I wonder if they'll miss us."

She refused to leave the house until the last cart had gone down the road at which Helen must no longer look in hope. She watched the slow departure of the cart and held to the garden gate, rubbing it with her hands. She looked up at the long house with its wise, unblinking eyes. She had to leave it: George was waiting for her at the farm, but the house was like a part of her, and she was not complete when she turned away from it.

There was daylight on the moor, but when she dipped into the larch-wood she found it was already night, and night lay on the cobbled courtyard, on the farmhouse, and on George, who waited in the doorway.

"You're like you were before," he said. "A silver star coming through the trees—coming to me." He took her hand. "I don't know why you do it," he murmured, and led her in.

They slept in a room papered with a pattern of roses and furnished with a great fourposted bed. It was the room in which George Halkett and his father had been born, the best bedroom for many generations. The china on the heavy washstand had pink roses on it, too, and the house was fragrant with real roses, burning wood, clean, scented linen. Jasmine grew round the window and nodded in.

"Are you going to be happy?" George asked her, when the warm darkness dropped on them like another coverlet, and she hardly knew that it was she who reassured him. Could it be Helen Caniper in this room with the low ceiling and farmhouse smells, this bridal chamber of the Halketts? Helen Caniper seemed to have disappeared.

She woke when she had been asleep for a little while, and at first she could not remember where she was; then the window darted out of the darkness and the furniture took on shapes. She looked up and saw the looming canopy of the bed, she heard George breathing beside her, and suddenly she felt suffocated by the draperies and the low ceiling and the remembrance of the big pink roses growing on the wall.

She slid to the edge of the bed and out of it. The carpet was harsh to her feet, but, by the window, the bare boards soothed them.

There were dark clouds floating against the sky, and the larches looked like another cloud dropped down until she saw their crests, spear-like and piercing: they hid the moor in its livery of night.

She turned her head and listened to the sleeper, who did not stir except to breathe. She wanted to see her moor and the house where the Pinderwells were walking and wondering at its emptiness. George would not hear her if she dressed and left the room, and, having done so, she stood outside the door and listened before she fumbled her way along the passages.

She sped through the larches, but when her feet touched the heather they went more slowly, and now it was she who might have been a cloud, trailing across the moor. So she went until she saw the house, and then she ran towards it, startling the rabbits, hearing the blur of wings, and feeling the ping or flutter of insects against her face.

The doors were locked, but the kitchen window was not hasped, and through it she climbed. The room had an unfamiliar look: it was dismantled, and ghostly heaps of straw and paper lay where the men had left them, yet this was still her home: nothing could exile her.

She went into the hall and into each bare room, but she could not go upstairs. It was bad enough to see Mr. Pinderwell walking up and down, and she could not face the children whom she had deserted. She sat on the stairs, and the darkness seemed to shift about her. She thought of the bedroom she had left, and it seemed to her that there would never be a night when she would not leave it to find her own, nor a day when, as she worked in the hollow, her heart would not be here. Yet she was Helen Halkett, and she belonged to Halkett's Farm.

She rose and walked into the kitchen and slipped her hand along the mantelshelf to find a box of matches she had left there.

She was going to end the struggle. She could not burn Zebedee, but she could burn the house. The rooms where he had made love to her should stand no longer, and so her spirit might find a habitation where her body lived.

She piled paper and straw against the windows and the doors, and set a lighted match to them; then she went to the moor and waited. She might have done it in a dream, for her indifference: it was no more to her than having lighted a few twigs in the heather; but when she saw the flames climbing up like red and yellow giants, she was afraid. There were hundreds of giants, throwing up hands and arms and trying to reach the roof. They fought with each other as they struggled, and the dark sky made a mirror for their fights.

The poplars were being scorched, and she cried out at that discovery. Oh, the poplars! the poplars! How they must suffer! And how their leaves would drop, black and shrivelled, a black harvest to strew the lawn. She thought she heard the shouting of the Pinderwells, but she knew their agony would be short, and already they were silent. The poplars were still in pain, and she ran to the front of the house that she might not see them.

There was a figure coming up the track. It was John, with his trousers pulled over his night things.

"God! What's up?" he cried.

"It's the house—only the house burning. There's no one there."

He looked into the face that was all black and white, like cinders; then at the flames, red and yellow, like live coals, and he held her by the arm because he did not like the look of her.

A man came running up. It was Halkett's William.

"Have you seen the master? He went round by the back."

"Go and look for him. Tell him his wife's here. I'll search the front."

Both men ran, shouting, but it was Helen who saw George at the window of Mildred Caniper's room.

She rushed into the garden where the heat was scorching, she heard his joyful "Helen!" as he saw her, and she held out her arms to him and called his name.

She saw him look back.

"I'll have to jump!" he shouted.

"Oh, George, come quickly!"

There were flames all round him as he leapt, and there were small ones licking his clothes when he fell at her feet.

"His neck's broke," William said.

They carried him on to the moor, and there he lay in the heather. She would not have him touched. She crouched beside him, watching the flames grow and lessen, and when only smoke rose from the blackened heap, she still sat on.

"I'm waiting for Zebedee," she said.

John sent for him, and he came, flogging his horse as a merciful man may, and when she saw him on the road, she went to meet him.

She put both hands on the shaft. "I set the house on fire," she said, looking up. "I didn't think of George. He was asleep. I had to burn it. But I've killed him, too. First there was Notya, and now George. I've killed them both. His neck is broken. William said, 'His neck's broke,' that's all, but he cried. Come and see him. He hasn't moved, but he was too big to die. I've killed him, but I held my arms out to him when he jumped."

Printed in Great Britain
by Amazon